L.A. Justice

L.A. Justice

Christopher Darden

and Dick Lochte

WARNER BOOKS

A Time Warner Company

Copyright © 2000 by Darden Family Inc.
All rights reserved.

Warner Books, Inc., 1271 Avenue of the Americas, New York, NY 10020
Visit our Web site at www.twbookmark. com

W A Time Warner Company

Printed in the United States of America

First Printing: January 2001

10 9 8 7 6 5 4 3 2 1

Library of Congress Cataloging-in-Publication Data

Darden, Christopher A.
    L.A. justice / by Christopher Darden and Dick Lochte.
        p. cm.
    ISBN-0-446-52327-5
    1. Afro-American public prosecutors—Fiction. 2. Afro-American women lawyers—Fiction.
    3. Los Angeles (Calif.)—Fiction. 4. Afro-Americans—Fiction. I. Title: Los Angeles justice.
    II. Lochte, Dick. III. Title.

PS3554.A68 L18 2001
813'.54—dc21   00-039890

To Daddy.
C. D.

To Gerry and Bob,
fellow toilers at the keys.
D. L.

≡ ACKNOWLEDGMENTS ≡

My good friends, Detective Victor Brown, Hollywood Division, Los Angeles Police Department; Joseph Stoltman, West Harbor Intelligence, Inc., Laguna Niguel; and Gavin DeBecker, thanks for the ideas and inspiration. My agents and friends at the William Morris Agency, Norman Brokaw and Mel Berger, thanks for making my dreams a reality.

Christopher Darden

L.A. Justice

PART ONE

PRETRIAL MOTION

≡ 1 ≡

zzpt.

Zzzp; zzzpt.

The sound was close to his head. The crackle of crossed wires? Static electricity? *Zzzpt.* Really annoying. Not the sort of music a man with a hangover needed or craved.

Zzzpt.

If he opened his eyes he could see what was causing the irritating sound. But that would have required effort.

Lord, he felt awful. Two-hundred-dollar champagne wasn't supposed to leave you in this—wait a minute! He hadn't had that much to drink. Two or three glasses of merlot at the restaurant and maybe a sip or two of the Crystal at the house. He groaned, not only because of the pain that was like a spike driven into his forehead but also because he had no memory of how the evening had ended.

Not another blackout! On this night, of all nights.

Zzzpt.

How did he get home? He hadn't a clue.

He opened his eyes.

It was not the ceiling he usually saw upon waking. But it was a familiar ceiling nonetheless, high and shadowy in the dim glow of a lamp.

He was at the old house, lying on his back on the carpet in the den. Fully dressed. Judging by the shadows, it was still night. He hadn't been out very long.

He raised his left arm and squinted at his Cartier Tank. So blurry. *Two-what? Two-nineteen?* He sat up to a spinning room. His head throbbed. All around him were Shelli's rather silly drawings, torn from her sketchbook. Where was she? *Wrapped in the arms of Morpheus,* he imagined.

Zzzpt.

The noise was coming from a long metal object on the floor beside him. He watched a moth flutter against its glowing grid. *Zzzpt.*

"'As alluring as Lucifer's promise,'" he said, quoting one of his own poems. "'As dangerous as his flames.'" He reached out to turn the gizmo off, then changed his mind when he saw other flying insects. "No bugs, milady," he said.

Sister Mildred would be so upset with him. Drinking to excess. Purposeless decadence.

There was smoke in the air and a strange malignant, coppery odor. Smoke wasn't good. It irritated his fragile lungs.

Staying seated on the carpet, he surveyed the room. He sobered a bit when he spied the bugs' point of entry: two broken panes in a dark green French door that led to the patio. There was something on the surface of the door. It looked like oatmeal. With a dash of dark red.

He rose, the room seeming to shift under him. He took a cautious step and saw a woman's body slumped against the bottom of the door. "Oh, no!" he wailed. "Shelli, no!" He staggered forward and dropped to his knees beside the body, hands folded as if in prayer. There was no question that Shelli was dead. No movement, no breath, no—how would Sister Mildred put it?—no spiritual essence. Her poor, horribly damaged head was tilted back. One eye was filled with a dollop of her blood; more had drained down her neck, forming a pool at the bodice of her dress. The other eye seemed to be idly checking the corner of the ceiling for spiderwebs. *Oh, God, did I—could I?*

He began to cry, whether for himself or Shelli he wasn't sure. He gave himself over to the sorrow, welcomed it. Then came that fearsome wheeze, warning him that his lungs were failing.

His hand automatically went to the atomizer in his coat pocket.

One spray did the trick. It not only cleared the lungs, it cleared his head as well.

He saw the weapon resting several feet away under a table. He recognized the blue-metal gun, the walnut-colored handle, the name "Smith & Wesson" stamped on the side of its barrel. It had been a gift from his younger brother, Jeff—his gun-loving, animal-destroying younger brother.

Okay, my gun. But don't panic! The romantic does not panic. The romantic embraces adversity. Analyze.

The gun. He'd loaned it to Shelli. She'd been worried about living in the big house. Worries not exactly groundless, he now realized. He had no idea where she'd kept it. Ergo, she was the one who had planned to use it. On him? Why? What could he have done to make her seek a weapon?

Perhaps he'd done nothing. Shelli had her dark moods. Perhaps she . . .

He forced himself to study the ghastly wound, tasting the bile rising from his stomach. Shelli might have pressed the gun to her own head. But there was no way the weapon would have wound up so far from her body.

Wouldn't he have remembered if he'd murdered his own fiancée?

He looked at her left hand. A pale lily resting at her thigh. Unadorned.

Where was the ring? She'd accepted it, hadn't she? Hadn't they toasted their happiness? Or had that been a dream?

He touched the pocket of his coat, frowned and withdrew from it a gray felt case. Inside was the ring. The room was warm, but he felt a chill nonetheless. Had she refused the ring? Had he even offered it? Just for a second, the curtain lifted on his memory. He heard Shelli cry out "Monster!" Followed by the thunderous roar of the gun.

He shivered.

He *was* a monster. His beloved's lifeless flesh had not yet cooled, but he was beginning to worry about his own wretched hide. Such was his nature. A friend had once called him a rare combination of poet and pragmatist. He was that. Staring down at the weapon, he realized the time had come for pragmatism. Unlock and restore, Sister Mildred would say.

He took the ring from its box and, with mild effort, worked it onto the proper finger of the dead woman's left hand. Then he removed the silk handkerchief from his top jacket pocket and used it to pick up the gun. Was it his imagination, or did it vibrate as he wiped away the prints he'd no doubt left on its surface?

He placed it in the dead woman's extended right hand. It still wasn't quite what he wanted. He squatted beside the body and hooked the corpse's index finger into the trigger guard.

The body suddenly shifted and blood poured from its pooling place at the dead woman's neck.

"Aaaa!" he cried, staggering back, too late to avoid the splatters that hit his trouser leg and shoe.

The body slumped against the damaged French door. The head dropped forward, blood from the eye dripping down her cheek in vampire tears.

Panic hit him like a fever. He shook it off. Embrace the fear, he could hear Sister Mildred telling him. Use it.

He took a deep breath, let it out slowly. *Have to get away,* he ordered himself. *Nothing can be proved if you can just get away.*

He stumbled from the room and down the hall to the front door. The temperature in the house was unusually warm, but leaving it was like stepping into the first circle of Hades. It was hot and dry in Los Angeles, fire season, and the night air carried the choking musk of burning hillside. Bad for his asthma, but at least it replaced the coppery odor of poor Shelli's blood.

His Alfa-Romeo waited on the drive, its shiny black surface dulled by a powdering of ash from the fire in the hills. It was not the most reliable of machines. Still, it started right away. "My lucky night," he muttered ruefully.

Then he was away. Escaping down a deserted boulevard, placing as much distance as he could between himself and the horror.

The smoky air had filled his lungs with sand and cotton. He reached for the spray bottle in his coat pocket.

It wasn't there.

It wasn't in any of his pockets. He had to resort to the spare he kept in the Alfa's glove compartment.

Stay calm, he commanded himself, as his breathing returned to normal. *It doesn't matter if they find the atomizer in the room. You can always say you dropped it there earlier, before leaving for dinner.*

The thought of dinner made him realize he'd forgotten something infinitely more important than the spray.

He sighed. There wasn't anything he could do about that, either.

PART TWO

PRELIM

≡ 2 ≡

"McNeil, Homicide," the red-headed detective in the rumpled suit said into the phone. "We catch creeps while the city sleeps."

It was shortly before 3:00 A.M. The El Niño windstorms that had battered L.A. all week had mysteriously deserted the town, leaving the early morning hot and dry as dust. The heat usually meant an upswing in the crime rate, but somebody had forgotten to tell the bangers, boosters, and slayers. It had been the slowest night in Robbery-Homicide that Detective Virgil Sykes could recall.

He stood at the window of Parker Center, sipping a diet cola and watching a bus move along the quiet street five floors below like a lumbering dream machine in an uneventful nightmare. He was a tall, lithe African-American, surprisingly dapper for someone who'd been on-call for nine hours and counting. Stifling a yawn, he turned to his partner, who was at his desk, phone stuck to his ear.

Dan McNeil's watery, red-rimmed eyes locked on his. Without betraying any emotion, the pale Irishman gave him a nod. They had a go.

Thank you, Jesus, Virgil offered up silently. Several hours of sharing a nearly deserted squad room with the Mighty Mac had been tough duty. Not that he didn't love the older cop like a brother. Not that he didn't owe the guy big time for taking him on as a partner when he was fresh and inexperienced and not exactly the color of choice for redheaded—and yes, rednecked—Irish cops with ten years in. Not that Mac hadn't been there for him every minute of their six years together. It was just that lately his partner's private life, which had always resembled a toothpick construction resting on wet toilet paper, had come undone. His wife, Lynne, whom Virgil felt was in the same ballpark with Mother Teresa when it came to long-suffering good works, finally had had enough of Mac's boozing and screwing around. She'd grabbed the kids and the silverware and moved to her folks' home clear across the state in Yreka.

Since her departure, Virgil's tough, generous, joke-telling mentor had turned into an edgy, sleepless, hard-boozing drag-ass, beating the younger cop's ears with the same sour women-are-no-damn-good refrain, over and over. It was the sort of song that grew old fast, even if you weren't deep into a relationship with someone you loved and respected, which Virgil was.

A new case sometimes returned McNeil to form or at least got him off the anti-female soapbox for a while, which was why Virgil was so glad the call had come in. "What's the squeal?" he asked, as they grabbed their jackets and headed for the elevator.

"Female vic with fatal gunshot wound to the head," McNeil replied. "Probably pissed off her old man and paid the price. Okay, you can't live with 'em, but who says you can't kill 'em?"

≡ 3 ≡

Their destination was the Beckman house in Hancock Park, one of the city's quiet old-money neighborhoods. The two-story mock Tudor was something of a local landmark, owing its celebrity to its original owner, the silent-film pioneer and philanthropist Adrian Beckman, who had long since moved on to an even more tranquil address in Forest Lawn Cemetery.

When Virgil and McNeil arrived, the house, like its neighbors, was merely a very pricey hunk of real estate, nestled in shadows behind a wrought-iron fence. In just a few hours, when the media picked up the blood scent, the building would take on a notoriety beyond anything old man Beckman might have imagined.

Like harbingers of things to come, two gaudy vehicles were parked along the curb. The first was an LAPD blue-and-white. It had brought the two uniformed officers who'd discovered the victim's body while responding to a call to the Wilshire Division station. Virgil was curious about the phone call. Most people would have dialed 911. This "concerned citizen" had known exactly how to keep his identity a secret. He'd avoided the Caller ID setup on the 911 line by phoning the Wilshire station. He'd also informed the station operator up-front that it was not an emergency, thereby stopping her from running a trace. He'd reported the gunshots and broken the connection immediately. Why would somebody go to all that trouble?

Virgil parked behind the second car, a black-red-and-white two-door that belonged to SoCal Home Security.

"Looks like our man's doing his job," McNeil said, indicating the uniformed officer who was guarding the open gateway like a ticket collector at Dodger Stadium. He seemed to be arguing with two men in brown, members of the SoCal patrol. Beyond them the looming night-lighted building looked as welcoming as the barrel of a shotgun.

McNeil rolled out of the sedan, sniffing the air. The winds had fanned a fire in the Hollywood Hills the night before, covering the flatland with white ash and polluting the atmosphere enough to send the gentry rushing north or south along the ocean. "Smoke's thick enough to cure a ham," McNeil grumbled. "Even here in Fatcatland."

"Some things money can't buy," Virgil said. He got out of the car, wondering what it would be like to live in one of these old castles. What would Nikki, the love of his life, say if he showed up tomorrow and told her, "Honey, pack your bags, we're movin' on up to Hancock Park"?

Of course, depending on what was waiting for them inside the Beckman house, the neighborhood real estate might be taking a little dip.

McNeil sniffed again and wrinkled his pug nose. "Not only smoke, there's the stink of ama-choors in the air."

The policeman at the gate was pointing their way, evidently siccing the security guards on them. McNeil dropped his head and rolled it in a circular motion to get the kinks out. Then he straightened, ran a hand through his thinning red hair and greeted the guards. "Gentlemen," he said.

The shorter, more aggressive one offered his name and said, "Saw the blue-and-white. The Beckman house is on our beat. What's up?"

"What'd the officer tell you?"

"He wouldn't tell us shit. We're here to help. Like I say, this is on our beat."

"Oh, your *beat*?" McNeil said mockingly.

Virgil could see no reason to alienate these guys, who might have information they could use. Before McNeil could tell them to go fuck themselves, or worse, he said, "We don't have any answers ourselves right now. We'd appreciate it if you could hang out in your vehicle for a couple minutes while we see what the sitch is inside."

"Was it a break-in? There wasn't no alarm. If there'd been an alarm we'd of got a call."

"That's the kind of thing we need to know from you guys," Virgil said. From the corner of his eye, he spied his partner heading for the gate. "Sit tight. We'll get back to you."

As the guards reluctantly moved to their car, Virgil ran to catch up to McNeil, who asked heatedly, "The fuck you so nice to those wanna-bes?"

"Why piss 'em off?"

McNeil stared at him and smiled suddenly, Irish mug turning into a catcher's mitt with stubble. "Where's the Watchbird, Virg?"

Virgil opened his mouth to say that it wasn't his turn in the damned Watchbird, but McNeil hadn't waited for any conversation. He was at the gate, flashing his badge to the officer there.

Virgil returned to his car, conscious of the two khaki cops watching him with curiosity. He removed his suit jacket, draping it carefully over the driver's backrest, then walked to the rear of the sedan and popped the trunk lid.

Here goes nothing, he thought, and removed a lumpy, silvery vest. Just the perfect outfit for a nice hot morning. He slipped it on, securing it across his broad chest with Velcro fasteners. The lumps were, in fact, state-of-the-art technical gizmos, including a bar code stamp for identifying evidence and a laser range finder that measured distances and sizes. As he and McNeil had already proven, it had accuracy to within a quarter of an inch.

Next, he picked up a black plastic helmet. Before putting it on, he reached down into the truck and flipped the switch on a digital video recorder. He placed the helmet on his head, adjusted it until it was as comfortable as he'd ever been able to make it, then clicked on the transmit button that protruded from its right exterior. If everything was in working order, a microcamera in the helmet's crown would then be sending a picture of everything he saw back to the recorder, along with an accompanying audio track.

The vest-and-helmet combo was the brainchild of Altadine Industries of the Silicon Valley. Its creators called it the Watchbird. Virgil called it a pain in the ass.

During the years when he and McNeil had done mainly undercover work—before their promotions to investigators in Homicide Major Crimes—he'd spent days and weeks in outfits that ranged from freaky to funky and back again. Smelly Levi's. Booze-soaked T-shirts. Scuzzy jackets that he'd artfully stained with everything from beet juice to bay rum. All part of the job. He'd even worked in drag, shaving his legs and . . . other sections of his body, the better to apprehend a serial killer who'd been frequenting transvestite clubs.

This outfit was something else. It made him feel like some jagoff *Star Trek* groupie. Not for the first time he wondered why, out of all the lawmen in the state of California, he and McNeil had been lucky enough to have drawn one of the six test units. He figured it was God's way of telling him he needed a little humility.

But if those security jackrabbits so much as let out one giggle . . .

They didn't. They just gawked at him. So did the LAPD officer at the gate.

"Yo, Robocop." McNeil was standing just past the front door to the house. "Your super-sensors pickin' up the stiff yet?"

"Maybe they'll be pickin' you up," Virgil replied, noting unhappily that the house was only a few degrees cooler than the outside. He supposed it must cost an arm and a leg to keep a place that size air-conditioned. But if you could afford to live there, you sure as hell—

"I been chewin' the fat with Officer Tony DiBono," McNeil said, interrupting his thoughts. "The officer is a boot, but don't worry, he's read the book cover to cover. Says he's kept everything nice and clean for us."

"Good. He notify the lab?"

"They're on the way. DiBono may be just a year out of the Academy, but he—speak of the devil. . . ."

A stocky, smug-looking young policeman joined them from the rear of the house. McNeil did the introductions. DiBono seemed fascinated by the Watchbird. "That gonna be standard issue?" he wanted to know.

"Right now we're just testing it," Virgil said. "Guess we should put it to work, huh?"

The officer took that as a request to provide them with a motor-mouth recap of events. He and Officer Martin Holtz, the gatekeeper, had arrived at 2:29 A.M., just a few minutes after an anonymous caller had reported gunshots inside the house.

The front door had been slightly ajar. They'd knocked and shouted their identification into the building. Getting no reply, they'd entered and followed the light to a room at the rear where they'd found the dead woman.

"Somebody did a real number on her," DiBono said. "Set it up to look like a suicide."

"But you're sure it's murder?" Virgil asked.

"No way could she have put *two* bullets into her head like that," DiBono said with a wiseguy smile.

"We got a budding criminologist here," McNeil said.

"Why don't you show us?" Virgil suggested.

Walking down the hall, McNeil asked the young cop, "Nobody else home?"

"No, sir," DiBono said. "I checked soon as I secured the murder scene. Here we are. I've been very careful to protect the integrity of the room."

"You're a goddamned wonder," McNeil said.

Virgil stood in the doorway, trying to ignore the odor of congealing blood while he scanned the room. It looked like an artist's studio. Framed paintings on the walls. Modern stuff. Splashes of color. A naked easel stood in a corner of the room. Near it was an L-shaped glass-and-metal desk. The short section of desktop was taken up with a computer monitor and a keyboard, both inactive. The long section was occupied by a phone, neatly stacked papers, a modern lamp that looked to Virgil like a Lego construction on a heavy metal base, and an empty bottle of champagne.

" 'Louis Roederer Crystal,' " Virgil read aloud. "Expensive."

"I'm a whiskey man myself," McNeil grumbled.

A casual couch, covered in white canvas, squatted against one wall. A thick dark carpet covered most of the hardwood floor. It was littered with pastel sketches.

The body was in a heap near a pair of French doors. Two panes of glass were broken in the right door at about the five-foot mark, directly above the corpse.

Virgil chose to keep the dead woman for later. He focused on the sketches. They looked like feet with wings at their heels. McNeil began to sing "Come Fly with Me," doing a passing-fair imitation of the late, great Chairman of the Board.

"Watchbird's watchin' you," Virgil said as a reminder.

His partner shrugged as if that were of no consequence.

Virgil scanned the area again. A champagne glass rested on its side on the carpet. He looked around the room. "Anybody see another glass?" he asked.

"What?" McNeil asked.

"I got one champagne glass right here. Should be another somewhere. Solitary drinkers usually don't go in for expensive champagne."

They couldn't turn up any other glass. Virgil asked DiBono if the room was exactly as he had found it.

"Pretty much," the patrol officer said. "I sure didn't remove any glass."

"You didn't touch anything?" Virgil asked.

DiBono's eyes shifted nervously to the French doors.

"Something about the doors?" McNeil asked.

"I, uh, unlocked 'em to go out behind the house. Didn't find anything out there, so I came back in. Relocked the doors. I was careful." He held up his hands to show that he was wearing latex gloves matching those the detectives had on.

"Doors were locked from the inside, but you thought you'd find something out there, huh?" McNeil asked. "Something worth disturbing the corpse?"

"I didn't disturb anything," DiBono said. "I used the door on the left."

"Didn't move her at all?" Virgil asked.

"No way," the officer said defensively. "Look, I was just being thorough."

"Touch anything else with those magic gloves?" McNeil asked.

"No. Uh, yeah. That bug zapper." He pointed to a metal object a few feet from the corpse. "It was making this noise, so I clicked it off."

"What kind of noise?" McNeil asked.

"You know. *Zap.* Bugs musta come in through the broken windows. The zapper was turning 'em into crispy critters."

"You queer for bugs?" McNeil asked.

DiBono looked confused. "Do I like 'em? No."

"Good answer," McNeil said. He moved to get a better look at the body.

Virgil was sweating under the vest and helmet. He wondered if the manufacturers had accounted for sweat when they rigged the wiring. He didn't want to wind up being zapped like a bug. He bent over the electronic insect killer, giving his camera a good, clear look. "You move this when you turned it off?" he asked the officer.

"No, sir," DiBono replied smartly. "Just pushed that red switch."

"Oh, mama!" McNeil exclaimed, checking out the corpse. "This is my favorite kind of lady. No sass. Low maintenance."

DiBono's eyes opened wide.

"Never mind him, Officer," Virgil said. "Anything else you touch?"

"Uh, wallet on the table over there. I, uh, flipped it open. Driver's license belongs to a woman named Dietz. Shelli Dietz. That's Shelli with an 'i'."

"Of course it is. Hi, Shelli," McNeil addressed the corpse. "You're looking good."

"Probably hers, the wallet," Officer DiBono said. "Age and description seem to fit. But there's a Santa Monica address."

"Looky here, partner."

McNeil was hunkering beside a small two-tone green object on the floor near the body. Virgil moved in on it.

"Some kinda spray deal," he said, squinting at the print on the plastic atomizer. "Serevet."

"Where did *that* come from?" DiBono asked.

"Maybe Shelli used it, maybe the killer," McNeil told him. "I say it's a goddamn clue."

"Resting on top of bloodstains," Virgil said. "Left after the murder."

"Maybe during," McNeil added.

"Maybe during," Virgil agreed.

"Dunno how I missed it," DiBono said. "I went over this place pretty good."

"Thanks, Officer," Virgil said. "We'll take it from here."

"You can see what I mean about the position of the wound being all wrong for sui—"

"Yeah. Thanks."

The young patrolman backed out of the room, giving them every opportunity to change their minds and tell him he could stick around. When they didn't, he nodded and said, "Okay, then, I'll, uh, go check the periphery."

"Good idea," McNeil said. He straightened and took a step back from the body. "That kid's so wet behind the ears I'm surprised his collar hasn't shrunk, but he's right about suicide. One bullet took off the top of her head, busted the window; other looks like it's still in there. Either should have done the job, thereby making it improbable she got off an accurate second shot. You wanna take her picture?"

"In a minute," Virgil said. Using his fancy laser measurer, he registered precise distances, reading the results aloud for the benefit of the recorder. "Room is twenty-five feet, six inches by twenty feet, two inches. Distance of body from interior entrance: nineteen feet, four inches, pressed fast against doors leading to patio. Brain particles and broken window five feet, seven inches above floor."

Virgil stepped past the zapper. Bending his knees, he lowered his camera-headgear to a level where it might capture every detail of the dead woman's body. Simultaneously, he described what the camera was seeing. "Female. Caucasian. In her thirties, probably." Her head was bent, chin touching chest, offering a clear view of the damaged skull. The missing part was decorating the broken French door behind her. The pistol—a Smith & Wesson 9 mm—was resting in her right hand. Her other hand lay on her thigh. A diamond sparkled from her ring finger. She was wearing some kind of long summer dress. Indian or Mexican. Purple with black patterns on it. Pulled back exposing her legs.

"I don't know about you, partner," McNeil said from directly behind him, "but I feel a song comin' on."

Virgil took a backward step, forcing the older detective away from the corpse.

"So what do you think?" McNeil asked.

"Judging by the height of the broken glass, she must've been standing when she was shot." He was starting to study the probable trajectory of the bullets when DiBono called to them from the doorway.

"What's up?" McNeil asked him.

"I got to wondering about the name and address in the wallet. So I asked the SoCal guys to pull a sheet on this place. The Dietz woman has been paying the monthlies for about a year."

"Good work."

The officer looked uncomfortable.

"Something else?" Virgil asked.

"Maybe I, uh, quick-searched the place a little too quick. She, uh, wasn't living here alone."

It only took a few minutes to find the other occupant. McNeil drew the lucky section of the house. "Bingo!" he shouted to Virgil and the two uniforms.

According to information Shelli Dietz had supplied SoCal, her son, Adam Noyes, was ten years old. He looked younger, hiding in the closet of an empty room upstairs. Curly auburn hair, large green eyes, skin the color of maple sugar, suggesting that his father was probably not Caucasian. Dressed in gray pajamas with a drawing of the Disney Tarzan on the pocket. Curled in a ball, hugging his legs, rocking back and forth.

"I told him who we were," McNeil said. "Nothing. Shock, probably. Better get somebody here for him."

"Hey, Adam!" Virgil called.

"Mosquitoes," the boy said.

Virgil looked at McNeil, who shrugged. "No mosquitoes around here," he said.

"I'm allergic," the boy said.

"I know how that is," Virgil said. "Got stung by a bee once. Looked like Eddie Murphy in *The Nutty Professor*."

The boy stopped rocking. He turned his curly head toward the black detective. "What's that?" he asked, pointing at the shiny helmet. He seemed perfectly calm now.

"Something new. It's a camera and a lot of other stuff."

"How's it work?" Adam asked.

"Come on out and we'll talk about it."

Tentatively, the boy unlocked his fingers and stretched out his legs. "Randy's not still here, is he?"

"Who's that?" Virgil asked.

"Randy Bingham. This is his house."

"He's not around," Virgil said, helping the boy stand. "He lives here?"

"No," Adam said. He was a handsome little boy. "We live here. My mom and me. He just spends a lot of time here." He pointed at the helmet. "That's only a cam, right? Transmits to a deck somewhere near."

"Deck's in the car," Virgil said. "Randy was here tonight?"

"Uh-huh. He and my mom had another big shouting match. They woke me, yelling at each other. I listened for a while. Then I went back to sleep, I guess. I woke up again a while later. Mosquitoes were buzzing, so I got out of bed and ran in here to get away from them."

Virgil studied the boy, trying to get a fix on the kind of emotional shape he was in. He seemed okay. Maybe a little anxious, but who wouldn't be? "What woke you up the second time?"

"Loud noises, I think. Doors slamming. Maybe a dream, but it woke me." He looked past Virgil and McNeil to Officers DiBono and Holtz standing at the door in their blue uniforms gawking at him. "Policemen?" he asked. "Where's my mom?"

"You wanna field that one, partner?" McNeil asked Virgil.

FROM PATIENCE'S SPOKEN DIARY: TUESDAY MORNING, AUGUST 3

Hello, Sony, old friend. Time to blab to you again.

Spent the evening at the Vic, in that funky suite with the wall sconces that look like funeral flowers, watching the wicked Pickett go through his song and dance. Ricky G the Beloved says to take it real slow around Pickett, that he's hyper about some new scam and is showing signs of going agro. The G-man is getting paranoid in his old age. Or maybe it's just love. Ha-ha.

It was new-girl night at the Vic. Hickabillys, all of 'em. Virgin Marys, real dumbsters. Recruited by Stephen and Jay Jay, who were there, of course, all G'ed up in their superduds. Chester Molesters. Slouching on the dirty-white silk sofa, looking very movie star and hormonal, as usual.

A few customers were lurking in another room, checking the new crop on the vid screens. Didn't want to get too up close and personal. The Pickman sure knew they were there. He's such a ham. He was wearing his black leather outfit with the silver buckle that Ricky says makes him look like the front end of a Mercedes. Pickett thinks that's a compliment.

Anyway, he got things going by slapping this big, freckle-faced hottie who was talking too much. Carrie, I think her name was. That ring of his raised a big welt on her cheek. It sure got the attention of the other girls. Then he forced that poor burnout Gloria to stand up.

She was sooo out of it. Glazed eyes. Mouth kinda slack, Pickett started running his fingers down her arm. I could see the goose bumps clear across the room. "Well, young ladies," he said, using this dumb kind of exaggerated way of talking that he thinks is so cute. "Allow me to introduce Gloria as a final note of caution before you enter your new life."

He tilted his head and the diamond in his left ear winked like it was real.

"Eight months ago, Gloria was standing right where you are," he said. "But she didn't see the possibilities. She wasn't listenin'—didn't hear me right. She made some unwise career moves. Like telling a john to go fuck himself. That's a no-no, ladies."

He turned Gloria around till her back was to us. He lifted her long black hair and the new Marys all "oohed" and "ahhed" at the scar along the nape of her neck. It's called keloided. Lumpy, like a pink worm crawled in there and died.

Pickett dropped her hair back into place and patted it gently. "But she still didn't get the message. Did you, babe?"

The look Gloria gave him was so sad.

Pickett told them she tried to extort money from another john. That was his take on it. Actually, Gloria had fallen for the john and thought he felt the same way. She asked him for some money to get herself straight. Naturally, the john complained to management.

"Sho' us your foot, baby," Pickett ordered.

Like a sleepwalker, Gloria stepped out of her slippers and let him raise her right leg so that they could see the scar along the sole of her foot. I looked away. I happen to know it still makes her limp and some days it gets so sore, she just stays in her room and won't come out.

"Don't no bitch ever walk away from me," Pickett told them. "Now she knows we got her sussed as a troublemaker. We been patient, but no more Mr. Nice Guy. Next time she acts up . . ." He used his finger to trace a diagonal line down the side of Gloria's face from her eyebrow to her chin. Like I said, he is such a ham.

The Marys were speechless. Then one of them, this skinny

blonde, ran over to Stephen and said, "You'd never let him do that to me, would you, baby?"

What a chickenhead. Stephen gave her a shove, so hard she stumbled back and fell on the floor and did the crybaby thing. "C'mon, Pickett," Stephen said. "Don't wanna be late for our human potential class."

I think he was kidding, but you never know with these guys. They're always finding new places to meet girls.

Pickett wrapped it up. He gave the Marys the same old lines I now know by heart, about how all their needs will be taken care of. Bullshit like that.

Then the boys in the back room made their choices and the rest of the girls hit the streets for the first time. I felt sorry for them, what with the heat and the smoke and ashes falling down from the fire in the hills and all. Ricky G took me to dinner. Thank goodness the devilmobile has AC—this El Niño is really sucky. Later, we went over to the Green Carnation to watch the gays dance and grope. Then we went to Ricky's and did a little blow, had a little sex.

All in all, not a bad night.

And now . . . back into the vault you go.

≡ 4 ≡

I t was 9:20 A.M. when Deputy District Attorney Nikki Hill arrived
on the eighteenth floor of the Criminal Courts Building in downtown
Los Angeles. Her clerk, Jeb Lacy, a young black man standing six-foot-
four-inches tall and weighing in at barely one hundred and seventy
pounds, was at his desk, watching her with some anxiety through rim-
less glasses. He shook his recently shaved head and said with more than
a hint of reproach, "The meeting started ten minutes ago."

"Shit," Nikki replied, shoving her briefcase and purse at him as she
headed toward the conference room.

She'd been late several times that month. She'd done everything she
could to get there by nine. Her alarm had gone off at 6:30 A.M. She'd
dragged herself from the bed, and almost by rote staggered into the
kitchen to fix a dish of medicated dog chow for her housemate, Bird,
an eighty-pound Bouvier, who, if his vet was to be believed, was suffering from diverticulosis.

"Next he'll be telling me you've got the gout," she'd said to the big
dog as he attacked his breakfast.

By 6:45, Nikki had climbed into a mildly funky jogging outfit she
could live with for one more workout before it hit the Biz bag. Most
mornings, she drove to a park in nearby Manhattan Beach where she

got her heart pumping by struggling up a five-story-high sand dune. But experience had taught her that sand dunes and El Niño forces didn't mix and though the winds seemed to have stopped she'd settled for just a neighborhood jog. Actually, it was a two-mile sprint from her front door down the hill across Slauson Avenue to La Tijera Boulevard and back up again. Letting the big dog set the pace—as if she had any choice—she'd jogged in the warm early morning past her neighbors' expensive homes.

Once again, she'd marveled at her good fortune in finding a house in the upscale African-American community of Ladera Heights. So, big deal if her mortgage payments didn't leave her with enough money to furnish the place *and* eat. Who needed furniture? Besides, she and Bird might be getting another roommate one of these days and he had some lovely sofas and chairs, if a little heavy on the macho-leather.

The thought of Virgil Sykes moving in had taken her mind off what she was doing and Bird had to brush up against her, panting, to make her notice how hot and dry the jog back up the hill had become.

By 7:45, still on schedule, she'd showered, powdered, detangled her hair and was seated at the kitchen counter in a pale violet robe, sipping black coffee while listening to an all-news FM station and speed-reading the metro section of the morning *L.A. Times*. Her daily plan called for another fifteen minutes of current events, twenty minutes to dress, say good-bye to Bird, and be on her way downtown to the Criminal Courts Building. That would put her at her desk in the District Attorney's office at just a minute or two before 9 A.M., which would have been ideal.

She hadn't quite finished her coffee or the paper when Virgil arrived, in desperate need of a woman's touch after a weary and depressing night on duty. There went her schedule. There went her good intentions. There went her violet robe.

Acting District Attorney Raymond Wise glared at Nikki as she entered the crowded conference room and found an empty chair at the far end of the table. Wise was thin and pale with a long, bland, angular face, high forehead, and lank dull-brown hair. He was a man of two personalities that she had labeled "Dr. Jazz" and "Mr. Snide." In the office he was the latter, bent and dour, with an acid tongue and a total lack of social grace; but in the courtroom, Nikki had seen him morph into a straight-backed, avuncular, sincere and honorable seeker of justice, the bane of many a smug attorney with a seemingly bullet-proof defense.

At the moment, he was definitely in his Mr. Snide mode. He purposely stared at his watch and said, "Well, Ms. Hill, what is it this morning? Car break down? Dog eat your alarm clock? Bad hair day?"

The other deputy D.A.'s turned to her. Some faces reflected sympathy. Most were smiling at her discomfort. Theirs was a competitive office.

Her immediate reaction was to say, "The reason I'm late, Ray, is just good old early morning sex, something you know nothing about—morning, noon, or nighttime version." But she'd been working with Wise long enough to ignore his pettiness and bullshit. And she *had* been guilty of tardiness all month, ever since Virgil went on his late-night schedule. "Sorry," she replied.

"We've been talking about a murder in Hancock Park last night," Wise told her. "Fem vic named Shelli Dietz. As I was just informing your associates, who got here on time, the police feel they have a suspect whose name is—"

"Randolph J. Bingham, the third," Nikki said.

"Christ," Wise exclaimed. "I haven't even decided if there's enough to indict. It's on the news already?"

"I don't think so," Nikki said. "Least, I didn't hear it on the drive downtown. I got my information directly from the police." Virgil had been lying in bed, yawning and telling her about the murder while she dressed. "That's sort of why I was late."

"Don't tell me they're blabbing—"

"No blabbing," she said without blinking an eye. "A very confidential source direct to this department and nowhere else."

Wise stared at her and nodded, pleased but trying not to show it. It was an election year and Nikki knew his razor-blade mind sliced and diced every piece of information that might have an effect on the vot-

ers. The two candidates opposing him, a public defender named Louis
Corrigan and former D.A. Seymour Kehoe, had thus far offered no serious threat to his job security. However, a high-profile murder trial involving a member of the Bingham family—the same Binghams of Bingham Industries and Bingham Boulevard and Bingham Plaza fame—could
change the playing field. "What else did you hear?" he asked, dropping
all sarcasm.

"The police think that at about two A.M., for reasons unknown, Bingham decided to shoot the vic in the head twice and then stick the gun
in her hand to fake a suicide."

"Yes, yes," Wise said impatiently. "Lieutenant Corben told me that
much."

A balding, middle-aged deputy asked, "What evidence do they have?"

"Nothing hard," Nikki said. "Bingham was with the vic earlier in
the evening. Last known contact."

"Motive?" This came from the newest deputy, a Hawaiian named
Kalimona.

"Judging by the sheer dumbness of the suicide setup," Nikki said,
"the homicide detectives are thinking drugs might be involved."

"Get your source to keep you posted," Wise ordered.

"Yes, sir," Nikki said, saluting.

Wise didn't seem to notice the salute. "I wonder how they made the
Bingham connection so quickly," he said.

"Witness," Nikki said.

"What witness?" Wise was on the edge of his chair. The others at
the table were equally intrigued.

She told them about the victim's son, Adam, and what he'd said to
the police about hearing an argument and loud noises.

"How old is the kid?" Kalimona asked.

"Ten. But from what I hear, a mature ten."

"Where is he now?" Wise asked.

"DCS has him." The Department of Children's Services. "They're
shaking the bushes for relatives."

"Wonder why Corben didn't tell me about the kid," Wise said.

Nikki thought it was probably one of the little power games the

LAPD played. Their office played them, too. "Maybe he's going to let Louis Corrigan break the news," she said.

Wise was not amused. "Find out what you can about the Noyes boy," he said to her. "See if he'll stand up in court."

"Excuse me, Ray." The interruption came from a deputy seated at Wise's right. Dana Lowery was a large-boned but whippet-thin woman, two inches taller than Nikki's five-eight. She cut quite a dramatic figure. Mainly it was her hair. Early in her career, her go-for-the-jugular style of prosecution had prompted a convicted felon's mother to whack her across the scalp with a hardwood walking cane. The result had been a concussion, several stitches, and a shock of white hair against her normal brunette that she wore like a badge of honor. Thanks to the hair, sunken eyes, and prominent cheekbones that seemed on the verge of breaking through her pale skin, she possessed more than passing resemblance to a certain mythic cartoon character. The similarity did not go unnoticed around the office where her associates referred to her as "Cruella."

"I assumed this would be *my* case," she said.

"Where'd you get that idea?" Wise asked.

"When you need a win," she said, as if the answer should have been obvious, "you send in a winner."

"The body's still warm, honey," Wise said nastily. "There's been no formal arrest. Maybe Mr. Bingham has an alibi. It's a little premature—"

"That's why you're sending Nikki to talk to the witness?"

"If you bothered to notice what your associates have been doing around here, Dana, you'd know that Nikki has been in Family Violence for nearly a year. She works with the people at DCS all the time, so she's the logical person to send over there. This, by the way, has nothing whatsoever to do with who will or who will not represent this office should I decide to put Bingham on trial. I'm not about to appoint a lead counsel who can't make it to court on time."

It was a typical Wise reply, perversely designed to put both Dana Lowery and Nikki in their places. For the rest of the meeting the two women remained moodily silent.

●   ●   ●

Nikki was loading her briefcase for her visit to the Department of Children's Services when Dana appeared at her office door. "Minute?" she asked.

"Sure. C'mon in."

Dana closed the door before taking a chair. "I'll make this short and sweet," she said. "Ray has to go."

"The man does have a way of ingratiating himself." The closed door made Nikki uneasy. It also was filling her small office space with Dana's cloying perfume.

"I've been having talks with the heads of the Police Officers' Guild," Dana said, her voice a conspiratorial whisper. The POG, a powerful political force, had been opposed to Wise almost from the start, mainly because of the reputation he'd forged as a deputy who delighted in prosecuting cops. "Right now they're backing Kehoe."

"That's going in the wrong direction," Nikki said. Seymour Kehoe had been a do-nothing Acting District Attorney.

"He's a fossil, he's incompetent"—Dana flashed a triumphant smile—"and he's toast. POG is dumping him and backing me."

Nikki was surprised. "Well, isn't that something!" she managed to reply.

"What I want to know is: Are you with me, Nikki?"

"Beg pardon?"

"It's going to be Wise or me."

Nikki frowned. Some choice! An irascible jackass, who was annoying as hell but left her alone as long as she produced, versus a dragon lady who was certain to keep her heel to everybody's neck. "I think I'll go to Switzerland this war," she said.

Dana's eyes flashed in annoyance. "You're not just another warm body," she said. "Your association with the Maddie Gray case and the general cleanup in this office have made you something of a celebrity. Your backing could be key."

"There's always a lot of political intrigue slowing things down around here," Nikki said. "I try to step around it."

"That won't be possible this time," Dana said.

"We'll see."

Dana cocked her head to one side. "What's Ray promised you? Director?"

"Ray hasn't promised me a thing. Wouldn't matter if he did. I'd tell him the same as I just told you."

"I'll put it in writing: In return for your support, you will serve as my director of Central Operations."

Nikki knew that the key word in that sentence was "serve." "It's a tempting offer," she lied, "but no thanks."

"Thinking of going for the top job yourself?"

"Hell, every one of us thinks about it," Nikki said. "But between the thinking and the doing is a long, rocky road that I'm not inclined to travel right now."

Dana rose to her feet, obviously peeved. "I suppose you'll go running to Ray to tell him all about our conversation."

"The only running I'm doing is to the DCS."

"Right," Dana said sarcastically, jerking the door open. "Remember, my enemy's friend is my enemy."

Nikki raised her right hand and made a "V" with her index and middle fingers. "Peace, sister," she said.

"Fuck you," Dana replied as she strode from the room, nearly knocking over Nikki's clerk in the process.

"What's with Cruella?" Jeb asked.

"Probably woke up on the wrong side of the coffin this morning," Nikki said. "I'd better head out to the DCS."

"You don't wanna do that," Jeb said. "Adam Noyes isn't with 'em anymore." He glanced at the notepad in his hand. "One Nicholas Jastrum, of the firm of Jastrum, Park, Wells, filed a guardian ad litem petition."

"That was fast," Nikki said.

"Happens that way when you got the kind of money young Master Noyes does."

"Guess we'd better set up a meeting with Jastrum."

Jeb grinned. "I'm waiting for him to return my call."

"Full of soul and in control," Nikki said.

Jeb dropped his head in feigned humility. "Long as you've got a few minutes, want me to see if Janice Breem is available?" Janice Breem was one of three witnesses in a bar-fight murder case. A lock.

"Hold off on that. I'd better prep for my meeting with the Noyes boy."

Jeb started to say something, then censored himself.

Nikki noticed. "The way this clerking deal works," she said, "you ask questions when you get confused."

"Okay. I don't understand. A minute ago, you were all set to meet with the boy. Now you say you need to prepare."

"Yep. Now we got lawyers mixed up in it. That always complicates matters."

"How do you prepare for that?"

She smiled. "As my grandma used to tell me, Jeb, an ounce of gossip sometimes weighs more than a pound of truth. I'm going to see how much heavy dish I can get on Mr. Nicholas Jastrum."

FROM PATIENCE'S SPOKEN DIARY: TUESDAY, AUGUST 3

More news, but this is a quickie 'cause I'm on the run. Gonna be hopping aboard the silver bird to San Fran with Ricky for a few days' frolic. I'm starting to feel like it really might happen for us. The G-man has this honey in San Fran, which would ordinarily mean I'd be staying right here, servicing my regulars. But everything is different now.

I knew I'd find true love if I kept lurking around, looking sweet and virginal. Ha-ha. Earlier today, Ricky G called Detective Liver Spot to give him the bad news that he'd have to get his own rocks off tonight. The Liver did not take it well. Usually Ricky has this the-customer-is-always-right philosophy, but the guy's reaction was so extreme G-man told him their "arrangement" was "kaput." Those were his exact words. Then he slammed down the phone and said, "Imagine the balls on that putz, threatening me. With all I've got on him." Then he stared at me. He was still angry, but the slap took me by surprise. "You musta been too nice to the bastard," he told me.

I tried not to cry.

The thing about Ricky is that he doesn't stay mad. It's like a wave washes over him. He took me in his arms and kissed my face where I could still feel the sting of his hand. He said he was sorry. He said he'd remembered he had told me to be nice to the john. "The peckerwood could do us some good, things get rough. But screw that. He tries to get in your pants again," Ricky warned, "you tell me about it."

Then it got very romantic. He was ultra cool. We did some coke and some other stuff baked just that morning. The lovemaking was so fine. My God, it was like those pukey romance novels but for real. Happening to me.

Then he got the phone call giving him the flight time. He should be back any second to pick me up.

So now, Sony, old pal, it's time for thrills and chills in the city by the bay.

≡ 5 ≡

Lt. Foster Corben, the head of Major Crimes, was a big man with a square head topped by close-cut sand-colored hair. His eyes were hooded but watchful, his nose a short right triangle above a thin-lipped mouth that seemed too small for his massive jaw. He sat at his desk in a surprisingly neat office, the sleeves of his starched white shirt rolled evenly to his elbows. "Your job is to interrogate the man," he was instructing Virgil and McNeil. "We don't punch a Bingham's ticket on just the word of a ten-year-old kid."

The room was filled with the rich aroma of recently brewed coffee, courtesy of a percolator that the detectives in his command had given Corben the previous Christmas. Virgil sniffed the air and longed for his cup, back at his desk cooling. Drawn from the office machine, it was surely more bitter than Corben's, and staler, but with less than four hours' sleep to his credit the detective yearned for its caffeinated jolt.

"Too bad the media had to spread the word about Dietz being murdered," Virgil said. "Might have helped if the killer still thought we were buyin' his suicide setup."

"Yeah, this place has got more leaks than an army latrine," Corben said in weary resignation. "Better to concentrate on things we can control. Like going easy on Bingham until we have our ducks in a row."

"We got the spray bottle of asthma medicine," McNeil said.

Corben nodded. "When we're sure it belongs to Bingham, then we might invite him down. Anything on the weapon?"

"Still checking," McNeil said.

"Okay, then. Be very cordial, gentlemen. Your job is to collect information only."

"If he confesses," McNeil asked, "should we try and talk him out of it?"

Corben sighed. "Play it friendly. Get me, Mac?"

He waited for McNeil's halfhearted nod, then levered himself out of his chair and moved to a bowl of goldfish that sat on his filing cabinet. Virgil looked at his partner. When Corben focused his attention on his fish, it was a signal to leave.

Randolph Bingham III was not at his home on the Venice Canal. Nor was he at his office in the Bingham Building on Eighth Street in downtown L.A., the young woman at the receptionist's kiosk informed them. She was more handsome than pretty, with a halo of fluffy blond hair circled by a no-nonsense telephone headset. What Virgil could see of her was dressed in a ruffled white blouse under a gray blazer that had black piping and the Bingham Inc. logo over her heart. Her large brown eyes held his as she listened to the instructions her earphones were receiving from the building's executive suite.

Eventually, she smiled and said, "Mr. Bingham, senior, will see you, gentlemen. The last elevator to your right will take you directly to the sixteenth floor."

There they were met by a smartly dressed black woman in her thirties, her hair processed and worn close to the scalp, like the late Josephine Baker's. She flashed a professional smile and informed them that she was "Divina George, Mr. Bingham's assistant." She ushered them past the semicircular desk of another gray-blazered receptionist, and down a long, thickly carpeted hall to a corner office.

It was bigger than the squad room.

Wooden, not metallic, blinds covered two walls, forming a carpet-to-ceiling right angle of protection from the morning sun. The two dark green interior walls were being used to display the heads of various unfortunate wild beasts, mounted weapons, and documents and photographs in uniform black frames. To the right of the door, a looming, furious brown bear glared at them with bright, glassy eyes. Other stuffed birds and animals were scattered on tables and pedestals, along with leafy plants and trees. The dimly lit room was so dense with objects it took Virgil a few seconds to spot the dapper man seated behind a massive wooden desk.

Divina George knocked once on the open door and said, "Detectives Daniel McNeil and Virgil Sykes to see you, sir."

Randolph J. Bingham II leapt spryly to his feet and bounced toward them, a short, wiry man in a tan silk sport coat, blue Oxford button-down shirt with yellow tie and dark brown trousers. Virgil, who was good at the age game, guessed him to be in his early sixties. "Welcome to the veldt, gentlemen," he said in a high, musical, almost effeminate voice, his inverted-triangular face breaking into a V-shaped smile.

He shook their hands energetically. "Let's take this over to Borneo," he said, leading them to a conversation pit guarded by a bristling mountain lion. "I do most of my hunting in the Dark Continent, but Suzie there is a local cat. Bagged her for a friend up near Mulholland after she filleted two of his dogs."

McNeil whispered to Virgil, "Another friggin' looney tune."

"Anyone care for coffee or a soft drink?" Divina George asked, glaring at McNeil.

Both detectives declined.

Bingham eyed his assistant speculatively as she left the room. Virgil wondered if the little man had lust in his heart or was pondering what caliber load it might take to bring her down.

Bingham turned to him. "Any idea what tribe your people came from?" he asked.

"No clue," Virgil said.

"Hard to tell," Bingham said, observing him carefully. "Masai, maybe. The Caucasian influence throws off the bone structure."

Virgil didn't much care for a discussion of his family history. He said, "We'd like to talk to your son, Mr. Bingham."

The dapper man blinked and settled back in his chair. "I assume this is about Shelli. Rand is terribly upset by her death."

"Any idea where we can find him?" Virgil asked.

"Find him? Oh, right. Of course. He is in the care of his . . . religious counselor."

"That would be. . . ?"

"What is it you want from him exactly?"

"Whatever he can tell us about last night."

Bingham raised his eyebrows. "I know he and Shelli were together earlier in the evening and parted shortly after dinner."

"What makes you think that?" McNeil asked.

"I talked to him at ten, or thereabouts. He was getting ready to leave her house on his way home."

"He must be a good boy, keeping you posted on his romantic progress," McNeil said.

Bingham studied the red-haired detective. Virgil knew his partner was misreading the man, mistaking cordiality and eccentricity for weakness. Virgil had met men like Randolph Bingham II before, men who'd almost forgotten how to raise their voices because they so seldom had to.

"He doesn't call that often," the little man replied to McNeil's question as if he were taking it seriously. "He was eager to tell me the news that Shelli had just agreed to become his wife."

McNeil's reddish eyebrows went up. "No kiddin'?" he said. "People are still doing that?"

Virgil said, "He sounded pretty happy about it?"

"Ecstatic. Rand isn't the sort to get enthusiastic about any—"

Suddenly, the floor seemed to drop. The blinds clacked against the windows. The walls of the building groaned like a ship's hull and Bingham's stuffed creatures tottered on their bases. The bear did a pirouette before settling down.

None of the men saw the bear. They were staring at one another. Bingham and McNeil were showing the normal amount of apprehension, but Virgil was frozen, his body coated with icy sweat, his last cup of coffee rising harsh and sour into his throat. No matter how long

he lived in southern California, he would never get used to the trem-
blers.

He clutched the arm of his chair, waiting for the aftershock.

"That was a big boy," Bingham said heartily. "At least a four-pointer.
I think this hot weather brings 'em on. You all right, Detective Sykes?"

"Fine," Virgil replied. "We were—"

The aftershock hit. More creaking and rocking.

Bingham was looking at him with concern. "Lemme get Div . . . Ms.
George to bring you some water. Maybe a seltzer?"

Virgil's heart was pounding. He shook his head. "No. It's okay."

He saw the worried frown on McNeil's face and repeated, "It's okay."
But he'd lost his place in the interrogation.

McNeil understood that and took up the slack. "Mr. Bingham, before God started hiccupping, you were saying your son told you he and
the Dietz woman had just set the date, huh?"

"Not set the date, exactly."

"She was wearing a nice engagement ring," McNeil said. "Your boy
must've given it to her earlier that night, eh?"

"I don't recall his mentioning a ring, but that seems a logical surmise."

"Was this good news, Mr. Bingham?" McNeil asked.

"Of course."

"An older woman with a kid in tow who's part black. You considered her pretty good daughter-in-law material?"

Bingham's eyes shifted to Virgil, who was trying not to think about
when the next trembler might hit. "Rand's thirty-two years old," the
little man said. "Shelli was thirty-five. Not exactly summer and winter.
I liked her. Wouldn't have leased the house to her, if I hadn't. She'd
turned those drawings of hers into quite a success. She had substance,
the kind of woman Rand needed. And Adam's a clever little rascal.
Bright as a button. I hope he's got good help to get him through this
nightmare."

He leaned forward. "The thing to keep in mind, gentlemen, is that
my son was totally in love with Shelli. If you've got any misconception
about that, you will waste a great deal of your time."

"Any idea who might have wanted to kill Ms. Dietz?" Virgil asked, his voice a dry croak.

"None whatsoever. We live in difficult times. I used to be amused by the phrase so common on news shows, 'senseless murder.' I would wonder, how could a murder be sensible? These days, people kill people for no reason at all."

"Just for the hell of it, huh?" McNeil said. "Like going out and shooting an elephant or a tiger."

That one caught the old man off-guard, but he continued to smile impassively.

"Your son take any drugs?" Virgil asked.

"Lord, no."

"Any ailments?"

"Has his share of colds. That what you mean?"

"What about asthma?"

Bingham hesitated, then replied with a nod. "Bronchial asthma," the old man said, as if he were trying to distance it from the common variety.

"We really have to talk with him," Virgil said.

"About what?"

"His mood, now that the wedding is off," McNeil said.

Bingham's enigmatic smile remained in place. Virgil wondered what it would take to get rid of it. A heart attack, maybe.

The door was thrown open and a youthful, taller, heavier version of Bingham senior stormed into the room. "You okay, Dad? That was a five point—" He stopped, seeing the detectives. "Sorry. I didn't know you were busy."

"We've weathered the quake, thank you," Bingham said. "This is my younger son, Jeffrey. Detectives Sykes and McNeil."

Jeffrey Bingham didn't offer to shake their hands. He glanced at McNeil and through Virgil, who was familiar with that particular reaction. The cellophane effect.

"Detectives, huh? About Shelli?" Jeffrey asked McNeil.

"You knew Ms. Dietz?" McNeil asked back.

"Keats brought her around," he said sullenly.

"Keats?"

"Jeffrey's nickname for his brother," the little man said. He turned to Virgil. "There was a poet named Keats. John Keats. From England."

Fed up with the man's patronizing bullshit, Virgil said, "No wonder he and Ms. Dietz got together."

"How's that?"

"Keats and Shelli," Virgil said.

Bingham stared at him, smile still in place.

"How'd you feel about Shelli joining the family?" McNeil asked Jeffrey.

"It wasn't any concern of mine." He turned to his father. "Call me when you're free, Dad," he said and headed for the door.

"We might need to talk with you later," McNeil said.

The impatient young man left the room without acknowledging the statement.

"How can we reach Randolph's religious adviser?" Virgil asked.

"Her name is Mildred Lupton. Sister Mildred is her designation, I believe. Ms. George has the information."

"What sort of religion does Sister Mildred represent?"

"I haven't the foggiest idea," Bingham said, his smile broadening. "Nothing too organized, I'm sure."

≡ 6 ≡

The legal offices of the firm of Jastrum, Park, Wells were in Century City, twenty-seven floors off the still shifting ground. Nikki was seated at a glass-and-chrome table in a conference room, staring through a floor-to-ceiling window at another swaying high-rise across the Avenue of the Stars. The sway of their building was moving them in the opposite direction, doubling the disorienting effect of the quake's aftershock.

If it had been up to Nikki she would not have been in that seismically active high-rise at that ill-fated time. She believed that elegant law offices were the last places an honest deputy district attorney should set foot. Signs of wealth and prestige and power were everywhere—the polished parquet floor peeking from behind vaguely somber Oriental carpets, the soft glove-leather chairs, and tasteful works of art, the sleek contemporary desk with its smoky two-inch-thick glass top. Such surroundings and the air of unhurried efficiency seemed designed to compromise, or at least demoralize, an underpaid and overworked lawyer for the county.

Adam Noyes's attorney, Nicholas Jastrum, had insisted that the meeting take place in his office. So she was there, waiting for the building and her stomach to subside. The little boy sat across from her, his back to the window, staring down at the vibrating glass tabletop. His thin body, garbed in yellow Polo shirt and khaki slacks, had gone rigid. Jastrum and Adam's nanny, Jenny Mapes, seemed to be too much under the spell of the swaying buildings to notice the boy's reaction to the quake, so Nikki reached out and placed a comforting hand on his arm. He lifted sea green eyes to hers. His front teeth were small and slightly separated. They gave his face a boyish goofiness that his large intelligent eyes denied. He smiled and she felt his arm relax.

"What's your name again?" he asked.

"Nikki Hill."

"And he's Nick," the boy said, drawing the youthful lawyer into their conversation.

"These damn quakes," Nick Jastrum said, slowly unfreezing.

"I keep saying I'm gonna leave this crazy place," Jenny said. In another decade, she'd be an earth-mother type, Nikki thought. At the moment, she was a tall and fleshy twenty-year-old whose unseasonable black dress intensified her chalky complexion and matched her spiky bottle-black hair.

"Where do you go that's safe?" Jastrum asked. "When I was at Harvard Law, we had fires and snowstorms, so what can you do?" Nikki's friend Sue Fells, who worked for the firm, had described the young lawyer, the grandson of the founding Jastrum, as an arrogant, handsome, opinionated yutz who couldn't go twenty minutes without bringing Harvard Law into the conversation. *Bingo on all counts.* Sue had mentioned something else about Nick Jastrum that Nikki suspected she would have to address before their meeting ended.

"Hey, Adam, yo?" Jastrum asked, setting the cause of Ebonics back about fifty years. "You aw'right, man?"

"Ah'm cool, bro," Adam replied mockingly. He winked at Nikki. She found him completely engaging.

"Well, I think that wraps it up, Ms. Hill," Jastrum said.

"Wraps what up? I've only been here thirty minutes, and ten of that was waiting for you in the reception area."

"We don't want to wear the kid out." He lowered his voice and whispered, "He's been through enough." As if Adam couldn't hear better than both of them.

"I want to answer her questions," the boy said. He turned to Nikki. "Then afterward, can you tell me about some of your trials?"

The quid pro quo caught her off-guard. "I . . . sure, I guess." She hoped she could think of one or two that might be appropriate to discuss with a ten-year-old. Maybe some that would serve as cautionary tales. "Right now, though, I'd like you to tell me about last night."

"I heard Mom and Randy shouting at each other."

"You were sleeping, Adam," Jastrum said. "I bet it was a dream."

"I lay in bed listening to them for a long time."

"How can you be sure whose voice you were hearing?" Jastrum asked. "Couldn't it have been some new visitor? Or even the TV?"

"Mr. Jastrum," Nikki said, "you mind letting Adam tell it his way?"

Jastrum responded with pouty silence.

"I know Randy's voice," Adam said. "I know what it sounds like when he's loud and angry."

"You've heard him angry before?" Nikki asked.

"Sure. He does a lot of acting out."

She smiled. "How do you know about 'acting out'?"

The boy gave her a sheepish look. "I used to do that when I was real little. When I didn't get my way. I got over it, but I don't think Randy did."

"You ever *see* him get mad at your mom?"

"We went to San Francisco one time for a couple of days. My mom took me to the aquarium while Randy did . . . I don't know what he did. Some kind of business. But when we got back, Randy was stomping around the hotel room, really mad, because we were a little late. And he hit her."

"Hit your mom?"

"Slapped her."

"In front of you?"

"Uh-huh. I tried to punch him, but he just pushed me away. Mom was crying, too. He gets mad easy."

"When was this, Adam?" Jastrum asked.

"When? Last year."

"You sure this really happened?" the lawyer asked. "That you didn't just make it up?"

"Mr. Jastrum, what are you trying to do?" Nikki asked.

"Playing devil's advocate."

"Let me suggest an appropriate place for you to go play it."

"Oh, really?" Jastrum said in a tone of annoyance. "Well, that's it. This meeting's over. Jenny, take Adam back to the apartment."

Jenny Mapes moved behind Adam's chair, but the boy didn't stand. "I want to tell her about Randy," he said. "And I want to hear about the stuff she does."

"Hey, Adam," Jastrum said, "the Nickster knows what's best for his main man."

"Main man?" Adam gave him a disgusted look. "You're supposed to be my lawyer, right?"

Jastrum straightened and dropped the soul brother act like a hot penny. "I'm the lawyer your mother appointed to look after your best interests."

"My mom never even met you."

"She was a client of this firm," Jastrum said, his face flushed. "So was your dad."

"Now *I'm* the client," Adam said.

"No. Your mother's estate is the client."

Nikki had had enough. "You're right, Mr. Jastrum," she said. "No sense putting Adam through this any longer."

The boy registered surprise and disappointment.

She took his hand, squeezed it, and brought a grin back to his face when she said, "We'll talk tomorrow."

Jastrum started to comment. Instead he pasted a smile on his face, raised his right arm, and said to Adam, "High-five me, my man."

The boy shook his head in disgust and turned to Jenny. "Ready?" he asked.

The spike-haired nanny gave Jastrum a questioning look and he nodded vigorously. "So long, Adam," he said.

"Bye," the boy replied solemnly. He paused at the door and turned to Nikki. "Tomorrow, do we have to do it here?"

"We'll figure something out," she said.

"The park by the place where we're staying looks nice."

"Maybe the park."

The heavy glass door to the conference room had barely swung shut when Jastrum said, "Little bastard."

"Orphan. Not bastard."

"Yeah. Well, whatever, you won't be meeting with him again."

"Wow." She gave him a wide smile. "So you've got a plan to stop a district attorney from questioning a willing witness in a murder case, huh? That what they're teaching at Harvard Law these days?"

He glared at her. "You really want to put that little boy on the stand? Isn't losing his mother enough? Right now, he's got reporters and TV newspeople climbing over each other to get to him."

"Please, Mr. Jastrum. I just saw an example of your concern for Adam."

"I resent your fucking attitude, *Ms.* Hill, and I'm going to convey my feelings to Ray Wise."

She wondered what Wise's reaction would be. Would he back her or turn chickenshit? Not that it mattered. Jastrum wouldn't be talking to him. She said, "You're going to have to get somebody else from the firm to do the hands-on with Adam."

"Yes? Dream on, lady."

"Www, dot, Poetsource, dot, com."

He frowned.

"A nice, handsome Web page for a mail-order company," she continued. "Got some lovely art, pretty colors. Nice order form. You can buy books that'll help you with your own poems, send in your work and get it appraised by experts. All for a fee, of course."

"Your point?"

"It's Randolph Bingham's operation."

"I still don't—"

"You're an investor in Poetsource," Nikki said.

"A few of us threw some money into a hat and Rand used it to start up his poetry thing. It was a lark."

"A lark that clears around six hundred grand a year," she said. "Love that World Wide Web."

"Where are you going with all this?"

"You're doing business with a man who may have had something to do with the murder of Adam's mother."

"That's ridiculous. Rand Bingham's no murderer."

"You may be right. But Adam says he heard Mr. Bingham shouting at his mother on the night she was killed."

Jastrum glared at her. "Maybe he heard it and maybe he didn't. The bottom line is that this firm does not represent the Binghams. Unfortunately. My connection to Rand is tangential. I may have helped him with some start-up capital. Big deal."

"Your definition of tangential is a little different from mine. You and he have been close friends since you were five years old. Both went to Andover. In the same house at Harvard. But the main reason you're going to have to recuse yourself is that you're in business with him."

"That's your opinion."

"No. That's the law. Maybe you slept through that class. Anyway, you should be happy to let somebody else deal with Adam. For some strange reason, he thinks you're an asshole."

"Like I give a damn what the little twerp thinks."

"According to my figures," Nikki said, "what with Homeboy Software, the company his father founded, and the royalties and subsidiary rights to the literary properties his mother left him, the little twerp is worth about eighty-five million dollars."

"The estate is. Maybe more. So what? Adam has no say in the matter until he's twenty-one."

"Right this minute, he could be phoning some hungry lawyer who'll be overjoyed to challenge your guardian ad litem petition. The next step would be to mess with the will and tie this firm up in so many knots, you'll think you've been macraméd. Why risk all that because you and the boy don't hit it off? Find somebody who can get along with Adam and your firm can keep on keeping on, billing the estate at six hundred dollars an hour."

The young lawyer relaxed suddenly and gave her a knowing smile. "Somebody who can get along with Adam, huh? Gee, would you be thinking of leaving the D.A.'s office, Ms. Hill?"

"No. I like my job. All I'm trying to do is get it done."

He was silent for a moment, evidently considering his position. She decided to push him just a bit more. "Do your father and the other partners know about your financial connection to Randolph Bingham?"

He glared at her.

"You could always give up your interest in Poetsource," she said. "If Bingham goes on trial, it could be bad for business anyway. Or it could mean lots more hits on that old Web site; people are so intrigued by murder."

"I suppose someone else *could* handle Adam," he said, almost choking on the words.

"Somebody who really likes kids. They can always tell. I'll call you tomorrow to set up a time for my meeting with the boy. We'll have to figure out a place, too. I'm not coming back here." She didn't wait for his reply.

Striding past richly appointed offices, she spied the familiar large, impressive form of Jesse K. Fallon, the attorney the media had labeled the "Black Melvin Belli." Some people said he was a mind reader. The year before, they'd been on opposite sides in a murder case, an experience that had half-convinced Nikki that those people were right. He nodded to her in a courtly manner and smiled. She returned the nod and moved on quickly. *Stay out of my head, old man,* she thought. *Nothing here for you today.*

≡ 7 ≡

Virgil waited for a break in the southbound traffic along the Pacific Coast Highway, then pushed the sedan into a one-eighty from the center divider.

"Christ, it's nearly three and I'm roasting in here," McNeil complained.

"Maybe if you shut your window, the AC could do a better job."

"I need fresh air," McNeil said. "Hey, nice digs, huh?"

The headquarters for the Church of the Romantic was a three-story weathered-wood-and-glass building separated from the PCH by a semi-crowded parking lot. Virgil guided the sedan past the gate and found an empty slot between an Eddie Bauer Ford Expedition and a Toyota 4Runner so new it was still wearing its inflated sticker price.

They'd received a crash course in the history of the church from a rotisserie-baseball buddy of Virgil's who taught philosophy at UC–Dominguez Hills. Its founder, the late Brother Matthew Lupton, had been a publicist at MGM who was pink-slipped during one of the studio's many transitions. Armed with severance pay, some costumes lifted from Wardrobe and an interesting new wrinkle on fundamentalist evangelism, he began a television ministry that combined balm for the soul with aerobic exercise for the body. According to the philosophy professor, the ministry's show, *The Health and Glory Hour*, beamed out each week across the nation from southern California, featuring shapely young men and women in colorful tights writhing aerobically while the charismatic Brother Matthew thumped the Bible, peddled holistic placebos, and passed the hat.

TV provided the church with more money than Lupton had ever dreamed possible. In 1987, when he moved on to meet his maker, his widow, known to the flock as Sister Mildred, a former actress from the 1960s (*Beach Blanket Rumble, Bikinis in Outer Space*), used a small hunk of the donations to take advantage of a momentary drop in the value of southern California real estate. She purchased a sizable section of the same beachfront where she once wiggled her bikini before the cameras.

"I understand you can drop thirty pounds and all your sins here in two weeks," McNeil said as they got out of the sedan. "Comes to about a grand a pound. Sins are free."

"Sins you don't pay for, huh? That'll be the day," Virgil said.

They'd explained to Ms. George at Bingham's office that they preferred to drop in on the church unannounced, but Sister Mildred didn't seem too surprised to find them standing in her office.

The curvaceous starlet was still in evidence in the rounded, serene woman whose unlined heart-shaped face was topped by ringlets of gray hair. "I hope you haven't made the trip for nothing," she said.

"Randolph Bingham isn't here?" Virgil asked.

"Oh, he's here," she said. "But he may not wish to speak with you."

She walked them to a small waiting room that smelled of patchouli incense. "Make yourselves comfortable while I tell Randy you're here."

McNeil opened his mouth to say something, but Virgil shook his head. When they were alone, he explained, "If he refuses to talk, we've got enough probable cause to get a warrant. It might even work better that way."

When Sister Mildred returned, she told them Bingham was eager to cooperate and led them upstairs to a communal dining room to await his arrival. Wooden chairs were tucked under round tables. The walls were filled with paintings and photographs of nature in revolt. Storms, fires, earthquakes, and tornadoes. Not exactly subjects to aid digestion, Virgil thought.

A much more appropriate view was provided by a series of sliding glass doors, open to sand and surf and cool, salty breezes wafting in from the ocean. He stared out at an expanse of beach, occupied by twenty or more black-and-white-striped tents stretched along the shore. Men and women, some of them African-American (which surprised him, because the "Church" didn't strike him as multicultural), rested on deck chairs or towels, wearing thongs and sandals. There seemed to be no interaction, just private meditation.

"Holy Bikinis, Batman," McNeil said.

Sister Mildred ignored the comment, pointing to a table near the open doors. "That should be a nice cool spot."

She strolled to a sideboard and poured two glasses of lemonade.

"Your church seems a lot more laid-back than mine, Sister Mildred," McNeil said, accepting his drink.

"That's the whole point," she said. "You don't celebrate individual freedom by enforcing a structured environment. We maintain that same sort of freedom in opening our doors to everyone. Even policemen."

"I'll keep that in mind," McNeil said.

"Randy will be with you in a minute."

Virgil watched her glide from the room. He stood and strolled through the doors to the balcony. A man wearing an open multicolored robe and a red bikini swimsuit flopped his sandals toward the building. His thin body was deeply tanned. Large mirrored sunglasses covered a sizable portion of his triangular face.

"That our boy?" McNeil was standing beside him.

"Has the Bingham V-shaped head," Virgil said.

"Sunburned poet, huh? These romantics got their own style of mourning."

They were both seated, with a small cassette recorder on the table in front of them, when Randolph Bingham III entered the room, led by Sister Mildred.

She did the introductions, then said, "Randy has asked me to join you."

"Unh-unh," McNeil said. "We'll speak with him solo."

"I . . . want Sister Mildred here," Bingham said. "She's like my doctor."

The young man seemed scattered, as if his timing mechanism had thrown a few cogs. Maybe grief trauma, Virgil thought. Or maybe he'd been popping some pills out there in the sun. "No problem," the detective said, starting the recorder.

His partner glared at him, then shifted his attention to Bingham. "Mind losing the sunglasses?"

"The glare . . . of course, if you feel it's important." His eyes were green, like his father's. He squinted, then stood up so suddenly Virgil's hand moved toward his gun. Bingham was only repositioning his chair to put his back to the sun. "What . . . what exactly do you gentlemen need from me?"

"This must be a rough time for you, Mr. Bingham," Virgil said. "We'll try to make it short."

"I appreciate that."

"You seem a little jumpy, Mr. B.," McNeil said, staring at the tanned man. "You on any kind of medication?"

Bingham opened his mouth, but Sister Mildred interrupted him. "The only drugs allowed under this roof, Detective, are those that have been legally prescribed for reasons of health."

"Well, gee, I didn't mean to suggest you were runnin' a crack house, ma'am." He turned to Bingham. "Legal drugs is what I meant."

"As of today, I'm on Prozac."

"That it?"

Bingham nodded.

"Your father said you had a bronchial condition," Virgil said.

"Oh, yes. Bronchial asthma. I have my spray, of course. Serevet. And I take Accolate twice a day."

"Good," McNeil said. "Glad we cleared that up. Now, why don't you just tell us about last night?"

Bingham faltered, his eyes filling with tears. Sister Mildred's hand rested on his arm. It seemed to give him strength. "Sh-shouldn't my lawyer be here?" he asked.

McNeil's eyes went from the tape recorder to Virgil.

"We're not here to accuse you of anything," Virgil said to the young man. "We're only trying to find out how Ms. Dietz spent the evening. You were with her for most of it. But if you'd feel more comfortable with a lawyer present . . ."

Bingham looked at his companion. "Sister Mildred is comfort enough."

"Okay," Virgil said. "Then if you could run through the events of the night—?"

"I arrived at the house at seven," Bingham said, sniffling. "I'd made a reservation at Campanille, but Adam's nanny wasn't available, so we wound up at a place he likes on Melrose instead. Techno's."

"What happened to the nanny?"

"She was visiting her family in . . . Visalia? Somewhere like that. Anyway, the boy was with us and we got back to the house around nine. The three of us watched TV in the den. Then Adam went upstairs to get ready for bed."

"What'd you watch?" McNeil asked.

"Some show Adam likes about a policeman who has the heightened senses of jungle animals."

"Sounds like you, partner," McNeil said.

"What happened after the show?" Virgil asked Bingham.

"Shelli took Adam upstairs to make sure he went directly to bed and didn't get sidetracked by his computer. By the time she got back, I'd . . ." He lost steam again and looked to Sister Mildred for support.

"Harmony saps the creative spirit, Randy," she said, smiling beatifically. "Embrace the conflict."

McNeil rolled his eyes but remained quiet.

"By the time Shelli got back," Bingham said, "I was all set. I'd poured the champagne and placed a jewel box on the center of the coffee table. She opened the box and saw the engagement ring inside. I asked her to marry me."

"And she said?" Virgil prompted.

"She said it was what she wanted, too." His eyes closed and his head dropped, pointy chin digging into the collar of his robe.

"And then?"

Bingham opened his eyes "We . . . kissed, held each other. We cried. Happy tears. I put the ring on her finger and we kissed again. I suggested we go upstairs and tell Adam, but Shelli said she thought it would be better if we waited."

"Why?"

"Adam was very depen——oh, Jesus, what the kid must be going through. How's he doing?"

"I've been told he's doing all right," Virgil said.

"If he needs anything . . ."

"You were saying Shelli Dietz didn't want you to tell Adam about the marriage plans."

"She just didn't want to hit him with it out of the blue like that."

"Was your proposal a surprise to Ms. Dietz?"

"No. We'd been discussing it for a while. But Adam wasn't expecting it and she wanted to prepare him a little for a new dad."

"You and he get along all right?" McNeil asked.

"Sure. He's a good kid."

"A truthful kid?" Virgil asked.

Bingham frowned. "Far as I know, yes. Why?"

Virgil ignored the question. "You and Ms. Dietz did a little celebrating, then?"

The tanned man hesitated, then nodded.

"You left the house when, exactly?"

"Ten-fifteen, ten-thirty."

"Your father said you phoned him a little before that."

Bingham nodded. "That's correct."

"Did you and Ms. Dietz have an argument that night?"

"No." The frown was back. "Did Dad say—"

"Randy," Sister Mildred interrupted. "Unlock. Restore."

Bingham closed his eyes.

"Did you raise your voice at the house?" Virgil asked. "Maybe in a rush of happiness?"

"No. We were purposely keeping it low. The boy was asleep upstairs. We didn't want to disturb him."

"On your drive home," McNeil said, "I don't suppose you stopped for gas or a pizza or anything like that?"

"No. I drove directly home."

"Anybody see you? A neighbor?"

"Not that I know of." He leaned forward. "Are you accusing me of having something to do with Shelli's death?"

"Actually, we're trying to eliminate you from the list of suspects," Virgil said.

"I loved her. She loved me. I'd never have done anything to hurt her."

"Can you think of anybody who might have wanted to hurt her?"

"No. Shelli didn't make enemies. People liked her. Sister?"

"We all loved Shelli," Sister Mildred said.

"She was a member of this church?"

"No, not exactly a member," Sister Mildred said. "She wasn't a believer in any sort of organized religion, even one as open as ours. But she and Adam came here with Randy every so often."

"What about your family, Mr. Bingham?" Virgil asked. "Your father and mother and brother, they liked her, too?"

"Dad loved Shelli almost as much as I did," Bingham said. "My mother died some time ago."

"And your brother?" Virgil asked.

"Jeffrey . . . tends to be a bit overprotective, as if I were *his* younger brother."

"He didn't approve of Ms. Dietz?"

"Shelli was slightly older than I. And she had a child. My brother is a true conservative." He smiled. "We're alike in many ways, but not in that. And not in religion. He prefers to worship tradition, while I believe in the true democracy of individualism. Every human experience is valid."

"Even murder?" Virgil asked.

Bingham blinked and turned to Sister Mildred. "We believe that too much harmony dulls the human spirit," she said. "Therefore we prefer conflict over harmony. However, we neither encourage nor condone any form of antisocial behavior.

"I think it might be best if we let Randy get back to his meditation now."

"He'll get back to it when we're finished," McNeil said.

"We're just about through," Virgil said, earning a hostile glare from his partner. "Mr. Bingham, you said you and Ms. Dietz drank champagne. Clink glasses and all that?"

Bingham nodded.

"We only found one glass. Any idea what happened to the other one?"

Bingham looked genuinely puzzled. "No."

"Well, that about does it," Virgil said, turning off the tape recorder. "Thank you both for your cooperation."

Driving back to the city via the PCH, McNeil said, "You really spread your cheeks back there."

"You hear him confess?" Virgil asked.

"No."

"As I recall, our orders were to question him, unless he happened to confess."

"You didn't have to put up with the old broad's shit."

"Wasn't for her we'd still be there waiting for Bingham's lawyer to show up, and we would've gotten the same information, or less."

"You got bupkis."

"Me?" Virgil said hotly. "Somebody give you the day off?" For nearly all of their years together, McNeil had led their interrogations, with Virgil acting as backup. During the past few months, that order had been reversed. Virgil had assumed it was because the older detective was demonstrating his trust. Lately, however, McNeil's criticism had become so harsh that Virgil began to feel as if he were being set up.

"The old bitch pissed me off," McNeil mumbled. "She reminded me of my wife."

"She wasn't anything like your wife."

"She had tits, didn't she?" McNeil replied.

•   •   •

"I been thinking of putting in for a new partner," Virgil said to Nikki that night as the two of them lay in her bed. He was staring at the TV set across the room, but he wasn't all that interested in what Kim Basinger was saying to David Letterman about man's inhumanity to animals.

Nikki looked up from her novel. "I hope you're not talking about me," she said.

He grinned. "No, baby. I'm talking about the partner I don't sleep with."

"Isn't he close to retirement?"

"Two years away. I don't think I can put up with him that long."

"You talk to him about it?"

"I guess I'm gonna have to." He yawned. "You about finished reading?"

"With you working nights, I been using these junky novels to put me to sleep."

"Well, toss that thing on the floor, woman," he said. "I've got something that's much mo' bettah."

"A video?" she asked with a grin.

≡ 8 ≡

Virgil was gone when Nikki returned from her morning workout with the big dog. Since she'd left him still in bed, mumbling about taking her to breakfast, she assumed something unexpected must have come up. She wondered if it involved the Dietz murder.

Just before 8 A.M., dressed and ready for the daily battle, she phoned him. She didn't bother listening to his voice-mail instructions. She'd heard them before.

She was annoyed.

Initially she was annoyed at Virgil for not having left a note. Then she was annoyed with herself for being annoyed with him. She clearly understood that in both their jobs the emergency call took precedence over social niceties. Still, damn it, if there was action on Dietz, she wanted to know about it. It could impact on her meeting later that morning with Adam Noyes.

The meeting! She'd have to check with Jastrum to find out when the boy would be available. Then it would be up to her clerk to work her schedule around it. Jeb would squawk, of course. *What about the other six murder cases*, he'd complain. *Do we just blow them off? Or the five spousal abuses, the rapes, child welfare, the trip to McLaren Hall?*

He was right, she supposed. She was giving Adam Noyes special attention. She wasn't precisely sure why.

Bird's gruff bark made her realize she'd been hunkering beside his bowl with an open can of his special food in her hand for several minutes. The big dog was staring at her impatiently.

"Like you'd starve to death if you missed a meal," she said, spooning half of the can into the dish. "Try to keep this in your mouth and off your beard."

Instead of dashing to the bowl, as usual, Bird raised his big head, apparently offended by the comment.

"Yeah, well, pout and go hungry," she told him.

She'd barely reentered the house when she heard the animal lapping away. Such was the beauty of pets: They made you smile, no matter what kind of mood you were in.

The smile had faded by the time she arrived at her office. The heat of the morning had overpowered her Mazda RX7's air conditioner and the car's muffler had shaken loose and sounded like a Harley on steroids—so loud she could barely hear the news. What she had heard had nothing to do with Shelli Dietz's murder.

At her desk she had another earful of Virgil's voice-mail instructions. She wished he had a cellular phone; he'd been holding out, annoyed that the department expected detectives to carry them without any form of reimbursement.

Failing to reach him, she called the offices of Jastrum, Park, Wells.

A young woman with a clipped British accent who identified herself as Nicholas Jastrum's assistant informed her that "Adam Noyes will be expecting you at ten A.M. at his temporary quarters."

"And where might they be?" Nikki asked, trying not to mock the woman.

"The Stanford Apartments on the Wilshire corridor," Jastrum's assistant replied. She pronounced the name of the boulevard "Wil-shyer." Her twangy air of superiority made Nikki feel she was being chided for not doing her homework.

"Will Mr. Jastrum be joining us on the corridor?" she asked, knowing the answer.

"I'm afraid his shed-yool will not permit."

"You really from England?"

"I beg your pah-don!" the woman said indignantly.

"Didn't think so," Nikki said and replaced the receiver.

Jeb reacted to news of the ten o'clock meeting with expected frustration, a very tall skeleton hovering over her desk with a frown on his dark brown face. "What about the Clemsons?" he asked, referring to a spousal-abuse case. "We've postponed them twice already."

"Third time's the charm," Nikki said.

"She got beat up pretty bad."

"That was then," Nikki said. "I spoke with her yesterday. Now she doesn't want her hubby going to jail. She says if we can just scare him a little, everything'll be fine. That sort of lowers Mrs. Clemson on my list of things to do. You see what I'm saying?"

"You the man," Jeb said, then added, "in any case, you're gonna have to rush back here. The Not-So-Great White Father has invited you to be in his office at eleven."

"About Dietz?" she asked.

Jeb shrugged. "Don't know. You got me too busy changing your schedule around to stay tuned in to the office hot line."

Even before he was out the door, Nikki was dialing Wise's extension. More frustration. Jeri, the friendlier of the D.A.'s two secretaries, informed her that he'd left orders not to be disturbed.

"Sounds serious," Nikki said, fishing.

"He's with his campaign advisers," Jeri said.

"What's our eleven o'clock all about?"

"Don't know, girlfriend. He didn't say."

≡ 9 ≡

The doorman at the Stanford Apartments had sideburns almost to his chin and was dressed in a purple uniform with white-and-yellow piping on the coat lapels. The designer of that outfit must've been on something spectacularly illegal, Nikki thought. Standing ramrod stiff, the man was not quite as tall as she and four inches of that was purple, yellow, and white hat.

"I'm here to see John Chase," she informed him. It was the name the law firm was using to keep Adam Noyes hidden from the media.

"Are you Ms. Hill?"

She nodded.

"They said to tell you they'd be in the park."

"They?"

"Young Mr. Chase, his nanny, and the older gentleman," he said, shifting his attention to a well-dressed matron approaching the building.

The park was directly across Wilshire Boulevard, small and surprisingly green in the midst of the current heat wave. It took her nearly a minute to realize why the grounds looked so unusually pristine: there were no representatives of the city's homeless population camping out on the grass. It was an election year, time to "Take Back Our Streets and Parks." At least until the votes were counted.

Where did the homeless go? she wondered. One of these days, they just might get it together enough to form a coalition, march on City Hall, demand their rights to sleep on whatever park grass they felt like.

She was stopped from this fanciful notion by the sight of Adam Noyes, standing on a sun-splashed section of emerald lawn. The tall oaks surrounding him seemed determined to keep the park moderately cool and shady, but he'd found a patch of smog-faded blue sky and was using a handheld device to send a winged object in its general direction. He was wearing jeans, an orange T-shirt, basketball shoes of an impossibly elaborate interweaving of canvas, plastic, rubber, and metal, and a Dodgers baseball cap that hid his curly hair.

"Well, Ms. Hill," a familiar baritone said. "Right on time."

She turned to discover the legendary attorney Jesse K. Fallon seated on a shaded bench, blessing her with a beatific smile. She had had ample opportunity to observe him the year before, during her prosecution of his client, the entertainer Dyana Cooper. The man on the bench was looking a little different. Gone were the tailored three-piece suit, immaculate white shirt, power-red tie, and polished black shoes. In their place were a red-and-white-checked shirt covered by a faded red windbreaker, slightly rumpled khaki pants, and, most surprising of all, worn and scuffed white sneakers. On his head was a floppy white golf hat that bore a patch reading "Pebble Beach Open."

"My day off," he said. He was probably reacting to the expression on her face, but she was once again reminded of his mind-reading capability.

"I was expecting a clerk or a junior member of the firm."

"Seemed like easy duty. Spending some time with a bright little multimillionaire," he said, patting the bench next to him. "Join me. Give Adam a few more minutes of childhood."

"Where's Jenny?" she asked, sitting down.

"Off on a search for sodas for us. Have to keep up our fluids in this heat. What's your opinion of Ms. Mapes?"

"I haven't seen enough of her to have an opinion."

"I'm not overwhelmed by my first impression," he said. "But perhaps I'm judging the book by its cover."

Nikki shifted her attention to Adam, who had used his remote control to bring the flying object down to within a few feet of the grass. It hovered there, then released a round bomb that fell to the ground with a loud crashing sound. Adam picked up the bomb, reattached it to the underside of the still hovering jet plane or alien spaceship, whatever it was. Then the strange craft shot forward, traveling up and away. "That's an amazing toy," Nikki said.

"It's a Homeboy prototype. Unlike any other remote-controlled craft on the market, it is multidirectional and has nearly unlimited hovering capability."

"Some kinda gizmo, all right."

"He designed it," Fallon said.

"Get outta here!" she exclaimed. "He's ten years old."

"Going on forty," Fallon replied with a grin. "An exceptional little boy."

They watched Adam bring the plane in for a perfect landing on the grass.

"You see it, too, don't you?" he asked.

"Beg pardon?"

"His uniqueness," Fallon said. "I have a son and two daughters. The boy went to Yale, the girls to Brown. One is still there. They're intellectually curious, good-natured, and a father's pride and joy. Adam is something else, however. There's no telling how far he can go, how much he can achieve."

As if sensing that he was the topic of discussion, Adam turned and stared at them. His face, which had been closed in concentration, relaxed suddenly. With a shout of "Nikki!" he ran toward her, throwing his arms around her waist and hugging her. She hugged him back.

"You came," the boy said happily. "Like you said you would."

"That surprises you?"

"People don't always mean what they say," Adam replied, stiffening a little and pulling away.

Fallon was watching them thoughtfully.

"That's some plane you're flying," Nikki said, indicating the toy on the grass.

"It's *Plane* Nine from Outer Space. You know, named after the bad old movie, *Plan Nine from Outer Space*," he said. "Is it okay if I test it just a little bit more before we talk?"

"Sure."

"Then do you have some stories about cases you've tried?"

"Uh-huh." She'd thought of a couple that didn't involve anything too unsavory.

"Great," he said, racing across the lawn to his Plane Nine.

"How much time did you spend with Adam yesterday?" Fallon asked her.

"Your associate didn't give me a lot. Thirty minutes, tops."

"Had you met him before?"

"No. Why?"

Fallon smiled. "He seems to have bonded with you more than with Ms. Mapes, who's been caring for him for more than a year."

Adam had picked up the plane and was brushing grass and dirt from its wheels. He looked at them. "I'll take just two more test runs. Okay?"

"Sure," Nikki replied. She turned to Fallon and lowered her voice. "Have you located any family? Grandparents? Aunts or uncles?"

He shook his head. "No. You know about his father, the one who started Homeboy?"

"Not any more than that."

"Brilliant man, but not smart enough to stay away from narcotics. Sober, he was an ideal husband and father. Drugged . . . well, not so ideal."

"Physically abusive?"

"Oh, yes."

"Adam, too?"

Fallon's pale blue eyes registered genuine sadness as he nodded.

"How bad?" she asked, shifting her gaze to the boy playing in the patch of sunlight.

"Various abrasions and contusions. These we know about because, I am ashamed to say, my firm successfully defended Jerome Noyes against an assault charge."

"Shelli Dietz had her husband arrested?"

"No," Fallon said. "It was one of his mistresses. Claimed he broke her nose. Someone in your office—is there a Guidry?—handled the prosecution. He compiled a rather complete list of the late Jerome Noyes's reputed episodes of violence. Though unsubstantiated and therefore not allowed in the trial, they were nonetheless shocking. If Jerome were still alive, I imagine he might have edged Randolph Bingham out of the prime suspect spotlight."

"Some women seem to be drawn to abusive relationships," Nikki said.

"Indeed. In any case, neither Jerome nor Shelli had any living blood relations other than their son."

"Did Jerome OD?" Nikki asked.

"He drank turpentine."

"Straight or on the rocks?" She watched Adam swat at a flying insect.

"It happened in a cabin in the Sequoias. I call it a cabin. Actually, it's a two-story building that's part of the estate. The family had gone there to ski. Noyes imbibed some drugs and grabbed a bottle that he thought contained tequila. He was too high to do anything but roll around the floor until he expired."

"Where was his wife while that was going on?"

"She and Adam were upstairs, in the bedroom. They were hiding, actually. Noyes turned nasty when he was high."

Nikki frowned. "Maybe she decided to get back at him with a turpentine margarita."

Fallon shrugged. "Unlikely, but we'll never know."

She looked at the boy. "Poor little dude."

"True enough. We've got to be very careful not to let the trial add to his history of woe."

Nikki's bullshit sensors began to vibrate. Her cynicism must have shown, because Fallon added, "Don't misunderstand me, Ms. Hill. I have no intention of trying to dissuade you from putting Adam on the stand. Quite the contrary. If Randolph Bingham has robbed the boy of a mother's love, I sincerely hope he is made to pay dearly for it. It's what Adam wants, too."

"Then what are you saying?"

"Only that my firm is dedicated to protecting the boy's interests. The members of the media have been relentless, but we've managed to keep Adam from both the nightly news and the tabloids. The trial will stir them up again. That's my problem. Our task, yours and mine, will be to prepare the boy for whatever Bingham's defense may throw at him when you put him on the stand."

She stared at Fallon, looking for some sign of guile and finding not a trace. "I'm not sure I'll be that closely involved in the trial," she said.

"Raymond Wise isn't a complete fool, is he?"

She felt her cheeks burning. A schoolgirl reacting to a compliment from a respected teacher. A daughter—she nipped that thought in the bud. "No. But there are a lot of other prosecutors in the office."

"You're here now," Fallon said. "I think we can assume we'll be working together."

"There may not even be a trial," she said. "The police don't feel they have enough evidence to arrest Bingham."

Fallon frowned and looked away from her.

"What's the matter?"

"Bingham was arrested this morning for the murder."

She gawked at him. When she thought about it later, she hoped that her mouth hadn't been hanging open.

"Since you weren't notified, I fear I may have overestimated Mr. Wise's acumen," Jesse Fallon said. "Perhaps we won't be working together after all."

≡ 10 ≡

Go right on in, Nikki," Wise's secretary Jeri said when she arrived for the eleven o'clock meeting.

Head Deputy Peter Daspit was making an exit, frowning, as she entered. Wise was at his desk, looking just as troubled. "Shut the door," he ordered.

They were alone in the room. The fact that this was apparently a private meeting was surprising enough to defuse her annoyance at being kept out of the loop on Bingham's arrest. At least momentarily. "Where is everybody?" she asked, taking one of the uncomfortable leather chairs facing the D.A.'s desk.

"I postponed the general meeting a half hour. I wanted to speak with you first."

She waited expectantly. Maybe Fallon had been right and Wise was about to tell her she was going to be prosecuting Randolph Bingham.

He took a deep breath and said, "It's been a rather hectic morning. I'm not sure if you're aware of the situation . . . ?" He paused, looking at her.

"The situation?" she asked, lobbing the ball back into his court.

"That idiot Curland from the Police Officers' Guild issued a press statement that POG was withdrawing their support from Seymour

Kehoe. The assumption is that they have another candidate in mind. I gather it's not going to be me."

Nikki returned his stare without comment.

"Anything you want to tell me?" he asked.

"About the POG?" she replied, a bit testily. "I don't know anything about those people. What's on your mind, Ray?"

He winced, then blurted out, "Can I count on your support in this election?"

"*That's* why we're having this talk?" she asked.

"I . . . I was hoping," Wise hemmed and hawed, "since we've been through so much together . . ."

Save this jive for whoever's going to be prosecuting Randolph Bingham, she thought. What she said was, "Ray, I'm here to work, not play politics."

"You think I've been a lousy D.A.?"

"You're a good enough lawyer that you wouldn't ask the question without knowing the answer."

"Then why not back me?"

"This political stuff is too messy. I just don't want to get involved in it."

He stared at her, genuinely disappointed. "At least you won't be against me, right?" he asked hopefully.

"Right," she said. "Is that it?"

He glanced at his watch. "Heard anything new on Bingham's arrest?"

She felt heat rising to her face. "Oh? Has he been arrested?"

"Of course he has," he said. "This morning. I assumed you knew."

"You assumed? Why?"

"You have this mysterious police source. I assumed you were being kept up to speed."

Damn. She knew him well enough to realize he was being sincere. She'd been blaming him for one of the few slights of which he hadn't been guilty.

"You talk to the Noyes boy today?" he asked.

She nodded. "He's a together kid and he knows what he heard. He'll do fine."

"I think we've got a good case," Wise said. "Crime of passion. Bingham gets a snootful of champagne. Dietz pisses him off. Bang, bang."

"Had she been drinking too?" Nikki asked.

"Oh, yes. Over the inebriation line."

Nikki frowned.

"What's the matter?" Wise asked.

"They only found one champagne glass at the scene," she said.

"He was drinking from the bottle," Wise said. "His prints were all over it."

"This educated, supposedly sensitive and poetic guy slugs down champagne from the bottle to celebrate his engagement?"

"Your sensitive poet put two slugs in his fiancée's skull, then tried to make it look like suicide."

"That bothers me, too. He proposes to her. She says yes. He shoots her. Then this supposedly intelligent man sets up a seriously dumb fake suicide."

"Bingham may be no retard, but he's no mental giant either," Wise said. "He's the member of a cult, for cripe's sake. And he was drunk. Don't try to figure out a murderer's mind. It can drive you crazy. We've got another solid witness, by the way."

"To the murder?"

"We're not *that* lucky," Wise said. "We'll hash all this out at the meeting and figure out where we go from here." He slumped in his chair. "Sure you won't change your mind about the campaign?"

Nikki stared at him. Was he suggesting a quid pro quo: her backing in return for a seat at the prosecution table? It didn't matter. She wouldn't take that deal.

Outside the office, she was stopped by Dana Lowery, who had arrived early for the 11:30 meeting. "You and the gimp talking about anybody I know?" Dana asked sarcastically.

"Now, Dana," Nikki replied, moving past her with a smile, "how could anybody you know be worth talking about?"

≡ 11 ≡

At 6:30 that morning, Virgil had been lying in a half sleep in Nikki's big bed, marveling at the sudden quiet, now that mistress and mastiff had left for their run. Nothing but the steady thrum of central air. He stretched and rolled over, smelling the scent of Blue Gardenia on her pillow, relishing the memory of their night of lovema—

From the night table came the trill of the telephone.

He grabbed for it, knocking over a glass, spilling water on his arm and a section of the bed.

He paid no attention to the wetness, focusing on the white Princess phone in his hand.

"Uh . . . hello?"

"Virgil. That you?" He just had the voice IDed when his caller added, "It's me, Mac. I'm at work."

"What the hell you doing down there so early?"

"I, uh, slept here, partner. The house seemed kinda empty. I got this broad who comes over when it gets too rough, but she wasn't answering her phone. So I hung out with the night squad. Used the dogwatch cot." Virgil thought that the reason McNeil kept his house was that, in spite of continuing evidence to the contrary, he held on to the hope that his wife would someday return. "It's a good thing, too, 'cause we got some action on Bingham."

"The report on the gun come in?"

"You bet. Guess whose signature is on the registration? A hint: It's the same guy whose prints are on the unused rounds."

"Bingham?"

"Randolph J. 'Randy' Bingham, the toid himself."

"Fine. I'll be down in an hour."

"Good. 'Cause you and me got a date with Mr. Gus Prosser."

"Who he?"

"A law-abiding neighbor of the victim who's gonna put that asshole poet-murderer in our clutches, to do with as we please."

"No. It was later than that," Gus Prosser was saying in the study of his Hancock Park home. "Like I told the officer when I phoned this morning, it was after two."

He was an elderly man who obviously took proper care of himself. His lined face was deep-tanned, his snow-white hair freshly sculpted into a sort of meringue spread over his scalp. Prosser was wearing a crisp white, pleated Mexican shirt-jacket over lemon-colored silk slacks. White slip-ons kept the thick nap of his study carpet from tickling his sockless feet.

From where he sat, Virgil could look past the leaded-glass windows of the book-lined study to where the morning sun was natural-heating the pastel waters in a lap pool. He shifted his attention back to Prosser. "You usually up that late?" he asked.

"Most nights," Prosser said. He'd insisted the two detectives join him in a cup of tea. Virgil sipped his. McNeil left his untouched on Prosser's desktop, next to their scratched and battered Panasonic cassette recorder that seemed to be performing adequately enough. "I've always liked nighttime," Prosser continued. "Did most of my best work then. I don't suppose you gentlemen are old enough to remember the film *Beyond Passion*? Lana Tuner, Michael Rennie, and a very young, very handsome Roger Moore? Cinemascope. No matter. My first 'A' script. I was proud of it."

"You just happened to be looking out of the window?" McNeil asked.

The old man hesitated. "I . . . was here in the den. Spend most of my time here with my best friend." He gestured to the huge television set that occupied a section of bookshelf and held sway over most of the small, comfortable room. There was a soft chocolate-colored leather chair and ottoman facing it that seemed to be the old man's favorite resting place.

"Not much reason for me to use the remainder of the house since Georgina passed away," Prosser said. "Anyway, I was watching television and thought I heard something. A car backfire. Street's usually quiet that time of night."

"Around two," McNeil said.

"Yes. I didn't go to the front of the house right away. I suppose I was arguing with myself whether I should bother getting up, but . . . a writer, even a forcibly retired one, is a creature of curiosity. I dragged myself to the living room at the front of the house, keeping the lights off, of course, and looked out on the street.

"It was quiet. Peaceful. I started to return to the den when I noticed the way the moonlight fell on the velvet loveseat and I could almost see Georgina sitting there with the boy playing on the floor at her feet." He smiled. "He's forty-seven now, Gus junior."

McNeil shifted on his chair. "But you looked out of the window again?" he asked.

"Yes. There was another noise. A car door slamming. I looked out and saw the Bingham boy in his black sports car."

"Randolph Bingham, the third. You're sure?" McNeil asked.

"The Binghams were our neighbors for many years. Ever since old man Beckman died and the place went on the market. They were newlyweds, younger than Georgina and I. I remember when Randy was born. His brother too. The family lived there till six or seven years ago when they moved to Holmby Hills and put the Beckman place up for lease." He shook his head. "Old man Beckman, I call him. When he died, he was four years younger than I am now."

"When you saw Randolph Bingham on Tuesday morning, he was where exactly?" Virgil asked.

"In his car. Pulling out of the Beckman driveway."

"You had a clear view of him?"

"Oh yes. The top was down on his little car and he drove right under the streetlamp. And, before you ask, with my glasses, my eyesight is pretty damn good."

"You're familiar with his car?"

"I know the car. It's been in and out of Beckman's on many occasions since Mrs. Dietz moved in."

McNeil's beeper sounded. He groped for it in his pocket, then glanced at its readout. "Corben," he told Virgil, before turning to their host. "Can I use your phone?"

The lieutenant limited the conversation to the basics. "They found blood matching the vic's type on a pair of pants and shoes in Bingham's closet. Time to bring him in."

McNeil's eyes brightened when he passed along the news to Virgil. "Let's roll," he said, as they walked to the garden where Prosser had gone to give them privacy for the call.

"In a minute," Virgil told him.

The old man was sitting at a wrought-iron table, observing the foliage. Virgil took a chair across from him and placed the recorder on the table. "At around two-fifteen this morning, someone reported gunshots from your neighbor's house," he said, "but they didn't leave their name. Was that you, Mr. Prosser?"

"Me? No. I wasn't even sure they were shots until I saw about the murder on TV."

"You called the Homicide Department to report seeing Randolph Bingham."

"That's correct."

"Why not 911?"

Prosser's eyes opened wide. "Isn't that the emergency number?" he asked. "I didn't feel this was an emergency."

McNeil looked at Virgil and picked up the tape recorder, making an elaborate gesture of clicking it off to indicate they should be on their way. "Thanks, Mr. Prosser," he said. "We'll be needing you to sign a statement of what you've just told us. And I imagine the district attorney's office will want to talk with you before too long."

"I'll be here," Prosser said.

"You're certain about the time you saw Randolph Bingham in his car?" Virgil asked.

"Oh, yes."

"Because of the TV?"

The old man faltered. "Y-yes. Precisely that."

"What program were you watching?" Virgil asked. Behind him, McNeil groaned impatiently.

"Is that important?" Prosser wondered.

"The time is important," Virgil said.

"The early morning news. I was watching the early morning news on channel ten. It goes on at two. I'd been watching it for just a few minutes when I heard the sound."

"Do you remember which specific news story was on?"

Again, the old man hesitated before replying, "Something about the fires in the hills and the weather."

"Thank you, sir," McNeil quickly interjected, grabbing and shaking the old man's hand. "Let's go, partner."

"What the hell was that all about?" McNeil asked when they were in the car. "The old fart gave us what we needed. What were you going for?"

Virgil shrugged. "You pick up any weird vibes in there?" he asked.

"Naw. It all worked for me," McNeil said, shoving the tape recorder roughly into the glove compartment.

"Well, it means that both Binghams lied to us. The old man didn't get any call at ten-thirty."

"Maybe our boy Randy left early and put through the call to dear old dad. Then he got to thinking about the joys of marriage and went back and killed her to save himself some agony."

"Something hinky about Prosser," Virgil said.

"Not our problem," McNeil said. "Kee-rist. This is a gift—an eye-witness who puts our boy on the scene at murder time. Don't piss on it."

"You're probably right," Virgil said.

"No 'probably' about it," his partner replied, relaxing a little. "C'mon, give it the goose. I can't wait to put the grab on the Rand man."

Sister Mildred was not pleased by their reappearance at her beach-front establishment. Rather brusquely, she asked a heavily muscled and tattooed staff member named Ramon to show them the way to Randolph Bingham's quarters.

As they climbed the dark wooden stairs to the building's third floor, McNeil asked, "Where'd you pick up the amateur body art, Ray-moan? Soledad?"

The guide gave him a bored glance. "If you must know, it was Kuwait, after Schwartzkopf and me won the war," he said. "Got laid up in Mercy Hospital trying to kick this infection the DOD said wasn't caused by no chemicals. An intern did the tats." He looked down at his arm, where a red dragon puffed blue-gray smoke. "Don't see nothing amateur about it."

Bingham answered the door wearing a tan Polo shirt and dark blue shorts. His feet were bare. He stepped back into the room and picked up the phone receiver that he'd rested on a table beside the unmade bed. "They're here," he said, and replaced the receiver on its cradle.

"Sister Mildred, letting me know you were on the way up," he explained to the detectives.

"Randolph J. Bingham, the third, we're arresting you for the murder of Shelli Dietz," Virgil said without inflection.

"Can I put on long trousers?"

Virgil held up a hand, suggesting that Bingham remain where he was in silence, then began reciting the Miranda warning. When he was finished, he said, "You can put on your pants now."

"I didn't kill Shelli. I loved her," Bingham told them. "That's all I have to say without a lawyer."

They waited for him to change clothes and put on socks and shoes.

Then they walked him down the stairs, uncuffed, as if they were pals heading out to lunch together.

Ramon remained at the front of the building watching them drive away.

"Kuwait," McNeil said contemptuously. "Yeah, right. Like I'm a schmuck who doesn't know a Soledad dragon when I see one."

≡ 12 ≡

Peter will be in charge of the prosecution of young Mr. Bingham," Ray Wise informed the members of his staff who were assembled in the main conference room. Nikki was seated down the table, across from Dana Lowery, who alternated between glaring at Wise and scratching notes on a legal pad as if she were inflicting wounds.

Peter Daspit, the thirty-six-year-old head deputy D.A., accepted his boss's announcement with a nod of customary false modesty. He was a square-jawed young man of only moderate intelligence who made an effort to convey an image of rugged masculinity. His blond hair was cut close, marine-style. His myopic eyesight was corrected by contact lenses. The special heels on his shoes pushed his height to over six feet. His dark-colored lightweight suits had a bit more padding in the shoulders than was currently in vogue, the better to give him a V-shaped upper torso.

Well, hell, Nikki thought. *It seems to work for women jurors. Even for some men.* Daspit was, in her mind, the perfect vanilla prosecutor. He was prepared, spoke well, and had a knack for presenting his case in clear, simplistic terms that even the least attentive juror could easily assimilate. On the minus side was an absence of passion. Some prosecutors could get a conviction from a dog walk by displaying a sense of moral outrage, or by using flowery language or charm or, in rare instances, by indulging in old-fashioned groveling. As far as Nikki could tell, these implements were missing from Daspit's toolbox. She'd never seen him really involved in a case. Which was probably the key to his success. If they felt the situation demanded it, many prosecutors could be talked into going to trial with less than a fifty-fifty chance of conviction. Daspit weighed each case with absolute dispassion. Child molester. Mass murderer. Church burner. It was of little consequence to Peter Daspit. The only things that impressed him were physical evidence and witnesses.

Both were present in the case against Randolph Bingham III.

"It looks pretty solid," he told those assembled. "We've placed Bingham at the scene at approximately the time of the murder. The victim's son heard him shouting at the Dietz woman earlier that evening and also heard a loud noise, presumably the gun firing." He smiled. "The murder weapon, a Smith & Wesson 9 mm, was registered to Bingham, and his prints tell us he's the one who loaded it. Premeditation. Murder One.

"We've also got his asthma spray on the scene. And we've found bloodstains on his pants and shoes that match the vic's type. They're working on the DNA composition, but even without it, this case is as close to open-and-shut as I've ever seen."

Wise looks less certain, Nikki thought. He had his future riding on the trial. Barring a lurid murder involving some crackhead movie star or sex-crazed local politician, the Bingham trial would be the event that kept him in office or booted him out forever. "We shouldn't be too overconfident," he warned his head deputy. He added solemnly, "The Bingham family has hired Gerald Wheeler."

"That cornpone jackass with his shoestring tie," Dana sneered. "You're worried about *him*?"

"That cornpone jackass hasn't lost a case in twenty-two years," Wise said.

"In the South," she said. "In Georgia, for Christ's sake. Emerson"—she indicated a deputy farther down the table—"could win a case in Georgia."

There was some laughter. Not from deputy Errol Emerson and not from Wise. "Wheeler's a brilliant attorney," the D.A. said flatly. "His firm is the largest in Atlanta. There's a reason old man Bingham selected him."

"The reason is called desperation," Dana said. "The case is a lock. Bingham couldn't get anybody else."

"You know that for a fact?" Wise asked.

Dana grinned. "Uh-huh. I've spent the last two hours finding out quite a bit about the Binghams and their psycho son. By the time we go to trial, Peter and I will be—"

"Whoa!" Wise shouted. "I missed a beat here. You and Peter?"

Dana seemed surprised by the question. "Why, yes. I'll be in second chair."

Wise opened his mouth and then closed it again. He shifted his stare from Dana to Daspit, who took that moment to study the wood grain of the conference table.

The D.A. returned his attention to Dana. "You and Peter stick around after the meeting," he said stiffly. "We'll talk about this."

He called for progress reports from some of the other deputy D.A.'s, made a few comments, and after inquiring if anyone had any further business, dismissed the staff.

Nikki was halfway to the door when Wise told her to stay, too. She returned to the conference table where she found Dana Lowery glaring at her. "You told him, you bitch," she snapped.

"You're wrong," Nikki said without emotion as she took her chair.

"What're you talking about?" Wise asked.

"Girl stuff," Nikki said, staring at Dana.

Wise wheeled on Daspit. "Forgive me if I've gone senile, Peter," he said, "but did we have any discussion about who'd be trying Bingham with you?"

"No," Daspit answered. "But Dana's up on the whole thing and I assumed—"

"Oh, I see," Wise said. "Dana's up on it. Was that revelation accompanied by a lapdance in your office?"

"That's goddamned insulting, Ray," Dana said.

"I'll tell you what's insulting," Wise replied. "Your trying an end run around me to dine out on Bingham."

"I deserve this case."

"I'll be the judge of that," Wise said.

"You know, don't you?" Dana said.

"Know what?" Wise asked, frowning. Daspit's blandly handsome face looked confused.

"You know damn well I'm going for your job," she said nastily. "With the backing of the POG."

Wise stared at her wordlessly. Daspit's chin dropped.

Dana shoved her chair back and, turning to Nikki, spat out, "You bitch."

"I realize, coming from you, 'bitch' is like a compliment," Nikki replied. "But call me that one more time and I'm going to get rid of that skunk hair for you, strand by strand."

Dana stared at her for a beat, then turned to Wise. "You can take *this* trial away from me, Ray. But you can't stop me. I'll find myself something better."

She grabbed her tablet and jammed it into her leather briefcase, then strode angrily from the conference room.

The others watched her exit. There was silence for a few seconds, then Daspit said, "I swear to God, Ray, I didn't know a thing about her running for D.A."

"You going to back her, Peter?"

"Of course not."

Wise turned to Nikki. "Why's she so pissed off at you?"

"Her mirror must have told her I was the fairest in the land."

Wise smiled for the first time that morning. "Well, now that we're past the unpleasant interruptions, let's get down to business. You two will be jointly responsible for the prosecution of Randolph Bingham." He looked at Daspit. "Are we all on track?"

"Sure," Daspit said, nodding to both of them. "Nikki and I have beaten 'em before."

"I'd like to hear more about this other witness," Nikki said. "And the bloodstains and the weapon."

"Peter will bring you up to speed," Wise said. Then he turned to his head deputy. "Give us a minute alone, Peter. Nikki will catch up with you."

Daspit's face subtly shifted from surprise to suspicion before settling back into its usual bland mask. Nikki thought she might have to work at it to keep their relationship compatible.

When the door had closed behind his head deputy, Wise said, "You knew about Dana going for my job, didn't you?"

"Didn't *you*?" she asked back.

"Of course," he said. "Why else am I paying those so-called campaign experts? So she went to you, asked you to back her?"

"Something like that."

"Judging by her attitude, I assume you said no."

Nikki nodded.

"I want to clarify a point," he said. "Even if she weren't running against me, I still would have picked you over her for the Bingham trial."

"Oh?"

"You're a better prosecutor. You know how to enlist juror sympathy. Dana's Dragon Lady routine doesn't play. Besides," he said with a grin, "considering that Wheeler is a cracker with a drawl so thick you couldn't cut it with a hacksaw, I'll be expecting you to put as many of your people as you can in that jury box."

"My people, huh? And you call *Wheeler* a cracker?"

"Just having my little joke," he said, backpedaling about an inch. "You know how I am."

She did, of course. But sometimes she forgot.

FROM PATIENCE'S SPOKEN DIARY, WEDNESDAY, AUGUST 4
Oh, well.

I guess I was hoping too hard. Here I sit in the hotel john, waiting for this little Chink in the next room to wake up and make more demands on my tender and aching body. Ricky is with his S.F. slutfriend, Candi. I guess it was a mistake to think he might be my Prince Charming. He just wanted me here to service this so-called Japanese businessman he and Pickett have got something going with.

Last night, we all went to this place called Baccus where you eat and then play with tech toys. My "date," Mr. Nakamura—"just call me Nakki"—is some kind of importer. Not blow or guns or anything illegal. Maybe computer stuff. I dunno. But he's filthy rich and Ricky says he's bankrolling them in some new kind of private club, sorta like this Baccus, I guess, because Pickett was making notes.

The food was a weird kind of Asian-Mex mix that tasted better than it sounds. The games I couldn't really get into. Too complicated. One was like a quiz show where you team up with somebody to answer questions that appear on a big-screen TV and you have to press some buttons. Maybe I'd have liked it more if things had been a little different. My partner was Nakki, who seemed more interested in pressing my button than the one on the table. Ricky G and Candi were sitting across from us, like la-di-da lovebirds. They won the game, too.

Pickett was teamed with Amber and he was in good-behavior mode and almost charming, because of Nakki, no doubt. Jay Jay was with some local he picked up at the hotel, a nonpro who didn't know what the hell was really going on and thought it was like a sorority party until he started feeling her up and she complained and had to be slapped around a little.

Anyhow, we're playing this dumb game and Nakki's got his little hand working in my lap. Whispering in my ear what he's going to do to me later. Like that's a real turn-on. Look in the mirror, Nakman!

And Ricky and Slutface are just happy as rainbows. Earlier he and I had a little . . . scene. I was so bummed about Candi. Ricky swore that he showed Nakki both my picture and Candi's and the Japster picked me. "That's 'cause he knows quality," Ricky told me.

A year ago, I might have bought that bullshit and not done the stupid thing. But I was angry, so I did the stupid thing.

Ricky G gave me a handful of new Franklins and told me to go out and buy something nice to wear to the party; he left to go to slutface Candi's.

I sat around the hotel room for a while, getting more and more tassed off. Then I made an el-dee call to my Big Badge john in LaLa. I'm not sure why. I guess when somebody treats you like shit, you just want to find somebody you're sure is gonna stroke you. Then maybe you can treat *them* like shit.

BBj wasn't at home, so I left a message on his machine. Some message, I swear. I'm pretty good with the phone sex. Maybe, when my looks start to go, if I'm not with someone who'll take care of me, I'll have that to fall back on. Anyway, I gave it to him, industrial strength. He's into sex talk. I could imagine him coming home from the job and playing back the message, getting off on the spot.

I wound up telling him I was planning on leaving Ricky (what a doof I am!) and I was hoping he might help me out until I could sort of get my act together, maybe do the phone sex thing or something where I wouldn't have to work so hard.

Now, I can see that wasn't the smartest idea. I mean, I don't honestly think I could spend more time with him than it takes to fuck him. He gets mean sometimes when he's drunk, and he's usually drunk. Why'd I call the Big Badge? I can be such a romantic asshole. When I get back to the city, I'll phone him and try to—uh-oh, Nakki's up and making grunt noises. Duty calls. Time to put you back in your hidey-hole, old pal.

≡ 13 ≡

Virgil was ignoring the television monitor, preferring to watch Nikki sitting across the room from him. She, along with Dan McNeil and Peter Daspit, were in the latter's office to view the tape made by the Watchbird's camera of the crime scene on the morning of Shelli Dietz's murder.

Virgil had seen the tape before. Even if he hadn't, he would still have been more interested in watching Nikki than a TV set. He loved just looking at her, charting her unconscious expressions, filing them away for mental replay during the hours when they were apart.

She leaned forward suddenly, staring hard at the screen, her face transformed by a special smile. Warm. Comforting. But something more. The expression seemed familiar to him somehow, yet he was certain she'd never blessed him with quite that same lovely smile.

She was looking at the video image of Adam Noyes.

"Kid's a handsome little mutt," McNeil said, as Adam was abruptly replaced by millions of wiggling and blinking dots. "Oughta have his own show."

Daspit used a remote control to click off the set. "Interesting tape," he said. "But it presents us with a few problems." He stared at McNeil. "You happy about your performance, Detective?"

Virgil saw his partner's face start to redden. "What's wrong with it?" McNeil asked.

"How about your psycho comments about the corpse and womankind in general?"

"We were at the murder scene," McNeil replied, "not a tea party. It's nasty business and it gets to you. Some guys throw up. I mouth off."

"Too bad you didn't throw up, McNeil. That might have gotten you a little sympathy from the jurors instead of animosity." He shook his head. "We can't risk using the tape. Let's hope the defense doesn't."

"I doubt they will," Nikki said. "The close-ups of Shelli Dietz's body are really grim."

Daspit nodded. "They're enough to prompt a lynching. I wish we could use 'em. I also wish we didn't have to worry about Bingham's lawyers throwing this trial off-track by attacking Detective McNeil for his sexism and cynicism.

"Maybe I should ask, Detective: You a racist, too?"

"No." McNeil's reply sounded like a dry cough. Virgil saw his partner tense and said a silent prayer that the big man wouldn't give in to his emotions and leap across the desk to smash the smug face of the head deputy D.A.

"That's something, I guess," Daspit said, turning to Virgil. "When do you plan to interrogate Bingham?"

"Late this afternoon," Virgil said. "Assuming his lawyer gets here by then. He's flying in from Atlanta."

"Lieutenant Corben said it would be okay if somebody from this office took notes," Daspit said.

McNeil remained rigid in his chair. Virgil nodded and stood up. "We'd better be getting back," he said.

The idea seemed to please Daspit. "Thanks for dropping by," he said. "And, Detective McNeil, next time you're at a crime scene, remember: You could be on *Candid Camera*."

Nikki winked at Virgil and he smiled back.

•   •   •

"Daspit's a pussy-mouth," McNeil said, as the elevator carried them to the Criminal Courts Building lobby.

Virgil didn't much care for the man, either. However, in this instance, he thought the head deputy's complaints had been legitimate. "You're going to be taking a lot of shit on the stand from Bingham's lawyer because of the tape," he said.

"We shoulda just scrubbed it, claimed the damned thing didn't work." When Virgil didn't reply, he added, "Fucking lawyers. All of 'em assholes . . . except for your girlfriend, of course."

Virgil and Nikki had never tried to keep their romance an absolute secret; they dined out together, went to films, and on Sundays, attended services at Faithful Central Baptist Missionary. However, because their occupations were so interlocked, and because some might feel that an intimate relationship would compromise their work, they had agreed not to publicize their situation.

Virgil doubted that Lieutenant Corben or the other members of the Major Crimes unit knew he was keeping time with a deputy D.A. But he'd made no attempt to hide that knowledge from his partner.

"Thank her for me for not piling on," McNeil said.

Virgil could imagine what she'd have to say about his partner when he saw her that night. As they turned the corner, heading toward Parker Center, he said, "I know you been going through some tough times, Mac, but you're getting close to the edge of really fucking up."

McNeil nodded. "I've bottomed out, partner. Things are changing and I'm starting to climb back up."

He was looking a little better. His eyes, while not crystal clear, were showing some white mixed with the pink. He'd brushed a few of the cowlicks out of his hair, and the blue suit he was wearing, though rumpled, had no obvious stains on it. "I'm here to help, if you need me," Virgil told him.

"Yeah. I know," McNeil replied, flashing him a ghost of the smile the younger detective remembered from better days.

≡ 14 ≡

Nikki was in her kitchen, the only room in her ranch-style home beside the bedroom that was properly furnished, when Virgil called. It was nearly nine o'clock and Bird stirred sleepily on a section of the kitchen floor that benefited directly from the central air-conditioning. The radio, turned low, was offering one of Lauryn Hill's odd mixtures of hip-hop and soul.

"On my way," Virgil said.

"How'd it go?" she asked. Daspit had decided to attend the Bingham interrogation. That gave her the time to put her notes on Adam Noyes together, study the transcription of the detectives' interview with eyewitness Gus Prosser, and still be able to stop off at the supermarket and get home before Bird started gnawing on the lawn chairs.

"It went about the way you'd figure. Bingham said he didn't do it."

"What's Wheeler like?" she asked.

"He's got that good ole boy look. The modified cowboy hat."

"I think they call that a planter's hat."

"Yeah? Well, with his planter's hat and his shirt with the little gold arrows weighing down his collar points, the string tie, and his alligator boots, he looks like he oughta be on cable TV. Your second thought is that he's kinda chubby and maybe sorta slow. Then you realize he's more muscle than fat and the reason he doesn't do much talking is that he's listening real hard. I'll tell you more about it when I get there. Which'll be in less than twenty minutes if I make the traffic lights."

He let himself in, harrumphed at the groggy dog lumbering to his feet, and took Nikki in his arms and kissed her. It was a kiss that suggested the day had been long and difficult and that being there with her was definitely the best part of it. Reluctantly, he let her go when Bird forced himself between them.

Nikki headed for the counter where a bottle of merlot was breathing, not quite as heavily as she. Virgil removed his jacket, rolled up his sleeves, and washed his hands at the sink.

He followed her into the dining room where she placed their full wineglasses on the cloth-draped card table they'd been eating off for nearly a year. "You ever going to get furniture for this place, Red?" he asked.

"Red" was short for Redbone, used to describe light brown skin with a rosy cast. She'd never cared for the designation until Virgil started using it. "That beautiful dining room set in your apartment is just gathering dust," she replied. "Along with that lovely leather couch that would fit just fine in the living room."

She said it playfully. They'd had several discussions about his moving in. It made sense economically. Though the house had been a bargain considering the value of the property in Ladera Heights, the monthly notes were still taking a large bite out of her budget. The rent on his Hollywood apartment was nearly as high.

It also made sense romantically. Neither had any doubts about that.

The problem was his, as she saw it. He told her he preferred his neighborhood, where, unlike the resolutely residential Heights, one could walk to restaurants and drugstores and even movie theaters. She thought his reluctance had more to do with an inability to surrender the last vestige of his bachelorhood, the scene of countless sexual conquests and other manly memories.

He'd suggested she move in with him in Hollywood and put her house on the market. But to her mind it was foolish for a young couple to be renting when they could be living in their own home in one of the city's more prestigious locations. More important, though his apartment might be big enough for the two of them (and Bird, of course), it was not fit for a family. Lately, with her biological clock ticking loud enough to drown out Metallica, a family was definitely on her mind.

Virgil responded to her comment with a sheepish smile. "On the other hand," he said, "this little table is kinda intimate and cozy, don't you think?"

"You still subscribe to *Perfect Ten*, I bet," she said, shaking her head as she returned to the kitchen for their food, Bird at her heels. "You're getting more and more like that pathetic woman-hating McNeil character."

"Hey, don't put me in that bag. I love women. Always have."

"So I've heard," she said, placing a covered bowl on the table and returning to the kitchen for more.

"Anyway," Virgil called to her, "with Mac it's the separation thing with his wife."

"It's something," she said, depositing two smaller bowls and heading off again. "Man belongs in a cage."

"Actually, I think he's coming around," Virgil said. "He's seeing a lady tonight."

"That'll be some major event. Where's he taking her, Hooters?"

"Probably back to his place to watch *Red Shoe Diary* and suck toes."

"You men," she said in exaggerated disgust.

Bird, apparently bored by their conversation, flopped onto the dining room carpet, making wet smacking noises with his tongue and the roof of his mouth.

She'd prepared a roasted chicken with corn bread stuffing, which Virgil devoured as if he hadn't eaten in weeks. She was hungry herself, but she managed between bites to ask him about the Bingham interrogation.

"Bottom line, he says he's innocent," Virgil replied. "He also denies having any kind of argument with her that night. Claims Dietz was alive and well when he left the place shortly after ten."

"Don't suppose you told him about the neighbor who saw him leave at two?"

"No. Daspit is saving that for later. We just got his lie on record. Didn't mention Adam Noyes's statement about him shouting at Dietz either. Mac did ask him if he'd ever hit the woman or yelled at the kid. He denied that, too. Inquired about the boy, wanted to know how he was. Said he'd like to see him. We told him that wasn't in the cards."

"Bingham's locked up, right?" she asked, her voice rising in concern.

"Yep. It was a no-bail warrant. But Wheeler's definitely a smooth operator, and money does have a loud voice in this town."

"Are you arranging for Adam's protection?"

"You think he's at risk from Bingham?"

She made a vague gesture with her hand. "He's . . . a witness for the prosecution."

"So's Gus Prosser," Virgil said, dragging a chunk of chicken through the gravy. "His statement's more damaging than the boy's. But we're not talking about a drug cartel here, or a Mafia deal. I don't see them as being in any real danger. Even if Bingham gets out on bail."

Nikki knew there was little chance of that. Not with him being locked up on a no-bail. "I suppose you're right," she said, staring at the food on her plate. Her appetite had deserted her.

Virgil's was still in full force. He hummed contentedly as he filled and emptied his fork. "Bingham said he sorta remembers his little bro giving him a handgun years ago," he told Nikki, "but he didn't know if it was a Smith & Wesson 9 mm. And he didn't know what happened to it. He seemed really shook up when we told him it was the murder weapon. Right about then is when Wheeler closed us down."

"Was anyone with Wheeler?" She knew the Georgia lawyer would have to associate himself with a California attorney to try a case in the state.

"Handsome woman. A little thin for my taste, but her dress fit her like it was tailor-made. Strictly high price tag. Name's Gentry, I think."

Mimi Gentry. A partner in the firm of Kastile, Long and Gentry. Nikki had shared a courtroom with her before. Gentry was a spider— one of those defense attorneys who took their time spinning their webs to catch up witnesses, then striking swiftly and with deadly precision. Protecting Adam Noyes from Mimi Gentry could require some work.

"Uh, I don't suppose you have any more chicken back in the kitchen?" Virgil asked.

"Here. Take some of mine," she said. "I'm not very hungry."

Later, they sipped black coffee on the rear patio, sitting on lawn chairs she'd bought on impulse at a drugstore three months before. An FM broadcast of one of R. Kelly's more soulful efforts mixed with the singing of the crickets and cicadas. Heat lightning flashed in the dark sky.

"Some spread, honey," Virgil said with a sigh of satisfaction.

"Thank my grandma Tyrell's recipes."

"Giblets in the corn bread stuffing?" he speculated.

"Oh, yeah. Mushrooms, too, and a few ingredients I'm forced to keep secret from anyone who isn't a member of the family."

He leaned forward in his chair. The secluded hilltop patio offered an unhindered view of the inky sky above and the shimmering lights of Inglewood below. He ignored them to stare at her. "Suppose I do move some of my fine furniture in here," he said. "That be good enough to buy me a list of what went into that stuffing?"

She laughed. "Depends on whether you'd be accompanying the furniture."

"I go where my leather couch goes."

They both stopped smiling at the same time. "I think I'm being serious," she said.

"Yeah, I know," he replied. "It's time we got a little more serious."

He stood and reached for her hand, urging her from the chair. The big dog was inside the house standing at the glass patio door, looking at her disapprovingly. She turned away from him and let Virgil lead her across the flagstone patio and down the sloping grassy hillside. He paused at a spot approximately halfway between the house and a low chain-link safety fence that guarded the edge of the hilltop property. Bird couldn't see them now. No one could, unless some ghosts from a cemetery down the hill were curious enough to rise from their rest.

Virgil pulled her down on the grass beside him.

They kissed, a long, sensual kiss, during which they wound up lying on the ground like the two hands of a large clock. The grass beneath her back still carried some of the day's warmth, but a cool breeze had at least momentarily replaced the hot dry breath of El Niño.

She felt his large, strong hand on her flat stomach. Nothing tentative or hesitant about it. He tugged her blouse free from her slacks.

Then his hand worked its way up the blouse performing the double duty of caressing her and undoing the pearl buttons. She was not wearing a bra. Her nipples stiffened in the breeze. His lips deserted hers in search of the ultra-sensitive extended tip of her right breast.

His lips and tongue played with that for a while, his eager fingers undoing the button of her slacks and unlocking the zipper.

She arched the lower part of her body, making it easier for him to push down the slacks far enough for her to kick free of them.

His lips were on hers again as his hand slipped past her stomach under her black silk panties, long powerful fingers rubbing and caressing until the longest found a moist nesting place.

They were not new lovers, but this was a new experience, making love under a rumbling dark sky. A tremor of excitement electrified her body. She moved against him, clawing at his shirt. "Easy, Red," he whispered, as if the night could hear them.

Naked, they melted into each other. When, at last, she screamed in joy, lightning flashed across the velvet sky.

"That's definitely the way it should be done," he said, still breathing hard as they lay side by side on their backs, holding hands. A wisp of wind dried their perspiring bodies.

"You finished, then?" she asked merrily.

He moved her hand. "That feel finished?"

"Guess not," she said, rolling on her side, smiling at the clean line of his profile. "You know what I'm thinking?"

He turned his head, stared at her luminous brown eyes, her parted lips. "What?" he asked.

"I'm thinking . . . we couldn't be doing this in your backyard in Hollywood."

≡ 15 ≡

On Wednesday, August 11, a few days before Randolph Bingham's preliminary hearing, Jesse Fallon phoned Nikki to ask if she could spare a few minutes for a meeting with Adam Noyes.

"Has something happened?" she asked with alarm. "Is he hurt?"

Fallon hesitated before answering, "No. Not hurt. But he's had a little scare and I think it would be good for him if you dropped by. I've something to discuss with you myself."

She glanced at her schedule. "I can be there in an hour." She replaced the phone and called Jeb with the news he loved to hear: he'd have to reschedule her two o'clock.

The boy's suite was on the fourth floor of the Sanford Apartments. Fallon greeted her at the door.

"Thanks for coming," he said.

"What's up?"

"We had an incident in the park this morning," he said.

"What kind of incident?" she asked, looking past him to an empty, very neat sitting room.

"Adam was bitten by a bug."

"A bug?" she repeated, confused.

"He thinks a spider. It was very . . . unsettling."

She took in the elderly man's furrowed brow. "Unsettling for him or for you?"

"Both of us, I'm afraid," Fallon said. "Adam insisted we call in his doctor who didn't think it was anything serious. He left a prescription that Jenny is getting filled. The boy's in the bedroom. He's been asking for you. We'll talk afterward."

He led Nikki to the bedroom where Adam was resting on a tufted chair, his right leg extended on a matching ottoman. "Nikki!" he yelled excitedly. "A spider bit me and I can feel his toxins moving through my veins."

"Feels weird, I bet."

The boy nodded his head emphatically. "Here's where I was bitten." There was a bump the size of a marble on his right ankle. The brown skin surrounding the bite looked red and tender.

"A spider did that?" Nikki asked.

"Black widow," Adam answered.

"Maybe a spider," Fallon said. "But not a black widow, Adam."

Anger aged the boy's face for just a second. If Nikki had blinked, she might have missed it. "I can feel the toxins," the boy insisted.

Fallon shrugged. "The doctor said the salve will do the trick."

"Maybe you ought to take a little rest," Nikki suggested.

"No. Please. Sit here with me." He reached down and lifted his foot to one side, making room on the ottoman.

Nikki did as he requested. He blessed her with a grateful smile, then said excitedly, "It was a black widow. I saw the red spot on its back. I'm surprised I'm not sicker."

"Maybe she didn't get a chance to do a full job of biting you."

"I'm very allergic to bites. I hope my foot is okay when I have to go to court."

"That won't be for a while," Nikki said.

"I thought the . . . pre-thing . . . was this week."

"The arraignment," Nikki said. "Right. We won't need you for that. One of the detectives who took your statement can simply read it to the judge."

"Oh." He seemed disappointed. Then he brightened. "Do you have some new *weirdos* to tell me about?"

During a previous meeting, Nikki had responded to the boy's request for crime stories with some of the G-rated material in her mental files. These had been tales about seriously stupid criminals, like the bankrobber who was arrested trying to make his getaway while pushing his stalled car. Adam had lumped them under the general heading of "weirdos."

"Before Nikki gets into that, I'd like to borrow her for a few minutes," Fallon said.

"Why?" The boy looked at him with suspicion.

"I need her advice."

"About me?"

"There are several subjects to discuss," Fallon said amiably.

"Can't you do it here?" the boy asked.

"Lawyer stuff," Fallon said.

"Nikki?"

Adam was asking her for verification, but all she said was, "I'll be back in a flash."

"Well, okay. Can you get me the remote for my Van-AM?"

"Your what?"

"Another Homeboy toy," Fallon said, retrieving a bright red plastic rectangle from the bed and handing it to the boy.

Adam pressed a few buttons on its surface and from somewhere under the bed came the romping, stomping sound of 2Pac's "California Love." As the boy worked the toggle, the music grew louder and to Nikki's amazement its source, a miniature Chevy van, rolled from under the bed, heading for them.

"It's simple," Adam said. "You just put a radio receiver in a remote-controlled car. Have your music follow you all around."

"Very clever," Nikki said.

"You should see some of the stuff," Adam said. "I've got a catalog . . ."

"Give me a minute with Mr. Fallon first. Then you can show it to me."

"Okay," he said. "Don't forget the weirdos."

•   •   •

Nikki assumed they'd have their chat in the sitting room, but Fallon led her to the corridor outside of the apartment. "I just want to make sure we're not overheard," he said.

"You think he's got the apartment bugged?" Nikki asked sarcastically.

"One never knows."

"What's going on?"

"The situation in the park today following the bug bite convinced me to take a few steps on Adam's behalf. One of them may impinge upon his effectiveness as your witness."

"I'm listening."

"Adam went totally out of control," Fallon said. "Screaming, yelling. In a complete state of panic."

"He's a little boy who was bitten by a spider."

"I'm not talking about tears and fear. He raced out of the park, totally unmindful of the traffic or anything else. It took both the doorman and myself to get him up here, kicking and screaming. It was enough to convince me that he should see a therapist."

It wasn't news Nikki wanted to hear. "As it is, Bingham's lawyers will be playing that old tune about kids not being reliable witnesses," she said. "They're gonna love finding out the boy's in therapy."

"It's not a decision I'm making out of hand," Fallon said. "I've noticed other things. An absence of affect. He obviously misses his mother, but I get the feeling it's mainly because her death has been an inconvenience for him. Sorrow doesn't seem to be part of his package. As for tolerance, he barely acknowledges me and he treats Jenny Mapes like a slave. He does seem to have a genuine fondness for you, but that could change in a heartbeat. His mood is mercurial."

Nikki knew that Fallon possessed a fair amount of ego. She wondered if Adam had challenged that in some way. "Your attitude toward the boy seems a little mercurial, too," she said.

"I've spent time with him," he said. "I still think he's a brilliant young man with limitless potential. But I believe his mother's death has taken a toll and I'd feel more comfortable if the extent of that toll were to be weighed by an expert."

"I don't suppose you could wait until after he testifies at the trial?" Nikki asked.

"If you were responsible for his care, what would you do?"

She sighed.

"I'm also going to replace the Mapes girl," Fallon said. "He runs roughshod over her. I'm leaning toward a settled married couple."

"Sounds good. But it might get a little crowded in there," Nikki said, indicating the apartment.

Fallon smiled. "We're looking for a small cottage in Beverly Hills or Brentwood. If you hear of anything..."

"Sure," she said. "We'd better get back inside, before he gets corrupted by too much radio."

"You think I'm being overprotective?" Fallon asked.

"I don't know. I don't really have a lot of experience with kids."

"Will that be changing one of these years?"

She smiled at the thought. "To use your phrase, one never knows," she said.

FROM PATIENCE'S SPOKEN DIARY—THURSDAY, AUGUST 12

How do I manage to screw everything up all the time?

My bags are packed in the next room. My Big Badge john is coming to pick me up, take me away from all this.

And Ricky calls.

He wants me to go with him to some place in Japland I can't even pronounce. More of his business deal. We'll be there a month or so. I'll be with *him*. No trade off to Nakki this time. No slut-face Candi. That's history, he says.

He tells me he loves me.

Shit!

Can I believe him?

My BBj'll be here any minute. What do I do?

≡ 16 ≡

As Virgil saw it, Nikki's nearly total immersion in preparation for the trial was both a blessing and a curse. The curse part was that everything else got put on hold, including their blissfully relaxed, unpressured evenings together. The blessing came during those rare periods when she'd purposely put the case on hold, opening a brief window of opportunity for romance that they used to full advantage. Lovely lovemaking. No time for discussions of their future, or the state of the world.

Or who would move in with whom.

The fact is, though he'd never admit it to Nikki, he just didn't feel right about moving into her house. It was *her* place. True, there was no pink-and-white tufted furniture. No furniture at all, to speak of. No lace drapes. The house did not look like a lady place, which would have been totally out of the question. It was big and comfortable and away from the noise and disruption of street life. Still, it was the idea: A man doesn't live under his girlfriend's roof unless he's a male whore or a mack.

Absolutely certain neither description fit him, he was glad the moving-in thing had been taken off the table temporarily. What they did talk about, when they weren't making love, was mostly the progress of the case against Randolph Bingham.

This was the first time in their relatively short relationship that they'd worked the same murder. From Bingham's preliminary court appearance, through his arraignment and on up to the date of his trial, they were together but apart in courtrooms and lunchrooms and offices. She seemed to have no difficulty keeping her feelings for him hidden under a professional blanket while they were on the job. He, on the other hand, had to struggle to keep his mind on the planning and plotting.

He was so focused on staying balanced between Nikki and the work that he didn't notice what was happening with his partner. He woke up to it one day when they were having lunch at a falafel joint in Westwood. He stared across the table at a reasonably well-groomed but very solemn McNeil. The older detective's suit had been pressed recently. The coat and pants matched. His eyes were clear. But his face was gray and the wrinkles in it had deepened. The man looked like he had aged twenty years.

"You okay?" Virgil asked.

"Sure. What do you mean?"

"You just . . . look different."

"Different how?" McNeil asked.

"Like you need a little color, maybe."

McNeil smiled. "That's funny. We never discussed color before."

Virgil started to explain, but McNeil waved him back. "I know what you're saying, Virg. I'm feeling my years. I'll be ready for retirement. The deal is this: Climbing back up after you've hit bottom takes a hell of a lot more energy than sliding down.

"I hired this Vietnamese housekeeper, comes in twice a week now. I get home and the place is spotless. My dirty clothes are in a bundle for me to take to the laundry. There's food in the fridge. Nothing for me to do but eat, watch the tube, and sleep. I been off booze for nearly two months. My body's not used to all this good living, I guess."

"Been to a doctor?"

"What for? I don't ache." He wiggled his fingers, raised and lowered his arms. "Everything works."

"Still seeing that lady?"

"What lady you talking about?" McNeil asked, frowning.

"The one you mentioned a while back."

"Oh. That was just a delusion. No. No ladies. Well, partner, you about ready to rejoin the world?" He picked up the check for the lunch, looked at the total, and did a mock shiver. "I'll handle this," he said.

Virgil shook his head. "Man, you really are going through some changes."

"Good for the soul," McNeil told him.

≡ 17 ≡

In addition to Nikki and Daspit, there were seven other lawyers assigned to the prosecution of Randolph Bingham. Each had an area of expertise, from forensics to jury selection. While they lightened the workload, their presence didn't lessen the pressure that Nikki was under. Quite the opposite. She felt it was up to her and to Daspit to make the best use of all of their team's efforts.

She'd always been slightly obsessive about her work. In prepping the state's case against Bingham, she became nearly oblivious to other aspects of her day-to-day existence. She thanked the Lord that her man was understanding, that he accepted their long periods apart without question, that he realized her silences in his presence had no bearing on their relationship. At least she hoped he did.

On a Sunday a few weeks before the trial, she and Virgil and her best friend, Loreen Battles, had brunch at an outdoor café after church service.

"You know, Virgil," the outspoken Loreen said, her narrow, fox-like face wearing its usual intense expression, "way back when your girlfriend was just startin' out at the district attorney's, a bunch of us ladies used to go out clubbin' every Friday night."

"Not this again," Nikki said.

Loreen gave her a raised eyebrow look and continued on. "Now, Miss Nikki gets her first big case. What was it? The Puddy Tat Rapist?"

Nikki nodded.

"I heard about him," Virgil said, grinning. "The man's a legend."

"Broke into women's homes—"

"Liked oral sex," Virgil said. "And his 'victims' didn't report him because he was so good at it."

"Man had calluses on his tongue, I heard," Loreen said.

"Rape is an antisocial act," Nikki said, obviously not amused. "An act of violence."

"True enough. Anyway, girlfriend is prosecutin' Puddy Tat and it gets on the TV. Her picture's in the paper. Friday comes 'round, no sign of Nikki. Next Friday, no Nikki. Friday after that, no Nikki. No word neither and we can't get her to return our calls. Nothing. So we say, well, the hell with Missy Too-Important-for-Her-Old-Friends. The sisters and I, we keep meeting and going out and havin' our fun.

"So, finally, trial's over. She's put the Puddy Tat in a place where he's gonna be the rap*ee* instead of the rap*er*. The next Friday night rolls around and Miss Nicolette shows up all apologetic about how she's sorry but she was so busy workin' on the trial she just couldn't do anything else. La, la, la. She hopes we understand it wasn't that she was stuck on herself or anything like that. La, la, la. Can't we just pick up where we left off? So the sisters and me, we take a vote and tell her sure, we want her back in the group. And so it goes for a couple months, when I see in the paper that Nikki's been given another big murder trial. That white woman shot her husband and her mother-in-law in the movie show parking lot, claimed some black men did it."

"The Littman trial," Nikki said.

"Whatever, I see Nikki's going to be prosecutin' that woman and here's what I did, Virgil. I sat down and sent her a telegram. Tell him what it said, sister."

"You tell him," Nikki said. "It's your story."

"It said, 'Congratulations on the new trial . . . and good-bye again.' "

Virgil chuckled and took Nikki's hand. "So it's an established pattern, huh? It's not just me?"

"Ohhh, girl. You don't mean to tell me you cut your man off, too? A man this fine?"

"Maybe I should just leave," Nikki said, only half-pretending to be annoyed. "Then the two people I most care about in this world can feel free to really dis me."

"You know we just funnin'," Loreen said. "If I be dissin' anybody, it's this man here."

"Me?" Virgil asked.

"In the year I've known you, you never once offered to put me together with any of your brothers in blue. Must be some eligible *dicks* looking for a single woman with her own very successful business." Loreen was the owner of a popular beauty salon.

Virgil was at a loss for words.

"Your partner a married man?" Loreen asked.

Nikki almost choked on her latte. "Loreen and McNeil," she said. "Now that'd be a matchup."

"You want to explain yourself?" Loreen asked, eyes flashing.

"You got your concept of the ideal man?" Nikki said. "Tall, virile, young, black. McNeil is the opposite of that."

She saw the frown on Virgil's face and realized she may have gone too far. He said, "Whatever he is, he's still my partner."

"I didn't mean to bring the party down," Loreen said quickly. "Let's just move on to something more up-spirited. Like that story in the *Inquirer*." The tabloid had exposed an adulterous affair involving a popular African-American politician and one of the currently reigning white sex goddesses.

Nikki said she hadn't heard about it.

Loreen's jaw dropped. "Haven't heard about it? The talk shows have been carryin' on about it all week."

"I don't watch those things even when I've got the time," Nikki said. "It's all junk. No real information."

"All right," Loreen said. "Hard news. What's shaking on the Melrose hooker?"

The battered body of a young woman, thought to be a prostitute, had been dumped at an outdoor table at Jimbo's sometime during the midnight-to-6 A.M. period that the Melrose Avenue coffee shop was closed. The reason for media interest in the murder had nothing to do with who the victim was or the all-too-common act of violence that had taken her life. It stemmed from the fact that her corpse had been discovered by radio shock-jock Jack Sylvestre in the course of his daily pre-dawn jog. As might be expected, the murder, the proliferation of violence, the incompetence of the LAPD, and the heroism of some celebrities unafraid to perform their civic duties, had become the hot topics on Sylvestre's show. Minus the last mentioned, these subjects were being picked up by other media outlets as well.

"It's not my case," Virgil said, "so I don't know much except that they're looking for her pimp."

Loreen turned to Nikki. "I don't imagine you'll get that trial, too. Probably be beneath you anyway."

"Get off my case, woman," Nikki said. "And get yourself a life, instead of spending so much time on gossip trash."

"That Jack Sylvestre has his way, the hooker trial could turn out to be big," Loreen said. "Maybe bigger than the one that's got you ignoring your friends and your man."

"I'm not . . ." Nikki began, a bit heatedly. She stopped because Loreen was clapping her hands and rocking in her chair, laughing.

"You see, Virgil," Nikki said, trying not to smile, "this is what I've been putting up with most of my life."

"What? Just because I offered you some friendly career advice, pointing out what's hot and what's not?"

"I don't care what's hot," Nikki said, "and I don't care what happens with Jack Sylvestre and his dead hooker. It's none of my business."

There would come a time when she'd remember that conversation and desperately wish that she'd been right.

PART THREE

OPENING ARGUMENTS

≡ 18 ≡

Richard "Ricky" Geruso reclaimed his passport, loaded his picked-over luggage onto the cart he'd rented and pushed it away from Customs into the bustling international terminal at LAX. He was staggering a bit, as if he'd spent the past twenty-seven days snorting coke and getting his ashes hauled. Which pretty well summed it up. Owing to the seventeen-hour time difference between Tokyo and Los Angeles, he was ahead of the city by nearly a day. Thanks to his recent sybaritic excesses and the usual jet lag, all he wanted was to lay back and spend that time and more with the sweet little lady he now realized he loved.

Never in his life had Ricky felt this way about a bitch. Even with all those sexy geisha broads and the mounds of coke, whatever sanity still sparking in his skull had been focused on her.

He didn't care that she'd stood him up on the longest and most important business trip he'd ever taken. He realized he'd been an asshole and hadn't treated her right. He was sorry for that and sorry for every time he'd slapped her around and treated her like dogshit. Hell, he was a big enough man to tell her he was sorry. He was going to stop, take three breaths, and count to ten before he hit her again. He was in love.

His red-rimmed eyes scanned the faces of those waiting to greet their loved ones. He relaxed when he spotted the two guys standing about a foot taller than the rest of the crowd, grinning at him like fucking dodos. Both were wearing Dino rayon shirts, silk slacks, and genuine authentic 1950s Tony Curtis–inspired Bolo hairstyles—crew cut on top and long and oily on the sides, swept back into d.a.'s.

Stephen, the blond one, called out to him. "Hey, Rickster, welcome home!"

The swarthy one, Jay Jay, scurried through the crowd to take the cart from him. "It went okay in Toyotaville, we hear." Ricky led the way toward the exit, as Stephen shoved people out of his way to catch up.

"It went okay," the weary traveler told Jay Jay. "Patience in the limo?"

Jay Jay hesitated, then said, "No, she ain't."

"Then where? I tole you to bring her."

"Rick-man," Stephen said, joining them, "you're lookin' beauty."

"I look like last week's clams. Jay Jay says you didn't bring my lady."

"Well, no. We didn't."

"Wasn't that my request?"

"Yeah," Stephen said, holding the heavy glass door open for Ricky, then pointing him to the waiting pearl gray stretch limo idling in the no-stopping zone. "Pickett'll explain. He's waitin' to hear all about the deal."

A chauffeur in black suit and black cap hopped from the limo and opened the rear door. Continuing with what seemed like one fluid motion, he took the luggage cart from Jay Jay's fingers and wheeled it to the rear of the vehicle.

"The deal's fine," Ricky said, getting into the limo. "No problem with the fucking deal."

Jay Jay and Stephen followed him in. They sat on the jump seats, giving Ricky the full backseat to himself. Stephen said, "Jay Jay and me, we want you to know we appreciate this opportunity you guys are giving us."

Ricky didn't seem to have heard him. "She really that pissed at me?" he asked.

Jay Jay and Stephen shifted in their seats. They were obviously uncomfortable with this discussion. Neither they nor Ricky seemed to notice that the vehicle was moving into the stream of airport traffic.

"All this time I'm out of the country and she's still got a hard-on about the bitch in San Fran?" Ricky asked, not expecting an answer. "Won't even come down here to welcome me back?" He scowled at the two men. "You fucking guys couldn't handle this one little thing for me?"

"It's . . . there wasn't nothing we could do," Stephen said.

"There's some real money quiff we've been roundin' up while you're away," Jay Jay said with fake enthusiasm. "Young, tasty. Maybe we shoulda brought a couple with, just to take the edge off the ride back. But it didn't seem right, considerin' the circumstances."

"Whaddya talking about?" Ricky said, leaning forward suddenly and grabbing the front of Jay Jay's shirt. "What circumstances?"

Jay Jay looked helplessly at Stephen.

"Patience is dead, Ricky," Stephen said.

Ricky froze. He forgot his fist was still clamped on Jay Jay's shirt. He turned to Stephen and in a terrifyingly quiet voice said, "What?"

"She's gone." The tall man's face registered regret, as close as it would come to genuine sorrow.

Ricky's hand dropped from Jay Jay's shirt. "How. . . ?" he began, still speaking in a dreamy tone of incomprehension so unusual it frightened the other two men.

"She got whacked," Jay Jay said, absently smoothing out the wrinkles on his Dino special. "Whoever did her dumped her body outside Jimbo's in the middle of the night. Like she wanted to be first in line for a breakfast burger. This radio asshole, Jack Sylvestre, found her body while he was out for an early morning jog."

Ricky heard the words, but his mind couldn't process them. "When?" he asked.

Jay Jay started to answer, but Stephen held up his hand and said, "A while ago."

"Guess nobody thought I'd be interested," Ricky said, his voice rising an octave or two. "I'm on the horn to Pickett two, three times a day and he don't think to tell me my woman is dead?"

"Uh, I'm not sure he understands how it was with you two," Stephen said, wincing as though he were walking barefoot on hard pebbles.

"I guess you're right," Ricky said. "Else he wouldn't have killed her."

The other two men registered alarm. "Shit," Stephen said, "Pickett didn't do the job on her."

"He's never offed a bitch," Jay Jay added. "He just, you know, messes 'em up a little."

Ricky wasn't listening. "She moved out of the hotel," he said, nodding to himself. "Pickett decided to make an example of her. It's how he operates."

"C'mon, Rick," Stephen begged, "don't go off the fucking deep end. Pickett didn't have nothing to do—"

"You guys carrying?" Ricky demanded.

"Huh?" Jay Jay asked.

"We don't carry," Stephen said.

"Don't fuck with me," Ricky said, bending down quickly and grabbing Stephen's left ankle. He pulled up the silk pants, exposing electric blue socks and a pale shinbone. He dropped the leg in disgust. "Where you keeping it?"

"It's the daytime," Stephen said, offended at Ricky's display of distrust. "I don't carry in the daytime. Sure as hell not to the airport where they got the machines."

"I need a piece," Ricky said. "I'm gonna kill that motherfucker."

"Oh, shit," Jay Jay said. "Think about it, Ricky. You were running her, not him. She splits, it's your deal. He wouldn't have crossed that line."

"This town's got more loonies than palm trees," Stephen added. "Coulda been a john that did her. Coulda been this asshole Sylvestre."

Some of the words sunk in. Ricky was quiet for a while. The other two men had just started to relax when he said, "Tell me everything."

Jay Jay and Stephen exchanged confused glances. Stephen asked, "Like what?"

"Start with what killed her. Was it a knife?"

Stephen blinked, knowing where Ricky was going with the question. "No. No knife. If Pickett had done it, like by mistake going too far, she'd have been sporting some nasty cuts. Patience was handled heavy. Neck snapped, is what killed her."

"No cuts, you're sure? You see the . . . body?"

"No. The cops told us," Jay Jay said.

"The cops?"

"Yeah," Jay Jay said. "The dicks pulled us in when they found out she was a working girl."

"All this going on and nobody tells me nothing," Ricky said, shaking his head.

"There wasn't nothing you could do, Ricky," Stephen said. "And Pickett thought that—" He stopped, censoring himself.

"Pickett wanted me to keep my mind on the deal."

"I guess."

"How'd they make her as a working girl?" Ricky asked. "And what brought 'em to you guys?"

"Some cop recognized her," Stephen said.

Ricky tensed. "What cop?"

"Liverdais," Stephen said. "Claimed he'd busted her a while back, is how he knew her."

"Eugene Liverdais," Ricky said. "Vice. Unclean Eugene. Yeah, he knew her, all right. About once a week, the prick. Till I put a cork in it."

The limo had been driving down Sunset, crawling through the traffic. Its destination was an ancient milk white, elaborately Regency Moderne hotel. A perpetually glowing, blue neon sign over its main portal spelled out its name in cursive, "The Victoria."

The vehicle abruptly turned right and descended into the hotel's underground parking level. It glided past several parked cars and stopped at the elevator. The driver had their door open within seconds. Ricky made no move to get out. "Tell me about the homicide cops," he asked.

"Jamokes," Stephen said. "No style. One was named Greene, the other Fido, or something like that."

Ricky frowned.

"Pickett's waiting," Stephen said.

"There's some calls I gotta make," Ricky said. "Gimme your celly."

Stephen removed a bright yellow cellular phone the size of a cigarette pack from his pocket. "Maybe you oughta check in with Pickett first, huh?"

Ricky glared at him and hopped from the limo.

By the time the other two had stumbled out behind him, he was heading for the street exit, punching keys on the cell phone. "What do we tell Pickett?" Stephen asked.

"Tell him whatever you want," Ricky said. "No—tell him I'm in fucking mourning. That's what you tell him."

≡ 19 ≡

Five bucks says he's unbuttoned," Peter Daspit whispered to Nikki, gesturing toward the judge's empty bench. Behind them, the small courtroom had reached full capacity.

Nikki considered the bet. During the course of forty years of service to the community, Jarmon Proody, the judge assigned to case # A094969, *The People vs. Randolph J. Bingham III*, had made frequent court appearances with his official robe purposely unbuttoned. He also was known to smoke while on the bench. These were his ways of showing the world his opinion of judicial formality. They also had led some defendants to the conclusion that the gray-haired jurist favored a liberal interpretation of the law. Some days he did, and some days his rulings put him to the right of Judge Roy Bean. One was never too sure where one stood in Jarmon Proody's court.

"Opening day, room full of press," Nikki said. "Could go either way, but I think he'll be doing the button-up. You're on for five."

She glanced to her left, where Gerald Wheeler sat with his co-counsel Mimi Gentry and their client. They were certainly a well-turned-out threesome. The chunky, broad-chested attorney had opted for a personally tailored dark gray suit, creamy white shirt, and a subdued maroon tie. His warm brown eyes, enhanced by laugh lines, were set almost too far apart on his wide, seemingly guileless yet serious face. Gentry was in a little Lauren number that had probably set her back eight or nine hundred dollars, if she paid retail. She was a luminous beauty with a tall, graceful body whose minor modeling career had paid her law school tuition. Between them sat a sun-bronzed Randy Bingham, wearing a beige linen suit, white shirt, dark brown tie, and dazed expression. On first impression, the trio resembled a take-charge father and successful daughter determined to help a hapless family member who was being picked on by bullies.

This picture was a calculated one, of course. The only thing wrong was Bingham's tan, over which Wheeler had had no control. It would probably fade before trial's end.

Bingham's real father and brother were in the first row of spectators, directly behind the defense table. The elder Bingham sat upright on the hardwood seat, expressionless. His younger son—Jeffrey, Nikki recalled from her notes—had enough expression for both of them. He twisted and turned anxiously, his sallow face registering boredom, the annoyance of the arrogant. Suddenly his eyes locked on hers, and the petulance was replaced by pure anger.

Nikki thought she knew the reason for his hostility. She was a woman and she was black, to his mind a member of the underclass. And she was going to do her best to toss his big brother into prison for the rest of his natural life. She responded to Jeffrey Bingham's fury with an exaggerated, patronizing smile that he could paste in his memory book.

The atmosphere in the room changed. The crowd quieted to throat-clearing. Nikki turned to see the judge, hawk-like of countenance, seventy if he was a day, rushing to the bench, his robe flapping. And buttoned.

"Damn," Daspit mumbled as he rose from his chair. "Double up on tomorrow?"

"Least I can do," Nikki said, getting to her feet.

Proody, too experienced (*and too jaded*, Nikki thought), to drag out any part of the proceedings, quickly advised the crowded room to "please avail yourselves of the dubious benefits of those hardwood pews and stay seated." He quickly asked the defendant to rise.

"How do you plead?"

Bingham hesitated before replying.

Nikki couldn't recall how many times she'd observed this particular exchange, but this was the first time she'd ever heard any hesitation. "Inno—" Bingham finally began, before being prompted by a frowning Wheeler. "Not guilty."

"All righty, then," Judge Proody said, relaxing. He turned his sharp features on the prosecutors. "Mr. Daspit, Ms. Hill, it's magic time."

Daspit took the cue energetically, turning his practiced charm on full force for the benefit of the jury. As he moved smoothly through the opening statement he was eloquent, if not exactly mesmerizing. It reminded her of something her grandmother had once said while watching Liberace play piano on TV. "The man sure enough knows where the keys are, but the music's coming from his fingers, not his heart."

"Let me describe for you the tragic night of August the second," Daspit said. "It was a hot Monday night, the smoke from fires in the Hollywood Hills was still in the air. The defendant, Randolph J. Bingham the third, and his unsuspecting victim, Shelli Joanne Dietz-Noyes, and her ten-year-old son, Adam Noyes, returned to her home after dinner. Ms. Dietz-Noyes put the boy to bed and returned to the downstairs den where the defendant opened a bottle of very expensive champagne.

"We do not know precisely what went on while they drank. Mr. Bingham claims he asked Ms. Dietz-Noyes to marry him and she accepted happily. That fails to explain why, as we will hear from Adam Noyes, Mr. Bingham would have been shouting angrily at Ms. Dietz-Noyes, loudly enough to awaken the little boy. Nor does it explain why, just a few hours after she supposedly accepted his offer of marriage, her body was found in that same den with most of her skull blown away by bullets from Mr. Bingham's own weapon."

Nikki barely heard the last part of the sentence. The mention of Adam had started her mind drifting to her meeting with the boy, three days before.

• • •

As he had promised, Fallon had moved his youthful client. The new address was a pleasant cottage in Bel Air nestled among tall poplar trees behind a formidable vine-covered fence. The lawyer also had replaced the nanny, Jenny Mapes, with a middle-aged African-American couple, Sidney and Donia Davis, who had raised their own children and seemed to welcome the opportunity to care for another.

Donia Davis answered the bell. The plump, very black woman with her hair tied in a colorful kerchief explained that Fallon had been detained by some problem at his office. She'd barely introduced the deputy D.A. to her sturdy-looking, gray-haired husband when Adam rushed into the room, beaming. He grabbed Nikki's hand and dragged her through the house to see his "special place."

It was a large room dominated by a long wooden worktable equipped with a buzzsaw, two vises, and at one end, a line of electric sockets, most of them filled with cords from a variety of space-age tools. The rapping of Will Smith blasted from surround-sound quads.

"Some of the guys from Homeboy fixed it up for me," Adam said, raising his voice to be heard above the music.

Nikki strolled to pale wooden bookshelves that had been built around a desk where two computer monitors rested, along with a wireless keyboard and a thin, shiny mouse that looked like it belonged on Michael Jackson's hand. The shelves housed an assortment of sleek black audio-video components. "Is there something that turns down the sound?" Nikki asked loudly. "Give my eardrums a rest?"

Adam's hand went to a black plastic square attached to his belt. On the face of one of the decks, a multicolored bar chart was dancing to the music. It suddenly went black and Will Smith was cut off mid-rap.

"Much better," Nikki said.

"Music keeps me company while I work," Adam said.

She saw that the twin computer screens were filled with schematic drawings. The desktop was papered with sketches and notes and pages torn from newspapers and magazines. The magazines themselves were scattered on the floor near the desk. They ran the gamut from *Details* to *Mechanics Illustrated*. She bent to pick up a copy of something titled *American Warrior*. It was open to an article on Tasers and stun guns.

She unfolded its cover—a garish photo of a muscular soldier of fortune, wearing a crew cut, a generic khaki uniform, and a knife in his teeth. He was smashing through a door, surprising a foreign-looking gentleman who was in bed with a voluptuous, dark-skinned beauty. She flipped through the periodical, glimpsing weaponry, maps, mug shots of dictators, rugged all-terrain vehicles, and pages upon pages of classified ads.

"You planning to start your own war?" Nikki asked, holding up the magazine.

Adam grinned. "Not exactly," he said, taking it from her. "There's some interesting stuff in here. You know, for toys."

He led her past an art easel. Nikki thought it was the same one she'd seen on the video of the murder scene. It was empty now. The floor was covered by rubber matting that probably helped to reduce the danger of shocks and also saved wear and tear on your feet if you were on them all day. Which, judging by the clutter, Adam was. Everywhere she looked there were bits of electronic gadgetry, pieces of wood and plastic and metal. Nuts, bolts. Wire springs. Numerous hunks of computer circuitry. "Looks like Robby the Robot threw up in here," she said.

"Who's Robby the Robot?" Adam asked.

Nikki had to think. She couldn't connect the name to anything specific. "I'm not sure, some movie robot. I just meant to say there's a whole mess of stuff in here looks like the inside of a robot."

"You don't like it?" He looked crestfallen.

"I think it's a wonderful workshop."

His smile returned. "It's dope. Everything I need in one place."

"How long ago did you move in, Adam?"

"Three weeks," the boy said.

"And you . . . achieved all this in three weeks?"

"I wouldn't call this an achievement. I'm still just starting on most stuff."

So serious, she thought. "You like it here, huh?"

"Oh, yeah. I've never had a room like this to myself. Not even with my mom." He sobered suddenly. "I really miss her," he said. "That's okay, isn't it?"

"Sure."

"Sidney and Donia take good care of me now. It's not the same as my mom."

"No."

"Sidney was in Vietnam," Adam said. "Saigon City. I get the feeling he doesn't like to talk about it. He drives, so we leased a Grand Cherokee and we don't have to take cabs anymore."

"And Donia?"

He was silent.

"Something about Donia?" Nikki coaxed.

"With Jenny, I got to eat pizza or mac with cheese or a burger, which was dope. Donia cooks a lot of things like fish and chicken. That's bunk. She makes me eat at least three bites of salad, or at least pretend to. I just keep it in my mouth and go to the bathroom and spit it out."

"So that's a vote for Jenny?" Nikki asked, amused.

"The thing is, Jenny wasn't very smart. So I could pretty much get around her."

"Is that dope or bunk?"

He grinned. "What do you think?"

"I think if you eat pizza every night, you start looking like a pizza."

"Isn't it better for me to find that out for myself, 'stead of having to go puke my salad?"

"You're a bright boy, Adam. I can tell you know a lot more than most ten-year-olds. But Donia can still teach you something about your diet. Greens are good for you, even if you don't think so. We all need somebody to steer us in the right direction."

"Who steers you?"

It was a question she wasn't prepared to answer.

"You got a dad or a mom?" he prompted.

"My mother died having me," Nikki said.

"Oh?" he asked, intellectually interested. "That can happen?"

"Sometimes."

"And your dad?"

Her feelings about her father were too complex to begin to explain to a ten-year-old. Shortly after her birth, William Hill had placed her in the care of his mother. She had grown up both hating him for this apparent abandonment and desperately seeking to prove to him what a terrible mistake he had made. Only recently had they even talked. "My dad and I haven't been very close."

"He beat you?"

"No." *Not physically*, she thought.

"Mine was big on that. Beating up people. Me. My mom. Even some of the people at Homeboy. It was a good thing when he died."

That last statement was said so matter-of-factly she shivered.

"Do you have any brothers or sisters?" he asked.

"Nope." As soon as the word was out, she realized it was an unconscious lie. Her father's second marriage had produced a daughter, a teenager she barely knew. Not really a sister any more than his second wife was her mother.

"Ever wonder what that would be like, a brother or sister?"

"Sometimes," she said.

"Most of the kids I go to school with, they have brothers and sisters."

"You like school?" she asked. Fallon had told her that the boy attended a private school devoted to liberal education. He was in seventh grade, the youngest in his class by three years.

"I'm very good at math but not so good at spelling. I'm bored by spelling."

"Comes in handy when you're trying to write," she said.

"Writing bores me, too," he said. "Who needs to write?"

"People who want to communicate."

"My e-mail software has a spellchecker."

"Who do you e-mail?"

"Technical support people, who are usually clueless. Homeboy Software users, mainly. It's the best way to know what works and what doesn't."

"What about friends?" Nikki asked.

"I don't e-mail any friends."

"Actually, I was just wondering who your friends are," she said.

"From school, mainly," he said, looking away from her. "Around."

"Anybody special?"

"No." He brightened. "Unless it's you."

She couldn't help but smile. "I'd like to be your friend," she said.

"You probably have lots of 'em," he said.

"Not a lot."

"Boyfriends?" he asked.

"One," she said.

"Oh." With no change of expression, he shifted to another subject. "Want to see this thing I'm working on? I call it an 'Alien Box.'" He held up a square block composed of clear Lucite panels. Each panel contained bits of colored plastic floating in some kind of liquid. As he turned the block, the plastic pieces moved to form images that resembled animated space creatures.

"Looks like a winner," she said.

"Randy's going to go to jail for killing my mom, isn't he?" His face was expressionless, but his green eyes seemed to darken.

"Guilty people should pay for their crimes," she said, promising him nothing she couldn't guarantee.

"You send lots of guilty people to jail?"

"As many as I can. Sometimes I miss."

"You work downtown, right?" he asked.

"Criminal Courts Building."

"That's where I'll be testifying?"

She nodded.

"Can I visit you sometime?"

"Not much to see down there," she said.

"I'd like to watch a trial. . . ."

"Mr. Bingham has informed the investigating officers that he left the victim's home at ten-thirty P.M." Daspit's slightly droning voice brought Nikki back to the courtroom. "Perhaps the defendant did leave at that hour, but, if so, he must have returned. Because, just minutes after two-fourteen A.M., when gunshots coming from Ms. Dietz-Noyes's home were reported to the Los Angeles Police Department, a neighbor saw Bingham running from the murder house, hopping into his fancy Alfa sports car, and driving away. Could the neighbor have been mistaken? No way, as you will discover when he takes the stand.

"Very soon, you will hear Homicide Detective Virgil Sykes describe the scene of the crime as he and his partner arrived in response to the report of gunshots. . . ."

Daspit moved on, following his plan to finish just before the noon break, providing the jury with food for thought along with their lunch.

Before that happened, Nikki was distracted once again, this time by a tap on the shoulder. She was surprised to see her clerk, Jeb Lacy, crouching beside her. He handed her a scribbled note.

It read: "Det. Sykes shot. Rushed to emergency at Midway."

≡ 20 ≡

Virgil had arrived at work that Wednesday to discover that one of his and McNeil's colder cases had hopped to the front burner. Over a year before, they'd been assigned the murder of a Beverly Hills internist named Charles Furst. The middle-aged doctor had been shot in the head twice while apparently asleep in bed at his ranch-style home in Mandeville Canyon.

There had been no sign of a break-in or struggle. Witnesses and evidence indicated that Dr. Furst, thrice-divorced, had entertained a variety of female guests at his home. There was nothing to suggest that he had been entertaining the night of the shooting, however. Just the opposite. One set of dinner dishes. One used towel in the bathroom. One used pillow on the bed, bloodied by the wounds, the other still fresh from the maid's morning laundering. Even the old reliable raised toilet seat indicated that Furst had spent the evening alone.

Nothing of value had been missing from the apartment, according to his most recent ex-wife. Virgil and McNeil had checked her out, along with the other former Mrs. Fursts, and more than thirty women (most, but not all, single) whose names had been in the doctor's little black book. All were possible suspects, but none came close to edging into the "probable" category, not even the two call girls he hired on occasion.

Ditto his business associates and his patients. Aside from earning somewhere in the neighborhood of $750,000 a year and possessing a libido that laughed at Viagra, Dr. Furst, apparently, had lived an average sort of life. Neither his friends nor his enemies had felt very strongly about him. The women said they found him attentive, entertaining and fun to be with but not a potential life partner; the doctor was quick to inform them that, after three marriage mistakes, he was just interested in having a good time.

With no clues, no motive, a missing weapon, and no prime suspect, the detectives eventually found themselves at a dead end.

Until that morning.

The gun used to murder Dr. Charles Furst had turned up as part of the evidence confiscated from the apartment of a burglar named Artie Olfax.

Olfax was a tense black man of indeterminate age. Virgil studied the small, wiry two-timer sitting on the metal chair in Interrogation and figured he could pass for ten years either side of forty. However old he was, this was his third strike, so he looked to be spending the rest of his years behind bars.

He didn't mind talking to them. There was no request for his court-appointed lawyer to be present. He'd been nabbed in the act. How much worse off could he be?

"Well, you could be facing murder," McNeil told him.

"Murder? You crazy. Who I murder?"

"A doctor. Last year. In a house in Mandeville Canyon."

"You crazy. I never do no work in Mandeville. Floor plans too fucked up in the canyons. You get yourself in a box, no back access. Just canyon wall."

"Your gun killed the man," Virgil said.

"What gun? I don't carry no gun. Got no use for 'em."

"Beretta Centurion," Virgil said. "Just like I got at home. Only mine didn't shoot that doctor."

"Gun's not mine," Olfax squawked. "Ask them guys who went through my place. Nothing there's mine. All loot."

"Where'd you pick it up?" McNeil asked, keeping it casual, like the question didn't mean much.

Olfax cocked his head to one side. "I tell you, what I get?"

"Peace of mind," Virgil said.

"Fuck that. How about . . . immunity?"

McNeil chuckled. "How about . . . death penalty?"

"I don't use no guns," Olfax whined.

"Then tell us where you picked it up," Virgil said. When Olfax remained silent, he added, "You give us an address, I'll try to get you immunity on that break-in."

"On *that* one? What the fuck good is that?"

"Hey, brother, you do the crime . . ."

"Well, shit, that's no good. I'm still gonna go up on strike three."

"That's all I can do," Virgil said. "Better'n a sharp stick in the eye."

"Well, shit," Olfax repeated.

He gave up the address.

It was the smallest home on that block of Georgiana Street in Santa Monica. Virgil parked so that he blocked the Infiniti that rested in the driveway, just in case. He and McNeil had recognized the address. It belonged to Geena Laurence, a plump but still handsome blonde in her mid-forties, who'd been the dead doctor's first wife. "How long ago was their divorce?" McNeil had asked on the drive over.

"Nineteen years. She remarried a guy named Kenneth Laurence, had a kid. A whole different life."

"She waits nineteen years to bump the guy off?"

"Looks that way," Virgil said. "Laurence himself died last year. Maybe that kick-started something that ended with her killing the doc. Come to think of it, we'd better see what we can dig up on Laurence's death."

"Good point," McNeil said.

The doorbell was answered by a teenage version of Geena Laurence, wearing cutoffs, a tank top, and several diamonds lining the upper ridge of her right ear; a matching one had been implanted in the right side of her nose. In spite of the jewelry, which Virgil viewed as a turnoff, he was stirred by the girl's languid sexiness.

"Is Ms. Laurence in?" he asked.

"I'm Ms. Laurence. My friends call me Jilly. Who are you?"

Virgil did the introductions. "It's your mother we're looking for," he said.

"Come on in." She eyed him appraisingly. "Maybe I can change your mind."

She led them to the large living room.

"We were here about a year ago," Virgil said, "but you weren't."

"I guess not," she said, smiling. "I'd have remembered. When was it exactly?"

"Last May."

"I must've been in school."

"Jilly, who was that at—?" Geena Laurence said, entering the room. She seemed surprised but not particularly disturbed to see them. "You're police detectives, right? I'm sorry, I don't remember your names."

"This is Detective Sykes," Jilly told her. "And Detective McGee."

"McNeil," he corrected.

"Is there something I can help you with?"

"You had a robbery here a week ago?" Virgil asked.

"Yes. The damn house was empty. Jill and I were spending the weekend at the Springs."

"We've recovered some of the items that were stolen," McNeil said.

She seemed relieved, then puzzled. "But I thought you were homicide detectives."

"Robbery-Homicide," McNeil said merrily. "Here's the list of stuff the perpetrator had in his collection. You mind checking off the things he picked up from this address?"

Geena Laurence took the list and the pen McNeil had provided to a chair beside an antique writing desk in the living room. She picked up a pair of glasses that looked to Virgil like ninety-nine-cent-store material and studied the list. "He was a busy boy."

"Yes, ma'am."

It took her less than five minutes to go through the list. When she handed it back to McNeil, he gave it a quick glance and passed it to Virgil.

"That's it?" McNeil asked her. "Nothing you missed?"

"Isn't it enough? Fourteen items including the silver-backed hand mirror that belonged to my grandmother."

Virgil moved closer to her, pointing at the paper. "What about that?"

"A Beretta Centurion? What is that, a gun of some sort?"

"Yes, ma'am," McNeil said. "Definitely a gun."

Geena Laurence looked up from the sheet with a puzzled frown. "Jilly, by any chance do you—" She saw that her daughter had left the room. "I don't know anything about a gun," she continued.

"That jibes with the list of stolen items you gave to the officers investigating the break-in," McNeil said. "No gun. But the Beretta was stolen from here."

"Why would you think that?"

"The thief said it was."

"He must have been mistaken."

"You have a room upstairs with framed pictures on the wall?" Virgil asked. "Trophies? The thief said he was tempted by the trophies, but it's not always easy to find somebody who wants metals for their melt-down value."

"It's . . . Ken's room. My late husband's room. I still haven't got around to . . ." She made a vague gesture with her hand.

"In the closet of that room," McNeil said, "there's a wooden box lined in velvet. The Beretta was in there. Thief says he left the box. It could still be up there. Why don't we go see?"

As if in a trance, Geena Laurence rose from the chair. Forgetting to remove the cheap eyeglasses, she said, "Follow me."

Virgil and McNeil exchanged glances. This was not going well. Assuming that she had murdered Dr. Furst, her inviting them to find the gun case could mean only one thing: She'd gotten rid of it.

As they climbed the stairs, Virgil said, "The gun was registered in your husband's name."

"Ken liked guns," she said as they reached the top of the stairs. "I don't. I thought we'd gotten rid of them all. I still don't understand why you're so concerned about this one."

"The gun was used to murder Charles Furst," Virgil said.

He was trying to shake her, but he wasn't ready for her reaction. Her knees seemed to give out and she slumped forward. He grabbed her upper arms and kept her from falling. "Oh, my God!" she wailed, pulling back from him. "You think I...? Why would I kill Charlie? It was so long ago."

"Let's see if we can find that gun case," McNeil said. "Then we'll talk about who killed good old Charlie."

Geena backed away from them, in the direction of the stairwell. "No. I didn't do anything."

"Ms. Laurence," Virgil said, "don't make this any harder on all of us than it has to be."

"Me murder Charlie? Why would you think such a thing?"

"That's what we've gotta talk about," McNeil said.

Her frightened eyes shifted from them to something down the hall behind them. She screamed, "No, Jilly, no!"

"Aw, shit," Virgil said, knowing in that split-second the mistake he'd made. His fingers wrapped around his Police Special even as he started to turn.

McNeil stiff-armed him, knocking him to the side, off-balance.

Virgil couldn't tell if the sound of the shots came before he felt the bullet enter his body or after. He experienced no immediate pain, then a fireball began to radiate from his left shoulder and a sharp stinging sensation cut across his head. He tottered at the top of the stairwell, then took a backward step into nothing and fell helplessly, banging against the stairwell railing. He slid down the rail for a few feet, then started rolling down the carpeted stairs on his back, gathering speed until, upper body throbbing in pain, he crashed into a wall and was still.

Above him, more gunshots exploded and a woman screamed.

Then he heard and felt nothing.

≡ 21 ≡

Damn you, Virgil Sykes."

It sounded like somebody he knew. Was she crying? She was mad at him but she was crying for him. That was as goofy as a shithouse rat.

"Did he say something?" Another familiar voice, male this time.

"Sounded to me like 'shithouse rat,'" the woman replied, no longer crying. She seemed happy, as if the words had given her hope.

His eyelids were stuck together. He wasn't sure he could pry them apart. He gave it one more try and they popped open.

He was staring up at white. Room color. White ceiling, white walls. To his right was a plastic bottle hooked to a metal pole. To his left, an intense bright light flooded into the room.

Two people moved closer, leaned over him.

One was a beautiful black woman, the other an ugly white man. He was happy to see them both.

"Well, hell, he's okay," the white man said in mock disgust.

"You wanna go let the doctor know?" the woman asked.

"Sure."

The white man departed.

"Hi, honey," Virgil croaked. "Got a hamburger on you?"

"You bastard," she said, crying happy tears now. "You had me so worried."

"Umm?" He couldn't quite figure out if she was mad at him or not.

"You've been unconscious for nearly twenty-three hours," Nikki said.

"Oh." He started to sit up.

"No," she said. "You just lie there with your head on the pillow."

"Yeah. Not quite . . . here."

"You've been shot," she told him. "Twice."

"No shit?"

"You lost a little piece of your big head."

He attempted to bring his left hand to his head and a stab of pain shot up his arm. He groaned.

"You sprained your wrist when you fell."

"What did I . . . ?" He lost track of his question.

"A seventeen-year-old girl shot you in the head and the shoulder. She mighta done more damage, but McNeil pushed you out of the direct line of fire." She hesitated. "He killed the girl."

"Good," Virgil said. His head was starting to ache, too.

"She murdered that doctor. Dr. Furst. Blamed him for her father's death."

Movement in the room. McNeil was back.

"Thanks for . . . you know," Virgil croaked out to him.

"My pleasure," McNeil said, grinning. "Doc'll be here in however long it takes him to sink the last putt at Brentwood."

"Didn't girl . . . shoot the doc?" Virgil asked, muddled.

"You got feathers in your head, partner. Remember our case? Doc Furst? The little bitch shot him. It's *your* doc who's at the country club banging golf balls."

Virgil blinked. The effect of the drugs seemed to be wearing off enough for him to get the drift of the conversation. "Furst was horndog," he said, trying to keep his mind off his aches. "Girl was sexy. He was . . . easy target."

"Look who's talking," McNeil said.

"Why shoot . . . me?" Virgil asked. "You're bigger . . . meaner."

"That's what you get for flirting with her," McNeil said. "She didn't even know I was there."

"Flirting with a seventeen-year-old?" Nikki asked.

"Don't . . . listen to him," Virgil said. He lifted the arm that didn't hurt, held out his hand to McNeil, who grabbed it in both his paws. "You okay?"

"Me?" McNeil replied, grinning. "Right as rain. The broad's mother is squawking, but Corben doesn't think there'll be any serious fallout, considering how much the kid messed you up."

"I mean . . . inside. You okay?"

"Oh, hell, yeah. The girl's old man raised her to be a gun nut. Sweetheart of the NRA and a homicidal whacko to boot. It was like stepping on a scorpion."

McNeil's pieface broke into a wide grin. "Well, now that I know I'm not gonna have to break in a new partner, I'll be getting back to work. Nice seeing you, Nikki."

When he'd gone, Nikki said, "Your partner's a little scary."

Virgil tried to smile without much success. He wanted to tell her that putting up with McNeil's bad behavior was a small price to pay for his life. But it was a complex thought. It seemed much easier just to float into sleep.

≡ 22 ≡

Ricky and Pickett sat at a table at the rear of Buffy's, the latest in an endless succession of trendy restaurants that opened and closed along Melrose Avenue. The place was decorated to resemble a cemetery at night—black walls with trompe l'oeil tombstones. An assortment of plaster statues, fanged and hairy monsters in the main, had been placed strategically throughout the room, while from the ceiling hung a phosphorous moon, a few stars, and a layer of some gauzy fabric Ricky assumed was supposed to look like fog.

He scanned the room. An upscale crowd was enjoying lunch, served by young waiters and waitresses in Gap wear and ghostly whiteface. "What the fuck is this place?" he asked.

"It's run by some pukes from the Valley," Pickett replied, idly watching a waitress slink past their table. "They rippin' off some hot TV show. Probably get sued, but it won't matter, 'cause by then they'll have made their loot, put it where it can't be touched, and nobody'll give a shit one way or the other. Tha's the beauty of the restaurant business out here. Hit-and-run."

"I hate this place," Ricky said. He flashed his fake Rolex. "And the broad's late."

"Figures," Pickett said.

The "broad" was Sylvia Stern, a writer for the *Los Angeles Times*'s business section. She had her own part to play in Pickett's new plan. Personally, Ricky was fed up with the plan; it had cost him too much already. If he had been in L.A. where he belonged, Patience would still be—no. He had to let it go. She was dead. During the past two days, he'd thought the whole thing through. He had to move on with his life. After he made the bastard who'd killed her pay.

"Nakki say when we'd be gettin' the down?" Pickett asked.

"By the fifteenth," Ricky answered dispiritedly.

"Hey, Rick, snap out of it before she gets here, okay? We need to go into this full force."

"I'm wearin' a fucking sport coat cost me a thousand bucks, for Christ's sake," Ricky said. "You're wearing a fucking Armani. Are we businessmen, or what?"

"This is serious," Pickett said. "You remember what you're supposed to call me?"

"Massah?" Ricky said. "Big bossman?"

"Damn it, don't fuck around," Pickett said. "We got to have the right front for the plan to work."

The plan. Pickett's plan. The way Ricky saw it, they'd been doing fine when they had the girls out on the street. He'd let Pickett talk him into expanding their operation, moving to a better class of johns. He had to admit that had worked out. More money and, considering the clout of some of their clients, they'd built themselves a nice little power base. He knew the city was cracking down on pimps, coming up with all sorts of new laws designed to put procurers out of business. It was time to consider some other possible ways to turn a buck. Still, this latest move seemed like too big a jump. The month he'd spent in Tokyo told him their new partners were in an entirely different league.

"Here she comes," Pickett said, getting to his feet.

Sylvia Stern was a tall, plain woman who moved like a man. But Ricky didn't think she was a dyke. One, she was wearing a dress. Two, she was wearing makeup. Three, she seemed to be flirting with his partner, which he doubted a dyke would do, even for a news story.

Pickett had decided that for purposes of their fledgling company,

Wonderbar, Inc., they would be L. J. Pickett and Richard A. Geruso, President and CEO, respectively. This seemed fine to Sylvia Stern, who placed a minirecorder on approximately the center of the table. She asked L.J. what he was drinking—a mimosa—and ordered one for herself. Then she turned on the machine.

It had been agreed that Pickett, a man of thespian experience, would do most of the talking. Ricky, Richard, was merely to nod every now and then and try to look like someone who'd taken a business course.

The first questions were harmless little puffballs. Where were they from? How did they meet? What were their backgrounds? Pickett lied smoothly and gracefully, concocting a tale about two young men from different parts of the country—Chicago's South Side (L.J.) and New York's Queens (Richard)—who'd traveled to the West Coast seeking fortune, if not fame. They'd been thrown together in a pro-am golf tourney at Torrey Pines. "Richard was looking for something a little more exciting than his accounting chores," Pickett said, "and I was in need of someone who could free me from the business side of my employment services company."

Actually, Pickett was from Hattiesburg, Mississippi, and Ricky from Boston and they'd met at the Hot Box Club on La Cienega, watching naked women dance and pick up folded dollar bills from the bar without using their hands.

"Where'd you get your B.A., Richard?" Sylvia asked between nibbles of her angel-hair pasta.

Ricky almost choked on a piece of steak. "I . . . uh . . . NYU."

Sylvia nodded and turned to Pickett. "And now I want to hear all about Wonderbar."

"Well," Pickett said, feigning coyness, "I don't want to get too specific, but it's a whole new adventure in night-out entertainment. We've figured out a way to combine dining and drinking and enjoying entertainment with state-of-the-art electronics."

"Give me an example," Sylvia said, taking a notepad from her purse.

"Okay." Pickett reached under the table for his briefcase and came up with a black plastic palmtop computer. He pressed a button on its front and the screen glowed, went to black, and returned with the words "Welcome to Wonderbar."

"This is our menu," he said. "Try it."

"What do I do?"

"Just press the button."

Sylvia pressed the button. Suddenly images appeared on the small screen. Photographs of mouth-watering dishes complete with full descriptions, including calories and fat content. And prices.

"You make your selection by pressing that other button," Pickett said. "When you're finished picking out your food and drink, you rest the machine on the table and your waiter arrives and accesses your selection via a microwave transfer."

"Interesting," Sylvia said, scribbling away. "But there are clubs using these same sort of gizmos. Baccus and Entros in San Francisco, and—"

"Are you married, Sylvia?" Pickett asked, cutting her off.

She stopped writing, evidently surprised by the question. "Not at present," she said.

"Then you might be amused by this little game you won't find at Baccus. Something we've planned for our evening happy hours." He turned the machine on again, punched a button twice, and was greeted by the words "Welcome to Psych-a-Mate."

This was replaced by a screen full of questions with multiple choices for answers. Pickett slid a black plastic stylus from its niche in the side of the machine. "These twenty-five questions have been selected to provide a psychological profile. If your palmtop is in close proximity to a palmtop with a matching profile, both machines will start to hum. Sort of a Y2K icebreaker." He smiled. "And, assuming you're both telling truth, you've got instant compatibility."

"But who tells the truth when you're playing games?" Sylvia asked him, smiling coquettishly.

"I always do," he replied so sincerely even Ricky came near believing him.

They went through a few more dog and pony routines, then Pickett offered to show the woman the site of the first of a proposed chain of Wonderbars. "It's right down the street. Where the Sez Who? Café used to be."

They left Ricky to pay the tab.

He took his time catching up with them. By then they were on the second floor of the now-gutted Sez Who?, a spot where Ricky had had drinks with Patience only a few months before.

Sylvia was asking about funding.

"International," Pickett said, being careful not to get any sawdust on his cuffs.

"German?"

"Japanese," Pickett said.

"Sony? Matsushita?" Sylvia prompted.

"Close," Pickett said and changed the subject.

Ricky stared at his partner. Toshiro Nakamura's operation was about as close to Matsushita as Pickett was to Colin Powell. Nakki made his loot in bathhouses and traveler hotels where you went to bed on a wooden slab. He operated nearly a dozen clubs in and around Tokyo that were, as far as Ricky was concerned, the Japanese equivalent of an American lapdance operation.

Ricky spotted something across the room—a beer label stuck to the bottom pane of a window overlooking Melrose. He'd put it there. They'd been sitting at a table right next to the window, him and Patience. She'd been wearing a tube top, showing lots of chest. He'd peeled the label and stuck it on her right tit. "Milk from that spigot, Bud from this one," he'd said.

She hadn't been amused. "Take it off," she'd said.

He'd obeyed and stuck it on the window.

He was peeling it off when Pickett returned from escorting the reporter to the street. "The fuck you doing?"

"Souvenir," Ricky said, placing the label carefully in his shirt pocket. "Sylvia gonna give us a good write-up?"

"I suspect. I'm taking her to dinner."

"I still don't see what we get out of a story on the business page."

"It's all perception, Ricky. If you're on the business page, you're in business. If the article says you're legit, you are legit, my man. And if, after a good night's humpin', the article says your legit business is about to fly to the moon, a lot of folks will be throwing money at us to get in on the maiden voyage."

Ricky shrugged. Maybe Pickett was right. He didn't much care. The only thing he did care about was vengeance. "You gonna be able to fuck Mrs. Ed?" he asked idly. "Horsy-faced bitch like that?"

"Fucking is never a problem," Pickett said. "Being nice to her afterward is gonna be the bear."

≡ 23 ≡

Anybody know when Sykes will be released from the hospital?" the D.A. asked the two prosecutors seated in his office.

"They're not saying," Nikki offered. "One bullet passed through his body but it clipped the top of a bone called the scapula. His doctor wants to make sure there's no infection or any nasty complications. And they always like to check head wounds for a while."

"Well, hell," Daspit grumbled. "Who's left to take us through the crime scene on Monday? We can't risk using Numbnuts."

"Forgive me, Frank," Wise said, "but the world is filled with numbnuts. Could you be more specific?"

"McNeil," Daspit said. "The guy's a loose cannon. He's on record as a woman-hater and he's just shot and killed a teenage girl."

"He took out a killer who was firing down on him and his partner," Nikki corrected. She knew in her heart that they couldn't use McNeil, but she felt she owed the detective some defense.

"Forget McNeil," Wise said. "At least until Internal Affairs is finished with him."

"Internal Affairs?" Nikki was surprised. "They must not have much to do, spending time on this one."

Wise screwed up his face as if he were suffering from an attack of heartburn. "The girl's mother is screaming that McNeil went postal and murdered her daughter. Nonsense, of course. Jill Laurence was armed and dangerous. All they have to do is look at the holes in Sykes."

"The problem is one of excess," Daspit said.

"Meaning?" Nikki asked.

"Mrs. Laurence claims he subdued her daughter with his first shot," Daspit said. "Taking her out was excessive."

"Mrs. Laurence is probably not the best judge," Nikki suggested.

"It's a nuisance claim," Wise said with a dismissive shrug. "It'll go away. Still, it's too risky putting McNeil on the stand. What about the uniforms on the scene?"

"DiBono is an inexperienced flannelmouth," Daspit said. "The other one is nonverbal."

"Then DiBono it is," Wise said.

"You want to take him?" Daspit asked Nikki.

The question caught her off-guard. Her mind was still on McNeil and the IAG investigation. "If you don't think you can handle him, I'll do it," Daspit said.

"What's the big deal about handling him?" Nikki asked.

"He's a courtroom virgin. It's going to take work to keep him from bending over for Wheeler."

"A little courtroom virginity might be refreshing," she said.

"Good," Wise said. "Problem solved. Now we can all get back to work."

Nikki took an extra minute gathering her notes. When Daspit had left the room, she asked the D.A., "Who in the office is looking into the claim against McNeil?"

Wise grinned. "Dana's been asking for work."

"You sicced her on McNeil?"

"It's perfect. She'll be busting her ass to dig up something that'll get her media time. That shooting was about as righteous as any I can recall. There's no way it'll ever wind up in court. She'll be spinning her wheels and out of my hair."

"Don't underestimate her," Nikki said.

"Don't you underestimate *me*," he said, punctuating the statement with a self-satisfied wink.

Nikki returned to the hospital to discover that Virgil had a new roommate, an elderly man with two broken legs. Nikki nodded to him and navigated around the curtain separating him from the detective.

Virgil was sitting up in bed, the plaster on his head looking more startling than it had against the white pillow. A sling held his sprained right arm in place. A bandage she hadn't noticed before was visible under the thin hospital gown at his left shoulder. A copy of *Sports Illustrated* was open on his lap.

Nikki gestured toward the curtain and whispered, "What's with the legs?"

"Tried to ride his grandson's skateboard," Virgil whispered back. "Me, turning my back on a murderer, I guess they figured we had that death wish thing in common. What's that you got?"

She was holding something behind her back. Something in a paper sack.

"Wait a minute," he said, sniffing the air. "Smells like . . ."

She removed a 6-ounce cheeseburger from the bag.

"Oh, baby," he said, grinning. "You know what I like."

He reached out his left hand and winced, drawing it back. "Damn," he said. "I keep forgetting. I gotta be real careful about moving my arm."

"Take your time," she said, handing him the sandwich.

"How's about a kiss before the onions kick in." She bent down for an awkward embrace. "Twice as nice as your mother's advice," he said.

"It'd be four times as nice if you didn't have those bristles on your face."

"I'm at the mercy of strangers," he said. "Don't know as I'd trust any of these mean-lookin' nurses with a razor to my throat."

"I'll get your electric from your apartment."

"Don't worry about it. Maybe I'll grow a beard."

"Something in that apartment you don't want me to see?" She was only half-kidding.

"'Course not, honey. Can you give me some help here?"

He was struggling to unwrap the burger using only one hand. She took care of that for him, then removed several paper napkins from the bag and spread them out on the magazine on his lap.

He chewed his first bite, savored it, and swallowed. "Simple pleasures," he said.

"Want me to move that water glass?"

"Water and a burger really don't make it."

"I'll see what I can find," she said.

When she returned with a cola, he said, "No beer, huh?"

She glared at him. "There's a bar right down the hall for the ambulatories. Ale on tap. Nurses pouring and busing tables. Couple of surgeons in their scrubs sipping martinis."

She plucked the straw from his water glass and stuck it into the cola, holding it out to him. He took a long pull, swallowed, and said, "Hits the spot."

She sat beside him, watching attentively as he ate the hamburger and holding out the cola when he asked.

"No angel of mercy ever looked so fine," he said as she gathered the resulting trash and deposited it in the wastebasket beside the bed. "How're things goin' in the courtroom?"

"Okay, I guess," she said, returning to the chair beside him. "Wheeler's hard to read. His opening statement was pretty general: Bingham didn't commit the murder. He loved Shelli Dietz. Like that. He floated the possibility that Dietz may have had another boyfriend who went nuts when he heard about the marriage. Don't suppose you came across any such animal in your investigation?"

"Nope. 'Course, she did business with several men. Guy named Phillips who was her art representative. Since he hit on me, I doubt he'd be getting buckwild with any female of the species. Gallery owner named . . . Martell. Mac has all the information. It's jive anyway. This unknown boyfriend just happened to use Bingham's gun tryin' to fake a suicide?"

"Yeah, the gun," Nikki said. "Wheeler says Bingham gave it to Dietz to protect her. This make-believe boyfriend could have found it in the house."

"Lame. They got any proof the gun was at Dietz's?"

"Hope not. It's our story he brought it with him. Makes it premeditated. They're also going to have to explain Bingham's spray bottle with Shelli Dietz's blood on it."

"And the witnesses," Virgil said.

"Wheeler will say they're confused and/or mistaken."

"The kid maybe, but my man Gus is 'bout it."

"You don't know Adam very well, if you think he could be confused about what he heard," she said. "What's your opinion of Officer DiBono?"

"Why?"

"With you out of commission, we're going to use him."

"What about Mac? He's got more experience on the stand."

She told him about Geena Laurence's assertion that McNeil had killed her daughter unnecessarily.

"What bullshit," Virgil said.

"I agree. Still, you've got to admit Mac's got his own weird ways. We just didn't want him Fuhrmanizing us."

"So now you've got to deal with a gee-whiz baby cop."

"That's about it. What do you think?"

"He's gung-ho, big on using his mouth. You might want to tell him to stick to 'yes' and 'no' when Wheeler starts in on him."

Nikki nodded. "On the videotape, it looked like he made a couple mistakes at the crime scene."

"Yeah. He opened a locked door, poked around a little, touched a couple items he shouldn't have. And, he missed the boy upstairs. Thought the house was empty. He's just fresh. Nothing evil."

"You know how it works," she said. "Wheeler will be blowing everything up to Godzilla-size just to stir the pot."

Virgil sighed. "Could mess up DiBono's plan for a long career."

"I'll do what I can to help him through it."

"How bad off is my partner?"

"Wise is convinced the charge is bogus."

"Good."

"Not completely. He's so convinced he assigned the case to Dana Lowery to keep her busy going nowhere. Problem is she's a motivated pit bull. She finds one string dangling on that shooting, she'll use it to hang McNeil out to dry."

"That Laurence girl drew down on us. Mac shot her. What could be more righteous than that?"

"Nothing, far as I can see," Nikki told him. "But Cruella's going to be using a microscope."

≡ 24 ≡

Officer Anthony DiBono, a third-generation member of the LAPD, had graduated from the police academy at the top of his class the previous year. This Nikki learned on a Friday morning spent with the young man in her office. She also discovered that, though he was not precisely the courtroom virgin Peter Daspit had predicted, when it came to dealing with a defense attorney of Gerald Wheeler's skill, he didn't know his ass from a hot rock.

"I appreciate your offering to help me, ma'am," he said to Nikki, "but I'm pretty sure I can hold my own."

Nikki was sensitive enough to both racism and sexism to realize that the brash young officer was exhibiting neither, merely hubris.

"Humor me, Officer," she said, getting to her feet. "Let me ask you a few questions that Bingham's defense attorneys are likely to bring up."

He nodded, but remained rigid and impatient in his chair, looking up at her.

"You've been a policeman long, Officer DiBono?"

"Like I just told you—"

"No," she interrupted. "We're playacting here. I'm Randolph Bingham's lawyer. You've just taken the stand and are facing me for the first time. Got it?"

"Yeah. I've, ah, been a member of the Los Angeles Police Department for one year and two months."

"Seen a lot of murders?"

He hesitated. "Some," he said.

"How many?"

"I don't know. Twenty-five maybe."

"Pretty bloody?"

"Usually," DiBono said, shifting in his chair.

"You're used to it by now?"

"Yeah, you could say that."

"No butterflies in the stomach?"

"No."

"Maybe you like it?"

"Huh?"

"Maybe you like looking at bodies?" Nikki asked.

"Like it? No." He was frowning now.

"You a married man, Officer?"

"No."

"Girlfriend?"

"No."

"You're a handsome man. City's full of beautiful women. No girlfriend?"

"I go out with girls. I just don't have anybody special right now."

"You consider yourself a pretty good policeman?"

"Yes."

"How'd you do at the academy?"

"Top of my class."

"Didn't make many mistakes, huh?"

"No, ma'am," he said with a smile. "Mistakes are costly."

"What about on the job? Any major screwups?"

"No, ma'am. You can check my record."

"Minor screwups?"

"No, ma'am."

"No little mistakes?"

"No, ma'am."

"Good, good. Let me ask you a question about procedure. Say, you're the patrol officer who's first to arrive at a crime scene. What's the key rule to remember?"

The young policeman stared at her. "Don't touch anything," he said flatly.

"So, as a top graduate of the academy, Officer DiBono, I assume you didn't touch anything at the scene of the Dietz murder."

"I . . . there was a—"

"Did you touch anything?"

"Well, there was this door leading—"

"DID YOU TOUCH ANYTHING?"

"I, ah, opened a door. To make sure—"

"You opened a door. Okay. Did you touch anything else?"

"I . . . there was a wallet lying—"

"Let me see if I understand this, Officer DiBono. The primary rule is 'Don't touch anything.' You touched a door and a wallet. So you'd have to call those mistakes, wouldn't you?"

"Not mistakes, exactly." DiBono ducked his head. He was blinking nervously.

"What would you call 'em?" she asked.

"A, uh, I was wearing latex gloves."

"I see. Then the rule at the academy is 'Don't touch anything—unless you're wearing latex gloves'?"

"No. Not exactly."

"You're under oath, Officer. Did you make mistakes?"

"I guess so," he mumbled.

"I'm sorry. I didn't hear that and I'm sure the court stenographer didn't hear it. Could you say that louder, please?"

"They were mistakes," he said clearly.

"So you lied earlier when you said you didn't make any mistakes."

"Lie? No, I don't lie."

"As I recall, I asked if you made any little mistakes and you said, 'No. No mistakes.' Now you say you made mistakes that have a definite bearing on this particular case. So which is it? Were you lying earlier or are you lying now?"

He glared at her, his face turning crimson. "I don't lie," he said through clenched teeth.

"Okay. We'll call it a fib, if you like. You do admit you disobeyed the key rule when you arrived at the scene of the Dietz murder: You messed with the evidence."

"I touched a door and I opened a wallet that was lying on a desk. I was wearing gloves and—"

"Would you call this a serious contamination of the evidence or a minor contamination of the evidence?"

"I wouldn't call it . . . any kind of contamination of the evidence."

"No. You probably wouldn't. But, as we've just discovered, you're a liar."

The young cop shot to his feet. "Fuck you!" he shouted. "And fuck your games. I don't have to sit here and take this shit. Put me on the stand. I can do it."

Nikki gave him a bored look. "And after they finish their cross, who's gonna mop up all the blood?"

He glared at her, momentarily speechless.

"Sit down, Officer," she said. "We got work to do."

≡ 25 ≡

Ricky arrived at the new office building on Sunset a little after noon. It was early for him, but Pickett had set up a meeting with some computer assholes who were going to demonstrate adult games they thought might work for Wonderbar. The problem Ricky had was that he really didn't give a shit about Wonderbar, while it seemed to be the only thing ringing Pickett's chimes. Their main source of income, the whores, had been left in the hands of Jay Jay and Stephen, who were occupying their old office in the Victoria.

He and Pickett were leasing space in a building that would have been too fucking expensive for lawyers. They had framed photographs on the wall that were supposed to be art but looked like bad camerawork to him. They had this hardass bitch secretary-receptionist named Annette, with a French accent she probably picked up hooking in New Orleans. All of it just added to his general depression.

"Good afternoon," Annette said as he dragged his ass through the reception area. "Mistair Pick-ett is expecting you in the conference room."

"You Mr. Geruso?"

Ricky turned to see a man getting to his feet from the visitor's couch. He was five-ten or -eleven, about Ricky's height, but his rumpled black suit hung on an undernourished frame. His white shirt had a frayed, dirt gray collar. His haggard face was tan but it was a worker's tan, not the Palm Springs variety. His hair was long and dank, chopped rather than cut. He was clutching a brown paper bag.

"This 'gentleman,'" Annette's voice dripped with distaste, "has been waiting to see you. He has no appointment."

"What's your story, Bo?" Ricky asked.

"I, uh, believe you was intimate with my little girl."

This was gonna be a day, sure enough, Ricky thought. He turned to Annette. "That monkey in the hat and shoulder boards by the door downstairs. See if you can get him or one of his pals to come up and throw this jagoff—"

"I'm Kermit Dahlberg," the visitor said. "Patience's daddy."

Rick gave him a skeptical look. "Sure. Dahlberg."

"Oh, the name." The haggard man ducked his head shyly. "My baby dropped the 'berg.' Did it legally. Didn't want to be taken for no Jew, I guess. Though that don't seem to be a drawback to folks in this here town of yours."

"Where you from, Mr. Dahl*berg*?"

"Bakersfield," the haggard man said.

It was the right answer, but Patience's hometown had been in the newspaper account of her murder. Ricky took his time exploring the lines and creases of the man's face, trying to see one hint of beautiful little Patience in the wreckage. It was the eyes, he decided. If you ignored the bloodshot pink, the irises had that same weird, light brown–almost gold color.

Annette's hand was on the phone. Ricky told her it was okay. "Come on into my office, Mr. Dahlberg."

"There is the meeting in the conference room," Annette protested.

"Tell 'em to start without me," Ricky said.

In his office he suggested that Kermit Dahlberg take a chair, indicating a tangle of tubing and leather resting beside his glass-top desk.

The old man sat down tentatively, as if he expected the chair to tip over backward. Ricky wasn't sure it wouldn't. Dahlberg was his first visitor. "What's on your mind?"

"It's about poor Patience."

"Uh-huh," Ricky said, waiting for the pitch.

"I know how it was with you two."

"How was it?"

"Sh-she loved you, Mr. Geruso."

"You know that, huh?" Ricky said. "She talk to you a lot?"

The haggard man shook his head. "No, sir. I never heard from her again, once she ran away from the house." He dropped his eyes.

"I guess that must've been because you treated her so nice," Ricky said.

"When her mama died, I did my best—"

"You beat her up and you took her to bed," Ricky said. "Don't know if I'd call that a personal best."

"I used to do me some hard drinkin'. Booze forced me into some shameful acts."

Ricky felt no anger toward the old man. Way back when he had first met Patience and she had told him why she'd left home, he'd heard that same story so many times it had barely raised a blip on his empathy meter. Now it was a little late, he supposed, to get bent out of shape over this bag of bones. Unless Daddy had seen Patience again. A month ago.

"You drive to L.A. pretty often, Mr. Dahlberg?" he asked.

"Got no call to travel anywhere. Been years since I seen this town. Then they phoned me about Patience and I drove down to pick up her things and see to her burial. I got Andy Oldbrook to fix up a coffin and arrange the funeral and the burial, same as his dad did for my dear wife. Now my whole family's resting in Oaklawn along with Patience's grandpa and grandma."

Ricky believed that anybody was capable of anything. But it was a long shot to think that this old wreck might have decided one night to drive to L.A. and kill his daughter. "Why'd you want to see me, Mr. Dahlberg?"

"I, uh, found this in her things." He held the brown bag out to Ricky.

It contained a small tape recorder and a collection of bright red cassettes in plastic cases, each labeled with dates. Ricky recognized Patience's precise handwriting. "You listened to this, I guess?" he said.

"Well, some. It's like my leetle girl's diary of her life here in Los Angeles. Things she did. People she met."

"In this city, if a working girl gets iced, they don't treat it like they do dead debutantes," Ricky said. "But I still don't see the cops letting you walk off with this tape shit if it had anything worthwhile on it."

"Uh, you see, Mr. Geruso, the cops don't know about these tapes. Yet."

"How'd you get 'em?"

Dahlberg's smile did nothing to improve his looks. "The law didn't do so good going over her leetle apartment. It was just the one room, and she'd barely moved in, so I guess they figgered they didn't have to put theyselves out much. But she was my leetle girl and I knowed how she liked her hidey-holes. These was in a bucket in the broom closet, covered up with dust rags."

"The cops didn't find 'em?"

"They were too busy emptying her drawers onto the floor, messin' up her foldin' bed, emptying out the fridge. Stealin' her cash."

"So here you are," Ricky said, "with your bag full of tapes."

"Memories," the haggard man said. "I'm not a rich man, Mr. Geruso." He was apparently unmindful of the hardening of Ricky's mouth, the flare of his nostrils. "Patience's burial, even more or less unattended as it was, cost me some money I really couldn't afford. On them tapes, she mentions you quite a lot and I was thinking maybe you might want to, uh, buy 'em off me. As a sort of keepsake, maybe?"

Ricky picked up the small machine, hefted it, placed it back on the desk. "A beat-up recorder, earphones," he said, "ten used, off-brand red cassettes. How much you think that might be worth, Mr. Dahlberg?"

"There's sentimental value," the haggard man said. "Maybe . . . a thousand dollars?"

He mentioned the amount so tentatively that Ricky almost laughed. Pathetic old bastard. He got out his roll and peeled off two one-hundred-dollar bills.

Dahlberg watched him place the bills on the desktop. "Oh, I

couldn't put so small a price on my daughter's memories," he said. "Especially her accounts of the . . . *work* she did for you and your partner, Mr. Pickett."

Ricky smiled. He reached out and took back one of the hundreds. Then he consulted his fake Rolex. "In one minute, I claim the other Franklin. And I break your arm. Forty-eight seconds. Forty-seven."

Dahlberg grabbed the bill angrily, stood, and headed for the door. "Y-you took advantage of my little girl. Now you're taking advantage of me."

Ricky didn't bother to reply. He was too busy watching Kermit Dahlberg closely. The low-rent jagoff didn't have a clue about how to squeeze a guy. If he was holding out a red cassette or two, Ricky doubted he'd be able to leave the room without using that threat for his exit line.

Dahlberg didn't say anything more, just shoved the bill in his pocket and left. *Good,* Ricky thought. Saved him the effort of having the old bastard slapped around, then sending Jay Jay and Stephen out to Bakersfield on a tape hunt.

He spread the red cassettes out on the desk. All were properly rewound, except one. Ricky figured that cassette, with less than half the tape transferred to the take-up reel, had been the only one the old man had bothered to listen to.

He snapped it into the machine and started to rewind.

He raised an eyebrow at the earphones and plucked a Kleenex from a box on the shelf behind him. Satisfied that both plastic earpieces were free of Kermit Dahlberg's taint, he put on the headset.

When the tape was fully rewound, he pressed "play."

It seemed an eternity before Patience's little girl voice sounded in his ear.

Well, here it is nighttime, Sony, old pal. Not much of a day. Three johns since lunch. I won't bore you with the gruesome details. One guy was truly coyote-ugly, you know, so ugly that if you got drunk and woke up with him sleeping on your arm, you'd rather bite your arm off than wake him up. I got through the experience by thinking of my darling Ricky. That's what gets me through all of it. I wonder where my darling is tonight.

Her "darling" was sitting in his office, listening to the slightly nasal voice of a dead girl and surprising himself by crying like a baby.

≡ 26 ≡

By three, Nikki and Officer DiBono were both ready to quit for the day. "Thanks for shaping me up," the young officer said, backing toward the door. "I'll do the job for you in court on Monday."

"You're bright, Officer, and you learn fast," Nikki said, "but you're still not quite ready. We can finish up tomorrow."

"Saturday? It's my day off. I was supposed—okay, tomorrow it is."

"Meet me here at ten o'clock. Shouldn't take us more than another hour or two."

He was clearly not thrilled at the prospect, but he nodded and made his exit. He'd barely left the room when Nikki's phone rang. It was the office receptionist, whose life seemed to be built around her perfect oxblood fingernails. "There's a handsome young man out here would like to see you," she said. "Says it's personal, not business."

Nikki knew it wasn't Virgil. They had spoken by phone at noon and he hadn't said anything about being released from the hospital. But if not him? Curiosity moved her quickly to the reception area.

Adam Noyes was standing there, shifting from one Nike-clad foot to the other anxiously. His face broke into a wide grin at the sight of her. "Hi, Nikki!" he shouted.

"Adam!" she said, returning his smile. She gave the room a quick search, saw neither Fallon nor Sidney. "This is a surprise."

"It's okay, isn't it? You said I could visit."

"Come on back to my office," she said.

In the corridor, they met Jeb with an armload of files. He looked at the boy questioningly. Nikki introduced them. "This your boyfriend?" Adam asked flatly.

Jeb laughed. "No, I'm her clerk," he said. "She just orders me around like her boyfriend."

"What's that mean?" the boy asked Nikki.

"That means he's going to go get you a Coke and me a coffee," Nikki said, herding Adam into her small office and closing the door.

He sat straight on the visitor's chair, his wide eyes taking in the room's general disorder—the scattered books and file folders, the wilting ficus in one corner, Nikki's high-back pink leather chair with the worn spot on the left armrest. Then he turned and saw the black-and-white photo that covered the back of her door. It was a life-size picture of an armed robber in a ski mask pointing his gun directly at the viewer. "Wow. Did you take that yourself?"

"No. It's something they use on the range for target practice. It keeps me on my toes."

She was smiling, but to the boy, everything was very serious. His eyes eagerly took in the rest of her office. "This room is sweet."

It wasn't exactly the word she would use, but she let it go. "Where's Sidney? Downstairs?"

Adam hesitated a beat before answering, "Home, I guess."

"Home? Who came downtown with you?"

"I took a cab," he said airily. "Sidney was busy."

"And he and Donia let you come here by yourself?"

"No big deal. The cab driver didn't have any problem getting here. He's waiting downstairs."

"Expensive," Nikki said.

"Just money," the boy said.

Nikki wondered what Sidney had been so busy doing that he let the boy drive to downtown L.A. in a cab. Should she call and find out? Was it any of her business?

"You have criminals up here?" Adam asked.

"Nope. We do most of our business a few flights down in the courtrooms or across the street at Parker Center. That's where the bad guys are held for questioning."

"My dad was arrested once."

"Oh?"

"For beating people up. They arrested him, but he wasn't in jail very long. Maybe a day. And later, they said that he wasn't guilty, which was pretty weird because I know for a fact he beat my mom." He lowered his eyes. "Me, too."

"How'd that make you feel?"

"You sound like the psychiatrist."

That would be a respected child therapist named Dr. Audrey Moore. Jesse Fallon had informed Nikki that Adam was seeing her three times a week. He didn't think that anyone on the Bingham defense knew that the boy was in therapy, but both he and Nikki understood that the sooner he appeared in court the better.

"You're seeing a psychiatrist?" Nikki asked.

"Uh-huh. She always asks me how I feel about things. How did I feel about everybody saying my dad didn't really hurt people? How I felt was angry. Then, Mom said it was okay for him to come back to live with us. I still can't figure that out."

"Sometimes people let their hearts rule their heads."

"What's that mean?"

"The facts tell you to stay away from somebody, but you want to be with them. So you convince yourself the facts are wrong."

"If a man did bad things to you, would you stick by him?" the boy asked.

She didn't want to disrespect his mother, but she didn't want to lie to him either. "Probably not," she said.

"I didn't think so."

Jeb arrived with their drinks. Before he could duck out, Nikki asked him to give Adam a tour of the offices.

The boy placed the can of Coke, unsampled, on the edge of Nikki's desk. "I was hoping *you* would take me around," he said to her. Jeb grinned and nodded his head in agreement.

"I'm in the middle of a trial," Nikki said. "Besides, Jeb's a better guide. He knows where all the bodies are buried around here."

"Bodies," the boy said, suddenly fascinated.

"Figure of speech," Jeb said. "But we'll visit a few places you might find of interest." He ushered the boy from the room, looking back at Nikki with a dark scowl.

They returned in less than an hour, Adam giving her a play-by-play of everything that had transpired. "Jeb took me to the conference room where you all meet to decide who you're going to put in jail. This bald-headed dude in a suit showed me his weapon. A Colt Mark five."

"Johnston," Jeb said, identifying the gunman as one of the D.A.'s investigators.

"And this other deputy. He keeps a box on his desk with the autopsy photos of every one of his 187 trial victims."

"You let LeCroix show Adam his gallery?" Nikki asked Jeb, frowning.

"I had to visit the men's room," Jeb said. "He found LeCroix on his own."

"Pictures of dead people look so weird," Adam said. "Real and not real. Anyway, then we went to see the courts. Some guy was being tried for selling crack. We watched that for a while, but it was just a bunch of talk. Then we met with one of the judges . . ."

"Matthews," Jeb said.

"Right. Judge Matthews. He gave me this." He showed Nikki a miniature wooden gavel, approximately three inches long. Written on it were the words, "Compliments of Judge Julius Matthews."

"He said any time I had a tough decision to make, I should stare at this for a while, then hammer it three times and then it'll come to me exactly what to decide."

"The judge should know," Nikki said. "He's been sitting on the bench for thirty-five years."

She was enjoying his enthusiasm so much she hated to end it. "Jeb," she said. "Give us a few minutes. Then I'd like you to take Adam downstairs to his cab."

"Catch you in five," Jeb said to Adam as he departed.

Nikki looked at the smiling boy sitting across from her, clutching the miniature gavel. "I phoned your house," she said.

His face didn't change.

"Donia thought you were in your lab working. You didn't tell either her or Sidney you were coming down here."

"They were both busy. So I just called a cab and came down."

"It's pretty rough out on the streets," she said. "You're a little young to be traveling around on your own."

"I'm ten," he said indignantly.

She tried to remember what it was like being ten. She and her friends had had a certain amount of freedom. No cabs, of course. They'd walked to school alone, taken buses to the movies or the mall. Her grandmother had sat her down and warned her about strangers and told her to stay mindful of her surroundings and that was that.

It had been a considerably less paranoid time, two decades ago. There were drugs and gangs and violence then. But not the drivebys or the predators of today.

She didn't feel it was her job to educate the boy in the wicked ways of the world. She definitely didn't want to be the one to tarnish his shining innocence or smother his self-confidence. But still . . .

"You shouldn't leave your house without checking in with Sidney or Donia," she said. "She got a little bent out of shape when I told her you were down here."

"She wouldn't have found out, if you hadn't told her. I would've just driven back home and shown up for dinner."

"Suppose she'd gone looking for you?"

"She wouldn't have. They don't disturb me when I'm in the lab workroom." In response to Nikki's frown, he added, "I sort of get into the zone when I work. If somebody comes in or buzzes me, it messes everything up. So they leave me alone, unless there's something planned in advance. Today, I didn't have to see the shrink or anything else, so I thought it would be a good time to come by here. I'm sorry if that was wrong and got you all upset."

"I'm not upset," Nikki said. "I'm just concerned about you." She was not unmindful of the way he'd shifted the conversation, putting her on the defensive. A very clever little boy. She wondered if she should tell Jesse Fallon about Adam's solo venture. No. She didn't want to cause the Davises a load of grief. A word in their ear should be enough.

There was a knock at the door. Jeb.

"Ready?" he asked.

Adam stood reluctantly. "See you soon?" he asked Nikki.

"I might stop by your house tomorrow evening," she said. "If you're not too busy in your workroom, I'll say hello."

The boy grinned at her, excited now. "Come by at dinner," he said. "There's always more than we can eat."

"Depends on what time I get away from here."

"You work on Saturday?"

"Don't you?"

He grinned again. She suddenly realized that she actually wanted to spend more time with him. He brought out maternal feelings she didn't know she possessed. She stood up and took a step toward the door. Her intention was to walk with them to the elevator. Adam suddenly hugged her awkwardly, pressing the side of his face against her chest. "Best friend," he whispered.

She smiled, but said nothing as he pulled away. Evidently, the smile was enough.

When Jeb returned from taking Adam downstairs, he asked, "You sure he's just ten?"

"So they tell me."

"Sorta has an eye for older women, huh?"

Nikki waved a dismissive hand. "That little boy's got a few years to go before puberty kicks in."

"I dunno," Jeb said, "even Wilt the Stilt had to start somewhere."

≡ 27 ≡

Virgil was awakened from a dreamless sleep by a voice calling his name.

There were four people standing by his bed. The nearest was a floor nurse he didn't think he knew. Reddish-orange hair. Glasses. "I'm sorry, Detective Sykes," she said, "these people say it's imperative they speak with you."

"I'm Deputy District Attorney Dana Lowery," the other woman said. "We've met at the office."

She did look familiar. Pale. Skinny. Jet-black hair with a shock of white in the middle. He just wasn't focusing fully. The tall well-dressed black man standing beside her looked familiar, too. He gave Virgil a sharp nod. The name popped into his head. Rafe Collins. Internal Affairs. They'd always gotten along okay, but he'd heard from others that Rafe played the "brother" game. Beneath an ethnocentric exterior he was 100 percent IAG shark. The shorter, whiter guy with the crew cut and oily skin was no doubt his partner.

"What . . . time?" Virgil asked, trying to use an elbow to lift himself up.

"Little after four," Lowery said. She turned to the nurse. "We can take it from here."

The nurse didn't seem totally convinced of that, but she left the room.

"Check the gomer," Lowery ordered the tall black man. He gave her a look, as if to say maybe she should do her own checking. She ignored it and, after a beat, he took a few backward steps, studied the patient with the broken legs on the other side of the divider and then rejoined the party.

"Makin' zees. This place is a real Rip Van Winkleville."

Virgil's head cleared enough for him to realize the reason for their visit even before Rafe said, "Got us a few questions about the shooting, brother."

"Okay."

"Tell us what happened, best you recall."

"Help me with the pillow?" With difficulty, Virgil was shimmying up to a sitting position. Rafe moved the pillow between him and the headboard of the bed. Virgil shifted around until he was comfortable before beginning to describe the events leading up to his and McNeil's violent visit to the home of Geena Laurence in Santa Monica.

He took his time, mainly because he knew the importance of making the statement as unambiguous as possible. Also, it amused him to test the patience of the self-important deputy D.A. While she tapped her toe, he described in detail the facts she undoubtedly already knew surrounding the murder of Dr. Charles Furst.

His throat felt dry, so he asked for water.

"Tony?" Rafe Collins said, and the unintroduced IAG man left to get the water.

The three stared at one another in silence until Collins's partner returned.

Virgil took the glass from him and said, "Thanks, Detective—?"

"Garibaldi," the man croaked.

"No shit? Well, thanks anyway." Virgil drank the tepid water, smacking his lips as if it were champagne. Then when he felt he'd pushed the deputy D.A. to the point of combustion, he continued his tale. "On the strength of the murder weapon having been in Ms. Laurence's home after the crime had been committed, Detective McNeil and I obtained a warrant for her arrest and a search of the property."

"And you used the warrant?" Lowery asked.

"We didn't have to. We identified ourselves and were invited inside by Jill Laurence. We talked briefly with Geena Laurence and she took us upstairs to look for the wooden box that Olfax had described as the gun case."

"You didn't think it strange, that this woman you believed to be a murderer would be so cooperative?"

"I thought she'd already unloaded the box and was just pulling our chain."

"And you weren't concerned that the girl, Jilly, had disappeared?"

"She wasn't our suspect. There was no reason for us to think she might be in her dead father's room ready to open up on us."

"Tell us about the shooting, brother."

"Geena Laurence led us upstairs to where the gun case was supposed to be. Before we got there, she pushed the issue of the gun. Why was it so important? I had a whole bunch of reasons for thinking she whacked the doctor and knew why it was important so I threw it out in the open: The gun killed Furst. This hit her hard. I was facing the stairs, talking to her, when she looked over my shoulder and freaked. I was turning to see what had rattled her when Detective McNeil pushed me, causing most of the shots fired by Jill Laurence to miss.

"You can check with my doctors, but I believe that one of her bullets passed through my upper torso right here." He used his free hand to indicate the approximate spot of entry below his shoulder. "The other ran along the side of my head, here. It is the opinion of everybody I've talked to that Detective McNeil saved my life."

"You see a gun in Jill Laurence's hand?" Rafe Collins asked.

"Yeah," Virgil said, without having to think.

"Did you draw your gun?" Dana Lowery asked.

"I think so. Not sure if it cleared the holster, me being shot and falling and all."

"Where was Geena Laurence when all this was going down, brother?"

"In the hall. I'd been holding her arm."

"The girl was behind you?"

"Yeah. The morning paper said she went to her father's room and found a gun. While Detective McNeil and I were talking with her mother in the upstairs hall, baby daughter came out of the room grabbing a grip."

"And McNeil was where?"

"To my right, as I turned."

"So, you figure he did what, brother? Looked back, piped the girl with a gun, shoved you with his left hand and drew and fired with his right?"

"That seems logical, but I really don't know."

Rafe opened his mouth to say something more, but Dana Lowery cut him off. "Let's talk about sounds, Detective," she said. "How many gunshots did you hear?"

"Four."

"You answered that quickly."

"Some things you don't forget."

"Did all of the gunshots come from the same place?"

It was an odd question. He considered it.

"What do you think, brother? Could be important."

Virgil frowned. "Why?"

Rafe turned to look at Lowery. She shook her head no. Rafe remained silent.

Virgil closed his eyes.

"Detective Sykes," Lowery said, "we're not finished here. Did all four gunshots come from the direction of Jilly Laurence?"

Virgil opened his eyes and stared at her. She was leaning forward intently. He suddenly understood the significance of the question. He honestly didn't know the answer, but he replied, "One of the shots sounded a little nearer to me than the others."

"But you're not certain?" Lowery asked, more annoyance in her voice than before.

"Yeah. The more I think about it, the more certain I am. The third shot."

Lowery glared at him, then turned on her heel and strode from the room.

Rafe rolled his eyes and said, "Sorry to mess up your nap, brother. Get better now."

He left, his nearly silent partner at his heels.

"Cruella and the shoeflies," Nikki said later that evening. "Some party."

She was in a good mood, mainly because his spirits were higher than they'd been in the morning. He looked more like himself, too. The large turban-like head bandage had been replaced by a king-size white Band-Aid. His eyes were brighter.

"Your co-worker wanted me to say I heard the girl stop shooting, once Mac started," he told her. "She wanted it so bad she could taste it, but I didn't give her that satisfaction."

"According to her mother," Nikki said, "Jill Laurence dropped her gun after she shot you. That's when your partner fired on her and killed her, when she was no longer a threat. If Cruella had gotten you to back that up, she'd have had her case. But if the Laurence girl was still shooting after McNeil fired one of his shots, well, then . . ."

Virgil's smile was as easy to read as the Mona Lisa's. She wondered how much he actually knew about the sequence of gunshots, but she wasn't about to solicit information that might jam her up later, she being an officer of the court. Instead, she asked what the doctors were saying about cutting him free.

"Maybe Sunday. I won't be back on the job for a while. But I'll be able to get out of the bed. Sit on a chair. Take a little walk."

"Great news," she said.

"Yeah, I've had my fill of hos-pi-tal. The word comes down, I'm out of here doing a buck fifty."

"You plan on recouping at the apartment?"

"I was hoping your place, maybe. It's all on ground level. No steps to climb. I could do a little bonding with Bird, maybe teach him to play poker."

She laughed. "I could put on a nurse outfit at night, bring you food and meds."

"And therapy," he said, grinning. "Lots of physical therapy."

"The trial will probably cut in on our therapy time," she warned.

He sighed. "Yeah. I'd still feel more comfortable at your place."

It was definitely the right thing to say. She moved her face closer to his to tell him so.

≡ 28 ≡

H*ello, L.A.,"* the deep, intimate voice was a dripping mixture of clotted honey and cynicism. *"It's eight a-em in our wide and wonderful smog heaven. The sun is shining on a be-yoo-ti-ful Saturday—the first day of Rosh Hashanah for all you chosen people. It's a crisp eighty-nine degrees, guaranteed to rise above the ninety-five mark by midday. This is Jack Sylvestre, your morning talk confessor, reminding you to drive carefully, the guy in the next lane may be packing heat."*

"Oh, no," the girl, whatever the fuck her name was, groaned from the circular bed. "Eight o'clock? What's goin' on?"

"Radio," Ricky said. He was sitting on the edge of the bed, slipping into his tassled alligators. He'd already passed on a morning shave (believing a few days' growth of beard made his face look thinner), showered, put on his slacks and Hawaiian shirt, a dukey rope around his neck.

"Looks like another gangsta bit the dust in a driveby in Inglewood last night," the voice announced from the radio. *"That makes four in the last four days. Awlright! We get two for one. One gangbanger dead; one gangbanger in jail for killing the first gangbanger. You homeboys still kickin' out there, it's payback time, right? While we wait, here's Jerry Vale to sing 'On the Street Where You Live.' Afterward, I want to hear your thoughts on the gang thang."*

"The guy gives me the creeps," Whatshername said. "Right-wing asshole hates the world."

Ricky looked at her, lying there on the rumpled and roiled beige satin sheets. Sweet, dimpled baby face. Eager little body, round, but hard and smooth as hand-polished wood. Clean, too. "I like Sylvestre," he said. "I listen to him every day."

It was the truth. At least for the past few days, ever since he learned that the talk jock had discovered Patience's body and was pushing the cops and the D.A. to find her killer. Before that, he'd thought the guy was an asshole, too.

The dimpled face showed a little confusion. "You like him? He's the big anticrime guy. Anti-drugs, anti-hookers, anti-everything."

"So?"

"Nothing," she said, putting the cat's grin back on her sweet face, in preparation for a shift in discussion topic. "That was some boo-yaa last night. The best."

It had been incredibly fine coke, all right. That's what it took to get Ricky out of the dumps. That and a hell of a lot of encouragement from his sex partner. "You were better than the boo, babe," he said, falling back on one of his patented responses.

She lifted a firm, tanned leg out to him, poking her toes under his shirt, tickling the flesh above his belt. "What are you doin' all dressed? Maggie's getting very excited."

He shifted away from the touch of her foot and stood. "Not now," he said. "Maybe tonight. Now I want you the fuck out of here."

The expression on her face changed to one of surprise. Then anger. He was too busy picking up her clothes from the floor to notice, tossing them on the bed without looking where he was throwing. Jerry Vale had finished his song and Sylvestre was back on the air, chatting with a caller about street gangs.

By the time Ricky turned to face the girl she'd managed to hide her fury behind a mask of indifference. "Come on," he said. "Chop-chop. Get moving." He crossed the room and yanked the drapes back, letting the beachfront morning brighten the room. He stared out at a placid ocean marked by little whitecap trails. It reminded him of a mirror decorated with lines of coke.

As if picking up his thought, the girl on the bed asked, "Did we, ah, use up all the stuff last night?"

"A little left," he said, turning away from the view. "You can have it when your ass is headed out the door."

She opened her mouth but decided not to say what was on her mind. Instead, she slipped into her slinks.

"Here's a pretty unusual story," Sylvestre was saying. *"One of the LAPD's finest apparently didn't shoot an unarmed teenager after all. According to this morn-ing's* L.A. Times, *the supposedly self-policing Police Department has issued a state-ment totally exonerating Detective Daniel Mc—"*

"I don't know how you can listen to this guy," the girl whose name was apparently Maggie said. "He's just nasty."

Instead of replying, Ricky turned up the volume on the radio.

"Okay, if you feel that way about it," she mumbled, adjusting the clasp to her platform shoes.

One ear to the radio, Ricky watched her as she circled the bed and bent to pick up her purse. Jay Jay had been right. She was special. It took special to get him going.

He grabbed two vials of coke from the top of the dresser and held them out to her.

She made no move to take them. "Can I say something?" she shouted above the sound of Sylvestre's voice.

Ricky looked at her for a beat, and turned down the volume on the radio. "Sure," he said, "but make it swift." He'd been hurrying to meet with more of Pickett's bullshit suppliers at the office. Sylvestre's com-ment about the cops put the kibosh on that plan. It reminded him that he still hadn't looked up his old pal, Detective Eugene Liverdais, the vice louse who'd ID'd Patience's body. He had matters to discuss with Unclean Eugene.

"I don't want your dope," the girl said. "It's da bomb. But if there's a chance we might be getting together tonight, I want to be clear."

"Yeah?" he said, grinning in spite of himself.

"Usually fucking is just the in-and-out, you know." Her hand went under her tank top and began fondling her breast. She was giving him the full treatment. "Last night was more than that. You opened me up, Ricky. Made me feel like a female again."

"Yeah?"

"I, ah, well, you know, Carrie and I share at the Vic. And, well, one night we were talking about all the crap johns put us through and how dick really doesn't do it for us anymore and, well, we started . . . you know."

"You did each other?"

"Well, yeah. We've made it a few times since then. I was beginning to wonder maybe I was lez or something. But last night was sooo good . . . I just want to feel it again. Only clear. I want to feel every bit of it."

Ricky's mouth was dry. He'd already talked himself out of going to the office. Liverdais could wait, too. His fingers began lowering his zipper. "It's all here, babe," he told her.

She smiled and gave a little wiggle of pleasure as she moved toward him.

"Sure you don't want me to powder the doughnut?" he asked, unscrewing the cap on a cocaine vial.

"Well, since you asked . . ."

≡ 29 ≡

Nikki arrived at the Criminal Courts Building at ten to ten on Saturday morning. Daspit was in his office. He'd be presenting the forensic witnesses early in the week and she expected him to be at work, studying the autopsy results and criminologist reports. The surprise was that Dana Lowery was also on the floor. She passed Nikki in the hall without a word and entered her office, making a point of slamming the door behind her. Since there had been an official LAPD announcement exonerating Dan McNeil, Nikki wondered what Cruella was up to. Had Wise given her another dog walk? Was she working on her campaign?

In either case, it wasn't any of her business, Nikki thought. Her business was the thick-bodied young policeman who arrived in bright purple warm-up gear even before she finished her first cup of coffee.

She was always intrigued by the way new little pieces of information surfaced each time she went over material with a witness. That morning, Officer DiBono mentioned seeing a light in an upstairs window of the home across from the victim's house.

Had he noticed the address? He opened his murder book and read off the number of Gustave Prosser's home.

"Why'd you make note of it?" she asked.

"In that neighborhood, that early in the morning, there aren't a lot of lights on. Is it important?"

Instead of answering his question directly, she said, "Try to remember to mention it when you're on the stand." If he forgot, she would remind him with a question. It would corroborate Prosser's statement that he'd been awake and had seen Randolph Bingham leaving the crime scene.

From there, they went through every step DiBono and his partner took, from the time they got out of the prowl car to the arrival of the medical examiner. She smoothed a few rough spots, then moved on to the crime-scene items he'd disturbed.

He frowned. "Couldn't we just let that go?"

"It's covered on the videotape. The defense'll hit it if we don't."

"How do I—"

"Why did you open the French doors?" she asked.

"I guess I thought somebody might be back behind the house."

"So just say that. While it is standard practice that the crime scene should be kept as intact as possible, you felt that a search of the rear of the house outweighed the possible contamination of opening the French doors. The same goes for your checking the victim's wallet for some identification. And"—looking at her notes—"the bug catcher."

"I was wearing the gloves."

"Fine. Just say that. I assume you were able to exit through the French doors without disturbing the corpse?"

"Definitely."

"And the items you touched, you put them back exactly as you found them?"

The policeman nodded.

"The defense will still scream and shout about contamination, but by then we'll have taken most of the steam out of their engine."

DiBono didn't seem to share her confidence.

"I won't lie to you," she told him. "This is hardball all the way. Just remember three things: first, do not blow, no matter what they say to you. Even if they insult your mama, you stay Mr. Freeze. The calmer and more confident you are, the worse they look. Staying cool is the best revenge.

"Two, always answer in a full sentence. Not 'yes' or 'no' but a full sentence that is a direct reply to the question. Don't add anything you haven't been asked.

"And three, nobody's got a stopwatch on you. Take your time before saying anything. Count to five even if all they've asked is your name."

He stared at her and a crooked smile appeared on his face. He nodded his head.

"Now go back to your Saturday," she said, standing.

Since she was going out for a sandwich, she walked with him to the elevator. They passed two men in suits on the way. The tall one was African-American, the small Caucasian. DiBono nodded to them.

"You know those guys?" she asked as the men disappeared down the hall.

"IAG," he said, lip curled in a typical rank-and-file sign of disgust. "I don't remember their names, but I've seen 'em around."

They'd seemed vaguely familiar to Nikki, too.

Carrying her sack with a grilled chicken sandwich and a medium-sized diet cola back to her office, she noticed that Dana's door was now open. The Internal Affairs officers were seated in front of her desk. The tall man was saying, "Officially, we've got to move on. Case closed."

"The guy's been a cop for nearly twenty years. Surely—" Dana's eyes locked with Nikki's. The two men turned to stare at her, too. Obviously annoyed, Dana hopped up and rushed to the door. By the time it slammed shut, Nikki was already entering her own workspace, mumbling "paranoid she-witch."

≡ 30 ≡

It wasn't until Sunday that Ricky emerged from his beach house. Maggie the hard-body had kept him busy most of the previous day. When the sun set on the Malibu colony, her roommate, Carrie, had joined them for an all-nighter that made Nakki's geisha broads look like nuns. For sheer sexual invention, he'd buy American every time.

He'd kicked the broads out at eight that morning. They were still wired from the crank and roaring, but there was just so much happiness a man could stand. He'd snoozed until 11:30 and then spent an hour getting presentable enough to greet the day.

He stepped out onto the patio and scanned the beachfront. Some of his neighbors were taking in the sun. The skinny pale-faced bitch with green hair who had just moved into the house next door was out there with two other broads. She was some kind of rock songwriter. He hated fucking rock music; it was like Martians beating on tin with hammers. Still, he was always up for some strange. Maybe he'd join the girls when he got back.

He circled the house and clicked the remote button on his key chain. The door to the attached garage rolled up, exposing his blood-red Lamborghini Diablo. A while before the Tokyo trip, he'd put in a bid on the late Dean Martin's classic Ghia L6.4 that wound up ten grand shy of the mark. To compensate, he'd bought the Diablo. Paid hard cash. The smartass salesman hadn't batted an eye at the green. Told him he'd be surprised if one day somebody paid with a check.

Well, fuck him.

Four-hundred-and-ninety-two horses whinnied loudly under that shiny red hood as the Diablo galloped free of the building and made its presence known on the Pacific Coast Highway. Ricky aimed it in the direction of the canyon road to the San Fernando Valley. He hated the fucking Valley. People were weird there. Some said it was because there was so much smog, it did something to the brain cells. Ricky had a different take: Only an asshole would want to live in the Valley; ergo, the Valley was full of assholes. Simple as that.

Detective Eugene Liverdais lived in Canoga Park on a corner lot of one of those blocks where they didn't like pedestrian traffic, so they purposely forgot to put in sidewalks. His house was ranch-style, freshly painted flamingo pink with a gray frame. Geez, Ricky thought as he parked in front, Gene and his old lady must share the same shitty taste.

There were a couple of vehicles—a new Camry and a slightly battered Previa van—parked in the drive. The scent of scorched meat was in the air. The Liverdaises were entertaining. Good.

Ricky walked around the side of the house until he came to the gate of a waist-high pink wooden fence. What the hell purpose did a waist-high fence serve, he wondered. It didn't stop the world from looking into Liverdais's backyard. It sure as hell didn't stop Ricky from reaching over the gate, lifting the latch, and strolling on in.

It took him about fifteen seconds to get a fix on the party. It was family day. Five adults in the general vicinity of an elaborate barbecue setup, some little kids splashing in a kidney-shaped pool. Liverdais was standing by the grill poking a long fork at a huge, charred hunk of something. He was a hard-muscled guy with freckles and a big red nose and thin shoe polish–brown hair that barely covered his sun-pink scalp. He was wearing an apron adorned with a giant police badge that read "To Protect and Serve Bar-B-Q."

The hatchet-faced bleached blonde with the gigantic nay-nays was probably Liverdais's wife. The old geezer in a pale blue leisure suit (geez, did they still make those fuckers?) holding on to a can of Bud and the fat old dame with the blue-tint hair were somebody's parents. The wife's, probably. He couldn't imagine Unclean Eugene having folks.

That left the remaining adult, a mousy brunette in her thirties who was gawking at him. "Doreen," she said, "here's . . . somebody."

The bleached blonde swung around. The smile of welcome forming above her extended chin froze when she caught sight of Ricky. "Hello," she said. "Can I help you?"

Before Ricky could form a reply, Liverdais dropped his fork onto the grill and, wiping his hands on his apron, rushed toward him. "A friend of mine, Dor," he said. "Hiya doin', partner." He put out a hand and Ricky shook it. The cop embraced him around the neck, pulling him close. "My man." He smelled of mesquite smoke and bourbon and Old Spice. He kept a pleasant smile on his face while he whispered heatedly, "You come to my home, you prick?" as if he couldn't quite believe it.

Ricky slipped from the cop's grasp and took a backward step, looking around the yard appraisingly. "Nice place you got here, Gene."

"Iddin' it?"

The others were staring at them, except for the kids, who were busy screaming Marco! and Polo! in the pool.

"Sorry to bother you folks on a Sunday," Ricky said. "But I really need Gene's advice about something."

Liverdais's wife looked at her husband with some concern.

"It's okay, Dor," he said reassuringly. "I won't be long. Flip the meat in about four minutes, huh?"

The cop led him out of the yard through the gate. The adults watched them leave. The kids couldn't have cared less.

Liverdais paused beside the red Diablo. "You park your pimpmobile in front of my house, you son of a bitch?"

Anger sent a quick shot of adrenaline through Ricky's veins. Then it passed. The cop was an ignorant shit-for-brains. It figured he wouldn't know the difference between a Lamborghini and a pimpmobile. He lived in a flamingo-colored house in the fucking Valley.

"Want to take a spin?" Ricky asked.

"What I want is for you to get the hell out of here."

"We gotta talk," Ricky said. "We can do it in the car, or we can do it right here, with your family and your neighbors' ears hanging out."

"I'm not getting in that piece of shit. Come on."

As he walked toward the garage, the cop fingered a key chain. The garage door slid upward in jerky movements, exposing an Olds and a Volvo wagon, both recent models.

Liverdais went to the Olds and got in behind the wheel. He must have pressed his key chain again, because the garage door began to close. The darkening, tight quarters bothered Ricky, but he wasn't sure why. He wasn't afraid of the cop. He took the passenger seat in the Olds.

Liverdais had a Police Special in his hand, pointed at him.

Ricky tried to stay calm. Logic told him the man wouldn't take him out right there, with his family in the backyard. "Nice gun," he said.

"You wearing a wire, Ricky?" Liverdais asked, so softly it was almost a whisper.

Moving very slowly and carefully, Ricky unbuttoned his shirt and pulled it open, exposing his hairless, slightly sagging chest. "You in Dutch downtown?" he asked. "Or are you going paranoid-nuts?"

The cop leaned over and ran his free hand up and down Ricky's pant legs, not overlooking the crotch. Apparently satisfied, he slumped back against the door, keeping the gun aimed at Ricky as he buttoned up again. "Now, why don't you tell me what's on your mind and how much it's gonna cost me?" Liverdais asked.

It was a hundred-to-one shot. Maybe the odds weren't even that good. The old drunk who worked the desk at the hotel had given him a description of the guy who had helped Patience move out. It didn't sound much like Liverdais. Too old. Wrong color hair. But Ricky had sampled a few of Patience's tapes—before his own patience gave out—and he'd noticed references to a "Big Badge john."

"You kill Patience?" he asked.

Liverdais blinked. Then a grin twisted his mouth unpleasantly. "*That's* why you're here?" He relaxed. Ricky wondered what the guy was so worried about. It sure as hell had nothing to do with Patience's murder.

The cop snapped the gun onto metal clasps attached to a wooden panel hanging down from the Olds's dash. He pushed the panel back up under the dash where it caught with a snap. "Got the idea from an old Bogart movie," he said.

Ricky knew the movie, too. "Did you kill her, Gene?"

"Fuck no. Why would I kill her?"

"Why do those pigeons fly to Capistrano? Nature, I guess."

"I don't kill people," Liverdais said.

"I got a different impression a minute ago, when you drew down on me."

"That was just . . . show."

"About Patience, I'm not criticizing," Ricky said. "You probably had your reasons. Maybe she tried to hit you up for money." He cocked his head. "Hell, maybe you thought *she* was wearing a wire."

"This is bullshit. I never killed anybody. I sure as hell didn't kill Patience. I—liked her. You fuckin' well know that."

"I know you threatened me when I told you she wasn't going to be spreading for you anymore."

"That was just, that was the heat of the moment. I was pissed off." He frowned. "And I'm getting pissed off right now. Who the fuck do you think you are, anyway? Saying I killed her."

"How'd you happen to ID her body, Gene?"

"I'm a vice cop. Dead Jane Doe hooker comes in, who they gonna call?"

"How'd they know she was a hooker?"

"Patience was a sweet kid," Liverdais said with some sincerity. "She looked young and fresh, all things considered. Like a college girl. Only she didn't exactly dress like one. You remember I took her to the Springs?"

Ricky remembered. Liverdais had taken Patience to Palm Springs for a couple days. On the cuff, of course.

"Crotch shorts and see-through shirts are fine for the corner of Melrose, but the Springs . . . I had to borrow some outfits with a little more class from the broad my buddy was with. Luckily she was about Patience's size."

"When was the last time you saw her?" Ricky asked.

"When she was still breathing, you mean?"

"Yeah, that's what I mean."

"Just before you took her to San Fran. You remember: You canceled me out so she could be with you."

"She ever call you her Big Badge john?" he asked.

"Her what?"

"You know how she had her pet names for everybody. Like I was Ricky G. Were you her Big Badge john?"

The cop grinned. "I was the Liver-man."

Ricky remembered that Patience actually called him Chicken Liver. Well, shit, it had been a long shot.

"I don't get you, Ricky. What're you up to?"

"I'm gonna nail the bastard who killed her."

Liverdais nodded as if he understood. He probably figured it had something to do with pimp macho, Ricky thought. Taking care of business. Mess with my girls and you go down. Try explaining romance to a vice cop.

"You're a little late stirrin' up all this shit."

"I was out of the country when it happened," Ricky said.

"So I heard," Liverdais said. "I also heard you been back a few days. Why come to me now? Catch a wave?"

"I just been busy, is all," Ricky said. He didn't want to tell Liverdais the truth, that he had just come into possession of Patience's spoken diary with the Big Badge john reference.

"You ever give one of your cop pals a whack at Patience?" he asked.

"Hell, no. I cared for her." Liverdais leaned forward, grinning. "So what's been keepin' you so busy? Got a lotta new talent?"

"Pickett and I are opening this club," Ricky said.

"Lapdance?"

"No. Straight. A yup crowd-pleaser."

"Yeah? I got a few bucks doing nothing, long as the operation isn't a place I'd wind up raiding."

Ricky was surprised at the cop's interest. Maybe his partner was right about this being their ticket to the top. "I'd like to cut you in," he said. "Lemme fly it past Pickett."

Liverdais said, "Listen, I don't know what they're doing about Patience downtown. I could check around and let you know if they got any leads."

"I'd appreciate that."

"I better get back to the folks."

"Sure. Again, sorry I pulled you away."

They got out of the Olds. As Liverdais started the garage door motor, Ricky was struck by a possibility. "That trip to the Springs," he said, "your buddy who went with you, he a cop too?"

"Sure," Liverdais said. "Why?"

Ricky's mind went into overdrive. "It'd be good for our new place to have some lawmen in on the deal. Think *he* might want a piece of our club?"

"You sure there's nothing hinky?"

"Emmis. Pickett's got the full prospectus. It's clean as a nun's bib."

"Nuns don't wear bibs no more, Ricky."

"Churchwise, I been outta touch. Point is, I'm not about to jam you or your pal up with anything bent."

Liverdais studied him for a beat. "He could be interested," he said. "His old lady powdered on him and he's thinking about dumping his house. Might wind up with some cash to invest."

"Do I know him?" Ricky asked.

"I don't think so. He was in Vice before your time."

"Older guy, huh?"

"A couple years away from the handshake."

"What's his beat these days?"

"Big dog. Part of the Major Crimes unit. Name's Dan McNeil."

≡ 31 ≡

As the Good Book tells us, 'The fathers have eaten a sour grape,'" Doctor Reverend R. L. Johnson's powerful baritone sang throughout the Faithful Central Baptist Missionary, "'and the children's teeth are set on edge.'"

"Amen," Nikki heard herself saying along with the rest of the congregation. In the past, the quote from Jeremiah had always had a very personal relevance. But the year before, her father had taken the first awkward steps in repairing the damage of a lifetime of estrangement. Her teeth were no longer on edge, and from what she could see of William Hill, sitting with his second wife and daughter several rows ahead of her, he seemed much too self-satisfied to have dined on anything sour recently.

That morning the reverend's sermon seemed more applicable to Adam Noyes and his paternal legacy. The boy had inherited a brilliant mind and all the money he'd ever need. Emotionally, however, he was close to Chapter II. She'd had yet another example of that at dinner the night before.

It had been an awkward affair, at best.

Jesse Fallon had hired the Davises to care for Adam with the idea that the couple would add an element of family togetherness to his surroundings. That clearly was not working. To Adam they were hired hands, not parental figures. When all four of them ate together in the main dining room, it was Adam who sat at the head of the table, Adam who initiated or changed the topics of conversation, while the Davises acquiesced to his every request.

After dinner, while the boy watched an animated television show based on one of the Homeboy games and Sidney went into the garden for a smoke, Nikki helped Donia clear the table.

"How's it going?" she asked the middle-aged woman.

"He's a good boy," Donia said without pausing at her task.

"Tell me about his friends."

"There are only two, far as I can tell," Donia said. "A big boy, name of Maurice, and Juliet, she's closer to Adam's age."

"How old is Maurice?"

They carried stacks of dirty dishes into the kitchen. Donia put hers down and turned to Nikki. "That boy's in high school. Wears those baggy pants look like they're gonna fall off his skinny butt." She began scraping the dishes over the sink and placing them in the dishwasher.

"He and Adam get along okay?"

"Get along to get along."

Noting the woman's frown, Nikki asked. "You don't like Maurice and Juliet?"

Donia shrugged. "Seems to me they just come over here to use Adam's games."

"He doesn't play with them?"

"None of them play together. Maurice and Juliet use those little handheld machines. Might as well be home by themselves except, I guess, these aren't games you can buy on the street. They're things Adam's working on. He just sort of sits back and watches them. I asked him about it and he said he uses them to test the games."

"Does Adam play ball, do any kind of physical activity?"

"No sports. Sidney found that out right away. 'Throwing a ball around is a pointless waste of time,' the boy said. The two of them go jogging a couple times a week at the high-school track. Adam says that's not so bad, because he can listen to books on his Walkman."

"Is he hard on you and Sidney?"

Donia gave a little mirthless chuckle. "Family we used to work for, the husband and the nanny were using our quarters to carry on in. Wife liked to put white stuff up her nose and then start taking out her bad temper on me. Kids were spoiled little snots who ordered us around like we were some form of lower life. They had a pony they mistreated that Sidney had to care for and clean up after. Every so often, the husband would demand to see our measly bank statements to make sure we weren't stealing from him. And they made us wear uniforms.

"So, to answer your question, when Adam gets grumpy about what I serve for dinner or does a little ranting if we interrupt him while he's working, I suppose I'd have to say no, he's not real hard on us. If he's hard on anybody, it's himself."

"How's that?"

"The boy saves his real furies for when he can't do something he's set his heart on. He starts crying he gets so frustrated. The first time it happened, it liked to break my heart. I went to the boy and tried to hold and comfort him. He wouldn't let me. Just pulled away. Said I wasn't his mama."

Her voice broke and her eyes turned moist. Nikki got the idea that life with Adam was probably a little harder than Donia was willing to admit.

". . . and may the Good Lord Almighty go with you," Reverend Johnson exhorted his flock.

As Nikki followed the flow of the faithful to the main exit, her friend Loreen touched her elbow. "You up for some brunch, sister? All that talk about grapes got me hungry."

"I have to get back to my place and do some cleanup."

"So Virgil's stayin' at Chez Nikki?" Loreen chuckled. "Somethin' happenin' there?"

"He's just resting up."

"Well, girl, I hope I at least get a postcard from the honeymoon."

"Sister, if Virgil and I ever decide to go on a honeymoon," Nikki said, "you can believe I'm not gonna be wasting any time sending post-cards."

When the doorbell sounded at a little after five, Nikki had the house looking as good as a basically unfurnished place can. She took one last glance around the nearly empty living room, smiled proudly at its high-gloss wooden floor, adjusted her blouse, licked her lips to make them shiny, and opened the door.

The wounded city warrior stood there, arm in sling, white tape hiding his head wound. "Oh, baby," he nearly moaned, "you lookin' awful fine." He raised his good arm. "Come here. I'm not made of glass."

She allowed him to draw her to him.

They kissed.

Bird's ominous growl brought them both back to reality.

The big dog was in the doorway. Thanks to a trip to the groomer's, he looked clean and fluffy, a red ribbon bow attached to his collar un-dercutting his serious demeanor. He was glaring past them at Dan McNeil, who stood a few paces down the walkway, carrying Virgil's two pieces of luggage.

"I could just lob these into the house," McNeil said.

Nikki walked to him. "Put down a suitcase and shake my hand, Mac. That'll let Bird know you're a friend."

Amused, the cop lowered both bags to the walkway. He held out his arms. "Might as well make him think I'm a good friend."

"Let's not overdo it," she said, taking his hand and facing Bird with a smile.

An automobile engine growled and McNeil turned just as a red sports car zoomed past. He dropped her hand and ran to the street. Nikki was surprised he could move so fast.

He returned repeating the plate number just loud enough to hear, with a "bastard" thrown in for good measure. He saw Nikki and Vir-gil staring at him. "Guy's been following me since I left my place this afternoon."

"I guess I do need to rest up," Virgil said. "I sure didn't see any shiny red sports car tailing us."

"I spotted him on my way to the hospital," McNeil said, following them inside the house with the luggage, "and again on the drive here."

"Any idea who he is?" Nikki asked.

"Just another asshole asking for trouble."

Nikki tried to convince the detective to join them for dinner, but McNeil wouldn't hear of it. "The main theme of our conversation on the way here," he said, "was how much my partner wants to be alone with you. Or as alone as he can be with the hellhound over there."

"And you want to run that guy's plates," Virgil said.

"Yeah. That, too."

"Using that obvious a car means he's either a flake or he wants you to know who he is."

"We'll see," McNeil said. "You two have a nice evening."

As he passed Bird, the dog issued a low, rumbling growl. The detective growled back, and the big animal cocked his head in surprise. "Nice doggie," McNeil said and left the house.

Virgil was perched on a stool at the kitchen counter, a frown on his face.

"You okay?" Nikki asked.

"Stalkers always got something on their mind," he said. "Mac's put a lot of people in the joint. Most of 'em get out, sooner or later."

"Your partner didn't reach middle age by being stupid. He can take care of himself."

"I'm living proof of that, I guess," he said and put a smile on his face. "Well, now, here we are all alone with the whole evening ahead of us."

She returned his smile, knowing him well enough to realize that, because of some jackass in a red car, they weren't really alone at all.

≡ 32 ≡

Virgil woke the next morning to discover Bird sitting on his haunches in the middle of the bedroom, staring at him intently. "What you looking at, fur ball?" he asked.

The clock read 8:20 A.M.

"Mom's gone off to court, huh?" Virgil asked as he slowly eased himself out of the bed. His wounds were healing well, the doctor had informed him, but they were still painful enough to cause him some discomfort.

Well, he had medication for that.

Wearing just his boxers, he shuffled into the kitchen, found the pill bottle, and filled a glass with tap water filtered through some *Star Wars* device stuck on the end of the faucet.

Nikki had left him coffee and a note. "Bird could use a walk. Doctor says you could, too." It also mentioned something about her loving him.

Virgil plucked the phone from the kitchen wall and dialed Major Crimes. The desk sergeant informed him that McNeil had been in that morning. "I don't see him around now."

"You run a plate for him?" Virgil asked.

"Not this week," the sergeant said.

"I'd like you to run one for me, then." Virgil gave him the numbers and letters he'd heard from McNeil.

"Will do. Getting antsy on sick leave, huh?"

"Somethin' like that. Call you back in a few."

Virgil replaced the receiver and Bird got to his feet expectantly. "Okay, dawg, just lemme slip on some pants and shoes."

They took an easy stroll down the hill, continuing on to a nearby mall. The trip back was a little more taxing but the detective kept reassuring himself there was nothing wrong with his legs.

Home again, Bird beelined to his water dish and Virgil headed for the phone.

The desk sergeant had the information. The car, a "Lam-bor-geenny," was licensed to "a pimp named Richard Anthony Geruso." The sergeant gave him a Malibu address.

"What makes you think he's a pimp? You run him?"

"Yep. Only one hit. Four years ago. Pandering. Didn't stick."

"Nothing current?"

"Want I should call Foxy in Vice?"

"No. That's okay," Virgil said. "Thanks, Sarge."

He hung up the phone, wondering why the name Richard Geruso seemed familiar. He remembered names; he didn't always remember contexts. Was it in the paper?

He entered the tiny bedroom Nikki had converted into an office. Typically, it was a bare-bones deal: a small table supporting a phone, lamp, and laptop computer, an office chair on rollers, a cheap bookcase loaded with law volumes.

He sat down and studied the two cords emerging from the rear of the laptop. One was connected to a wall plug, the other to a phone jack. So far so good. He automatically reached out to the machine with both hands and was abruptly reminded of his sling.

"Damn," he muttered.

Using just his right hand, he managed to unlatch the lid of the laptop and flip it up. Operating the keys would be another matter. He carefully slid his arm from the sling and flexed his fingers. Feeling just mild pain, he rested his elbow on the arm of the chair and his left hand on the keyboard. Now if the machine was user-friendly . . .

It took him a few minutes to find the hiding place of the power button and a little longer to realize that you didn't just click it, you had to keep it depressed for twenty seconds before it did anything.

A series of images flashed across the screen, the last accompanied by a musical flourish, compliments of the shy and humble folks at Microsoft. Then the monitor's surface glowed a royal blue, broken by four little icons identified as "Address Book," "Banking," "Personal," and "Internet."

As intrigued as he was by "Personal," he opted for "Internet."

More clicks, the harsh sound of electronic dialing, the even harsher sound of modems having a chat. The screen was suddenly filled with what looked like a checklist of information—dates, time, stock market reports, news headlines.

A needle of pain shot from his wrist as he typed in the name "Richard Geruso." He ignored it and hit the "enter" button. The search engine quickly poked its nose into the Internet's many corners and rewarded him with twelve hits. Only one involved the Richard Geruso he was interested in.

It was a very recent article in the *Los Angeles Times*'s business section. Geruso and one Luther Pickett were about to open a new Hollywood hot spot called Wonderbar. There was a picture of Geruso and Pickett posed in front of the site of their enterprise.

Virgil hadn't had a clear view of the driver of the sports car, but the white man in the photo, with his thick, razor-cut black hair and soft pale face seemed vaguely familiar. He looked a little bored. His partner, Pickett, was smiling enough for both of them. There was nothing about either man to suggest how they earned their coin.

The article indicated that Geruso had had a successful career as an accountant. He wondered if that was the euphemism for pimp these days. Probably not. More likely, the reporter hadn't bothered to check up on anything that Geruso or Pickett had told her.

He clicked the screen back to the search page and this time typed in "Luther Pickett."

Two hits. One was the article he'd just read. The other was from the *Times*'s metro section, nearly a month before. A piece about a murdered woman named Patience Dahl. The reporter referred to the victim as "an unemployed actress," but Virgil was up on the crime enough to know she'd been a holly, a prostitute. He scanned the piece. A paragraph near the bottom caught his eye. "The victim's father and her friends have expressed shock and disbelief. Businessman Luther Pickett, CEO of Wonderbar, Inc., for whom she'd worked part-time, described her as 'a sweet, very caring young woman who deserved all the best life has to offer.'"

Virgil turned off the computer.

Okay. A ho' who'd been working for a couple macks named Pickett and Geruso had gotten herself killed six weeks ago. Now, all of a sudden, the pimps were opening a club on Melrose, and Geruso was tailing McNeil. He lifted the phone and dialed Major Crimes again.

His partner was still among the absent.

This time, Virgil left a request for a call back.

≡ 33 ≡

Offisah Dee-Bona," Defense Attorney Gerald Wheeler asked, pushing his southern drawl to its avuncular limits, Nikki thought, "might theah be any other little pieces of crucial evidence you messed with on that tragic mornin'?"

The policeman swallowed hard and replied, "Actually, sir, I didn't mess with any crucial evidence. And my name is DiBono."

"Forgive me, Offisah Dee-Bo-No. Let me restate. In addition to your pawing of the door handles and the victim's wallet and the metal insect eradicatah, was theah anything else you may have . . . disturbed with your rather large and ungainly hands?"

The policeman's face was turning a bright red.

Marinate, Nikki prayed. Do not blow and blow our case.

DiBono seemed to be counting. Then he said, "Those were the only items I touched."

"And, as you continue to tell us, you were wearing gloves?"

"I was wearing gloves, yes, sir."

"Is it possible, in the course of all that pawing around, you got some of the victim's blood on your famous gloves?"

"No, sir, that is not possible."

"Not possible, Offisah? Not even when you went through that door to the patio, brushing right past that poor dead woman? Maybe one of the gloves just brushed against her for a second?"

"No, sir."

"Asked and answered, Your Honor," Nikki said.

"At least twice," the judge noted to Wheeler. "This going anywhere?"

"I hope so, Your Honor," Wheeler said.

"So do I," the judge said. "Carry on, with the knowledge that my patience is finite."

"Thank you, Your Honor. Offisah Dee-Bo-No, I don't suppose you still possess your famous gloves?"

"No, sir. Like I told somebody from your office a couple days ago, I tossed 'em."

"Why is that?"

"I use a fresh pair of gloves for each crime scene."

"They were dirty, then? Maybe bloody?"

"No, sir. Not bloody."

"But we'll never really know, will we, now that you've destroyed them?"

"I guess not."

"Nor will we ever know if you picked up that az-mah bottle with your bloody gloves and contam—"

"Objection, Your Honor," Nikki interrupted. "This is all conjecture."

"Sustained," Judge Jarmon Proody bellowed, his hawk-like profile and dark frown adding emphasis to his ruling. "Move on to matters of substance, Mr. Wheeler."

"Young Offisah Dee-Bo-No, would you consider your survey of the crime scene to be competent?"

"Yes, sir, I would."

"Yet you have stated that you overlooked the aforementioned az-mah spray bottle?"

"I was paying more attention to the victim's body and the—"

"You didn't see the spray bottle, did you?"

"I . . . didn't see the bottle, sir."

"Is it possible that the spray bottle simply wasn't theah at the time?"

"Objection. Calls for speculation."

"Your Honor," Wheeler complained, "Offisah Dee-Bo-No has testified to his competence as an observer. Surely he knows if he was capable of overlooking an obvious item like that spray bottle or if it wasn't there when he surveyed the room."

Judge Proody nodded. "I'll overrule. Please answer the question, Officer."

"I—The spray bottle must have been there," DiBono said. "There was no way anybody could have put it there later. I just didn't see it."

"There was a little boy—the victim's son—in the house that mornin', right?"

"Yes, sir."

"You didn't see him either."

"He was . . . hiding in an upstairs closet."

"Well, it's a big ole house," Wheeler said. "Right?"

"Yes, sir. It is."

"Don't suppose there was anybody else hidin' arou' when you got there?"

"No, sir."

"How can you be sure?"

DiBono opened his mouth, but the defense attorney interrupted whatever he was about to say. "Sounds like there were lots of things you didn't see and didn't do right that morning, Offisah Dee-Bo-No." Wheeler looked at the judge. "I'm finished with this witless . . . ah, witness."

Judge Proody scowled at him, then turned to Nikki with a questioning look.

She stood up from the table. "Officer DiBono, since Mr. Wheeler threw out a bunch of wild and unsubstantiated theories about how his client's spray bottle wound up at the crime scene covered in the victim's blood, let's try to clarify matters. Did you put the spray bottle where it was found?"

"No, ma'am, I did not," DiBono replied with fervor.

"Did you touch the spray bottle at any time?"

"I did not touch it, ma'am."

"To your knowledge, did anyone place the spray bottle where it was found?"

"Other than Mr. Bingham, you mean?" DiBono asked.

"Objection, Your Honor. Speculation."

Before the judge could make his ruling Nikki said, "I'll withdraw the question. Officer, do you have knowledge of anyone, Mr. Bingham included, putting the spray bottle where it was found?"

"None of us could have planted it. Like I been saying all along, I led the two detectives back to the room. When Detective McNeil discovered the spray, I had a clear view of him. Nobody planted nothing."

It was considerably more than Nikki had asked. She wished the young cop had taken her advice and kept his answers short and simple. Too late for that now. "That's all I have for the officer, Your Honor," she said.

The judge dismissed DiBono and announced that the trial would resume after lunch.

"How bad was it?" Nikki asked Daspit.

"Could have been worse," he replied without emotion. "Considering what you had to work with, I don't think I could have done much better."

She opened her mouth, then quickly closed it. The trial had had a disastrous enough start. No sense compounding it by calling your co-counsel a conceited asshole.

≡ 34 ≡

Ricky Geruso edged open the bottom drawer of his desk a few inches, leaned back in his leather chair, and watched the big bastard barrel into his office, red-rimmed eyes blazing. The man was seriously miffed, ready to ignite at any second. Good.

"S'okay, Annette," Ricky said to the French receptionist who'd chased the guy to the door. "I invited Detective McNeil, sort of. Shut the door and leave us alone."

Annette raised a skeptical eyebrow and did as she was ordered.

"Take a load off, Detective," Ricky said, indicating a chair near his desk.

"What the fuck are you up to, creep?" McNeil demanded. He remained standing, moving closer.

"Me?" Ricky gave him a look of feigned innocence. "I'm not the one beat Patience to death."

"That's why you're following me around? You think I killed Patience?" McNeil was leaning over the desk now. Ricky wondered if maybe he'd timed the whole thing badly. It had been forty-five minutes ago, give or take, when his scared-shitless housemaid had called the office with the news that an angry cop had been at his place at Malibu threatening to arrest her if she didn't tell him where Ricky was.

"So he's on his way?" Ricky had asked. "Don't worry, honey. It's okay."

He'd thought he could get everything going by the time McNeil arrived, but a key part of his plan was noticeably missing, why he couldn't guess. Could be a problem: The cop looked like he was ready to go caveman.

"C'mon. Sit down," Ricky said. "Let's talk about this."

"We got nothing to talk about, except you following me around town."

"I was in love with her," Ricky said. "I think maybe you were too."

"I don't know what the fuck you're talking about."

Ricky hesitated, then said, "You're not gonna try and tell me you didn't know Patience?"

"I knew her."

"You knew her pretty well. The hotel clerk says it was you helped her move out."

McNeil seemed to sag and Ricky realized everything was going to be just fine.

"I helped her move," the cop said.

"And then what?" Ricky asked.

"I drove her to her new place, helped her fix it up a little."

"She talk about me?"

"She mentioned a pimp who treated her like crap. A sleazebag who had her so terrorized she had to wait until he was on another continent to break away from him."

The words stung. "You were gonna make an honest woman of her?" Ricky asked.

"I'm too old to be that stupid," McNeil said.

"Then what?"

"I liked her. That's all there was to it. Not that it's any of your fucking business."

Ricky studied the guy. He sure as hell seemed sincere. But he had to be the one. There wasn't anybody else. "Well, it was sorta my business," Ricky said. "Before I went legit."

McNeil looked around the room. "This is legit?"

"It's what she wanted, and that's why I'm doing it," Ricky said piously.

He was improvising but he thought there might be some truth in it. And it was cooling down the madman. "She was a sweetheart."

The cop nodded. He backed into the chair and sat. "Yeah. She was."

"But she could also piss you off," Ricky said.

McNeil shrugged. "That's your story. We got along great, the little time we had."

"She make up a pet name for you?"

"Nothing special. 'Mac.'"

"She seeing anybody else but you, Mac? Another cop, maybe?"

"I didn't think so. And don't call me 'Mac.'"

"Gene Liverdais?"

"The way she talked about Gene, I can't believe she'd have had anything more to do with him."

Ricky was a little disappointed that the cop was answering his questions. He didn't think a guilty man would do that. Still, McNeil was the last man standing in the suspect room, so Ricky pushed it. "What about the night she bought it? You with her that night?"

The cop shook his head sadly. "I was on duty. She told me she was gonna take in a movie."

"How come after her death you never told your brother cops you were tight with her?"

"What would have been the point?" McNeil said. "I had nothing to help 'em."

"And they might've tagged you for the crime."

"That's bullshit," McNeil said.

"Let's suppose for a minute Patience kept a diary," Ricky said. "And in that diary she named you as the guy she was gonna see the night she was killed."

"I told you, I was working that night."

"Why would Patience lie?" Ricky asked.

"Maybe it's somebody else who's lying," McNeil said. "About there being a diary."

"Ten grand," Ricky said.

"What?"

"Ten grand. That's what the diary'll cost you."

"You scumbag." McNeil was on his feet again, eyes fiery. He grabbed Ricky's shirtfront and dragged him onto the desk. "I oughta snap your fucking neck."

Ricky felt a tingle of fear, but he was too far along to pull back now. "That what you did with Patience?" he managed to squawk.

The office door opened and two men in suits walked in. One was black, the other white. The tall black man said, "Let him go, Detective."

McNeil released his hold on Ricky's shirtfront. He glared at the black man. "IAG?"

The black man flashed a leather-covered ID. "I'm Detective Collins. My partner is Detective Garibaldi. Let's have your weapon, please."

"The hell you say."

"We're taking your weapon and then we're driving you down to head-quarters."

McNeil gave him a disgusted look and held his arms outstretched as if he were being crucified. Garibaldi moved close to him and unbuttoned his coat. Carefully, he lifted McNeil's Police Special from its holster.

He then patted the detective down, paying special attention to the calves and ankles.

"You guys took your time getting here," Ricky said. Liverdais had let it slip that his buddy McNeil was being investigated by Internal Affairs. He'd even inadvertently provided Ricky with Collins's name. Ricky had phoned the IAG detective as soon as he'd heard that McNeil was headed his way.

Collins waited for Garibaldi to make sure that McNeil was weapon-less, then asked Ricky, "He confess?"

"Not quite. But close." Ricky opened his bottom drawer and removed a tape recorder. He ejected the cassette from the tray and handed it to Collins. "Glad to help in your investigation."

As the three lawmen headed from his office, Ricky said, "No 'thank you'?"

No reply. He'd become a bit player in their drama.

He stared at the tape recorder on his desk. It had belonged to Pa-tience. He placed a hand on it and said, "We got him, baby. You and me, we got him good."

≡ 35 ≡

The afternoon session in Judge Proody's courtroom went about as
expected. Daspit took the coroner through the cause of death and a
criminalist through fingerprints and serology findings. The defense—in
the efficient form of Mimi Gentry—got the criminalist to admit there
was no way to accurately pinpoint the age of fingerprints. The presence of Randolph Bingham's prints at the crime scene only proved he
had been in that room, a stipulated fact. His prints on the remaining
shells in the murder weapon only indicated that he'd loaded the weapon
at some point in time, not that he had used it on Shelli Dietz.

As for the infamous spray atomizer, the criminalist had to admit
that its bloody presence did not provide positive proof that Bingham
was present at the time of the murder. It might have fallen from the
defendant's pocket earlier in the evening when Shelli Dietz was still very
much alive.

Daspit had asked the criminalist how an item as large as the atomizer might have fallen from the defendant's pocket without notice. The
criminalist had replied that such a thing may have taken place during
a struggle. Mimi Gentry got him to admit that the item could also
have fallen in the course of a hug or a kiss.

And so it went.

At 5:20, Nikki, Daspit and other members of the prosecution team had their daily meeting with the district attorney in his office. Among the topics for discussion were two new additions to the Wheeler and Company witness list: Jenny Mapes, Adam's former nanny, and one Charles Guidry.

"Guidry?" Wise asked, puzzled. "The guy who used to work here?"

The name clicked for Nikki. "Adam Noyes's father was accused of assault," she said. "Guidry tried the case and lost to Jesse Fallon."

"Why would Wheeler put *him* on the stand?" Wise asked.

"We'll have to ask Guidry," Daspit said.

"And the nanny?"

"Sounds like they're trying to muddy the vic," Nikki said. "If they can prove that Dietz was a little casual when it came to jumping the broomstick it'd help their scenario about another boyfriend doing her."

"And the nanny helps them how?" Wise asked.

"We considered putting her on the stand ourselves. To corroborate Adam's statement about Bingham's abusive nature and maybe say that he was the one who told her to get lost the night of the murder. She went in the opposite direction: Bingham was a real prince who treated Dietz better than she treated him."

"She say Dietz fucked around?" Wise asked.

"Not exactly. What she said was that Dietz liked to work next to nude—bra and panties, sometimes—no matter who was wandering by, the gardener, the pool guy, pizza man."

"Mapes actually see anything happen?"

"She said no, not at the house. But Dietz disappeared every so often in the afternoon and Mapes thought she had something going."

"Great. Have we checked the gardener and the pool guy?"

"The gardener is a sixty-six-year-old Asian-American who was home with his family the night of the murder," Nikki said. "The pool guy's got no real alibi, except that he's of the gay persuasion. Neither, by the way, is on the defense's witness list."

"Yet," Wise said. "Could Mapes be hot for Bingham herself?"

"Maybe. Or, in some screwed up way, she's pissed off at Dietz for getting herself killed and causing her to be out of work. Or Wheeler played with her head before I had a chance to. Or . . . maybe Dietz really did have something going in the afternoon."

"Was Dietz a nymph?" Wise said.

"Not much real evidence of that," Daspit said. "We know of only two other men she's seen since her husband died. They swear their relationships were very casual. And chaste. In other words, they're our witnesses, not Wheeler's."

Wise nodded. "But let's suppose the worst: The defense has evidence that Dietz was bending over for every swinging dick in town. How bad off would we be?"

Nikki shrugged. "It's a toss. The defense's scenario about an unknown lover would seem a little less fantastic, but we'd pick up points when it comes to Bingham's jealousy motive."

Wise relaxed. Then his press rep, Meg Fisher, appeared at the door. "The TV," she said tersely.

The D.A. opened a drawer, found his remote wand, and clicked on the television set in the built-in bookcase across the room. "Which channel?" he asked.

"Any of 'em," Meg replied.

They all watched as the monitor faded in on a press conference being held in front of their building. Dana Lowery, caught in the bright strobes of a half-dozen video cameras, was staring at them with a mixture of sheer joy and defiance. "I commend the Los Angeles Police Department for the professional and unswerving manner in which this arrest has been made."

"What arrest?" Wise shouted. "What the fuck is she talking about?"

"It should send a signal to criminals everywhere," Dana was saying, the lights forming a nimbus around her raven hair. "No one is above the law. Not in this county. Not with this police force, led by Chief Philip Ahern."

The camera pulled back to reveal the diminutive chief standing at Dana's side.

Wise was on his feet, screaming, "What is this?"

As if in reply, an unseen announcer informed the viewing audience, "Police Chief Philip Ahern and Deputy District Attorney Dana Lowery, announcing the arrest of a veteran member of the Los Angeles Police Department, Homicide Detective Daniel McNeil, for the eight-week-old brutal murder of young actress Patience Dahl."

"Get that backstabbing bitch in here!" Wise shouted to Meg.

"I'll do my best," the press secretary said.

The D.A. angrily clicked off the TV and flopped back onto his chair. He looked wretched.

Nikki wasn't feeling so upbeat herself. She knew how the news would affect Virgil. She hoped he wouldn't hear it before she got home. "I imagine that puts the cap on our meeting," she said, getting to her feet.

Wise nodded absently. It was all the encouragement any of them needed to pack up and head out.

As Nikki approached her office, Jeb held out his phone to her. "For you," he said. "The bf."

≡ 36 ≡

Earlier that evening, Virgil had been having another of his earth-quake dreams. In this one, he'd been propelled from his shaking bed into a Los Angeles crumbling before his eyes. High-rise buildings tottered and crashed. An overpass—he thought it might be the Santa Monica Freeway—tore apart, spilling multilanes of heavy traffic onto the streets far below. He could hear the crashes and screams and the terrible cracking sounds of the earth as it gaped open, swallowing people and cars and buildings. The pain pill he'd taken earlier had heightened the intensity of the nightmare while allowing him to float through it above the devastation, untouched but horrified.

Suddenly, the ability to defy gravity deserted him and he plummeted down, down into an open crevice in the torn earth.

He awoke gasping for air, legs jerking and pounding the mattress of Nikki's big bed. As the mixture of fear and disorientation drained away, it left him wasted and sore and groaning. Still, he thanked God that it had been only a dream.

The room had retained much of the heat from the afternoon sun. His T-shirt was damp and sticky. Blinking, he ran his tongue around a medicine-dry mouth.

He groaned again, using his good arm to sit up. "Ain't no way daytime sleep gives you any rest," he said.

As if to convince himself he'd been talking to the dog, he looked at the place on the carpet where he'd last seen Bird. It was vacant.

Virgil got out of bed slowly. His movements, especially with a head full of pharmaceutical cotton, were very deliberate.

Where was the dog? he wondered. Bird had not let him out of his sight since his arrival from the hospital. He staggered across the floor and down the hall.

The big dog was standing at attention facing the front door, as rigid as a pointer. Virgil's arrival did not distract him. There was a scuffling noise on the other side of the door and Bird shifted his body, his stump of a tail twitching anxiously, a low growl suggesting this was not a friendly visitor. The growl grew into a gruff bark. Virgil wondered if it had been an earlier bark that had brought him back from his nightmare.

He crossed to a window facing the street in time to see someone back away from the front door. The detective recognized the figure. "Bop!" he commanded the big dog, using the word Nikki had claimed would put the animal on hold.

Bird looked like he wasn't certain he had to obey, but he did stop barking. Virgil opened the front door just as the visitor was heading for a van. The vehicle had been painted a Day-Glo purple with the logo of "Team Homeboy" stenciled in bright yellow on the door.

"Adam!" Virgil called. "Adam Noyes!"

The boy stopped and turned. His expression changed from curiosity to confusion as he stared at Virgil standing in the doorway in his T-shirt and underwear. "I know you," he said. "You're the detective."

"Virgil Sykes," Virgil said, using the door to shield his boxers and bare legs from the world. "You caught me taking a nap."

The boy's attention shifted to the big dog who had appeared beside the detective. "I . . . I thought this was somebody else's house," Adam said.

"It is," Virgil said. Had Nikki mentioned anything about expecting the boy's visit? The medicine had been messing with his memory. At least, he hoped it was the medicine. "Come on in, while I throw on some clothes."

The door to the van opened and the driver got out. He was a large, hulking man in his early thirties, wearing wraparound shades and a loud Hawaiian print shirt. He flipped up the shades and asked, "Everything okay, Adam?"

"Uh-huh," Adam replied uncertainly. "This man's a policeman."

"Oh, yeah?" the big blond man said, staring at Virgil.

Virgil studied him briefly, noted the odd way the man's shirt folded above his right hip. Then he turned back to the boy. "You were looking for Nikki Hill, huh?" he asked.

Adam nodded.

"Well, won't you guys come in? We can give her a call, see how long she's gonna be."

The big man eyed the dog warily. "I'll stay with the van," he said, taking a cellular phone from his pocket and flipping it open. "Got some calls to make."

Virgil felt an odd sense of relief as the man stepped back into the van, slamming the door behind him.

Adam entered the house cautiously, eyes riveted on the dog. Virgil grabbed Bird's collar with his free hand. Using a bare foot to shut the front door, the detective said, "Get yourself a seat in the kitchen."

Virgil felt the big dog relax. Cautiously, he released his grip on the collar. Bird plopped to the carpet, eyeing the boy. Adam seemed to be returning his interest.

"I'll be back in a flash," Virgil told them both.

He moved quickly to the bedroom and found his slacks on the floor where he'd stepped out of them several hours before. His wilted sports shirt was tossed casually on top of a stuffed chair in the corner. He slipped his feet into his cordovan loafers, not bothering with socks.

When he returned to the kitchen the boy was looking at a cartoon show on the small TV that rested on the breakfast counter.

"Where's Bird?" Virgil asked.

"Outside chomping a turkey leg I found in the fridge." Adam seemed mesmerized by the animated squiggles and bursts of color on the TV.

The detective blinked, then turned to stare out of the sliding glass doors to the patio where the big dog rested, gnawing on a bone. "Got a way with animals, huh?"

"Dog's hungry, you feed him," Adam said. "You live here with Nikki?"

Virgil pointed to the cast on his arm. "Just till I mend."

"You're her boyfriend?"

"Uh-huh."

"Gonna get married?"

"I don't know," Virgil said, the question making him uncomfortable. "What time were you supposed to meet her?"

"Oh, she's not expecting me. Howard was just driving me to my house and I talked him into coming here first on the chance she might be home."

"Howard your bodyguard?" Virgil asked.

"Bodyguard?" Adam smiled. "Why would I need a bodyguard?"

"He carries a gun on his hip."

"Sure. He's, like, a security guard for Homeboy. The main security guard. Anyway, I . . . I wanted to talk with her about the trial. She said I may be taking the stand on Monday."

"I don't know what her schedule's like," Virgil said. He looked at the clock on the wall. Felix the Cat's short arm was nearing 5, the longer aimed at 11. "Why don't I give her a call, see what her plans are?"

"Okay, cool."

Virgil crossed the room to the phone. He had punched in part of Nikki's office number when Adam asked, "Isn't that your partner on the TV?"

On the screen, a handcuffed Dan McNeil was being led into Parker Center by Rafe Collins and his IAG shadow, Garibaldi. Mac looked dazed and disheveled.

Virgil put down the phone and ran to the TV. He turned up the volume on a newsman's in-progress description. ". . . but the extent of Detective McNeil's involvement in the girl's murder has yet to be determined."

Murder? Could they seriously be calling the Jill Laurence shooting a murder?

On the screen, a swarm of reporters bore down on the three men as they approached the front doors to the building. McNeil stopped suddenly and stared directly into the camera, as stunned and helpless as a deer caught in a speeding truck's headlights.

"Your partner kill somebody?" Adam asked, as casually as if he were inquiring about the score of a Dodgers' game.

Virgil couldn't reply. He was too busy trying to clear his head. His shoulder was starting to throb.

The video scene shifted to another photo op across the street. This one was more controlled, thanks to the intimidating presence of a squad of uniformed LAPD officers. They were holding back the more impulsive members of the media from getting too close to the main attractions—Police Chief Philip Ahern and Deputy District Attorney Dana Lowery.

TV lights focused on this odd couple—the diminutive man and the woman with the dramatically streaked hair—and logo-heavy microphones waved in front of their faces. Lowery congratulated the chief on the efficiency and speed with which he had acted in arresting a member of the LAPD.

Virgil was having trouble assimilating the information. Unconnected phrases seemed to penetrate his mind's cloudy confusion: "one of his own," "hiding behind a policeman's shield," "heinous crime," "speedy trial," "brutal beating."

Jill Laurence hadn't been beaten. Then he heard the name "Patience Dahl."

He turned down the television's sound, hoping the silence might help him recall who—the hooker! The one whose body had been found at the fast-food joint on Melrose. The guy following Mac had been her pimp.

"You okay?"

He'd forgotten about the boy. "Oh, yeah," he said to Adam.

"You going to call Nikki?"

"Right. Good idea." Nikki would know what the hell was going on.

He tapped out her number and waited impatiently for a connection. Jeb Lacy answered on the second ring. He told Virgil that Nikki was at a meeting in the D.A.'s office. "Got no idea how long it—hold on, you're in luck. Here she comes."

"You heard, huh?" were her first words. His reply must have betrayed his anxiety because she added, "You take it easy. I'm leaving now. Be there in half an hour."

"What've they got on him?" Virgil asked.

"I don't know. Ray doesn't know. This is Dana's show, top to bottom."

"Can you talk to her? See what you can pry loose?"

Nikki hesitated. "I'll try."

"Bounce a name off her. Richard Geruso."

"Who's he?"

"Remember that red sports car, the Lamborghini that was following Mac? It belongs to a pimp named Richard Geruso. The dead girl worked for him."

"I'll see what I can find out. Meanwhile, you just take it easy, okay? Don't do anything . . . rash."

"Can I speak with her?" Adam asked.

Again, he'd forgotten about the boy. "Don't hang up, Red. Somebody here wants to say hello." He handed off the receiver quickly, before she could divine, in that voodoo way she had, exactly what he was planning to do.

He moved quickly to the bedroom, found his wallet, badge, ID, keys, and small change on the bedside table and stuffed them into his pockets.

He moved down the hall but didn't reenter the kitchen. Instead, he stayed just beyond the boy's angle of view, watching his animated conversation. The kid had a thing for Nikki. Well, who wouldn't?

Adam suddenly looked serious, sitting up straighter on the stool beside the counter. "He went away somewhere. You want me to—? Oh, okay. I will."

Virgil waited for Adam to replace the receiver before he walked into the room. "Wha'sup?" he asked.

"Nikki says to tell you she's leaving the office right now and should be here soon."

"You waiting?"

"I've got to go. Nikki is going to try and meet with me tomorrow."

"So you and Howard with the gun headin' back to town now?"

"Guess so."

"Do me a big favor? Give me a lift to my car?"

"Whereabouts is it?"

Virgil wasn't sure, exactly. He'd asked McNeil to have the vehicle moved from the Parker Center lot to his apartment. He thought Mac had told him it had been done. Unless that had been in a dream. "In Hollywood. On Havenhurst north of Fountain."

"You sure you're well enough to drive?" The boy was frowning. "Nikki says you were hurt pretty bad."

"I can drive," Virgil said. "It's got an automatic shift. I just need the one hand."

"It's kinda on our way," Adam said.

"I think I've got a spare key." Virgil took out his ring, to check.

Adam stared at an object dangling from the chain. "What's that?" he asked. "Some kind of badge? It's tiny, but it looks real."

"It's an honorary badge from the Bay City Sheriff's Department," Virgil said. "I did some work for 'em a few years ago."

"It's neat."

Virgil worked the badge off his key ring and held it out to the boy. Adam looked at him quizzically.

"Take it," Virgil said. "It's okay. All it does is tear holes in my pockets."

"I'm going to keep this with me always," Adam said. "I mean it. Can I trade you something?"

Virgil smiled. "I'll settle on a lift to my car."

"You got it," Adam said, smiling at his new possession.

Bird must have sensed their imminent departure. He squeezed through his doggie door and joined them just in time to stare disapprovingly at Virgil. "When your momma gets here," the detective said to the big animal, "tell her not to worry, I'll be back in time for dinner."

• • •

The van descended the hill away from Nikki's home, with the driver, Howard, ignoring his new passenger and whispering into his cellular. Adam said to Virgil, "You look a little stressed."

"I've been sleeping all afternoon."

"Nikki sounded stressed, too."

"My friend's been arrested for something he didn't do. It's affecting both of us, I guess."

"You mean the detective? Your partner?"

Virgil nodded.

"What makes you think he didn't do what they say?"

"Because I know him."

"That why you need your car?"

Virgil smiled. "Everybody needs a car in L.A."

"Not me. I have people who drive me. You and Nikki going to try to help your friend?"

"However we can."

"Is Nikki going to be mad at me for taking you to your car?" Adam asked.

"No," Virgil replied without equivocation. He wasn't lying. Nikki was pretty tuned-in herself. When she arrived home and discovered he was gone, she'd know exactly who deserved the full brunt of her anger. That would not be Adam.

≡ 37 ≡

As Ricky Geruso strolled through the reception area of the new offices, heading out, Pickett called his name. His partner was standing in his office doorway, looking annoyed.

"Pick-man," Ricky said, "how'd your meeting go?"

"It went. Annette tells me you had cops runnin' in and out of here all afternoon."

"Annette, huh?" Ricky glanced at the neat, empty reception desk. "Where is she, anyway? I thought we paid her to work till six."

"Gettin' me some ribs, you must know. What's with the cops?"

"I caught Patience's killer for 'em."

"You did *what*?"

"I figured out who killed Patience. It was this son-of-a-bitch homicide dick named McNeil who'd been porkin' her. I, ah, got him down here and had some IAG cops put the grab on him."

Ricky had expected Pickett to be amused. Impressed, even. Instead, he was furious. "You dumb wop!" the big man shouted, taking a few steps into the reception room, forcing Ricky to take a step backward. "Getting mixed up with cops and murder just when we're about to make our move."

"It's okay," Ricky said without overwhelming conviction. "I'm in with the cops. It's win-win."

"What happened to your common sense, man? You bury it with that little bitch?"

"Easy on that 'bitch' stuff," Ricky said. "You know how it was with me and—"

"Shake the shit out of your head and follow me on this," Pickett interrupted him. "Let's say they get this McNeil into court. You gonna be testifying against him?"

"Well, I guess—"

"Sittin' up here in the witness box, dressed in one of your nice Eye-talian suits, polished shoes. Lookin' fine. Champion o' justice. Answering all the D.A.'s questions."

"So?"

"So then it's the cop's lawyer's turn. He's gonna get into your rela-tionship with Patience. He's gonna ask you about your occupation for the last bunch of years. He's gonna make you look like a low-rent pimp with a hard-on for law enforcement. He finishes with you, you'll be lucky they don't find *you* guilty of murderin' the ho'."

"I was in Japland," was all Ricky could think of to say. In fact, he hadn't foreseen that particular aspect of the trial.

"You shoulda stayed there," Pickett said nastily. "Hell, you're in the soup now, unless they got enough on this McNeil they won't need to put a pimp on the stand."

"The old fart at the hotel can ID him from when he helped Pa-tience move out. I think she stayed at McNeil's place for a while. Her prints will be there. Her blood, maybe."

Pickett's face relaxed. "Her blood would be nice. You wouldn't have any samples at your place you could scrape off?"

Ricky ignored the question. "The IAG cops were already on his case. He shot some broad last week."

"No shit?" Pickett asked. "I'm startin' to like this guy."

"Bastard killed Patience," Ricky reminded him.

"Yeah, well," Pickett said.

Ricky began to get a weird idea. What if the fucking cop didn't

kill Patience? He'd seemed really bummed by her death. What if
Pickett . . . ?

"You got anything else to help the cops make their case without
you?" Pickett asked.

"Like what?" Ricky replied, studying Pickett anew.

The black man made a vague gesture with his big right hand. "Hell,
I dunno. A belt you used to beat her with we could toss in his garbage
can."

"I never used a belt on her," Ricky said. He hesitated, then added,
"There are these tapes she made."

"What kinda tapes?"

"Like a diary she was talking into a recorder. Maybe twenty hours'
worth. I haven't listened to 'em all. Maybe she spells it out." Ricky suddenly was wondering if she might've spelled out another name. Pickett. Maybe he'd found out she was getting too close to the cop and
felt he had to do something about it. To protect his precious plan.

"I don't think they can use tape in a trial," Pickett said. " 'Less they
lucky enough to draw a judge don't know the law. There's our business,
too. She probably shot her mouth off about that on the tapes. Stuff
you and me don't want cops to hear."

"We could erase that part," Ricky said.

"Ain't as easy as it sounds," Pickett said. "I best take a listen to them
tapes myself."

Ricky knew that if he turned the tapes over to Pickett he'd never
see them again. His partner wouldn't bother listening to them; he'd simply burn them or feed them to the shredder. Regardless of what they
contained or didn't contain, Ricky didn't want them destroyed. Aside
from the possibility that they might provide the name of Patience's
murderer, they were his last physical connection to her. "I'll just get rid
of 'em," he lied.

Pickett gave him the hard eye. "Don't bullshit me, Richard," he said.

"I'll get rid of 'em."

"They here?"

"At my place."

"I go into your office, I won't find 'em in one of your desk drawers?"

Ricky's throat was dry, but he met Pickett's glare without blinking. The tapes and Patience's Sony were locked in the bottom left drawer of his desk. Next to them was a loaded Colt Mark IV, Series 80, the kind Navy SEALs use. Trouble with the gun was, once it was in his hand, he'd have to kill Pickett. Or, worse yet, Pickett would have to kill him.

"I'll get rid of 'em," he repeated.

Pickett cocked his head to one side, saying nothing, studying him.

The glass door to the offices opened and Annette entered carrying a large white bag mottled with grease stains that smelled of barbecue. She raised an eyebrow at Ricky and said, "I only bought enough for two. I did not know you'd still be here."

"Just going," Ricky said. "Bone appetite, you two."

The blazing red Diablo was parked in front, the garage guy standing on the sidewalk beside it, holding out the keys. The poor bastard must've been standing there for the past fifteen minutes, waiting for him. "Sorry, pally, I got hung up on the way down," Ricky said, slipping him a dead Lincoln.

He barely acknowledged the guy's mumbled thanks as he slid behind the wheel. His mind was elsewhere, wondering if Pickett would search his office for the tapes. He didn't think so. The black man was a hard-ass son of a bitch and dangerous as a rattler. But he wasn't dumb. He wouldn't do anything to cause a rift in their partnership so near the launch date of his goddamned Wonderbar. Unless he was certain Patience had fingered him for her murder.

Ricky was so absorbed in thought he didn't notice the car that pulled behind him as he passed. As he continued to ponder Pickett's potential for homicide, the vehicle stayed two car lengths behind the Diablo, joining him and the rest of the traffic heading west toward the Pacific.

PART FOUR

CLOSING ARGUMENTS

≡ 38 ≡

Nikki was dispiritedly nibbling on a chicken dinner she'd brought home from El Pollo Loco when Bird raised his big head. At the sound of a key in the front-door lock, he pushed himself from the floor of the kitchen and trotted off to investigate. Nikki glanced at the Felix clock, 9:17. She took a sip of her supermarket merlot and waited for Virgil to drag his sorry butt into the kitchen.

"Hi, baby," he said, bending down to kiss her unresponsive cheek. "Got my wheels."

"Guess the doctor was talking through his stethoscope when he told you to relax and take it easy."

"Doctor didn't realize my powers of recuperation."

She rolled her eyes, then gestured in the direction of the fridge. "Brought you a chicken dinner, but you're gonna have to nuke it if you want it hot. Or maybe you ate while you were out joyriding."

"Nope." He pulled the bag of chicken from the refrigerator, and transferred it to the microwave. "Been home a while, huh?"

"Nearly two hours. I had the mistaken idea you might want company. Instead, I find an empty house."

"I'm sorry, honey. I just felt I needed my car here."

"Why?"

"Man needs his car."

"Not a man who's been shot in the head and can only use one arm and who's on medication. Especially with a little boy in the passenger seat."

He winced. "You talked to Adam, huh?"

She stared at him. "Uh-huh. Since neither one of you was here, I called his house. He wasn't there. Donia was worried about him. Then about twenty minutes ago, he called back, told me you'd just dropped him off."

She watched him remove his dinner from the oven, slide the half-chicken from its bag, and poke at it with a finger. "Warm enough," he mumbled, mainly to himself. "Adam mention what we been doing?" he asked her.

" 'Following a bad dude in a red sports car.' On a fool's errand, endangering my key witness."

"He wanted to come along. It was his payback for driving me to my car."

"He's a child. You're supposedly an adult."

"He had his bodyguard with him."

"His what?"

"Some ex-cop named Howard Rule," Virgil said. "Not really a bodyguard. Works security for Homeboy. Okay guy, but a little weird. Got this scar on his face that won't quit."

"I still don't know what you were thinking."

"I was thinking about that sorry sack of shoes Geruso. The pimp's gotta be mixed up in this." He attacked the chicken as if it were a substitute for the sorry sack of shoes.

Nikki hesitated, then said, "He's mixed up in it all right. He tipped IAG they could pick up McNeil in his office."

"He set Mac up?" Virgil was gawking at her, mouth open in disbelief. "IAG so hard up they using pimps now?"

"Geruso's just part of McNeil's problem," Nikki said. "Cruella's got this hotel manager who saw him helping the vic move out. McNeil's phone bill turned up several working girls who claim the vic called them to brag about her new digs. They found all sorts of evidence at his house of their cohabitation. McNeil admits she was living there for a while."

"What else does he say?"

"I'm getting this thirdhand from Daspit. Dana's not talking to me about anything. McNeil says he met the vic on a trip to Vegas, when she was with some cop from Vice. Then, later, he bumped into her at the cleaners, if you can believe that, and asked her out on a date. Asked a hooker on a date!"

"And they got together, huh?"

"She's a hooker! She gonna say no to a cop? They went out a few more times and then she calls him to say she's leaving her pimp, the lovely Ricky Geruso, and wants McNeil's help."

"Mac say anything about the night she died?" Virgil asked, his mouth dry as sand.

"Only that he didn't kill her."

Virgil nodded.

"But he does admit to knocking her around one night. Next day, he felt bad, as woman-beaters often do," she said with some disdain. "The girl told him she wanted to move out and he went along with that plan and helped her find a place. Three days later she was dead."

"That's all they got? She lived with him?"

"They found blood, her type, in his bedroom and bathroom."

"That could be from the time he beat her."

Prior exposure. That was pretty much the excuse Randolph Bingham's defenders were floating. Nikki hoped it held more water in McNeil's case. "They're working on his car as we speak. If they find any trace evidence there, you can stick a fork in your partner."

"I got to talk to him."

"It's a little late tonight." She picked up her plate and utensils and took them to the sink. She was conscious of him watching her as she rinsed them and positioned them in the dishwasher.

"Yeah. I guess it is kinda late," he said.

"I'm going to bed," Nikki said, picking up a folder of notes for the next day in court. "I fixed you a place in the guest room."

"There's no bed in there."

"I dragged a cot from the garage and put some pillows and a blanket on it for you."

"Aw, honey. Don't be this way."

"You're not here when I come home. No note. Nothing to stop me from worrying. Then I find out you're joyriding with my witness, a little boy who should be at home having his dinner. Now you tell me you were following some stranger, 'stalking' would be the legal word. For what purpose? To catch him breaking the law so you can beat a confession out of him? To find out where he lives so you can break in to discover some miracle clue that'll save your partner's bacon? Grow up, Virgil."

"It's him who was stalking Mac."

"Even if you weren't under doctor's orders to slow down, you've got no business messing in that investigation."

He nodded. He wiped his fingers on his napkin and slid from the stool. "You're right, honey. I been actin' like an idiot."

She watched him approach, knowing he was planning on taking her in his arms. He was overestimating his charm and underestimating her mood. "You must think I'm the idiot," she said, "if you expect me to believe you're not going to keep after that man."

He stopped. The dreamy-eyed look he thought was so seductive—and in fact was—left his face, replaced by a solemn determination. "Mac saved my life. I gotta do something."

"He's got himself a good attorney, Desmond Porcello. He's beaten Cruella before. Best you can do for McNeil is pray and stay out of the way of the detectives working the case. Harassing Richard Geruso isn't going to help your partner and it sure isn't going to help you."

"You're right," he said, making another attempt to get around her anger. "You really gonna make me sleep all alone tonight?"

She didn't want to. She wanted him to come to her bed, where they would make love. She wanted them to make love one more time in the morning before she left for work and he remained in the house, resting his wounds. But she knew him too well. By giving in now, she would not only be forgiving him for frightening her by his

unexplained absence, she'd be giving her tacit approval to his vigi-
lante plan.

"C'mon, baby. You're not gonna make me sleep on some backbreakin'
little cot with a mattress skinny as blue milk?"

"You got your car now. You can always sleep there," she said and left
him standing with his mouth open and his good arm outstretched.

≡ 39 ≡

The morning started well enough in Judge Proody's courtroom.

Keeping her concern over Virgil at the back of her mind, Nikki presented the only two men the D.A.'s investigators had found, other than the defendant, who'd seen the late Shelli Dietz socially. Both testified to the fact that the relationships had been basically platonic. Though each would have preferred something a bit more physical, Dietz had given them no such encouragement. The purpose of their appearance was to combat the defense's allegations of the dead woman's promiscuity.

The defense, in turn, attempted to get them to admit at least a small suspicion that Shelli Dietz's reticence may have stemmed less from chastity than from sexual excess she was enjoying with other lovers. One-night stands, perhaps.

By her almost incessant objections, Nikki was able to keep most of Mimi Gentry's innuendo-loaded questions out of the court records, but not out of the jurors' memories.

During the lunch break, Nikki phoned home. She was not surprised when Virgil didn't answer.

•   •   •

The afternoon session began with Peter Daspit presenting their witness Gus Prosser.

At a rather tense breakfast that morning, Virgil had told her that, during his and McNeil's interrogation of the retired screenwriter, he'd sensed something a bit hinky about the man. Though he had nothing specific to offer, Nikki dutifully had reported his qualms to Daspit who'd replied, "One of the investigators has a hunch? What the hell should I do with a hunch?"

Proceed with caution, she thought but did not say. It was the sort of thing Daspit should have been able to figure out for himself.

Prosser gave off no negative vibes as he took the stand. To the contrary, he was a picture-perfect example of the ideal witness for the prosecution. Dressed in subdued elegance—somber blue suit, white shirt, and red-and-blue-striped tie—his white hair perfectly groomed, he suggested a wise, well-to-do grandfather, old enough to be believed, sharp enough to be reliable.

Prompted by Daspit's questions, he offered a brief biography and went on to describe the events of the early morning of the murder, ending by identifying "the young man at the defense table" as the person he saw leaving the scene of the crime at 2:19 A.M.

Mimi Gentry, looking as fresh and bright as if she hadn't spent most of the morning calling Shelli Dietz a nympho, began her cross by complimenting the witness. "I have to tell you, Mr. Prosser, *Beyond Passion* is one of my all-time favorite movies."

"Thank you," Prosser said, preening. "It's my best work, I think."

"I particularly liked the little girl who played Lana Turner's daughter," Gentry said. "What was her name?"

Prosser blinked and seemed to lose a little of his composure.

"Cut her off," Nikki whispered to Daspit.

"L-Linda Anne Jonas." The elderly man's suntanned face now bore a slightly green tinge.

"Object, Your Honor," Daspit called out. "Relevance?"

"The relevance will be apparent pretty quickly, Your Honor," Mimi Gentry said.

"See that it is, Ms. Gentry. You're on the clock."

The defense attorney nodded and turned to Prosser. "Linda Anne Jonas went on to star in another of your films, didn't she, sir?"

Prosser opened his mouth, but words failed to come. Instead, he nodded.

"Is that a yes?"

"Yes." Almost a whisper.

"Would you tell the court the name of that film?"

Daspit was on his feet again. "Your Honor, why are we discussing Mr. Prosser's films? What bearing could they possibly have on this trial?"

"Ms. Gentry?"

"Please bear with me one minute, Your Honor," she replied.

Judge Proody cocked his head and nodded. Daspit took his seat. Gentry repeated the question. Prosser replied in a voice too low for Nikki to hear.

"Speak up, sir," the judge requested.

"*The Pleasure Room*," Prosser said.

"It was a hard-core porno film, right, sir?"

"Your Honor?" Daspit complained.

"Ms. Gentry, where are you heading with this?"

"Goes to the witness's credibility, Your Honor."

"Then get there fast."

"You like porno movies, don't you, Mr. Prosser?"

The old man didn't reply.

Gentry strode to her table, picked up two sets of paper. She dropped one set in front of Daspit and carried the other to the judge's bench. "I'd like to put these into evidence, Your Honor. Printouts of Mr. Prosser's rentals from Forbidden Video."

"Sidebar, Your Honor!" Daspit almost yelled.

Nikki watched him approach the bench, joining Mimi Gentry. There was a short whispered discussion. The judge observed them both wryly, then said, "Carry on, Ms. Gentry. This item will be marked for the defense."

As Daspit marched back to the table, his poker face seemed totally unreadable. But Nikki knew they were in trouble.

"How many X-rated movies did you rent this month, Mr. Prosser?" Gentry asked.

While the old man fumbled, Nikki whispered to Daspit, "No objection?"

Daspit merely moved his head from side to side.

"Let me see if I can help you," Gentry said. "Looks like about fifty. Several a night?"

"Yes."

"You told us you were watching television just before you heard the noise, went to the window, and saw the black sports car?"

"Yes," Prosser said solemnly. He looked like he'd aged a decade in the past ten minutes.

"You also said, you'd been watching the news. That wasn't exactly true, was it?"

"I did watch the news."

"Maybe the early news. Not the two o'clock."

"The two o'clock news," he said shakily.

Gentry gave him a skeptical look, shrugged, and went on. "According to Forbidden Video, they delivered four films to your home that day. One was titled"—he consulted the sheet—"*Private Dick.*"

Laughter in the courtroom caused Judge Proody to raise an eyebrow and glare at the spectators.

"You aren't gonna do anything?" Nikki asked Daspit incredulously.

"Like what?" he asked flatly.

"Was that one of the films you were watching that night?" Gentry asked, drawing Nikki's attention back to the witness.

"It may have been."

"I'm sorry to have to admit that we screened all four films in our offices a few days ago," Gentry said. "They get pretty repetitious, don't they? All that moaning and bad jazz music?"

"I suppose some might think so," Prosser said, drawing himself up.

"By that fourth film, I found myself drifting off. That ever happen to you?"

"If I've had a long day, perhaps."

"What about that day? Was that a long one? Might you have been dozing a little when you heard that sound like a backfire?"

"No. I was wide awake."

"Let's talk a little about *Private Dick*. Could you give us a brief summary of the plot? Leaving out the salacious parts, if you please."

Prosser glanced at Daspit. When the deputy D.A. remained silent, he replied, "I—it's about a private detective who's hired by a millionaire to find his missing wife. The search leads the detective into several situations, some suspenseful, some humorous. Eventually, he meets a mysterious woman working in a bordello who seduces him. He falls in love with her and then discovers she's the millionaire's wife. She has run away because she has discovered her husband is a kingpin of organized crime."

"Not exactly *Chinatown*," Gentry noted.

"Little is," Prosser said.

"What kind of car does the detective drive, Mr. Prosser?"

"I don't recall."

"Sedan? Convertible? Sports car?"

"The last."

"Color?" Gentry asked.

"Black."

"Do you know the name of the manufacturer?"

"No. Those little cars all look pretty much the same," Prosser said. Nikki groaned.

"Could it have been the same car that Mr. Bingham drives?" Gentry asked.

"It seemed rounder."

"But you're not sure. It could have been the same make?"

"I suppose."

"There's a scene in the film where the detective is being shot at as he drives away from his employer's mansion at night. You remember that scene, Mr. Prosser?"

"That particular scene? I don't recall . . ."

"Is it possible, Mr. Prosser, that after watching three pornographic films, you might have dozed off, then been awakened by the sound of gunfire on the TV? You saw the private dick driving his black sports car on the screen and you confused that image with a memory of having seen Mr. Bingham in his car earlier that evening? Or at some other time?"

"No. That's not possible," Prosser said, anger causing red spots to appear at his cheeks. "I know what I saw. I'm not senile."

"No, you're not senile, sir. You're merely an old man who lives alone and watches porno all night.

"I'm finished with the witness, Your Honor."

Judging from the looks of accusation on the faces of some of the jury, they were finished with him, too.

≡ 40 ≡

What the hell, Virg, she was sweet. She made me feel good. That asshole Geruso was treating her like dirt. It didn't seem like any big deal, lettin' her stay at my place till she found a place of her own."

Virgil was alone with McNeil in the watch commander's office of the Bauchet Street lockup. If he'd been an ordinary citizen, even McNeil's attorney, Desmond Porcello, the meeting would have probably taken place in the interview room, but Virgil played his cop card, flashed his war wounds, and was extended the special courtesy of privacy. Not only did he want their conversation unobserved and unheard, he wanted to concentrate on his partner without distraction.

Since McNeil was being housed in K10, with total keep-away security, he was undamaged. But he was jumpy and he blinked nervously as Virgil calmly took him through his relationship with Patience Dahl. "I'm not gonna bullshit you that I didn't like having her at the house," he said. "She made me feel like a goddamn twenty-year-old."

"You beat on her a little," Virgil said.

"Once."

"Don't tell me: You had a few drinks and started feelin' like a forty-year-old again."

McNeil scowled, red blotches appearing on his face. Anger rash. "Something like that. You on my team, or what, Virg?"

"I'm here," Virgil said. "The way things are shapin' up, we may not get another chance to talk. So let's just put as much as we can on the table. Why'd you beat her?"

"She blew in about three one morning, coked to the gills, acting cute. We had an understanding. No tricking or using while she was under my roof."

"Who'd she been with?"

McNeil averted his eyes. "She wouldn't say."

"That why you hit her?"

"Why I hit her is because I was drunk. I was drunk because she wasn't home when I got there."

"What happened after you hit her?"

"She's crying. I'm suddenly sober as Santa Claus. I feel like shit. The next day she moves out."

"But you kept in contact?" Virgil asked.

"Yeah. Why not? I . . . liked her. Not just the sex. I liked being around her."

"You got no idea who killed her?"

The pale cop shook his head.

"Lemme see if I get this straight, Mac. You have some feelings for this girl. She's beat up and choked to death and you sorta shine it on."

"Soon as I heard about it, I figure it's her fucking pimp. She'd told me he was out of the country on business, but jets fly both ways. I poked around a little, found out he was definitely long gone when she died."

"That was it?" Virgil asked. "You didn't try any harder than that? Check out her johns? Talk to some of her ho' sisters?"

McNeil slumped back in his leather chair. "I turned chickenshit, partner," he said. "I didn't want to get messed up in it."

"You were living with the woman just a few days before she died. I'm surprised you didn't get called in right at the jump."

"The guys originally assigned to the murder are donkeys who handled it like they handle all hooker killings. I think they gave it a little more of their time because this talk-show asshole who found the body

228 CHRISTOPHER DARDEN AND DICK LOCHTE

kept yakking about it on the radio. But it was a going-nowhere investigation. Maybe they found out she'd been seeing a cop. But they didn't
follow up on it. I figured if I started pushing around, I could wind up
in the jackpot. So I chickened out."

"And now you're in the jackpot."

"Thanks to that prick Geruso."

"Tell me about him," Virgil said.

"He set me up for the IAG weasels."

"Why? What's his angle?"

McNeil looked genuinely puzzled. "I don't know. He says he loved
her. Maybe he did. Enough to get pissed at the guy who took her away
from him."

"Or he wants to take the heat off somebody else," Virgil said. "Like
his partner in crime."

"Yeah." McNeil leaned forward, energized by hope. "Maybe."

"I'll pay 'em a visit."

"Hold on, Virg. You're in no shape to mess around with these punks.
I'll get Porky to put somebody on it." "Porky" was Desmond Porcello,
his lawyer.

Actually, Virgil's head was throbbing a little and his arm felt stiff.
He said, "I can get the job done faster and better than some private
heat you'll be paying through the nose for."

"I don't want you getting messed up in this, Virg."

"Messed up how?" Virgil asked, trying not to wince because of his
sudden headache. "We talking pimps here. A cop comes callin', what
can they do?"

The receptionist at Wonderbar, Inc., was busy reading a fat paper-
back with rough-edged pages and a dull gray cover that carried the title
Tristesse. She was so wrapped up in it that he had to clear his throat
twice. That got her to shift her big brown eyes up from the novel.

"Cain I help you?" she asked, the words thick enough with accent
and attitude to suggest that neither English nor politeness were her first
languages.

"I sure hope so," Virgil said.

She stared at him, slowly dropped her sullenness and actually managed to twist her lips into a smile. She wasn't bad-looking when she smiled.

"I'd like to see Mr. Geruso."

"He's not in." She consulted a computer monitor resting on her desk. "Did you have an appointment, Mr.—?"

"Why don't I just park over here and wait for him," Virgil said, taking a few backward steps to a dark purple leather couch. He'd popped a pain pill about twenty minutes before and it was starting to pay off in a pleasant way.

"It's a little late in the day. I'm not sure he'll be back, Mr.—?"

"Bannana-fanna-fo-fanna," he said. The pill was making him giddy. He should have eaten.

"I beg your pardon?" she asked.

"It's Detective," Virgil said, showing her his badge. "Detective Coffin Ed Johnson. You can call me Coffin."

"Annette, were you able to set up an appointment for the Home—" The man who entered the room from the other office had an inch or two on Virgil's six-three. *Bigger and blacker*, the detective thought. And, at the moment, definitely less mellow.

He raised an eyebrow at Virgil's presence and the receptionist replied, "This is a gendarme, Detective Johnson."

"Oh, yeah? What's your business here, Detective?"

"I'd like to talk to Mr. Geruso about the death of a friend of his." Virgil wondered if he could take the big man down. Not one-armed.

"This is about the ho'?"

"Patience Dahl," Virgil clarified.

"Mr. Geruso doesn't know anything about the murder. He was out of the country when the woman got herself killed."

"I'd like to talk to *him* about it."

"Not today. He's gone."

"Gone where?"

"I didn't think to ask."

"Your name is Pickett?" Virgil asked. "Any relation to Wilson?"

"No." Not a hint of humor.

"Were you out of the country, too, when the Dahl girl was killed?"

"What's *your* name again? Johnson?"

"You got it."

"From Hollywood Homicide?"

Virgil grinned and said nothing.

"Well, Detective . . . Johnson, I have already had all the discussions I'm going to on that subject with you cops. Dig?"

"Sure," Virgil said, smiling genially. "It's Mr. Geruso I really want to see anyway."

"Like I say, he's gone for the day. Leave your card with Annette. He'll get back to you."

"I got time to waste and the scenery sure can't be beat." Virgil winked at Annette. "I'll just sit here on the chance he might come back."

"I don't think so," Pickett said. "I'm expecting some business associates any minute. I'd just as soon not have any cops loitering in the office when they arrive. So you can go now."

"Not very cordial," Virgil said, getting to his feet. "Usually a lack of cooperation with law enforcement indicates guilt of some sort. You guilty of anything, Mr. Pickett? Aside from your long, eventful career as a low-rent mack daddy?"

Pickett's eyes flashed, but he held on to his anger. Then he grinned, pointing at Virgil's bandage and sling. "Who put those hurts on you, Detective? I'd like to send him a little gift."

"It wasn't a him," Virgil said, "and the only gift she can use is flowers for her grave."

Pickett's smile grew wider. "Johnson, huh? Bullshit. I know who you are. You're the cop's partner. The one who got his ass shot by some schoolgirl. You a little off your beat, right? All by yourself, like the Lone Ranger. Well, show me some kinda paper or bone on outta here, Detective, before I have you thrown out."

There wasn't much Virgil could say to that. He didn't think he could whup the guy and he wasn't going to shoot him. As he sauntered from the office, Pickett called out, "Your boss know you get off givin' fake names and hasslin' taxpayers?"

Jesus, Virgil thought as he descended the stairs, *that sure went well.*

≡ 41 ≡

Nikki had come home from the office determined to do whatever was necessary to repair her relationship with Virgil. She had two reasons. The primary one was that she was in love with him. But she was a professional animal, too. Adam would be taking the stand the next day and she wanted to be at her absolute best when presenting his crucial testimony, without concern over her personal life affecting her concentration.

She would fix Virgil a nice dinner. Apologize for being too hard on him. Tell him she'd put away the fold-up bed. So what if he had behaved like a fool. Men did that, in the name of honor or courage or some such thing. The reality of the situation—that he was a wounded man who was running around against doctor's orders, sticking his nose into a murder investigation—was beside the point. He felt obliged to that jackass McNeil and she had to live with that.

Even if it killed him?

No. That was the big problem. She'd experienced the death of one lover, a wrenching of the heart that had almost destroyed her. Been there, done that.

Still, when he returned at nightfall, achy and angry, she tried to be the understanding, fully accepting, loving partner. She managed to do it until about fifteen minutes after dinner.

That's when he got to the part of his daily adventures in which he was faced down by Richard Geruso's business partner.

They were sitting on lawn chairs behind her house, sipping iced tea to keep cool while Bird chased fireflies. "Well, what were you expecting him to do," Nikki asked, "except kick you out of his office?"

"A confession would've been nice."

"But you weren't acting in any official capacity. You know well as I, even if he and Geruso confessed to a dozen murders, it wouldn't have done McNeil any good unless they were willing to admit it in a courtroom. So why go there in the first place?"

"I want him and Geruso to know somebody's on their ass."

"Sounds like you didn't make too big an impression."

His eyes narrowed. "Get off my case, woman!" he ordered.

She felt the heat of anger rising in her body. But she held her tongue. There were stronger words he could have used. And he was in discomfort from his damaged body. And she had stepped over the line by giving his already battered male pride another poke. "He was probably blowing smoke with that threat about calling your boss," she said. "Pimps don't do a lot of complaining to cops."

"Geruso did," Virgil said. "And Mac's in the can and nobody's doing nothing to help. Not the detectives working the case. Definitely not the shoeflies sniffin' the behind of your girlfriend D.A."

She continued to control her annoyance with him, even letting the girlfriend comment slide. "The Hollywood homicide detectives aren't about to roll over for Cruella," she said, trying to offer a ray of hope.

"It was never a twenty-four–seven case for them," he said.

"They sure can't be happy about pinning a murder tag next to a shield."

"I don't think they give a rat's ass one way or t'other." He stared at her and said belligerently, "What about you? You care what happens to Mac?"

"If it's important to you, it's important to me."

"Not what I asked. You care that an innocent cop, my partner, is being put through this shit by pimps?"

She considered the question for a few seconds, decided to reply something to the effect that McNeil had saved his life and naturally—

"'Bout it. You don't give a damn," he said impatiently, struggling out of the chair. "You don't like the man. You don't care what happens to him. Hell, you'll probably prosecute him if the other bitch falls out."

Other bitch? *Well*, she thought, *so much for good intentions.*

He was moving through the house now, Nikki following, the big dog keeping pace. "I don't know McNeil from a hot rock," she said to Virgil's departing back. "I don't know if he killed the girl or if he didn't. You say no, I'm willing to believe it. I do know he's a man out of sync, trying to mess up his life any way he can. Now he's messing up your life. Our life."

At the front door, he turned to her. "I'll get my stuff later," he said, an edge to his voice. "Just put it all in the *guest* bedroom."

"Bail out, huh?"

"No," he said in a softer tone, but also with less certainty. "I just want to sleep in my own bed for a while."

Maybe he was expecting her to plead with him not to go. She didn't think so. In any case, she wasn't about to. Instead, with misty eyes, she watched him drive away, so fast he left two smears of rubber on the street.

She dried her eyes on the back of her hand. The big dog watched her with curiosity as she closed the front door quietly and walked into the kitchen where the bottle of vodka rested on a counter. She stared at it for a while, then shook her head. Just because she was in love with a reckless fool didn't mean she should act recklessly, too.

It would not have been fair to Adam. There would be no hangover tomorrow morning. That was the easy part. The hard part would be to put thoughts about Virgil on hold. Hard, but not impossible.

She was reasonably alert and psyched the next morning when Jesse Fallon parked his white Mercedes sedan next to her Mazda RX7 in a self-park lot two blocks away from the Criminal Courts Building. The boy seemed strangely subdued, anxiety registering only in his shifting eyes.

Fallon, as dignified as a deacon, nodded to her and said, "He's ready to do his duty."

"That's good," Nikki said. "Have a solid breakfast, Adam?"

"I ate, like you told me. I don't remember—oh yeah, Donia fixed some kind of oatmeal deal with cut-up bananas."

"Fine, then let's go play dodge the media."

"Just a minute," Fallon said, looking off across the lot. "Here comes another member of the team."

A Day-Glo van emblazoned with the "Team Homeboy" logo drew to a stop beside Fallon's Mercedes. The man who got out was big and sandy-haired, his tan poplin suit straining to keep his body contained. "Nikki, this is Howard Rule, Homeboy's security officer. Nikki Hill."

Rule nodded. His sleepy green eyes stared at her. Not in a lascivious or insolent way. More like they were taking note of her features and filing them away for future reference. He nodded without offering his hand.

A thin white stripe of flesh traced his jawline from right ear to chin. She remembered Virgil's description, "a scar that wouldn't quit."

"If there's too long a wait for Adam to be called," Fallon said, "I may have to leave him in Howard's care."

"Looks like Howard can handle that," she said. "But he'd better leave his weapon in his van. That'll never fly in the courtroom."

She waited for the big man to lock his pistol in the van, then led them down Grand Avenue to an unmarked gray granite building. In its unoccupied main lobby they waited for a service elevator that took them to the basement. There, they traveled along a twisting and turning system of tunnels until they arrived at the basement of the Criminal Courts Building.

They passed the building's maintenance office and a space that had been converted to a makeshift gym, with some padded carpeting and an assortment of weights and exercise machines. A black man Nikki didn't recognize was lying with his back to a bench, working out with barbells. He paid them no mind.

"Ever lose anyone on this route?" Fallon asked, entering the freight elevator.

"Nobody I didn't want to lose," she replied.

At the fifth floor, she ushered them out of the elevator and into a nearly empty courtroom. Nikki nodded to the clerk as they continued on through a rear door that led to the judges' chambers.

They used the judges' special elevator to get to the ninth floor, then made their way to the chambers area.

"You can wait here with Mr. Fallon and Howard until they call for you," Nikki told the boy. "It shouldn't be long."

He gave her an odd, helpless look. "There's something I need to know right now."

"Sure, honey. What?" She was trying to keep the concern off her face.

"Where's the bathroom?"

She smiled. "Right down that hall."

The boy ran to the marked door.

"Think he might need your help," she said to the two men.

"The boy's ten, ma'am," Howard said.

"I just thought . . . he could be losing it in there. Getting sick."

The elderly lawyer smiled. "He's under control. I've never seen a boy more under control. Right, Howard?"

"Check," Howard said.

"I hope he stays that way when Wheeler and Gentry do their number on him."

"They won't know what hit 'em," Fallon said.

≡ 42 ≡

At 8:45 A.M., a white Bentley convertible, year undetermined, disappeared into the basement parking area of Pickett's office building with the big man himself behind the wheel. Parked across Sunset in his aging T-Bird, Virgil could hear the loud classical music from the Bentley's radio grow less and less audible, then cease.

He picked up a clean spiral notebook and carefully printed the time of Pickett's arrival. "Love to see the captains of industry get an early start on the business day," he muttered to himself.

The morning temperature was comfortable but the forecast was 100 degrees by noon. He was wearing a warm-weather outfit, short-sleeve white shirt over tan palm-beach slacks, Reebok sandals without socks. Two sleek black canisters rested on the passenger seat, one filled with hot coffee, one with cold tea. A small Styrofoam chest on the backseat contained bottled water, a couple of Jarlsburg cheese–and–olive sandwiches, a container of carrot chunks and Super Ice packets to keep them all cool and reasonably fresh. To complement all the fluids, a big-mouth gallon jug rested on the rubber mat below the passenger seat.

He was ready to spend as long as it took to get a fix on the comings and goings of the men he'd labeled the Pimp Brothers, Geruso and Pickett.

He yawned and opened his glove compartment, removing a bumblebee black-and-yellow Sony Walkman. He adjusted the headset, positioned his beloved foam rubber pillow behind his back, clicked on an oldies station and filled his head with the sounds of the Dramatics' "Me and Mrs. Jones."

In spite of the effort he'd made to keep his comfort level high, he felt a little out of it—remote. He'd taken a pain pill with his breakfast coffee, but he thought the weird otherworldly sensation he was experiencing was not merely an effect of the narcotic soothing his wounds. It was the Nikki thang. She'd accused him of bailing out, but he didn't think that was what he'd done.

He'd been pretty straight about it. He wanted to sleep in his own bed. Bullshit.

He had definitely bailed. Worse yet, he didn't feel bad about it. He loved her but he wasn't happy being around her these days. She put him on the defensive. He didn't like that, didn't like having to explain himself. He was a man of action, no explanations necessary. Any guy would understand why he was doing what he was doing.

There were women out there who could figure it out, too. Women more beautiful than Nikki. Or as beautiful. Who liked to go out on the town instead of working nights. Simple, uncomplicated, loyal, beautiful women. Out there, just waiting for a handsome, smooth-talking . . .

Damn it. This was the drug. This sure as hell was the drug doing his thinking for him. Putting dumb notions in his head.

He let the R&B harmonies chase those notions away while he stared at the building across the street.

Pickett's white Bentley nosed into the Sunset traffic at 10:21 A.M.

Virgil removed the headset and shifted behind the wheel. He put the T-Bird on hold as the convertible glided past, then swung into the lane behind it, joining the eastbound caravan.

The first stop was a building on Beverly Drive. Pickett entered a street door on which neatly printed letters spelled out T. WALLET & AS-SOCIATES, AIA. The acronym meant nothing to Virgil but like the address and the tasteful façade, it suggested legitimate enterprise. He

sighed. What had he expected? That Pickett would lead him to a cas-
tle in the hills where millionaires worked their wills on abducted teens?
Or maybe some hinky warehouse operation with a basement full of
wetbacks burning poppies?

Pickett emerged with a short white man in his forties carrying a clipboard. A little too round in his rumpled olive drab suit. Hair was thinning. Aviator sunglasses didn't do much for his moon face. A brown
wiggle-worm of a mustache covered most of his upper lip. Not Virgil's idea of a criminal associate.

They drove to a workplace under renovation on Melrose where a
busy crew was prepping the exterior for a repaint. The same location
that had been in the article in the *Times*. Pickett double-parked the Bentley in front and entered the building with the fat guy, waving his arms
angrily and ragging on the guy, who had a pencil out and was looking
unhappy as he jotted down notes on his clipboard.

Fifteen minutes later, Pickett returned to his car alone. Would've been
butter if he'd left the fat guy in a pool of blood at the back of the
house, but as Virgil drove past he could see the beach ball just past the
door, talking animatedly to some rawboned guy in a sawdust-covered
T-shirt and jeans.

Virgil followed Pickett to a wholesale grocery, then a slaughterhouse,
and finally, to a business in the Valley that had shady connections. A-
Plus Restaurant Supplies and Waste Removal was one of the waning
Mafia's last holdings in the city. Unfortunately, as Virgil knew quite
well, every restaurant in town used its services.

He was sitting in the T-Bird, the AC on meat-locker strength, watching the front of the A-Plus warehouse shimmer in the heat rising from
Van Nuys Boulevard, when there was a *tap-tap* on the passenger window.

A grinning man with a large sun-reddened nose, wearing a Panama
hat and a crisp short-sleeve shirt, wiggled his eyebrows at him. Virgil
knew the guy. Unclean Gene Liverdais, a vice cop who was a pal of
McNeil's. When he thought back on it later, he blamed the painkiller
for not immediately realizing what Liverdais was doing there.

Curious, he popped the lock on the passenger door and Unclean

Gene slid in beside him. "Oh, man, like stepping from Death Valley onto an iceberg. I love it."

"Wha'sup, Gene?"

"I heard you were on leave, Virg."

Virgil gave him a vague nod of the head, neither confirming nor denying.

"What the hell you doin' out here?" Liverdais asked.

"Just driving around."

"Like the guy in *Miss Daisy*, huh?"

Virgil stared at him. *Fucking redneck.* "Yeah, just like him."

"You not doing our friend any favor, you know."

"That so?" He still didn't get what Liverdais was doing in his car.

"Not doing yourself any favor either." The pale man shifted so that he could look at Virgil without turning his head. "You don't think Mac killed the hooker. I'm with you on that. But Pickett and Geruso didn't have anything to do with it either. You can take that to the bank."

"You mentioning the Pimp Brothers and goin' to the bank in the same breath, makes me wonder, Gene."

Angry blood rose in Liverdais's face. "Don't wonder too much, bro'. I'm here givin' you a break, because of Mac. Pickett wanted me to call Corben and dump you in the deep shit for fucking with an ongoing investigation."

"You and Pickett and Geruso pretty close, Gene?"

Liverdais glowered at him, wrinkled his nose, and said, "Naw, we're not close. I closed 'em down a bunch of times when they were in the whore business. They're clean now, opening a new club. It's legit and it looks good. I got some fuck-you bucks in it."

"So you're what, their not-exactly-silent partner?"

"Partner, no. Investor, yeah. You should see the list of investors. You'd be surprised who's on board. What I'm saying is you're wasting your time with these guys. You're pissing them off for no reason."

"Think they might offer me a piece of their club?" Virgil asked.

"You never know—oh, I see. You're fucking with me, right?"

"I think we fuckin' with each other."

Liverdais gave him a disgusted look. "Don't be an asshole, Virgil.

These guys are gonna mess you up. If you don't care about your career, think of Mac. He's gonna need you at full strength and clean-as-a-whistle in the courtroom."

"He's gonna need something, with friends like you."

Liverdais frowned. "Fuck you know about it?"

"I know Geruso put Mac in the jackpot."

Liverdais hesitated, then said, "Yeah, well, that was a mistake all around. It'll be corrected."

"Corrected how?"

"Just accept it as done." Liverdais opened the car door and stepped out into the heat. "Now get on outta here, Virgil. Don't make me have to take this to Corben. Do the right thing." He winked and slammed the door.

Virgil watched the vice cop walk back to his sedan and get behind the wheel. What to do? Corben would come down on him, without a doubt. How hard, he wasn't sure, but hard enough to clip his wings.

Hell, he wasn't accomplishing anything clocking Pickett's daily routine. He started the engine and swung out into a U-turn. He glanced at Liverdais's vehicle as he drove away. The vice cop was giving him a thumbs-up sign.

Fuck him and his *Miss Daisy, Do the Right Thing* movie references.

He drove to his apartment in a fury. He wasn't sure when he realized that the effect of the breakfast pill had worn off, but he knew it had. His shoulder was sore and his head ached. At least his mind seemed to be clear again. He tried to think of a way Richard Geruso was going to correct the mistake of fingering Mac. He also wondered what Nikki was doing and if she was thinking of him.

≡ 43 ≡

It was definitely Randy's voice," Adam was saying from the witness chair in the crowded courtroom.

Nikki had been right in saving him for last. He was a perfect prosecution witness. Amazingly poised and precise for a child his age. The jury loved him, she could tell.

She and the boy had begun with his descriptions of the times the defendant had demonstrated anger toward his mother, had shouted at her and even hit her. Then they'd moved on to the night of the murder. He'd given a detailed account of the dinner at Techno's Restaurant, during which "the games were fun. But my mom and Randy were very tense, like something wasn't right but they didn't want me to know about it."

Gerald Wheeler had objected to this bit of speculation and the judge had agreed, so Nikki had the boy provide specific examples of tension at that table. "When the food came, and I got back from playing the games, they'd sort of stopped talking to each other." And, "Finally, Mom hadn't quite finished eating, but Randy just paid the check and stood up and threw his napkin down at the table."

Movement from the defense table caught Nikki's eye. Bingham was shaking his head back and forth and Mimi Gentry was patting his hand to comfort him.

"Do you remember what time it was when you got back to your home?"

"I think Mom said it was ten o'clock. Something like that. I'd taken a shower before we went out, so I didn't have to have another one, which was fine with me. I went to bed."

"Fall right to sleep?"

"No. Actually, I played with Tetron for nearly an hour before I fell asleep."

"What's Tetron?"

"A game. The full title is Battles of Tetron. It's a parallel universe thing. There's a civil war and you choose a side and then try to win the battle."

"How can you be sure you played the game for over an hour before you slept?"

"It's got this readout of how long you've been playing."

"So after an hour, you turned off the game and went to sleep."

"I didn't turn it off," he said. "It has this feature built in: After sixty minutes of inactivity, it turns itself off."

"Did you sleep through the night?"

"No. The shouting woke me."

"Shouting from where?"

"Downstairs."

"Who was doing the shouting?"

"Randy."

"Your bedroom door was open or closed?"

"Open."

"You're sure it was Randy Bingham you heard?"

"Oh, yes. It was definitely Randy's voice."

"Did you hear your mother?"

"No. Just Randy, shouting at her."

"Could he have been shouting at someone else?"

"No. I heard him call her by name. Shelli. 'Damn it, Shelli!' is what he yelled."

"Any idea what time this was?"

"At least an hour after I fell asleep."

"So that would be midnight or so?"

"Yes."

"Then what happened?" Nikki asked.

"I wondered if I should go downstairs. But it sounded like just another argument. Nothing really serious. Maybe if I'd gone downstairs . . . but I didn't. I just lay there and after a while I fell asleep again."

"What woke you the second time?"

"A loud noise."

"Did you have any idea what it was at the time?"

"No. Not then. It just was . . . a noise. Then it was quiet. Except for the mosquitoes. I'm sort of allergic to bug bites. I heard the mosquitoes buzzing near my ear and I grabbed Tetron and jumped out of bed and went into the closet to get away from them."

"Was that something you did a lot, sleep in the closet to get away from mosquitoes?"

"Not a lot. Mom usually was pretty careful about keeping the doors and windows closed, because she knew about my allergy. But I'd done it before."

"How long did you stay in the closet?"

"Until the policeman came and told me . . . about my mother."

He looked like he was on the verge of tears, but he didn't cry.

"You okay, Adam?"

"Uh-huh."

"Adam, are you seeing a doctor regularly?"

"Uh-huh. Dr. Moore."

"What kind of doctor is she?"

"A therapist. I visit her two afternoons a week."

"Why are you seeing Dr. Moore?"

"She's helping me with my, um, bereavement therapy."

This was a half-truth. Dr. Moore was providing grief therapy. But, as she'd informed Fallon, she'd also discovered that Adam was unyielding in achieving goals he'd set for himself and had difficulty handling criticism. He also seemed to care very little about the feelings of oth-

ers. "In an adult," the doctor had explained, "these would be symp-
toms of a narcissistic personality disorder. In a child as brilliant as
Adam, they're probably nothing more than the unfortunate by-products
of precocity, something he'll discard as he matures." But they merited
careful monitoring. That was the main reason for the two sessions per
week.

Initially, Nikki and Fallon had gone back and forth about entering
Adam's therapy into the trial record. "Just the mention of mental disorder could undermine the effect of the boy's testimony," the elderly
lawyer had argued. "And providing Wheeler with the information could
be disastrous. If he's desperate enough, he might even suggest that a
boy with mental problems might also possess homicidal tendencies."

Nikki had set her jaw and replied, "If Wheeler tried to do that to
the orphaned little boy of the murder vic, I'd have those jurors looking at the cracker like he was John Wayne Gacy on a bad day."

"Perhaps, but let's not give him the opportunity," Fallon had said.

"Suppose he finds out about Dr. Moore on his own? Wouldn't it be
better if we presented it to the jury our way?"

Fallon hadn't been convinced. But a few days later, a phone call from
Dr. Moore had changed his mind. A private investigator had visited her
office inquiring about Adam. He'd learned nothing, the doctor insisted,
but Fallon suddenly saw the wisdom in Nikki's plan.

She moved back to give the boy a good view of the defense table
and asked, "Adam, up to the night of the murder, how'd you feel about
Randolph Bingham?"

"I liked him. Not when he got mad. But that wasn't very often. Most
of the time I liked him a lot."

"You have no reason to say anything about him that isn't true?"

"No way. I don't tell lies."

This was a slight departure from his reply to the question in her
office.

"Not even a little fib?" she asked.

His mouth went up in a crooked grin. "Well, everybody tells a lie
now and then. I mean I'd never tell a lie about anything important, that
might get somebody in trouble."

"Okay, Adam, thank you."

She returned to her seat in time to see Wheeler approach the boy, a warm smile on his face. "Sorry to have to keep you in that chair, Adam, but I've got a few questions to ask you. Okay?"

"Okay."

"You ever have nightmares when you dream?" the lawyer asked.

"Sure. Sometimes."

"What's the worst one you can remember?"

"I don't know. I remember being up high, flying maybe, and then suddenly, I couldn't do it anymore and started falling."

"You land?"

"No. I woke up."

"How'd you feel when you woke up? A little fuzzy? Like you weren't sure where you were?"

"No," Adam replied without hesitation. "I knew exactly where I was. In my bed."

Wheeler lost some of his smile. "Everybody takes a few seconds to recover from an intense dream," he said.

"Not me," Adam replied, staring straight at the attorney with child-like intensity.

Daspit chuckled softly beside Nikki.

The big lawyer raised his eyebrows and said, "Well, you're the exception, I guess. Lemme ask you something: On the night your mama went to heaven, what kind of clock did you have in your bedroom?"

"I didn't have any. I used to have one. It broke. I didn't really need it."

"Because you wear a watch?"

"No." Adam held up both arms, showing his wrists. "No watch. There was a clock in the kitchen and a digital readout on my computer monitors. I don't like watches. They get all sweaty."

Wheeler nodded as if he agreed about the sweatiness of watches.

"You told Ms. Hill you didn't tell lies about serious things," he said.

"That's true."

"You said you heard Mr. Bing—Randy talking loud at around midnight. Now that's about as serious as things get."

"That's why I told the truth."

"But if you didn't have any clock or watch in your bedroom, how do you know what time it was?"

"Because of Tetron," Adam said.

Wheeler's face fell. "Your game tells the time?"

"No. But, see, it was turned off when I woke up, and it turns itself off after an hour of inactivity. I mentioned this to Nikki, Miss Hill. You must not have been listening. So I know it was at least midnight. It might have been later. One o'clock. Two o'clock."

Wheeler turned to the defense table and cocked his head. He seemed momentarily speechless. Then he faced Adam again. "When you woke up the second time and heard the loud noise, you said the house fell quiet. Did you hear anyone at all?"

"No. Nothing. Just mosquitoes."

"You didn't hear Randy Bingham?"

"No."

"You have any reason to think he was in the house at that time?"

"He must have been, if he killed my mother."

"But we don't know that he did, do we?"

Wheeler shifted his bulk, cutting off Adam's view of Nikki.

"All we know for sure is that Randy Bingham took you and your mom out to dinner and spent a little time with her after you went to bed. Isn't that correct?"

"I guess it is."

"Did you know your mom was thinking of marrying Randy?"

"No. I didn't know that."

"If you had known, how would you have felt about it?"

"Your Honor," Nikki complained, "what's the relevance here?"

"Mr. Wheeler?" Judge Proody asked.

"Goes to the witness's credibility, Judge."

"Don't take all day with it."

"I won't, Your Honor. Adam, were you a little jealous of Randy Bingham?"

"I don't know what that means, exactly."

"He was taking up a lot of your mom's time, time she might have spent with you. I think I might have resented that. Did you?"

"No. It didn't have anything to do with me. It was between him and my mother. But I resent it now. Because of him, I'll never see her again."

"Your Honor," Wheeler said, trying desperately to keep any hint of whining or annoyance at the boy out of his voice.

The judge expunged Adam's last comment from the record and instructed the jury to ignore it. As if they could ignore the accusation of an orphaned child.

Wheeler knew when to call it a day.

"I'm finished here, Your Honor," he said.

" 'Finished' is the word," Daspit whispered gleefully to Nikki.

The judge dismissed Adam. Fallon must have been called away, because Howard Rule was waiting for him alone. Nikki watched them walk toward the door. Before they reached it, a spectator rushed to the boy and said something to him. It was Jeffrey Bingham, the defendant's brother, his face pale as milk.

Adam drew back and Howard placed a large hand against the man's chest. Bingham took two steps backward and returned to his seat.

Judge Proody said, "Mr. Daspit, Ms. Hill, is that about it?"

Daspit stood. "The prosecution rests, Your Honor."

Nikki continued to watch Adam, who was pointing at Jeffrey Bingham. Howard was staring at the man, his scarred face showing no sign of emotion. Then the security officer bent down, said something to the boy, and they made their exit.

"Then let's call a halt to these proceedings till the morrow," the judge said, a pack of cigarettes in his fist. He'd prepared the lawyers for the short day. A personal matter. Daspit told Nikki the judge was scheduled for a cystoscopic examination for an enlarged prostate; how he found out those things she would never understand.

While the judge, between puffs, instructed the jurors about discussing the case, Nikki ran to catch up to the boy and Howard.

≡ 44 ≡

"Hello, Virgil."

He couldn't believe his ears. Before the phone rang, he'd been lying on his couch, listening to D'Angelo singing about makin' love, trying to ignore a headache, and, in general, feeling frustrated and sorry for himself. "Hi, Nikki," he answered. "Been thinking about you."

"I've been thinking about you, too, Virgil. Is that D'Angelo in the background?"

"Yeah."

"Want to have dinner?" she asked.

He sat upright, too fast and pain shot from his shoulder down his arm. Wincing, he said, "Sure."

"It's quarter to six," she said. "Come over when you can. I'm at Adam's house."

"Where?"

"At Adam's house. In Bel Air."

"I remember," he said, his elation deflating like a punctured inner tube. "We, uh, gonna be able to talk over there?"

"Sure," she said. "Get here when you can."

It took him twenty minutes to shower, brush his teeth, throw on a shirt, slacks, and sandals. It took him another sixteen minutes to arrive at Adam's home off Bellagio Road.

Nikki greeted him at the door. Earlier that afternoon, he'd fallen asleep on the couch and dreamed of her, saw her lying on purple velvet, looking beautiful and seductive. She looked better than that now, in the flesh, wearing her lawyer duds, her thick hair not quite under control.

He wanted to take her in his arms, kiss her, tell her how much he loved her. He made the move, but she stepped back. He said, "I was hopin' we—"

"There's something else has priority," she said.

Perplexed, he followed her through a formal dining room, where three places were set for dinner, into a modern kitchen. Adam was watching Sidney Davis replace a small television set into its nest in the wall, while Sidney's wife, Donia, stirred a bowl of thick, off-white batter. He let Nikki reintroduce him to the Davises, deciding not to remind her of their previous meeting when he'd dropped the boy off after their ride.

In that uncanny way children have of saying what you don't want them to, Adam asked, "What's that bad guy, Geruso, been up to?"

"Nothing much," Virgil said, avoiding Nikki's glare but feeling it all the same.

"I got my own bad guy now," the boy said.

"Say what?"

"Jeffrey Bingham," Nikki said sharply.

"The younger brother?" Virgil was confused.

Nikki suddenly took Virgil's good arm. "Let me show you around the house."

"I'll come, too," Adam said.

"You stay here and help Sidney reinstall the TV," Nikki said.

She moved Virgil out of the room before the boy had a chance to argue and led the way through the house to the backyard. When finally they paused beside the pool, Virgil looked at her expectantly. Nikki said, "This thing with Jeffrey Bingham is the reason I asked you here."

"Oh," Virgil said, caught off-guard enough to let his disappointment show.

"One of the reasons," she amended. "He approached the boy in court today. He told him—his exact words, according to Adam—'Liars get their tongues cut off.'"

"Guy sounds a little psycho," Virgil said, trying to cope with the fact that she had not invited him here to shore up their romance.

"Wise isn't treating it as a serious threat. He says Adam must have misinterpreted Bingham's comment."

"That's possible, isn't it?"

"Not if you saw the guy, Virgil. He's pretty scary."

"You think he's really gonna try to cut off Adam's tongue?"

"I think he's capable of doing some kind of harm to the boy."

"Wise won't approve police protection?"

She shook her head. "No way. He was wavering, then that fool Peter Daspit started going on about Jeffrey Bingham being a respected young businessman probably blowing off steam, no big deal, just a sure sign that we're headed for a conviction. Bullshit, bullshit, bullshit."

"And you're lookin' to me for what?" Virgil asked.

"What's your professional opinion? Is Adam in danger?"

"I'd be a little more worried if Bingham's threat had been more realistic. A man says 'I'm gonna kill you,' he might mean it. A man says, 'I'm gonna get me a knife and hold you down and yank out your tongue so I can cut it off' . . ." He paused, remembering the elder Bingham's office with its great white hunter trophies and weapons. Who knew if his son went hunting with a knife?

"On the other hand," he said, "nobody ever got hurt being over-cautious."

"My point exactly," she said. "Will you do it?"

"Do what?"

"Stay here and watch over the boy till his security guy can get it together to move in for a while. You remember, with the scar. Howard Rule. He told Fallon he could start in a day or two."

His immediate reaction was to tell her no. He'd be of no use to Mac saddled with nursemaid duties. Still, he knew how important this was to her and he didn't want to let her down. At least not let her down hard.

"I'm not at full strength," he said. "I'm not even at half strength. Guardin' somebody, especially a very active little boy, is—"

He was interrupted mid-excuse by Adam appearing at the door. "Dinner's ready," he said.

"You're not going to do this for me?" Nikki asked Virgil.

"I didn't say I wouldn't." He cursed himself for not telling her his mind. "We'll talk about it some more, after the kid's bedtime."

"Talk about what?" Adam asked.

"Just stuff Nikki and I have to figure out," Virgil said. "What's for dinner?"

As she served them, Donia apologized for the fare, which was country chicken with cornmeal waffles. "Sorta breakfasty, but it's one of Adam's favorites."

The boy had taste, Virgil decided as he inhaled the myriad odors—lemon and dill and chives and even a hint of sherry. "The Davises aren't joining us?" he asked Nikki after Donia made her exit.

She shook her head. "They say they're more comfortable dining in the kitchen."

Must be confusing for them, he thought. The Integration Generation. All that crap going down in the fifties and sixties. The government telling you equality was your natural right, but the reality of the situation was that if you tried to exercise too much of that equality, you'd get your ass kicked. He used to see it in his daddy. The old man didn't want to be an Uncle Tom. But he wasn't sure he wanted to be a dead Medgar Evers either. Caught somewhere in between.

"You okay, Virgil?" Adam asked.

"Sure."

"You seem a little . . . quiet."

"I'm fine. When food's this good, I'd rather eat than talk."

"Car's okay?"

"Sure."

"Have you talked to your partner? Is he all right?"

"He's doing okay, all things considered." Spearing a small piece of chicken, Virgil asked Nikki, "You hear anything around the office about Mac?"

"No. But I'm not exactly a member of Dana's in-crowd."

"Wise doesn't mention the case?"

She shook her head. "It's Dana's show. Wise would throw a wrench into it, if he could. At this point, it's out of his hands. She's got a bunch of staffers working for her. The rest of us, Wise included, are out of the loop."

"Dana the one who looks like Cruella De Vil?" Adam asked.

"Uh-huh."

"Is she evil?"

Nikki grinned. "I'm not sure how evil she is. She's just going for the gold, the only way she knows how."

Adam turned to Virgil. "But the guy we followed, Geruso, he's evil. Right?"

Virgil swallowed the last of his chicken. Even if Gene Liverdais was telling it straight about Geruso trying to "correct his mistake," the man was a cockroach. "Yeah," he told Adam, "I think he qualifies. Him and the dude he works with."

"Why do you think he picked on Mac?" Nikki asked.

"To get the Dahl case closed."

"Could be he cared for the girl."

"That must be why he turned her out."

"Love is strange," Nikki said.

"No love motivatin' that man."

"He's evil," Adam said with finality. "A bad guy."

"Enough 'evil' talk," Nikki said. "Let's switch to something a little more fun."

"We could play 3-D chess," Adam said eagerly. "At least two of us could. The other can watch and play winner."

Before Virgil or Nikki could reply, the boy had bounded from the table, to get the 3-D chessboard.

"You play," Nikki said to Virgil. "I'll help Donia clear the table, then come back and watch."

She was up and disappearing into the kitchen with her hands full of dirty plates before he could explain that he had no idea how to play chess, regular or 3-D.

Adam returned with an electronic game board. He'd barely turned it on, filling the screen with a three-tiered chessboard, when the phone rang.

The ringing ceased almost immediately, somebody picking up the call elsewhere in the house. Adam turned the board to face Virgil. "Have you played this before?"

Virgil shook his head.

"It's not as hard as it seems," the boy said.

Virgil waited for him to continue. When he didn't, the detective looked up and saw that Adam was staring at Donia, who was approaching with a cordless phone.

"Somebody for you, Adam."

The boy seemed puzzled. "Who is it?"

"He didn't say. Just that it was important."

"Not too many people know this number," the boy said, taking the phone. He pressed the "talk" button and said, "This is Adam."

He listened for a few beats, then looked at Virgil in alarm. He held out the phone for the detective to hear.

". . . shoot you in the throat, the mouth, . . .the face—"

Virgil grabbed the phone from the boy. "Who the hell is this?" he demanded.

There was a click, then silence.

He dialed *69. No response. The call had come from either an access-blocked phone or a cellular.

Nikki returned to the table and saw the looks on their faces. "What happened?"

Virgil placed the phone on the table and said, "Adam's not gonna have to settle for a one-armed bodyguard. He just qualified for official police protection."

Nikki made two calls. The first was to Ray Wise, who reluctantly agreed to approve a police guard for the boy. He would not agree to send an investigator to Jeffrey Bingham's apartment. "Not on just the kid's say-so that the voice sounded like his."

The second call was to Jesse Fallon. Virgil heard Nikki assure the lawyer that the situation was under control. A police officer would be in the house and she was going to spend the night there herself. There was no need for him to come.

The boy was sound asleep in his bed by the time the LAPD officer arrived. He decided to occupy a couch in the study, from which to make tours of the interior and the grounds every half hour.

"Want me to stay?" Virgil asked Nikki at the front door.

She gave him a weary smile. "We need some time together. But not tonight."

"I figured. I just didn't want to walk away again without asking." He tried to draw her close with his good arm, but she twisted free. "Call me," she said.

"I will."

"Thanks for coming."

"Sure." He stared at her. "I love you."

"That's good. Call me," she said again.

Outside, sitting in his car waiting for the air conditioner to work its magic, he mumbled, "I tell her I love her and she says 'Good.' That's the same as her sayin' 'I love you' right back, isn't it?" Sighing, he put the car in gear and drove off into the hot, still, lonely L.A. night.

≡ 45 ≡

The defense began its case by calling former Deputy District Attorney Charles Guidry to the stand. He was a trim man in an expensive, dark gray suit, pale blue shirt, and yellow tie. His olive-complexioned, unlined face made him look younger than his forty-eight years. Nikki had discovered, during their brief conversation at his office, that since leaving the district attorney's office he had had an uneventful but fruitful career in contract law. She had also learned what Gerald Wheeler's first questions to him demonstrated: His sympathies were firmly with the deceased. Wheeler wasted no time in declaring him a hostile witness.

"At the time you were prosecuting Ms. Dietz's husband, Jerome Noyes, for assault on one Ms. Donna Childers, did any information surface regarding Ms. Dietz's personal life?"

"Our main interest was in Mr. Noyes's personal life," Guidry replied. "Ms. Dietz was not actually involved in the proceedings at all. The charges against Mr. Noyes had been made by Ms. Childers, who was his mistress at the time."

"Uh-huh. But the trial did turn up some information on Ms. Dietz, did it not?"

"One of our investigators testified that medical records suggested she had been physically abused by Mr. Noyes, as had their son, Adam."

Nikki felt more anger for the long-dead man and a renewed sadness for Adam.

"Yes, yes," Wheeler said, losing patience. "And what did Mr. Noyes testify about his wife?"

Guidry gave Wheeler a look of disgust. "He said what wife-beaters usually say, that she deserved it."

"Why specifically did he claim she deserved his wrath?" When Guidry hesitated, the defense attorney added, "If you're having trouble remembering, I can provide you with the trial record. You can read it to us."

With obvious reluctance, Guidry replied, "He said she had been unfaithful."

"Said it under oath, did he not?"

"Yes."

"I imagine you would have liked to have proven him a liar?"

"Yes," Guidry replied.

"Did you assign someone to investigate his claim?"

"Yes."

"And what did your investigator discover?"

"She'd been seeing another man."

"That's a quaint term, suh. 'Seeing.' What do you mean by it, exactly?"

"Objection, Your Honor," Nikki said. "What's the point of this line of questioning?"

"I've been wondering that myself," Judge Proody said. "Ms. Hill, why don't you and Mr. Wheeler join me here for a quick chat?"

Nikki approached the bench wondering why she always felt wary answering summons to sidebars even when she wasn't the one who was being put on the spot.

The jurist scowled at Wheeler and said in a low tone, "Let's assume you get this witness to say the late Ms. Dietz had hot pants, Counselor. Explain the relevance."

"We plan to prove that Ms. Dietz had several lovers, any one of whom might have murdered her after Mr. Bingham left her alive and well."

"There's no evidence that anyone else was there that night," Nikki said.

"Mr. Wheeler," the judge said, "do you plan on introducing us to these lovers? Or are you just gonna fantasize about 'em?"

"It's our plan to put them on the stand."

Judge Proody nodded. "All right. I'm overruling your objection, Ms. Hill."

When she returned to her seat, Daspit gave her a quizzical look.

"Wheeler says he's got witnesses who were knocking boots with Shelli Dietz," she whispered.

"We'd better check that list again."

"No kidding."

In the witness box, Charles Guidry was saying, "Our investigator established she'd spent several evenings in the company of a fellow artist named Charles de la Tour."

"Did they go to dinner, see a movie—what?"

"She visited his apartment."

"Thank you, Mr. Guidry."

As Wheeler walked to his table, Nikki rose and headed for the witness box.

"Let's get specific, Mr. Guidry. Was Mrs. Dietz sleeping with Mr. de la Tour?"

"Not to my knowledge," Guidry replied.

"She and Mr. de la Tour were both artists. The evenings spent in his apartment—could those have been business meetings?"

She heard Wheeler emit a loud chuckle. "Try to ignore the cynicism of the defense attorney, Mr. Guidry," she said. "He just assumes the worst of everybody."

Guidry smiled. "I have no reason to believe the meetings in Mr. de la Tour's apartment were anything but business," he said.

"Have you any actual involvement in the murder case we are presently trying?"

"No, I don't."

"Do you know anything about the case itself that would be of interest to the court?" she asked.

"Not to my knowledge," Guidry said.

"Then I have no further questions, Your Honor."

"I've just a few more," Wheeler said. He didn't bother to leave the defense table. "Mr. Guidry, do you have any idea where Mr. de la Tour is today?"

Guidry hesitated. "I read that he passed away. Maybe two years ago."

"By fair means or foul?"

"Automobile accident, as I recall."

"Pity. Else we mighta been able to get him to tell us about those 'business' meetin's in his *one-bedroom* apartment."

≡ 46 ≡

Virgil started out the day by dumping his pain pills down the toilet.

He wasn't used to failure and frustration on either the professional or personal front. This double-whammy convinced him that his compass had gone out of whack. He hoped it was a temporary condition brought on by the damned pills. He preferred pain to stupidity and ineffectualness. In fact, he wasn't feeling much pain.

His goal for the day was to get back on track. Nikki was in court, so until the noon recess there wasn't much he could do to straighten out that situation. He phoned Adam and discovered that the rest of the night had been uneventful. "A second policeman came by this morning and he and Officer Garnett, the one who'd been on duty all night, had breakfast with me. Nikki had already gone to work." The boy added, "Howard came by to rig up a recorder on the phone, in case I get another call, but it's really crude, not digital or anything."

Smiling, Virgil told the boy he'd drop by and see him when he could.

His next phone call was not so short or so pleasant.

It was to Porky Porcello, McNeil's lawyer. He and the partners in his firm had represented other members of the force and Virgil had met him a few times. An effective defense attorney with the kind face of a professional pitchman. He sounded like he was late for court. "What can I do for you, Detective?" he asked with an edge of impatience.

"You get any good news about Mac's case in the last day or so?"

"Good news? Like what?"

"Like Richard Geruso making a move to shift the weight off Mac?"

"What sort of move?"

"I don't know. And my source isn't very reliable."

"Mr. Geruso hasn't approached us."

"Could he have done something to shake up the D.A.'s case?"

"I can't imagine what it would be," Porcello said. "He's not really a player."

"Come again?"

"From what I've been able to divine from Lady Lowery's closed camp, he's being treated like a pariah."

"Isn't he responsible for Mac being in jail?"

"Oh, yes. He brought Mac to Dana's attention. Then she and her merry band of investigators and Internal Affairs ferrets dug up the dirt they needed to have him arraigned. Exit Mr. Geruso, who has morphed from whistle-blower to embarrassment. What made you think he wanted to help Mac?"

"A cop told me. I figured it for bullshit, but the cop's a friend of Mac's."

"What's his name?"

"Gene Liverdais."

"Detective Liverdais is on the list of witnesses for the prosecution."

Virgil felt a headache coming on. Or maybe it was just pieces of information breaking off and joining other pieces.

"Mac was a little surprised," the lawyer continued. "He said they were friends, but he also knew that Internal Affairs has been on Liverdais's case. My surmise is they found dirt on him and agreed to overlook it in return for his cooperation."

"Cooperate how?"

"He introduced Mac to Patience Dahl."

"Sweet mama! Liverdais knew her?"

"Intimately. But calm down, Detective. That ended a while before she died and he's got an ironclad for the time of the murder. Five other poker players. Four of them cops. Two of them genuine friends of Mac's."

"That son of a bitch. Handin' me that jive about Geruso's change of heart, just to get me off of . . ." A thought occurred to him. "Counselor, you got any idea what the IAG has on Liverdais?"

"Liverdais's Vice. I assume it has to do with hookers or drugs."

"Let's make another assumption," Virgil said, "since he was rompin' with a ho' from Geruso's stable and since Geruso's partner sicced him on me."

"A crooked cop, procurers, and Internal Affairs, all conspiring to bring down an honest cop," Porcello said. "I do like that scenario. What I need now is the glue that binds them together."

"Geruso could provide that."

"So could Liverdais or the other man, Pickett."

"Of the three, I'd say Geruso is the weakest. And he's responsible for Mac's problem. I'll feel him out."

"Okay. But understand, though the incarceration may be unpleasant for Mac, the case against him is weak. Don't do anything that Dana Lowery could use against us."

"Don't worry," Virgil said. "I'm just gonna sweet-talk the man a little."

"I'm sorry, sir. Monsieur Geruso is out of the office." The receptionist's French accent seemed even thicker over the telephone.

"Where can I reach him?" Virgil asked, using a gruff, slightly guttural voice.

"I'm afraid he's unavailable."

"Lissen, lady, I'm Inspector Faarnah, at the building on Melrose. I don't talk to Geruso in the next five minutes, I'm closing this construction down." He hoped that Geruso didn't happen to be at the construction site.

"*Who* are you?"

"Inspector Faarnah. I've counted forty-two code violations. I can nail a board over the front door now, but I wanted to talk to Geruso before I put him out of business."

"Actually, sir, I believe it is Monsieur Pickett you should speak with."

Damn, Virgil thought. "Minute," he told her. He placed his hand loosely over the speaker and called out to the wall of his apartment, "Geruso, you sure?" He said into the phone's speaker, "The construction chief says Geruso is the man."

"Really?" She sounded surprised. "Well, both he and Monsieur Pickett are attending a meeting in Beverly Hills."

"Good. If this bozo's got it wrong, I can talk to Pickett about it. What's the number?"

"I will have Monsieur Geruso phone—"

"Hold it!" Virgil shouted at the wall. Then back to the receptionist, "Look, lady, I can't waste any more time. They're trying to sneak uninsulated wiring though these drywalls. Maybe Geruso or Pickett can set 'em straight. All I can do is shut 'em down. Zat what you want?"

She wasn't easy. Virgil had to give her that.

"I would be glad to—"

"Let's have your name, lady. Case they try to come down on me for not giving proper notification before I send these boys home."

She hesitated only slightly. "Monsieur Geruso is at Selmar Advertising," she said angrily, following that with a phone number. Then she broke the connection.

Grinning, Virgil dialed the number. This receptionist was much more cordial and cooperative. She was happy to give him the ad agency's address.

Fifteen minutes later, he was pushing through the glass double doors to Selmar Advertising with offices in, if the bronze wall plaque were to be believed, Beverly Hills, New York, Chicago, Atlanta, London, Paris, Tokyo, and Beijing. The last was a recent addition, shinier than the rest.

The redheaded, green-eyed receptionist did not seem too impressed by his arm sling, faded Sir Mix A Lot "Let's G" T-shirt, khaki shorts, and sandals. "Yes?" she asked with her mouth, while the rest of her said "No."

"Ricky Geruso is in a meeting here," he said. "I have to talk to him."

The probability of his being an associate of Ricky Geruso, a client, earned him a smile. She lifted the imitation tortoiseshell telephone on her desk and asked, "Who shall I say wants him?"

"Gene Liverdais," Virgil replied, returning her smile.

She pressed two keys on the phone and relayed that information to the person who answered. "He's coming right out," the receptionist informed Virgil.

Geruso stormed through a door at the rear of the reception room, obviously annoyed. He looked around the room and grew even more annoyed. "Where is he?" he asked the receptionist.

Confused, she pointed to an advancing Virgil.

"What bullshit is this?" Ricky Geruso asked. Then he answered his own question. "You're the guy. McNeil's partner." He grinned. "Pickett really hates your ass."

Virgil had been planning on feeding him a lie about Liverdais selling him out to save himself from Internal Affairs. But the grin at Pickett's discomfort changed his mind.

"Your partner hates everybody's ass. Except his own."

"What's that supposed to mean?"

He had the man's attention. The receptionist's too. Her hand was moving toward the telephone.

"It means," he told Geruso, "Pickett's getting ready to throw you to the wolves."

"Bullshit," Geruso said, without much conviction.

The receptionist was whispering into the phone. To whom?

"He's tired of having a partner. I know. I've been keeping an eye on him, talking to people he talks to."

"Like who?"

Damn. *Throw out a name*, Virgil commanded himself, *any name*. "Miss Paris, France, in your office. You know Pickett's been doin her, right?"

He figured one of them had to be doing her. If it was Pickett,

Geruso would think he knew what he was talking about. If it was Geruso, he'd be jealous enough to want to know more.

"So? Pickett does anything that moves."

"He also tells her stuff. Like he wants you out of the business. Real bad."

Geruso stared at him for a beat. "She tells you what Pickett tells her?"

"Women like me, what can I say? My arm's the only part of me in a sling. Look, I got a way for you come out of this in good shape." He took a card from his pants pocket. "Here's my number. Gimme a call."

"Fuck you. You're scammin' me." But he took the card.

The rear door opened and Pickett stepped through it.

"You got nothing to lose," Virgil told Geruso. "Everything to gain."

Pickett walked stiffly to the receptionist and asked, "You got any se-curity guards in this building, honey? We may need 'em to eject that crazy bastard over there."

"Hey, Pickett!" Virgil called out. "My man. How about just one cho-rus of 'In the Midnight Hour'?"

Pickett glared at him.

"No? I guess I'll leave then." Virgil smiled at the totally perplexed receptionist and thanked her for all her help.

Then he got the hell out of there.

≡ 47 ≡

When Jennifer "Jenny" Mapes took the stand as a witness for Randolph Bingham's defense, Nikki was not surprised to see that Adam's former nanny had been treated to a makeover. Her spiky hair had been softened, cut to frame her face in a modified pixie. The jet-black wash-basin dye job had been replaced by a professional dark brown with highlights. Her makeup was subtle and the bra under her conservative designer dress did wonders to rein in her ample bosom.

Guided by Mimi Gentry, she soberly did her part in adding to the victim's defamation. "Shelli was sort of a free spirit, you know. Walked around the house with not much on, no matter who happened to be there. Topless, sometimes. Sometimes in bra and panties."

"What was her social life like? Active?"

"I'd call it active."

"She went out with lots of men, other than Mr. Bingham?" Mimi Gentry asked.

"When she and Ran—Mr. Bingham got serious, she blew off most of the others."

"But not all?"

"No. She still saw other guys every now and then."

"Had them to the house?"

"For dinner sometimes. Not a lot."

"Did they stay for more than dinner?"

It continued on in that general direction, with Nikki objecting to the Mapes girl's more offensive speculations, until Gentry returned to her chair, satisfied with the blanket of innuendo she'd woven.

Nikki wasted no time in punching holes in the blanket.

"Ms. Mapes, you said the murder victim went out with a lot of men before she and Mr. Bingham established a relationship. You did tell my co-counsel and myself that you'd never observed Ms. Dietz having sex with any of these men, right?"

"That's right."

"To your knowledge, did the murder victim ever have an intimate, sexual relationship with anyone other than the accused?"

"Well, her husband, I guess. There's Adam."

"Aside from that."

"No."

Nikki smiled. "Your comments about what the victim wore around the house, was this her usual manner of dress?"

"I don't understand the question."

"Did she go around topless all the time?"

"Not all the time. No."

"When she had friends over?"

"She didn't have friends over much."

"When she did?"

"No. She was dressed then."

"So when was it that she would take off her blouse?"

"Usually when she was working. Said it made her feel free. Something like that."

"In other words, she did it to facilitate her creative work, not for purposes of sending erotic signals to anybody who happened to be present?"

"I don't understand."

"Was she trying turn anybody on?"

"Well, the gardener is about a hundred and ten and the pool guy is gay. And she sure wasn't trying to turn *me* on."

"So that's a 'no' answer?"

"I guess."

Nikki decided to push her luck. "How do you feel about Randy Bingham? Do you like him?"

"He's a very nice man."

"Did you ever have romantic feelings toward him?"

"Roman—no. Not exactly. I mean, he was Shelli's, no."

"But you liked him?"

"Yes."

"Was it your impression that Shelli Dietz cared for him?"

"Well, yea-ah." She raised her inflection on the second syllable, Valley Girl–style. "She was going to marry him."

"You knew that."

"Sure. Everybody did."

"She told you?"

"No."

"Randy Bingham told you?" Nikki asked, a touch of surprise in her voice.

"Uh-huh."

"Did he tell Adam too?"

"No. Not when I was around."

"Where was Adam when Randy told you about his marriage plans?"

"Home, I guess."

"Where were you?"

"My apartment."

Nikki cocked her head. Had she gone out looking for quartz and stumbled onto gold? "Where was Randy?" she asked.

"His place. It was over the phone."

Nikki felt a slight letdown. But only slight. "Did you and he speak often on the phone?"

Jenny hesitated. "No. Just that once."

"Why did he call you?"

"He didn't. I called him."

"You have his phone number?"

"I . . . got it from Shelli's address book."

"And the reason you called him?"

"I just didn't think she was being fair."

"How was she unfair?" Nikki asked.

"She, you know, the other guys."

"The men she went out with?"

"Well, yea-ah."

"You felt that her seeing other men was unfair to Randy Bingham."

"Well, it *was*. And I just thought he should know."

"What did you tell him, exactly?"

"That Shelli was going out with other guys and, you know, slutting around."

"What was his reaction?"

"Objection!" Wheeler called out. "Calls for conjecture."

"I'll rephrase," Nikki said. "What did he say after you told him?"

"He thanked me, but said I shouldn't worry. Those men meant nothing to Shelli. He and Shelli were in love and they going to be married."

"When was this?" Nikki asked.

"It was after that Tuesday night Shelli went out with the creepy artist guy. I guess maybe the Wednesday before . . . it happened."

"The murder?"

"Uh-huh."

"So what you're saying is that six days before Shelli Dietz was murdered, you informed Randy Bingham that she was being unfaithful to him?"

"I guess."

Nikki stepped back from the stand. She'd heard athletes felt a physical rush of emotion when they entered the zone of perfection. She felt it now.

She was about to turn the witness back to the defense when she thought of one more thing she'd forgotten to ask the girl during their Q & A in Daspit's office. It was always a risk to raise a question in court without knowing the answer, but she couldn't see any danger in this particular one. And her luck was running full tilt.

"You told us you were visiting your aunt and cousin in Agoura the night of the murder." It was a suburban community west of Los An-geles. "Weren't you scheduled to sit with Adam that night?"

"At first, that was the plan. Then Shelli said she wouldn't be need-ing me that night. So I drove out to my aunt's."

"Do you know what made her change her mind?"

"We were all by the pool that Saturday, the Saturday before the . . . before it happened. Randy was talking to Shelli about them having din-ner on Monday night. He was acting very sweet and kinda shy and he said, 'Might as well give Miss Jenny the night off.' And Shelli said, 'Then it'll be three for dinner,' meaning that Adam would be having dinner with them. Randy said that'd be okay. So she told me I could have the night off. And I said that since I had Tuesdays off it meant I'd have two nights off in a row and she said 'Mazel tov.' "

"But it was actually Randy Bingham who suggested you take the night off?"

"I guess," Jenny Mapes answered, looking toward the defense table to see if she'd made some kind of mistake.

"Thank you, Ms. Mapes," Nikki said and returned to her chair.

Mimi Gentry took her time strolling toward her witness.

"Ms. Mapes, on that night you and Randy Bingham had your phone conversation about Ms. Dietz, did he sound surprised?"

"No."

"Did he sound hurt or upset?"

"Not really."

"The Saturday you just mentioned to Ms. Hill, that was three days after your phone conversation?"

"About that, I guess."

"What was the general mood on that day as far as you observed?"

"It was a good day. Everybody seemed happy."

"What about Ms. Dietz and Mr. Bingham? They were happy?"

"Sure. They got along great."

"You didn't sense any tension between them?"

"Nothing like that. They were very lovey. Holding hands."

"So, as far as you observed, your phone call to him may even have brought them closer together?"

"I hadn't thought about that, but that's true."

"Did you ever see Mr. Bingham get mad at Ms. Dietz?"

Jenny shook her head emphatically.

"Could you answer the question for the stenographer?" Gentry asked.

"I never saw him mad about anything, even when he had reason to."

Gentry's ears perked up. "What kind of reason?"

"Well, Shelli could be a real bi—a real difficult person when she was in one of her moods. But Mr. Bingham was always very nice to her."

"Adam Noyes testified that he saw Mr. Bingham strike his mother."

"Well, I never saw such a thing. Adam can get pretty heavy into fantasy."

Nikki was on her feet. "Speculation. Move to strike, Your Honor."

"Your Honor, Ms. Mapes is a professional childcare provider who observed Adam Noyes on a daily basis for a long time."

Judge Proody nodded. "Overruled. The statement stands. Continue, Ms. Gentry."

"I'm finished, Your Honor. Thank you, Ms. Mapes, for your honesty."

Nikki looked at the jury members. Some of them were scribbling in their notebooks. Some were idly watching Jenny Mapes walk across the room. One man looked like he was having stomach problems. What were they thinking?

≡ 48 ≡

Since Ricky Geruso was a night person, his nooners usually took place around 3:00 or 4:00 P.M.

That day, the lucky recipient of his attention was the baby-faced hooker, Maggie. Lately he'd been spending quite a lot of time in the little apartment she shared with Carrie at the Vic. Ordinarily, he preferred to get serviced on his home turf where he felt more in control. But the Hotel Victoria, which he and Pickett were within two hundred grand of owning outright, was sort of a home away from home. It had been his workplace for nearly four years. He felt comfortable there and it was convenient; just a few blocks from the new offices. He could hop into the Diablo and be at Maggie's door in less than five minutes.

She welcomed him appropriately.

She was wearing her Victoria's Secret teddy over her rooftop-bronzed skin and she smelled of Faconnable Eau de Toilette, his favorite cologne (a trick she told him she picked up from *Cosmo*). She was so adoring and eager that it almost made up for his disappointment that her roommate wouldn't be joining them.

To compensate, she gave him a massage, a "sensuous massage," based on an instructional video of the same name.

"That must be one hell of a tape," he said, after just a few minutes of lying facedown on towels spread over her bed while she rubbed scented oil into various nooks and crannies of his body.

"I've added a few little touches of my own," she cooed into his ear, leaning over him, completely naked now, letting her breasts do their own massaging.

"I needed this."

"I could tell. You were full of knots."

"Goddamn Pickett."

She did not join in with any anti-Pickett commentary. He liked that. It meant she was smart. A dumb cooze would've sided with him. Not Maggie. Maggie understood that the man was his partner. He could rag on the black son of a bitch all he wanted, but eventually, their differences would be settled in the name of good business. Then, a dumb cooze would wind up on the wrong side of the bed.

"Well, whatever's going on with you boys," Maggie said, chopping his back with the side of her hands, "it's got you tense as a steel cable."

"Guy's on my ass."

"Can't say I blame him. It's a nice ass to be on."

He smiled. "There's a difference. I like you on my ass, 'cause I can sort of spin around like this and—"

"Oh, baby." She closed her eyes. "it's like a steel cable."

A half hour and several lines of extraordinary coke later, he sniffed and said, "It's not my fault."

"What's not, baby?"

"The cop. The one who's bustin' Pick's chops."

"I think I'll visit the powder room, hon."

"Sure. Go." So she didn't want to hear about Pickett or the cop. That was okay. He probably shouldn't be talking to her about it. The cop, what was his name, Sykes? Fucking guy tracked him to the office of that PR fruitcake. Tried playing him with some bullshit about Pickett. Then Pickett sees 'em talking and puts the guy on the shit list.

"Know what I'm thinking," Pickett had told him when they got back to their office. "I'm thinking this Sykes is turning into a serious fly in my cornflakes."

"What's the guy's story, he can't let it rest?" Ricky had asked. "He and McNeil fuckbuddies, or what?"

"They're partners, Rick. 'Member what Bogart said about partners in that flick? Somebody fucks with your partner, you do something about it."

"Yeah, well, that's the movies," Ricky had said.

"You mean you wouldn't do something if somebody fucked with me?" Pickett had asked.

"Yeah, I'd do something," Ricky had replied, wondering if Pickett had overheard anything the cop had been telling him.

"Well, this prick Sykes is messing with your partner," Pickett had said. "So do something."

"Me? Like what?"

"Be creative."

"Kill him? A cop?" Ricky had asked, alarmed.

"Shit no. That'd just make things worse. You put McNeil on the spot. Do Sykes."

Ricky was pleased that Pickett had assumed he'd framed McNeil. It was a compliment of sorts. In the etiquette book of the underworld, dropping a dime on a guy was acceptable only if you'd framed him first. Still, he didn't want to make a habit out of fucking up cops.

"He's the fly in *your* cornflakes," he'd told Pickett. "Do him yourself."

Pickett had cocked his head and he smiled. "You're right," he'd said. "Time for me to take a hand in cleanin' up this shit you tracked to our door."

Ricky didn't like that particular smile of Pickett's. Showing teeth, like a shark swimming into chum. He wondered if that fucking cop had been on to something. Maybe Pickett *was* setting him up.

Maggie was back on the bed, beside him, strong little hands kneading that spot just below his neck. "Honey, you're all tense again," she said.

•   •   •

It was nearing 5:00 P.M. when Ricky's cell phone began chirping on the table beside Maggie's king-size. It was the French bitch announcing that Pickett needed him back at the office.

"Why?"

"There are people here from K-line Software. Monsieur Pickett says he needs you to 'crunch numbers.'"

"Yeah? Annette, tell me something. You know that cop Sykes?"

"He was in the office."

"Whaddaya think of him?"

"I don't," she replied. "Monsieur Pickett is anxious for you to get here."

She hung up. Ricky began to think she might be fucking the cop. And if that part was true . . .

He watched Maggie inhale a few lines off the other bedside table. Beautiful body, moist with sweat. It meant nothing to him. He was sexed out.

"Want some?" she asked.

"No. I gotta straighten up." He reached a hand into his pants pocket and felt Virgil Sykes's card. "I got a decision to make."

As Ricky got off the Victoria's elevator at the basement parking level, he heard a distinct two-part sound. *Twang-snap.* It was familiar. Nothing alarming. A tiny door opening and closing? Something like that.

He looked at the now silent parking area. It was still a little early for the after-work crowd. Just four other vehicles. A Camry, an Electra, an old Mustang convertible, some goofy looking hunk of tin he couldn't identify. Nothing in the same league as the Diablo.

He slid behind the sports car's steering wheel, smelled the satisfying expensive odor of new, butter-soft leather. He caught a whiff of something else, something abrasive. Ammonia? Some kind of cleaning shit. Phew. Time to go.

The machine's powerful engine started up immediately. He loved the roaring noise it made bouncing off the concrete walls and ceiling as the Diablo zoomed toward daylight. Then he was on Sunset, mixing with the traffic. He was passing a gas station at the La Cienega intersection when he suddenly realized what had caused the *twang-snap.* The closing of the little metal door leading to the sports car's gas cap.

But why would—?

It was as much of the question that his mind could form before the Diablo exploded in a flash of white and yellow and red, showering the traffic along Sunset with pieces of plastic and metal and rubber and chrome. And Ricky.

Virgil had spent the afternoon observing the Wonderbar building. He was parked half a block to the west along Sunset when the Pimp Brothers returned from the ad agency in the Bentley convertible. Pickett seemed to be giving his partner a full passel of angry words. Shortly thereafter, Ricky had left the building in his red sports car. Virgil toyed with the idea of following him, but decided against it. It was Pickett he was interested in. If nothing came of that, maybe he'd invite the snotty French receptionist to dinner. It would shake Pickett's tree and give Ricky food for thought.

At 4:30, when parked cars were no longer allowed on that particular stretch of Sunset, he moved to another vantage point, the deserted lot of a sour-luck hunk of real estate where restaurants and clubs opened and closed on nearly a quarterly basis. He'd barely gotten settled when there was a furious explosion on Sunset just to the east.

The T-Bird shook from the concussion. This was followed immediately by *pings* and *clangs* of metallic shards bouncing off the roof. A section of a license plate banged against the T-Bird's wide windshield, putting a spiderweb break in its upper right-hand corner.

In a startled reaction, Virgil banged his wounded shoulder against

the steering wheel so hard the pain nearly caused him to pull a blackout. But not quite.

When he began functioning again, he heard horns blaring and a
woman screaming. Traffic along Sunset was stopped. Pedestrians ran
past his car. A man stumbled by, keening, pressing his wadded windbreaker against a bloody forehead.

Feeling decidedly woozy, Virgil staggered from his car to help an elderly woman who'd fallen to the sidewalk. He could see no visible
wound, but her teeth were chattering and she seemed to be in shock.
He ran back to the car and found an old jacket that he draped over
the woman's upper torso. Her eyes were frantic. "You just lie still,
ma'am," he said in an amazingly soft voice. "Try to relax. The para-
medics will be here before you know it."

Hunkering beside her, he stared down Sunset. In the midst of the
traffic snarl, a thick bouquet of black smoke blossomed from the remains of a red sports car that looked like the same one Ricky Geruso
drove. Some idiots were adding to the congestion by abandoning their
stalled vehicles and running frantically from the scene. Virgil didn't think
there was enough left of the red car to make much of a second explosion.

The woman next to him was looking better. Her teeth chattering
had stopped. "That's it. Just rest," he told her. A siren sounded in the
distance. He stood.

"Thinkin' of fleein' the scene?" someone asked, right behind him.

Virgil turned to see Pickett, as unemotional as an obelisk, staring at
him. "What'd you use on poor Ricky's wheels?" the big man asked.
"TNT? Plastique?"

"Me? You think that's my work?" Virgil said.

"Oh, yeah," Pickett said.

"Why would I?"

Pickett shrugged. "The 'why' is not my problem. It's somethin' your
brothers in blue gonna have to figure out. Lessen' you wanna give it up
to 'em. I imagine they must be on their way."

Virgil looked down at the woman, who was now breathing normally.

The siren song of medical aid was growing louder. He glanced at his car, parked not fifty feet away, driver's door still invitingly open.

"That's a good move, brother," Pickett said. "You jus' get in your car and bone out. Take that alley behind the restaurant. Don't you worry none. Ole Pickett'll handle everything on this end."

Virgil walked to his car, slammed the door, and locked it. He walked back to join Pickett. The big man was grinning at him. *"We gonna wait till the midnight hour,"* he began singing.

≡ 50 ≡

By 8:30, Nikki had fed Bird, taken him for a walk through the neighborhood, and then fed herself. She was just putting four days' worth of dirty dishes into the washer when the phone rang. She thought it might be Virgil. Hoped it would be.

"I'd like to speak with Virgil Sykes, please." It was a woman's voice. Brusque to the point of rudeness. And familiar.

"Dana?"

"Is Detective Sykes there?"

"No, he isn't. What—?"

"Isn't he staying there?" Dana Lowery asked.

"What's going on, Dana?" Nikki asked.

"Nothing's going on. I'm trying to reach Virgil Sykes."

"Try *his* place."

"You deny that you and he are cohabiting?"

Lowery's prosecutorial tone prompted Nikki to ask, "You wouldn't be Linda Tripping me, by any chance?"

"I asked you a question," Lowery said.

"And I asked one right back at you," Nikki said. "Here's another. You and Gerald Wheeler been cohabiting?"

There was a popping noise on the other end. Was she turning off a tape recorder? Then: "What the fuck are you talking about?" Cruella asked.

"We were notified this afternoon that Wheeler was adding a name to his witness list. Daniel McNeil. Made me wonder if you and Wheeler weren't burning a little midnight oil together."

"I don't have to explain anything to you, Nikki. But I'll say this: Putting McNeil on the stand in the Bingham trial was totally Wheeler's idea. It will have no effect on my trial whatsoever."

Nikki knew that was jive, of course. The only reason Wheeler could have for calling up McNeil was to distract the jury. Don't pay any attention to the evidence piling up against my client; here's something much more significant: One of the first detectives on the crime scene, a man who had total access to all this so-called evidence, not only shot and killed a young girl, he is presently the main suspect in another murder. Wheeler will make McNeil look like the Son of Sam. The media would lap it up and spit it out all over the country, reaching every potential juror in southern California. But that would have no effect at all on Dana's prosecution of McNeil.

"Your problem, Dana, is that you underestimate people's intelligence and overestimate yours."

"And your problem is that you pick the wrong kind of playmates," Dana Lowery said before hanging up.

Nikki stared at the phone until it began to whistle. She depressed the plunger for a dial tone and punched in Virgil's number.

After three rings, his answering machine message began.

She hung up, wondering where he was. And whom he might be cohabiting with.

≡ 51 ≡

Thanks to the combined efforts of Luther Pickett and his receptionist, Annette Bovan, it took Virgil the better part of the evening to get clear of the two detectives assigned to Ricky Geruso's explosive departure. Most of the time he spent waiting alone in an ugly, barren interrogation room at Hollywood Division Homicide, staring at the one-way mirror and fuming while he waited for the beer-bellied veteran Wolstein and his thick-headed partner, Packfield, to join him.

Once they did, they stared at him poker-faced, as if daring him to deny Pickett's allegation that he was a rogue cop on temporary leave pending an investigation of the shooting of a young female. "There's no investigation," he explained with what he thought was saintly patience. "I'm on leave because I'm recuperating from wounds sustained in the line of duty. Mr. Pickett was also wrong about my being on a blood vendetta against him and the late Mr. Geruso. For the record, I have never threatened either of their lives and I did not plant a bomb in Mr. Geruso's automobile."

Not visibly impressed by his statement, Wolstein dragged himself from the room to see what he could find out about Virgil from Robbery-Homicide at Parker Center. He returned in fifteen minutes, eating a ham-and-cheese sandwich. "They say he's straight about the sick leave," he informed the tall, big-boned Packfield.

"But," Wolstein added, "considering how he got his injuries, I can see how Mr. Pickett might have been confused."

"Mr. Pickett wasn't confused," Virgil said. "Mr. Pickett is a lying son of a bitch."

"The French broad lying, too?" Packfield asked. "She backed him up."

"She works for the man. What else could she say?"

"Why would Pickett lie about you?" Wolstein seemed genuinely in the dark.

"Well, lemme see now. Why would a known felon lie about a policeman? Could it be to hide his own guilt?"

"He's a felon?" Packfield asked.

"Excuse me," Virgil said. "Make that a known *uncaught* felon. I was giving you guys the benefit of the doubt, seein' as he and Geruso have been running hookers out of a hotel in your district for the past half-dozen years."

"You got yourself a pretty lousy attitude, bud," Packfield said.

"Usually it's okay. It's not every day a couple of my fellow officers drag me down to their interrogation room and keep me there twiddlin' my thumbs for three hours, just on the word of a pimp."

With a sigh, Wolstein had pushed himself upright again and said, "Why don't I run over to Vice and see what they have to say about Pickett?"

Virgil watched him waddle from the room. "He the legman, huh?" he asked Packfield.

"He's got a physical coming up. He's trying to walk off some pounds."

"Man could walk to China," Virgil said, "and still be over the limit."

Wolstein returned gnawing on something that vaguely resembled a burrito. "Detective Sykes is on the money," he told Packfield. "Whitey Nordo in Vice says we must be spending too much time with dead bodies not to have heard of Pickett and Geruso. They're sorta legendary. Big rep for quality puss. Whitey's all broken up to hear his paisano Geruso is no longer with us."

"We better invite Pickett down here for a talk," Packfield said.

"Tonight?" Wolstein asked in surprise.

"Hell, no, not tonight," Packfield said, standing. "We're on golden time now."

"As long as we're all clear on who the bad guy is, okay if I go?" Virgil asked.

Packfield gave him a bored shrug and strolled from the room.

"No apology?"

"Settle for a ride back to your car?" Wolstein asked.

The section of Sunset Boulevard where Ricky Geruso had become one with the universe was cordoned off, setting up a nighttime traffic snarl that extended as far as La Brea. After creeping along for fifteen minutes, Wolstein said, "The hell with this," and hooked a left onto Fairfax. At Santa Monica Boulevard he began a westward flank along the slightly less-trafficked artery.

Eventually, he pulled to the curb at the corner of San Vincente and Sunset. "Okay if I drop you here?" Wolstein asked. "I can pull a U-ee, and work my way back the way we came."

"Sure," Virgil said, opening the door. Down the block, bright white lights illuminated the crime scene for those public servants unlucky enough to be spending their night searching for car and body particles. "What kind of explosive did it?" he asked the fat detective as he stepped from the car.

"Too soon to tell. Bomber really got some bang for his buck, though. You take care of yourself, now." Wolstein gave him a two-finger salute and performed his promised U-turn.

Virgil stood on the corner for a few seconds staring at the activity in the near distance. Then he walked down Sunset to reclaim his car. As he passed the building where Wonderbar had its offices, he noticed that lights were on at the western corner of the second floor. Pickett's office.

The son of a bitch was working late. Maybe he was working on the lovely Annette. Well, come morning the dynamic duo of Wolstein and Packfield would be treating him to their brand of dog-pound hospitality. Virgil continued on. He could see his car, waiting for him in the deserted parking lot. Instead of walking the thirty yards or so to reclaim it and be on his way, he paused, turned, and glared at the lighted windows.

He didn't need Nikki to be there to tell him he should just blow it off, that the best thing to do was put as much distance as he could between himself and anything connected to the late Ricky Geruso. But Pickett had grinned at him when the cops took him away, and he had an uncontrollable urge to remove that grin from the pimp's face.

He patted the hard lump under his shirt to satisfy himself that the gun Wolstein had been kind enough to return to him was still in the holster snapped to his belt. His confidence buoyed by the weapon, he crossed the boulevard, working his way through the barely moving vehicles.

The street entrance to the building was open. He strolled in and climbed the stairs to the second floor.

The glass door reading "Wonderbar, Inc.," was a few inches ajar. The faceplate of its lock had been pried away from the thick glass, with both surfaces scraped and gouged.

On the other side of the door, the light that spilled out of Pickett's private office was enough to show him that the reception area was deserted. There was no shadow motion from the lighted room to indicate the presence of anyone in there either.

Don't be a mule-headed fool, he could almost hear Nikki's voice in his ear. *Don't you go rushing in there.*

Reasons for not going in: A) He had no business whatsoever to be entering the scene of a break-in. B) The perp could still be in there, which would be a mess no matter who did what to whom because of A). C) He could get caught in the office and blamed for the break-in. On the other side of the ledger, there was actually only one reason for going in. Curiosity.

He reached under his shirt for his gun. Using his good shoulder to push the door open, he entered.

The French mistress of the telephone kept a very clean desktop, he noted. The whole reception area seemed surprisingly neat and orderly.

He moved quietly to Pickett's private office, stepped inside. Uninhabited. Some papers on the glass-and-chrome desk. The carpet was scuffed, but nothing looked very disturbed. A cabinet that matched the desk housed an assortment of new-looking electronic gear—TV monitor, stereo, CD player, both audio- and videocassette players. The average B & E perp would have left those shelves as clean as the receptionist's desk.

The other private office was dark. As Virgil approached it, he saw shards of police tape hanging from the jamb. Had to have been torn by the perp. Pickett would have used more care before entering his dead partner's office, would've taken the time to pry the tape loose and afterward would have reattached it.

Unless . . . Pickett had faked the break-in for the benefit of the police. That way he could cut their ribbon and get whatever he needed from Geruso's office. Virgil stepped over the threshold and used the tip of his gun to turn on the light.

The room had been thoroughly trashed. Drawers torn from desks and left where they fell. Locked cabinets pried open. Papers scattered. Fast, messy work. Not the work of a police crew—Geruso was a victim, not a suspect; if they had already searched his office, there would have been no need for the tape across the door.

He'd been in the office long enough. Pickett was a night person who could show up anytime. No sense pushing his luck.

He turned off the light with his gun barrel and was crossing the reception area to the front door when the phone rang in Pickett's office. His eyes went to Annette's desk. The buttons on her phone panel were dark.

It was a private line.

He entered Pickett's office in time to hear a click, then the harsh, accusing voice of the female caller. "Luther? It's me, damn it. Pick up. Where the hell are you? You said it would take you only a few minutes. You've been gone a fucking hour. The waiter's starting to hit on me." While the woman continued with a litany of complaints, Virgil noticed something disturbing: The random scuff marks he'd seen earlier on the carpet were actually parallel lines. A heavy object had been dragged across the room to a closed door.

The caller ended her harangue with a surprising mood swing. "If you're not here in fifteen minutes, I'll . . . be waiting for you at my place."

Man's a real Svengali, Virgil thought as he opened the door.

The light from the office fell on the mirrored walls of an elaborate bathroom. Gold fixtures gleamed on a black onyx washbasin. The floor consisted of black-and-white patterned tiles. On them just past the door lay Luther Pickett, body twisted, face frozen in pain and surprise. An object that looked like a huge shard of glass was buried in his upper abdomen. His still-wet blood dulled the bright colors of his Hawaiian shirt.

Virgil squatted to get a better look at the body and the weapon. The man was definitely deceased. It had happened fairly recently. The flesh wasn't cold. The big man's eyes were still wet with his tears. The object embedded in his stomach was long and tapered like an icicle. Smooth. Possibly not glass at all. Plastic? He wasn't about to touch it to find out. Better just bounce on out of here. A fresh corpse raised the ante considerably on the dangers of getting caught.

He was about to stand when he saw that Pickett's huge right fist was wrapped around an object. An audiocassette, brighter red than the big man's blood. Using toilet paper, Virgil moved a thumb the size of a Ballpark frank just enough to read the handwritten label: "March 12 through April 3." Dated that year.

The phone began to ring again, startling Virgil.

The same woman. "On second thought, mister man, I'm walking over there right now. And if I catch you with the fucking French whore down on her knees—"

Walking? She was that close? It was definitely time for him to be geese.

52

That night, Nikki drifted off to a fitful sleep. She awoke at 3:00 A.M. *Why*, she wondered, *is it always 3:00 A.M.?* She closed her eyes. Maybe she could go right back to dreamland. Fat chance. She began brooding over Dana's possible motives for trying to reach Virgil. She wanted to question him? Indict him? Fuck him? It was the time of morning when fretful images play on the psyche like a gloom video top-ten count-down.

Then, not by conscious choice, her worry about Virgil was replaced by the anxiety-producing realization that later that day she would be appearing before Judge Proody, trying to convince him to disallow McNeil's appearance as a defense witness.

She had to get back to sleep. She needed her favorite yes-doze pill— a glass of warm milk laced with vanilla extract and a healthy shot of Jack Daniel's, topped off with a sprinkle of nutmeg.

Bird, alerted by the kitchen activity, staggered in to join her. The only male she could count on. To reward his loyalty, she made him a present of a small chunk of cheddar that he gratefully gulped. He sat at her feet observing her adoringly, while she sipped her draught and perused, for the fourth time, the clips on McNeil's arrest and the few

bits of information available about the case Dana Lowery was building against him.

The hot-milk punch delivered another three hours of sleep. By 6:30,
she and the big dog were welcoming the day at a park in Manhattan
Beach. Nikki was working her way up the five-story mountain of sand,
while Bird bounced along the accompanying wooden stairwell.

At the crest, smug with their achievement, they rested their limbs,
backs to the ocean, and watched the sun rise into a sky full of plump
white clouds. Nikki ran her fingers through the animal's curly coat and
said, "The sun and those clouds remind you of anything? A nice big
egg, sunny-side up?"

Bird replied with a gleeful bark. He was hungry, too.

The effervescent mood resulting from her early workout was flat-
tened considerably by the news in the morning paper that entrepreneur
Luther Pickett had been found stabbed to death in his office six hours
after his business partner, Richard Geruso, had been blown apart in his
automobile. Geruso had been involved in McNeil's arrest. Was Dana
calling Virgil about his death?

Once again, she tried to phone him. Once again, she heard his
recorded voice informing her he wasn't home. This time, she left a message asking him to return her call.

She was definitely worried about the man now. Where could he possibly be, at, she checked the time, eight in the morning?

Eight? She leapt from the chair, rushing toward the shower.

She arrived at the Bauchet Street holding pen five minutes late for
the meeting she'd requested with McNeil and his lawyer, Desmond Porcello. The latter was waiting for her at the entrance to the interview
room. The round little man of the law was wearing, along with a fifty-
dollar haircut, a forest green suit, starched white shirt, green-and-blue
tie, and gold cuff links. Nearly everybody called him Porky, but Nikki
couldn't bring herself to use the nickname. Maybe if he hadn't looked
like Porky . . .

"Hi, Des," she said. "Sorry I'm late."

"No matter," he replied dryly. "What's five or ten minutes to a lawyer who's got to be in court in Santa Monica in less than an hour?"

"I'll make it quick," she promised as they checked their briefcases and waited to be allowed entry to the room.

"Remember," Porcello cautioned, "strictly Bingham. I hear just a whisper of the name Dahl and we're out of there."

"Agreed."

The large room was crowded. A professionally disinterested guard led McNeil to a vacant windowed cubicle. There was only one visitor's chair. Porcello gestured for Nikki to take it. When she hesitated, he said waspishly, "Sit, please. Nothing political, sexist, or racist intended. I've got a boil on my ass."

"That's telling me a little more than I need to know," she said, sitting down and facing McNeil. "How you holding up?" she asked him.

"I had a dream about a fifth of gin the other night," he said. "It's kept me going."

"The reason I'm here," she said, "is that in about an hour and a half, I'm going to try and convince a judge that you shouldn't be allowed to testify in the Randy Bingham trial. Des tells me you had a visitor."

"I get any more visitors," McNeil said, "they going to vote me Miss Congeniality. Not a title you want in here, by the way."

"Who've you been talking to?"

"This cherry pie named Mimi stopped by. She said she'd be happy to clear it with Porky, if I wanted, but she just had these few, really unimportant questions to ask. She showed a lot more leg than you do, Nikki."

"I'll wear short-shorts next time," Nikki said. She looked up at Porcello. "You okayed it?"

"I only found out about it after the fact," the round lawyer said, scowling at his client.

"What'd she ask you, Mac?"

"Did I ever happen to meet Shelli Dietz while she was still alive? Had I ever met her husband or her boy or any members of the Bingham family before the murder? Did any members of my family or any of my friends ever have any dealings with the Binghams? Did I ever purchase any Homeboy products?"

"And you replied?"

"No, no, no, no, and nice legs."

"Funny man," Porcello said. "Too bad 'funny' isn't a substitute for 'smart.'"

"I didn't think it was worth bothering you, Porky."

"Any time you're within earshot of a lawyer, it's important. Trust me. I know what deceitful, self-serving pricks we lawyers are. Even lady lawyers." He grinned at Nikki. "Especially lady lawyers."

She rolled her eyes and said, "Well, that's not exactly a disaster. Assuming that's as far as she went."

McNeil looked sheepish.

"There's more?"

The detective nodded.

"Damn it," Porcello said. "And you keep this from me? I ought to turn your case over to one of my clerks, right now. The one who keeps asking me what *habeas corpus* means."

"She said if I cooperated, she'd set up for one of those O.J. declarations of innocence from the stand. Then I wouldn't have to take the stand in my trial."

"Jesus!" Porcello exclaimed. "Please don't tell me you talked to her about our trial?"

"No. Of course not."

"Okay. We're getting off-topic," Porcello warned. "She say anything else about the Bingham trial?"

"She asked if that jackass DiBono had been alone with the body. I told her I had no knowledge of what went down there before we arrived."

"You shouldn't have said a damn thing," Porcello told him.

"What else did she want to know?" Nikki asked.

"Once we got on the scene, did DiBono have a chance to mess with the evidence? I told her I didn't think so. She looked surprised and said she assumed there had been opportunity during the search for the boy.

Not to my knowledge, I replied. And that was pretty much that. They seem to have a hard-on for DiBono."

"It's not about DiBono," Nikki said. "It's about whether *you* had the opportunity to plant evidence."

"Jesus, Mac," Porcello said with dismay. "You've taken part in enough interrogations to know the first rule, the only rule for a suspect, is to keep your mouth shut."

"It's kinda hard for me to think of myself as a suspect," McNeil said. "But what harm did I do? I just told her I didn't know anything."

"Any way you answer the question about DiBono at the crime scene," Nikki informed him, "you go on record. She and Wheeler can use this to convince the judge that you have information that the jury must be allowed to hear."

McNeil glared at both of them. "So I testify in the Bingham trial. What's the big fuckin' deal?"

"You want to tell him?" Nikki asked Porcello.

"Be my guest."

"The big fucking deal," she said testily, "is that once you take the stand, it will no longer be the Bingham trial. It will be the McNeil trial, with the probable outcome that Bingham will walk and you'll be put away.

"Your only chance of getting a reasonably fair trial of your own is if you stay clear of ours. I'm going to do everything I can to make that happen. Just don't cut my legs off by doing any more talking to Mimi Gentry, even if she shows up in a thong bikini."

McNeil nodded. "How bad did I fuck up?"

"There are a few things we can try," Nikki said. "I'll argue that your appearance on the stand would unnecessarily disrupt our trial. At the same time, it would compromise your right to a fair and honest trial. I'll state that you have no pertinent information to offer that was not available to the court through DiBono's testimony. And finally, I'll suggest we sit down and look at the videotape again, since it offers an accurate and complete eyewitness account of everything you and Virgil experienced while at the crime scene, untainted by the frailty of human memory. But if they want the human touch, let them call Virgil to the stand."

McNeil frowned. He was silent for a few seconds, then looked up at his lawyer. "Porky, you mind taking a walk? There's something kinda personal I have to discuss with Nikki."

Porcello shot her an accusing glance. She gave him a blank look and a shrug. He said to his client, "What part of 'keep your mouth shut' don't you understand?"

"This has got nothing to do with me," McNeil said. "It's about a mutual friend."

It was Nikki's turn to frown.

"Okay," Porcello said. "I've gotta run to Santa Monica anyway. You talk to this lady about our case and I will turn you over to my clerk. She's a really sweet kid who studied to be a nun before switching over to law. You can be her first client."

"He's okay, isn't he?" McNeil asked as they watched the plump lawyer make his exit.

"Yeah," she said. "He kicked my butt once. But I wasn't as good then as I am now."

"What about the bitch on my case?"

"Dana Lowery is . . . highly motivated. She's got hopes of using you to become the first lady D.A. in L.A. history. So if she loses, she loses big. But she tends to come on too strong. Des, on the other hand, plays it sorta cool. I think you're gonna be okay unless, of course, you killed that girl."

He started to open his mouth, but she held up a hand. "No. I'm sorry I said that. No need to defend yourself to me. We promised Des we wouldn't talk about your trial. What'd you want to tell me about Virgil?"

"Don't even think about putting him on the stand. Use me before you do that."

"Why?"

"He was just here an hour ago. To tell me about Geruso and Pick-ett, as if we don't get that kind of news in here ten minutes after it goes down. He also wanted to know if Porky had hired a gumshoe to do a background on them. I told him I didn't need to do that. I know their background. They were pimps."

"Virgil seem okay?" she asked.

"That's what I wanted to talk about. He didn't. Not at all. He hadn't slept. He seemed jumpy. I told him I was worried about the way he was behaving and he said he just needed a little sleep. But it's more than that, Nikki."

"What?" she asked.

McNeil lowered his voice. "Virgil said he found Pickett's body."

"He wasn't mentioned in the paper."

"That's because he wasn't there when the Hollywood police arrived. He didn't even notify them. Says he just hauled ass as soon as he stumbled across Pickett's corpse."

"Damn. Any wits see him go in or leave?"

"He doesn't think so. But the Strip was full of traffic and you don't want to put him on any witness stand where he can get blindsided. You know Virgil. He's not a guy who'll lie under oath. If he ever admits to being in that office at that time, he's gonna wind up in the room next to mine."

"Anything else I should know?"

"Two Hollywood Division dicks hauled him in as a suspect in the Geruso bombing."

She tried to keep her feelings off her face, but she could tell by the way McNeil softened his voice that she was not succeeding. "What made them think he might be involved?" she asked.

He hesitated. "He was in the vicinity when it went down. Keeping an eye on Pickett."

"Proximity usually isn't enough to get you a trip down," she said.

"No. Here's the bad part: Pickett sicced the cops on him, claimed Virg had a grudge against Geruso."

"So it's on the record that he was motivated to light a bomb under Geruso," she said. "And now he's got reason to get medieval on Pickett. And he winds up in the office with Pickett's fresh corpse."

"He thought he was helping me," McNeil said, his voice cracking in misery. "You've got to talk sense to him, Nikki. Maybe if he just chills till all this bullshit clears, he'll come out of it okay."

"You evidently weren't able to call him off. What makes you think he'll listen to me?"

"He's in love with you, for God's sake."

She did not share his confidence but she was not able to discuss her innermost feeling with even close friends. She certainly wasn't going to blurt them out to McNeil. "I'm not sure how much that matters. He's got a head like granite."

McNeil gave her a serious, dead-on look. "You don't want him in here, Nikki. Talk to him, plead with him, lie to him, fuck him, whatever it takes to keep him out of here. You do it."

Nothing like a little pressure.

It was 11:30 when Nikki left the judge's elevator at the CCB and headed toward Judge Proody's chambers. Virgil had still not returned her call. He was either not at home or not answering the phone. She hoped he was still a free man—out of jail and out of Cruella's clutches.

She paused at the judge's door to clear away her concerns about Virgil and psyche herself up with a few mental self-affirmations. She took a deep breath and exhaled, then opened the door.

She was greeted by the sound of men laughing together. "Mr. Wheeler's already with the judge," she was informed by the young male clerk seated at an antique desk in the book-lined outer office.

"So I hear," she said.

When she entered the judge's private chamber, the laughter stopped abruptly.

Judge Proody glared at her. He was leaning back in his chair, wearing tan slacks and a lime green pullover with a little golfer emblem over the heart. He gestured toward a tooled leather chair next to Wheeler, who was, as always, dressed for a cotillion.

Both men were chewing on cigars.

"We wanted to ask yoah permission befo' lightin' up," Wheeler said, giving her a smirky smile.

Off to a great start. "You're not going to offer me one?" she asked.

Wheeler patted his chest. "Sorry, ma'am, I didn't think to bring an extra."

She was the extra, she thought. "If I'm, late, I apologize," she said, sitting.

"You're right on time, Ms. Hill," Judge Proody said, lighting up. "Mr. Wheeler"—puff, puff— "showed up a little early. He's been"—puff, puff—"regaling me with some very funny anecdotes."

"I could use a few laughs this morning," Nikki said to Wheeler as the cigar smoke began to assail her sinuses.

"Well, ma'am, they're a little . . . too risqué for mixed company."

Mixed company. Beautiful.

"No more time for joking around anyhow," Judge Proody said, leaning forward, elbows on his desk. "Let's dispose of this totally unnecessary little diversion so we can get back to court, which is what they're paying us for."

Nikki's stomach did a little flip and her confidence level descended an inch lower than her heels. "Your Honor," she said. "I'd hate to think you'd made a decision without hearing arguments."

"You accusing me of prejudicial bias?" he asked, color rising to his face.

"No, sir. Just that Mr. Wheeler and I have prepared—"

"Okay, okay," the judge said impatiently. "Then let's hear what you have to say. That is, let's hear what Mr. Wheeler has to say."

Wheeler gave the judge an appreciative smile.

Nikki sighed.

≡ 53 ≡

When Virgil stepped from the elevator onto the fifth floor of Parker Center, he sensed subtle changes. In just the few days he'd been absent from his workplace, desks were no longer precisely where he remembered, the atmosphere was different, a little less charged, and people seemed preoccupied and even slightly rude.

Of course, he could have been the one who had changed. Being on the other side of an interrogation table, stumbling on a corpse and dipping out—those little experiences come back to haunt you when you're surrounded by blue, even when you're carrying a badge yourself.

There were surprisingly few detectives on duty in Robbery-Homicide. The bulletin board was full of open cases. *Must be a lot of field action,* he thought, as he nodded to the dicks who bothered to look up when he walked past. He paused by his and Mac's desks. They were littered with casually dumped interdepartmental memos, professional mail, and other bits of office flotsam that were the signs of inactivity. He gathered his junk mail with his free hand and dropped it into a green trash bin.

It was a few minutes before noon.

He strolled to the closed door of Lt. Corben's office and knocked. Corben was expecting him. He was there at Corben's request.

"You look like you're healing okay," the lieutenant said when Virgil had taken a chair across the desk from him.

"Yeah. Where is everybody?"

"Business is booming," Corben said.

"If you need me, I could come in a few hours a day."

"No, no. One more hot body won't matter that much. Keep enjoying the good life, rest up till you're 100 percent."

Virgil was a little confused. "Was that why you asked me down here? To tell me to stay home?"

"No, no," Corben said, smiling at the absurdity of that idea. "You have been taking it easy since the shooting, haven't you?"

Oh, shit. "Yeah, sure," Virgil said.

"We been getting some strange phone calls about you," Corben said.

Double oh, shit. "What kind of calls?" Virgil asked, not wanting to know the answer.

"You know an IAG guy named Collins?"

"He grilled me while I was still in the hospital."

"Prick. Well, he wanted to see your jacket, and I kept it from him as long as I could."

"But you had to turn it over?"

"Uh-huh." The way he said it was the closest Virgil had ever heard Corben come to an apology.

"Was there anything in there that I should worry about?" Virgil asked.

"Nothing I could see, but who knows, the way those guys do their business?"

"That it?"

"No," Corben said. "You know some guy named Wolstein from Hollywood Homicide?"

"I've met him."

"He wanted to know why you were on leave. Any idea why?"

Virgil didn't bat an eye. "Somebody was goofin' on him, told him I was on department suspension for helping Mac take down that Laurence girl."

"The broad who shot you? Who'd spread that kinda tale?"

"I don't know for sure," Virgil said, improvising. "My guess would be Collins, playin' some kind of Internal Affairs game."

Corben stared at him. "These IAG guys," he said at last, "they're like fucking ticks. Burrow in when you're not looking and, bang, you're down for the count. You want to be real careful not to let 'em bite you."

"Good advice, Lieutenant," Virgil said, getting to his feet. "I'll check my body parts."

Corben stood too, and guided him to the door. "You visit Mac lately?"

"This morning," Virgil said.

"You see, now, that's honorable but it's not smart. Not with Internal Affairs looking up your butt. I want you to stock up on food, booze, and a broad or two, and just don't go out of the house till you're feeling on top."

"I'll keep that in mind. Thanks."

Virgil was on his way out when two names on the open-file bulletin board caught his eye. "Richard Geruso" and "Luther Pickett." Both had been assigned that morning to detectives Duke Wasson and Pooch Puchinski.

Virgil made an abrupt left-face and marched to the coffee altar. He unhooked a mug that an old flame had bought for him years before during a visit to Chinatown. It was emblazoned "Virgil" in elaborate gold script and some Asian artisan's idea of what a Roman poet would look like. He filled it with thick, burned coffee and carried it to a desk where Wasson, a balding, weary-looking black man who'd recently been bumped up from office staff to detective, was painstakingly printing information in his murder book.

Reading upside down, Virgil made out the name "Pickett."

He sat down at Wasson's desk. The detective regarded him with tired, red-rimmed eyes. "Virgil. How they hanging?"

"You look like you been beatin' the bushes, huh, Duke?"

"Oh, yeah. Pooch is out on the bricks now, on ho' patrol."

"You covering Vice, too?"

"Naw. We just drew this pimp murder. It's been rough picking up some of the slack, what with you and Mac . . . off duty." He shifted his eyes, not sure if his comment was in some way insensitive.

Virgil let him off the hook. "I'm anxious to get back," he said. "I imagine Mac would rather be here, too."

"He okay?"

"Good as can be expected."

"It's a persecution. That's what it is."

Virgil sipped his coffee. "What's this pimp murder case you mentioned?" he asked idly.

"Like we don't have enough to do. Pooch and me just got thrown two H-wood homicides."

"Why the shift?"

"Like they tell us. All I know is, they're on our board now."

"That what you're workin' on?" Virgil asked, indicating the murder book with its powder blue cover.

"Uh-huh. Brother named Luther Pickett. No great loss to humanity. Pimp with . . . delusions of grandeur."

"Nice phrasing."

"My wife's got me on this self-improvement kick," Wasson said. "I'm takin'—*taking* these computer classes in English grammar and vocabulary." He chuckled. "Fuck Ebonics. Guess we all have our delusions of grandeur."

Virgil smiled. "Well, you got that vocabulary workin' full tilt." He conjured up a yawn to hide the fact that he was changing the subject, then asked, "The brother get popped, or what?"

"Jab and stab. Killer used this fancy combination paperweight and letter opener. Nasty utensil. Belonged to the vic. He kept it on his desk. Looks like the killer busted in through the front door of the vic's office, was goin'—*going* through drawers and cabinets and shit when Mr. Pickett showed up. Another example of bad timing in the extreme."

"Any suspects?"

"Haven't had time to make a list, but Gilbo says we should be leaning toward someone of the female persuasion."

The news that David Gilbo, one of the better criminologists, thought the murder had been committed by a woman relieved Virgil mightily.

That'd be one less on his scorecard if his name turned up in Duke and Pooch's investigation. "One of his ho's?" he asked.

"Prob'ly."

Virgil threw out a fishing line. "Pickett musta been a little mutt, huh?"

"No. Big som-bitch. Six-foot and then some, mainly bone and muscle. Oh, I see what you're . . . intimating. Hooker would have to be . . . massive."

"Somethin' like that."

"Not really. See, she used the double-whammy. Pepper spray and a Taser. Both of 'em state of the fuckin' art, brother. Spray was that new mighty stuff, have you doing the Stevie Wonder in seconds. And the Taser hooks dug out of his back are the new wireless variety. She put him down and then picked up the paperweight thing from his desk."

"I still don't see why Gilbo thinks—"

"There was a bite mark," Wasson said. "On the vic's left forearm. A woman thang. Also bruises on the vic's legs. The way Gilbo pictures it, Pickett surprised the killer in the midst of burglarizing the office, grabs her from behind and lifts her up. She gives him some kicks and a good hard bite and gets free long enough to pull the pepper spray from her purse or pocket and then the Taser. Now her choppers were at chest level, gnawing on his arm, and her heels were leaving their mark just above his ankles, she's maybe five-three or five-four."

"Saliva on the bite should narrow it down even more," Virgil said. "Prints?"

"An array," Wasson said glumly. "Pickett was getting ready to open some big-deal nightclub and the place was busy as the Forum with the Lakers in town. The secretary—and she's a piece of work, about as soft and . . . sentimental as your average shitcan seat—says people were coming and going all day. A, uh, multitude of prints."

"Sounds like you got your job cut out for you," Virgil said.

"It gets worse. Pickett's partner got himself blown up in his car yesterday and nobody around here puts much stock in coincidence."

"I was on Sunset when the guy's car blew," Virgil said.

"No shit? Real mess, huh?"

"Very messy."

"Drano bomb, according to SID. That fits in with the female theory."

"You lost me."

Wasson said, "It's an easy thing. You take one of them little plastic containers picture film comes in, toss out the film, put in some Comet and some Drano, drop it into a gas tank, and *kah-blooey.*"

"I know about Drano bombs," Virgil said patiently. "What I don't know is why it fits in with the female-killer theory."

"Comet. Drano. Kitchen stuff," Wasson said, like he was explaining to a child, "woman stuff. Anyways, it means Pooch and I gonna be having the dubious pleasure of interviewing the Pickett and Geruso stable of ho—demimondes."

Virgil was curious about the cassette he'd seen in Pickett's hand, but he felt he'd pushed Wasson as far as he could. Standing, he said, "Those lessons are doing you a world of good, Dukester. You startin' to sound just like a college professor."

Wasson smiled proudly, then put on a more serious demeanor. "You see Mac, tell him we're rooting for him."

Virgil said he'd pass the word along.

≡ 54 ≡

Nikki stuck her head into Daspit's office.

Daspit looked up from papers on his desk. He asked, "How'd it go with Prosser?"

"Short story," she said.

"Sit down," he said. "Tell me."

"I walk in on Prosser and Wheeler swapping good-ole-boy dirty jokes and chewing on cigars that Wheeler thoughtfully provided."

"Shit," Daspit said.

"Then the judge calls the meeting a waste of time. And I, in my wisdom, suggest that he should keep an open mind until we've presented our arguments. And this pisses him off no end."

"Holy shit."

"Begrudgingly, he says he'll listen to Wheeler's arguments."

"And yours?"

"That's the point. He wouldn't let me speak."

"Damn it. I should have gone with you."

She smiled. "Hop off that white horse, Lance, and get ready for the good news. The reason Proody won't let me speak is that he shoots Wheeler down like a big bird. Says to him, 'I hope you don't think a cigar, even a Davidos, and a couple of Viagra jokes are gonna get me to allow you to subjugate justice.'

"Wheeler starts sputtering about McNeil being in possession of crucial information and the judge, sittin' there in his little golf shirt, doesn't buy one word of it."

"You gotta love the guy," Daspit said. "And that was it?"

"That was it. Without McNeil, there's not much left for the defense to present. They're not giving us a whack at Randy. That leaves daddy and brother."

"They could rest this afternoon," Daspit said. "With Proody wearing his track shoes, we could be on deck for our closing arguments as early as Monday morning."

Nikki frowned. Closing arguments. She'd been working on hers, collecting notes and tear sheets all along, nearly two folders full, but it was far from final form. "No problem," she said, realizing any plans she'd had for the weekend, including a dinner with Loreen, would have to be scrapped.

"I wish I'd been there to see Proody wipe the smug smile off that cornpone son of a bitch's face," Daspit said.

"Wheeler was definitely on the ropes," Nikki said.

Daspit looked at his watch. "Let's go put him down for the count."

Randolph Bingham the elder sat stiffly and solemnly in the witness box. He'd dressed appropriately in a somber blue suit, white shirt, and pale yellow tie that allowed him to look dapper but also democratic enough not to raise the hackles of any millionaire-hating juror. The routine he and Wheeler had obviously worked long and hard to perfect went over well. He was the caring but observant father, a man who knew his son well and was convinced of his innocence.

"What was his relationship with the victim, Shelli Dietz?"

"He was in love with her. Unequivocal love."

"Could he have done what the prosecution would have us believe? Shoot his beloved and leave her to die in a pool of her own blood?"

"Of course not," Bingham replied. "There is no way my gentle son Randy could have done this monstrous thing."

"Thank you, sir," Wheeler said. "Your witness."

Nikki had come to court prepared to start her cross by pressing Bingham on his story about his son's phone call on the night of the murder. But for some reason, Wheeler had declined to introduce that so-called evidence and she was happy to ignore it also. She began by asking, "Mr. Bingham, would I be correct in saying that you are proud of your son Randolph?"

"I'm proud of both my sons."

"Nothing about Randolph has caused you any disappointment?"

"Well, I was hoping he'd express more interest in the family business. But his interests lie elsewhere."

"Could you be more specific about the 'elsewhere'?"

"He's . . . poetic. Aesthetic. He sees more in a rose than he does in a ledger book. Is that a disappointment? I suppose. But I'm also proud of him, proud of his . . . poetic insight, his humanity."

Before the elder Bingham could break out in a chorus of "The Best Little Boy in the World," Nikki asked, "Have you and Randolph had many arguments?"

"The usual, I suppose."

"How'd he feel about your hobby?"

"My hobby?"

"Hunting."

Bingham straightened in the chair. "It's a sport."

"Not one that poets usually go for. Did Randolph hunt with you?"

"When he was a boy. Not for the past ten or fifteen years. He never possessed a hunter's heart."

Nikki flashed on a human heart, stuffed and mounted, hanging on Randolph Bingham's wall. It was all she could do to keep from giggling. "But you taught him about guns?"

The elderly man hesitated, then said, "Yes."

"Shotguns?"

"Yes."

"Rifles?"

"Your Honor," Wheeler complained, "the question has been asked and answered."

"Move along, Ms. Hill," Judge Proody ordered.

"Mr. Bingham, did you feel Shelli Dietz was a good match for your son?"

"Of course. She was a wonderful woman. Bright, successful, a delight to be around."

"You disagree, then, with the defense witnesses who've pictured her as a woman of loose morals."

Bingham's eyes shifted to the defense table. Nikki took a sideways step to block his view of Wheeler.

"I . . ." he began. "That's something I, something beyond my knowledge."

"Did Randolph ever complain to you about her lack of morals?"

"Of course not."

"Did he ever mention to you that he suspected Ms. Dietz was seeing other men?"

"Never."

"Jenny Mapes has testified that she told him Ms. Dietz was, in her words, being unfaithful. How do you suppose your son would react to such news?"

"Objection. Calls for speculation."

"Your Honor," Nikki argued, "Mr. Bingham has stated that he has been very close to his son. All I'm asking is his expert opinion."

The judge nodded. "You may answer," he said to Bingham.

"I don't believe Rand would commit harm on any human being."

"The question was: How would he react to the news that his beloved was unfaithful?"

"He's a man. I imagine he might have been a bit angry, assuming he put any stock in the fantasies of a young woman. But that's a far cry from—"

"Thank you, sir," Nikki said, cutting him off. "One final question: Do you put any stock in Mr. Wheeler's fantasy about a mysterious homicidal lover showing up after your son left Ms. Dietz that night?"

"Your Honor," Wheeler began.

It was *a cheap shot*, she thought. "Withdraw the question. I'm finished with the witness."

•   •   •

Randy's brother, Jeffrey, was a sullen presence in the witness box, even when replying to Mimi Gentry's puffball questions. His recurring theme was that his brother was innocent and anyone who wasn't crystal clear on that point was an idiot or a villain.

When Nikki began her cross, his hostility level was near the boiling point.

"Don't twist my words!" he yelled in response to a question about his purchase of the murder weapon. Nikki was feeling pretty hostile herself. It was her intention to push his anger button hard enough for him to expose himself as a thug and a bully. It would satisfy her on a personal level to break the man who'd threatened Adam Noyes, and it would also end the defense phase of the trial on the right note, with the jury getting a glimpse of Bingham family arrogance and fury. She hoped she could get Jeffrey Bingham to take a swing at her.

"You told Ms. Gentry that you bought the gun," Nikki said.

"Yes. I gave it to Keats—that's what I call my brother—and he let Shelli Dietz borrow it."

"Did you see it at her home?"

"No. I've only been to the house once since she moved in."

"So you have no firsthand knowledge of her possession of the weapon?"

"Keats told me he gave it to her."

"But you have no proof of that, do you?" she asked.

"My brother doesn't lie."

"You have no proof of that either."

He glared at her. "That's it. I have nothing more to say to you."

"Mr. Bingham, I'm afraid you do have to answer my questions," she said sweetly. "This is a simple one. Do you love your brother?"

"Of course I do. He's my brother. Don't you love your brother?"

"The way this works," she said, "is that you have to answer my questions. I don't have to answer yours. Do you love your brother enough to feel protective about him?"

"This is ridiculous," Jeffrey Bingham said and slumped into silence.

Nikki shrugged and turned to the judge. "Your Honor?"

Judge Proody's robe was at half-mast and he looked like he was counting the minutes until adjournment. He was in no mood for petulance.

"Answer the question, son," he said, "or spend the weekend in jail."

Jeffrey Bingham seemed to undergo an internal struggle, with rationality coming out on top. "Do I feel I have to protect him?" he replied gruffly. "Yeah. Sometimes."

"Could you give us an example?"

He was silent for nearly half a minute.

"Do you understand the question?" Nikki asked.

"I'm thinking!" he almost shouted. Then he nodded his head. "Yeah. His Alfa. That's a perfect case. He saw it parked on a used-car lot, went in, and wrote out a check for the sticker price. No bargaining. No test-drive. Nothing but the check." Jeffrey sat back with a can-you-believe-it expression on his face.

"And you did what to protect your brother?" Nikki asked.

"I went back to the lot with him and got the owner to knock down the price and give Keats the extra money back."

"You got a used-car dealer to refund cash?"

Jeffrey's V-shaped face smiled for the first time since he'd sat down. "I can be very persuasive."

Nikki found herself in an awkward position. Jeffrey Bingham was reacting exactly the way she'd hoped he would. But she suddenly realized that it might have a disastrous result. Wheeler had missed a golden opportunity. It would be like falling off a log to convince the jury that the wrong Bingham brother was on trial. Jeffrey was overprotective, arrogant, hotheaded, and evidently capable of violence. He had threatened a little boy, for heaven's sake. If he had felt Shelli Dietz was taking advantage of Randy, luring him into marriage, he just might have confronted her and when his persuasiveness failed . . .

Nikki didn't believe this scenario—the evidence pointed to Randy, not Jeffrey—but it was certainly easier to float than the story about a secret lover. Had Wheeler considered raising the specter of Jeffrey's guilt and had Randy shot it down? No matter. The defense had not gone in that direction and, regardless of her personal animosity toward Jeffrey, she wasn't going to either. She suddenly wanted him off the stand and out of the jurors' sight.

"Nothing more, Your Honor," she said, returning to her table where Daspit was staring at her with eyebrows raised.

Judge Proody cast his glare at Wheeler.

The defense attorney seemed to have been caught off-guard by Nikki's abrupt conclusion.

"No further questions, Your Honor. The defense rests."

≡ 55 ≡

The bright light seemed to cut through Virgil's eye and go straight to his brain. He winced.

The man in white clicked off the penlight and muttered, "Hmm."

"Well, Doc. Am I ever gonna play the piano again?"

His doctor smiled. "Right now, it'll have to be a one-handed number. Be thankful we've removed your cast."

"Damn. I was hoping I could get rid of this sling, too."

"Virgil, two bullets with the velocity of . . . whatever the hell the velocity of bullets is, two bullets hit you. One penetrated your body; the other creased your skull. That's a whole lot of trauma for flesh and bone to handle. Don't wear hats and keep using the sling."

Virgil looked at himself in the mirror over the sink. "At least I got a smaller bandage." It was a rectangle of adhesive, not much larger than a Band-Aid and roughly the color of his light brown skin.

"Vanity, Mr. Sykes," the doctor said, leading him toward the door. "The wounds are healing nicely. Give the process time. If you rush it, you'll be delaying full recuperation. Don't overextend yourself. And don't ignore what I told you about getting lots of rest."

"I'm sleeping like a baby every night."

"Don't try to con your doctor. Especially after he's been shining a light in your bloodshot and tired eyes."

Out on the street at a little after 2:00 P.M., Virgil wasn't sure what to do. Go to a movie? Don't think so. Only losers and desperate people went to movies in the afternoon. Actually, he qualified under both categories, but he still didn't want to go to a movie. It was too early to hit a bar. He slipped behind the wheel of the T-bird and headed for his apartment.

He was creeping along, looking for a parking space, when he recognized the two men in a dark sedan several car-lengths in front of him. Rafe Collins and his IAG white shadow.

He braked, backed up, and did a U-turn.

He checked the sedan in his rearview mirror. It remained in place, fifty or so feet from the entrance to his apartment complex. What the hell did they want? Maybe he should just walk up to their car, get it over with, whatever it was.

No. He just wasn't down with that.

He drove.

Nowhere in particular. West on Fountain, past rows of apartment buildings. South on La Cienega, cruising the glitzy restaurants where the names and the motifs changed faster than the menus. When he'd first come to town, there'd been a garish yellow-and-black structure on La Cienega known as The Losers. It had a marquee, slightly askew, that the owner of the place reserved for the Loser of the Week. One week it would be an actor hit with a palimony suit. Another, a politician arrested for using crack cocaine. Once, the marquee boasted the name of a world-famous actress who'd failed in a suicide attempt.

Virgil looked at the seemingly endless rows of soulless minimalls and swanky restaurants and wondered which one had replaced The Losers. Maybe it wasn't gone. Maybe the owner had found another location.

He jerked the T-bird to the right, just missing the front bumper of a Camry creeping up behind him in the right lane. He turned down Olympic and pulled into a supermarket parking lot.

It was the pay phone he wanted.

He called information, asked for a number for The Losers Club or maybe The Losers Lounge.

What city?

Try 'em all.

It didn't take long. I'm sorry, sir, I have no listing for those names. Damn.

He looked at the phone. Should he call her? Naw. She'd be in court anyway.

He went to a movie instead.

≡ 56 ≡

Daspit disagreed with Nikki's assessment of the Jeffrey Bingham situation. "So the guy's a violent asshole," he said as he loaded his brief-case for the weekend. "That's no reason to think the jury would start to wonder if he might have killed the Dietz woman. The knockout drops in Dietz's body indicate premeditation, not a face-off that turned homicidal. Where's the evidence? The motive? The opportunity?"

"The possibility of Jeffrey's guilt occurred to me, Peter," she said, "and I respect evidence and motive more than the average juror. I didn't want to give them that element of doubt."

"You can't honestly think we're trying the wrong brother?"

"No. But we should have covered him. Suppose he's got a black sports car, too."

Daspit stopped packing to stare at her. "Could he have been screwing Dietz?"

She shook her head. "I think he's an uptight WASP who mainly gets it on with his own species, not ladies like Shelli. But"—she smiled—"for a minute there, you were playing with the possibility, too."

"No. Even when I still believed in Santa Claus, I didn't believe in Perry Mason," Daspit said, snapping his case shut. "Jeffrey probably has an alibi, anyway. You should have checked that with the investigating officers."

She started to remind him that one of the investigators was in prison and the other ... No, she didn't feel like going there, trying to explain, *Well, you see, Peter, he and I have been lovers, but now he's bailed and not returning my calls.* Instead she said, "I suppose I should have."

"Well, we ended soft," he said. "We'll have to firm that up with our closings. You clear on what you're doing?"

They'd had a slight disagreement about final arguments. Daspit had wanted to do the closing alone. Nikki countered that he could take opportunity and identity, but she felt she would be more effective covering Bingham's intent and motive. Especially since, through Jenny Mapes's cross-examination, she'd uncovered the strongest evidence to support the motive of jealousy and desire for vengeance. They went back and forth on it, but that's the way they finally agreed to split the summation.

Daspit evidently wasn't enchanted by the compromise.

"I'm clear," she replied, wondering if he'd have anything more to say about it before making his exit.

He didn't.

She returned to her office determined to prepare a closing argument that would make even a stiff-necked, pursed-lips, stone-faced Mr. Bland like Daspit jump up and boogie down. Or at least, considering who he was, do the turkey trot.

That night, she gave Bird an after-dinner walk past her neighbors' homes, stealing wistful glances at family tableaux framed in brightly lit picture windows. Husbands and wives. Children. Relatives, Friends. Dining. Watching television. Enjoying themselves. Thanking God it was Friday.

She and Bird returned home to share their family togetherness, the big dog lying flat from chin to hind legs on the floor, at his mistress's feet while she sat at her computer inputting bits of information gleaned from a hundred slips of paper.

From time to time, she'd glance at the silent phone, then return to the task at hand.

It was nearly midnight when she dragged her weary self to bed.

She and Bird did the sand mountain at dawn.

An hour later, she was back at the computer, going over the steps Randy Bingham took the night of the murder.

He arrives at seven. Is greeted by mother and son. Shelli spies the champagne. For later, he says. The guy's going to make their engagement official. She's down with that. We have Adam's testimony to substantiate her happiness at the start of the evening. Same source states that dinner starts pleasant, then gets tense. Why? Unknown.

They return to the Dietz home. The three watch television in the living room. Dietz goes upstairs to put the boy to bed. Bingham turns off the TV, strolls into the kitchen, pops the cork on the champagne, and grabs one glass from the shelf. Why the one glass?

Nikki had been bothered by that from the jump. Was it worth worrying about? She hoped not.

He takes the glass and the bottle into the den.

Shelli returns. Does he get down on one knee, our poetic, sensitive little killer, all the while thinking about that Smith & Wesson 9 mm? Showing her the engagement ring. Slipping it on her finger. Feeling her hug him joyfully, kiss him. Trust him.

He clinks the bottle against her glass. The damn bottle. Why the bottle? Hell, let's suppose he has a glass, which would make more sense. Why would he get rid of it after the murder? What could the glass have told us? He admits being there, drinking the champagne.

The usual reason for getting rid of the glass would be to destroy its contents.

Her mind took a strange sideways jog. Thinking outside the box.

What if Bingham's glass had been doctored? Could crazed Jenny Mapes have returned that night from Agoura to slip Randy a mickey and kill her employer in a jealous rage? Maybe Jeffrey Bingham dropped by at his brother's invitation to help them celebrate and decided in a fit of pique to kill Shelli and teach Randy a lesson? No! That way lay madness. Ignoring the ridiculousness of those theories, there'd been no hint of anyone present other than murderer and victim. Stick to the evidence. Get back in the groove.

Okay. Randy and Shelli drink champagne. He brings up what Jenny Mapes has told him about Shelli sleeping around. Shelli denies it, but that old cuckold aggression bubbles to the surface. He starts raving loud enough to disturb Adam's sleep. Shelli calms him down somehow. More champagne. More anger. He's really stoked now. He picks up the gu . . .

Hmmm. Where, oh, where had the gun been all this time? Where did it come from?

Did Bingham carry it under his shirt, hide it till he and Shelli were alone? Or had he really given it to her previously, in which case he'd retrieved it while she was upstairs with Adam?

Nikki played the questions over and over in her mind. Then she picked up the phone and dialed Daspit's home. He answered on the first ring. Probably sitting at his computer, too.

"What do you think about the gun?" she asked him. "Did Bingham really give it to Shelli Dietz?"

He was silent for a few seconds, then replied, "Nobody saw it at Dietz's. Not Mapes. Not the brother. Not Adam. We only have ole Randy's word for it—in one of his first interrogations—that he gave it to her. You got a problem with the gun?"

"No," she replied. "Just wondering how it wound up in the den, ready for Randy to use."

"One of three scenarios," he said. "It had been in his possession all along. He gave it to her and she gave it back, probably at his request. And three, he knew where she kept it."

"I'm thinking number three. I can't see him walking in there with a six pack under his shirt. I'd like to know where she was keeping the weapon, though."

"Why? What difference does it make?"

"I'd just like to get as complete a picture as I can of his actions that night. Did he have to follow her upstairs and root around in her bedroom for the gun? Was it hiding in a cabinet in the living room? Where?"

"You all right?" he asked.

"Yeah. Why?"

"You're making your job harder than it has to be," he said. "If he brought it or if he went looking for it at her place, it's still premeditation. This one isn't rocket science. We're favored to win. Don't psyche yourself out."

"You sound a little overconfident."

"Maybe we both better get back to work."

Yowsah, she thought. "Guess we'd better," she said.

She returned to her chronology.

The gun appears. Say Bingham gets it from some hidey-hole he knows about. He waves it at her. There was no evidence of a struggle. The gun goes off. Once. Twice.

Randy sobers up fast. Panics. Wipes the gun and places it in her hand and presses her fingers around it. He's an idiot. Doesn't know how easy it is to tell if she fired the weapon or not. He's never read a murder mystery. . . .

Stop that! He's a little drunk and he's panicked, so he's not thinking right. He gets out of there, double time.

It worked for her, after a fashion. Now she had to document Bingham's feelings of insane jealousy and rage over his girlfriend's betrayal that, ironically enough, probably had existed only in the rather simple mind of a young woman who had the hots for him herself.

At two o'clock on Sunday afternoon, her phone rang.

It was Adam Noyes.

"How you doing?" she asked.

"I'm fine. Wanna come to dinner? We're barbecuing."

She'd finished a rough version of her summation. She needed to shorten and sharpen it, and then practice it until she would be able to

walk into the courtroom on Monday, ready to lay it on the jury ver-
batim but sounding as if she were talking to them over the back fence.

"Wish I could, but I've gotta work. We're just about at the end of
the trial."

"I've been watching the TV," he said. "They make it sound like
you've been kicking defense butt."

She grinned. "And I want to keep my foot limber. That's why I'm
going to have to take a pass on dinner."

"Too bad," he said gloomily. "I want to see you and even though he
doesn't say so, I'm sure Virgil does, too."

"Virgil?" She was sitting straight in the chair.

"Uh-huh. He's staying here this weekend. Some people at his apartment he didn't want to talk to. It's been fun. Yesterday I showed him
around Homeboy. After dinner, he and Sidney and Howard and I played
poker until it was my bedtime. I think they kept at it for a while. Today
we're having barbecue."

"Sounds like the best of Boys Town."

"Wish you could come."

"So do I," she said. It was the truth. She considered asking him to
tell Virgil hello. She decided against it.

"Have fun," she said.

She hung up the phone and went back to work.

≡ 57 ≡

The movie that Virgil had wound up watching Friday afternoon was about a bunch of astronauts sent by the president of the United States into outer space to divert a giant meteor headed for Earth. It was a tough assignment, especially because one of the astronauts was an alien in disguise knocking off the real 'nauts, one by one.

There were twenty space travelers. Seventeen Caucasian actors, one Asian-American, no Latinos, and two African-Americans. That was about par, Virgil had thought. He'd made a bet with himself that neither black man was going to turn out to be the alien. The no-doubt white producers weren't about to make that kind of statement. He wasn't so certain about the Asian-American.

Sure enough, a black actor he didn't recognize bit the dust as the alien's second victim. The other, better-known one stuck around to die heroically helping to change the course of the meteor. The surface of the meteor had reminded Virgil of the burned crust of a cheese pizza.

When he'd left the theater, he'd gone directly to an Italian restaurant and had a pizza. Not just cheese, but mushrooms, sausages, and green peppers. Feeling fine, if a little bloated, he'd headed for his apartment at about 8:00 P.M.

Damned if the IAG sedan wasn't still there.

Screw those guys. He wasn't about to deal with them. That meant he could sneak into his apartment from the rear and not turn on any lights or the AC. Or he could go to a motel. Or . . .

Adam's house was bedroom city. Even with Howard Rule camped out there, three rooms were collecting dust. And he'd be earning his stay, adding one more set of professional eyes and ears to the job of keeping the premises threat-free.

Adam welcomed him happily. Howard gave a half-nod, which Virgil took as a warm acceptance. The security man introduced him to a young cop named Garnett, who was part of the round-the-clock protection the city was providing. The police officer looked competent. And bored.

"Not enough shakin' around here for one of us," Howard said, "much less two and now three. I might split a little later tonight, take care of some personal matters. Come back tomorrow night."

"Okay by me," Virgil said.

Garnett, a man of very few words, shrugged and left them sitting in the kitchen while he made a tour of the grounds.

Not for the first time, Virgil found himself fascinated by Howard's scar.

Rule caught him staring. He traced it with a thick finger. "Poster boy for safety razors," he said. "Watch out, or it can happen to you."

"How'd you get it, really?" Virgil asked.

"By being a dumb rookie when the King verdict broke," Rule said. "Got my ER experience the hard way that one evening."

"You talking about the King riots?" Adam asked.

Rule nodded. "You're too young to remember," he said.

"I was alive then. In 1992, this jury with no black people on it let these white cops go, even though there was a videotape of them whaling on a black motorist named Rodney King. That caused a riot."

"One way of looking at it," Howard said.

Virgil said nothing. The King riots had been tough enough to live through. He'd discovered long ago there was nothing to be gained by discussing them with white guys. Especially white guys who'd had their face sliced open in the course of the riots.

"She looked so sweet and innocent, too," Howard continued.

"She?" Adam asked.

"Couldn't have been older than . . . you. I bent down to move her out of the way of the crowd rolling down on us and she had this razor blade in her tiny hand."

Adam's eyes were like saucers. "Wow. What else?"

"What else? I started losing blood and that was my ticket away from the front line," Rule said. "But I get to remember it at least once a day when I shave."

At Virgil's suggestion, they retired to the kitchen, where he changed the subject to cases a little more upbeat. Adam drank hot cocoa and listened intently as the two men had coffee and talked about some of the more amusing things that had happened during their careers of fighting crime.

At nine o'clock, Howard left to pursue his "personal matters." Virgil walked upstairs with Adam. The boy hesitated at the door to his bedroom. "Would you do me a favor?" he asked.

"What's that?"

"Tell me a story."

"What kind of story?"

"That's up to you. Mom used to tell me stories when I'd go to bed. She was really good at it, because she was a professional. Donia tries, but her stories are pretty lame. Baby stories about bunny rabbits and stuff. I want to hear a story like you and Howard were telling."

"I'm a little burned out on cop stories," Virgil said.

"Okay, then something else."

"I got one about these astronauts who have to knock this meteor out of the way before it destroys Earth."

Adam frowned. "That's an old movie. I saw it years ago."

"This is newer. One of the 'nauts is an alien in disguise and he's killing off the others."

"Now you're talking. I want to hear it."

His bedroom turned out to be spacious, almost the size of Virgil's entire apartment, opening onto a balcony that overlooked the rear of the house. It was a surprisingly adult room. No TV. No computer. The walls were bare. No posters or pennants. The furnishings were adult, too. A king-size bed with a pale brown cover that looked like it was filled with down, a chest of drawers, and a mirrored walk-in closet that ran the length of one wall. The only signs that a young person inhabited the space were electronic games and robotic-looking toys on a night table beside the bed and a tape recorder and a pile of brightly colored cassettes on the floor beside his bed. Blues, yellows, reds.

The red cassettes reminded Virgil of the one clutched in Pickett's death grip. The image of the big man's corpse flashed before his eyes, accompanied by a chill that swept his body. A rabbit jumping over his grave, as they used to say when he was a boy back in Louisiana.

"What's the problem at your apartment?" Adam asked, chasing away the morbid image. He pulled his shirt over his head and tossed it onto the carpet.

Virgil went through the balcony door to give the boy some privacy. The night was warm. Below, the guard, Garnett, was strolling around the pool, heading for the fenced-in area at the rear of the property.

"There are people hanging around I don't want to talk to," Virgil said to Adam through the open door.

"In your apartment?"

"Not in the apartment. Waiting for me outside."

"Like reporters?" the boy asked. Virgil heard the bed squeak and walked back inside, closing the door on the still night, feeling the tickle of cool air from a nearby vent. Adam was in bed, clad in blue pajamas, half-covered by a tan sheet. The duvet was on the floor, spread across the rug like a downed parachute. Adam's clothes dotted the rug where he'd tossed them. The boy was used to people picking up after him. He said, "I know how it is when reporters get in your way and yell things at you."

"Yeah. These people are pests," Virgil said. "Just like reporters."

"You don't look so happy," the boy said.

"How happy should I look?"

"I read about what happened to that man, the one we followed who was trying to hurt your friend."

Ricky Geruso. Virgil was trying to forget that he'd made Adam a part of that bad business. If he hadn't, maybe he and Nikki would still be—no. *Don't go there.* What-ifs could sink you so low you couldn't climb back up. "Yeah," he said. "Man got himself blown up."

"Good," Adam said.

Actually, Virgil agreed with that sentiment, but some incipient daddy gene told him that wasn't the proper message to convey. "You shouldn't look at it that way," he said.

"What do you mean?"

"A man dies, it's not a good thing. No matter what kind of a man he was."

Adam gave him a puzzled look. "I don't understand. I read about this guy from long ago named Hitler. Everybody seemed happy to be rid of *him*. Killed millions of Jews. I'm Jewish on my mom's side."

"Hitler was no great shakes as a human being. You're right about that."

"There are people today, like that man who blew up that post office building. Wouldn't the world be better if he was dead?"

So here he was on a big Friday night, Virgil thought, arguing against capital punishment with a kid and losing. Probably because he believed in capital punishment.

"You want to hear about the alien and the astronauts?" he asked.

Virgil slept for fourteen hours. With the exception of being unconscious for a whole day after the shooting, it was the longest and deepest sleep that he could remember. He felt damn good, all things considered.

He ate breakfast alone in the kitchen. Orange juice. Eggs, bacon, toast. Coffee. Three cups of coffee, that took him through the always skinny Saturday *L.A. Times* and a conversation with Sidney about Michael Jordan's retirement, with both of them agreeing that the man was wealthy enough to stop doing commercials, which threatened to tarnish his legend.

Sidney generously loaned him a razor and by ten o'clock he was shaved, showered, and looking pretty good, even in yesterday's clothes. Searching for the boy, he encountered the policeman who'd replaced Garnett earlier that morning. Officer Louis Derkin was of average height, long-waisted, short-legged, heavily muscled with dark wiry hair, pale skin, and a prominent chin that carried a permanent stubble. He was sitting behind the house under an umbrella, sipping iced tea, a sheen of perspiration on his face.

After Virgil introduced himself, Derkin asked, "What's with the kid?"

"What do you mean?"

"He's a multimillionaire. Lives in this place. Has people to wait on him hand and foot. Here it is Saturday and, instead of kicking back, he's in there"—he indicated Adam's workroom—"grinding away. I don't get it."

"He likes what he's doing," Virgil said.

Derkin sighed. "I got kids sixteen and seventeen. Right now they're at home watching dumb cartoon shows, eating everything that's not nailed down, belching, farting, and not bringing in a thin dime. I get home from eight hours with Workaholic Junior in there and I feel like kicking my kids' butts."

Virgil smiled. "Howard Rule tells me that there haven't been any more threats or problems since that first phone call."

"Naw. It's been smooth as that pool," Derkin said, indicating the swimming pool with its bright aqua, glassy surface. "Speaking of which, it sure is tempting. It gets pretty hot out here."

"Why don't you go inside? It's air-conditioned."

"The kid says it, uh, inhibits his work, having me in the room with him. From here, I can keep an eye on him through the windows. It's okay. The umbrella helps and the lady, Donia, is nice enough to keep me in iced tea and lemonade."

"You can spend the afternoon inside," Virgil said. "I'm gonna take the kid somewhere fun."

"I should come along. You got your limb tied."

"I'll be okay. No sense doubling up."

"I'm on the job," he said.

"We'll be back in a few hours."

Virgil left the cop and walked to the rear door of the workshop. He knocked. He could hear a hip-hop beat vibrating through the door. He knocked louder. When that didn't work, he opened the door.

The music coming from the speakers was intense. Adam was bent over a workbench wearing some sort of goggles that circled the back of his head with a thick blue band. Virgil shouted, "Hey!"

"Damn it!" Adam screamed, tearing off the goggles and whirling in a fury. "I told you never . . ." He saw Virgil and did an instant chill. "I'm sorry, I didn't know it was you." He walked to the audio center and turned down the volume. He had a sheepish grin on his face. "I sorta get caught up in what I'm doing."

Virgil was considerably taken aback by the show of temperament. But he couldn't see the point in making a big deal of it. Instead, he stood at the work counter and asked, "What's all this?"

"Just another idea," the boy replied, indicating a thin plastic square topped by an intricate grillwork pattern of minute copper wiring. "Nothing that can't wait."

"I thought you might want to do something today," Virgil said.

"Sure. Like what?"

"Go out to Magic Mountain. Disney—" He stopped when he saw the boy's expression. "Not your style, huh?"

"How about I take you through Homeboy?" Adam said with considerably more eagerness.

"Deal," Virgil said. Fine with him. Less coming out of his wallet and they wouldn't have to put up with any crowds.

"I'll be ready in a couple of minutes," Adam said. "Meet you in the house."

Virgil let himself out. Even before the door shut, the music was back on full gain.

The tour of the Homeboy universe took a couple of hours. Virgil was impressed not only by the scope of the business but by the respect with which the weekend workers treated the boy. Adam was the 800-pound gorilla, of course, and if the incident in his workshop was any indication, not the easiest gorilla to get along with. But there seemed to be more to their reverence than just caution. Adam knew their jobs better than they did.

As they strolled down executive row, where his was the corner office, Adam stopped to point out a small, neat room that had only one wall decoration—a three-foot-by-eight-foot blowup of a front page of the *L.A. Times*. It was from the third morning of the King riots in 1992. In the right corner was a photo of a policeman seated in an emergency ward, stoically getting his face bandaged by a medic in scrubs. Howard Rule.

"This is Howard's office," Adam said.

"Figured," Virgil replied, his eyes taking in the clean desk, the stacked papers, the silver-framed black-and-white studio portrait of a woman posed, starlet-like, in a tight black gown against a velvet backdrop, her blond hair cascading down to her waist. The caption read, "To Howie, ever my handsome boy."

Virgil felt weird for having looked at the picture. There was something about the photo that was both intimate and offbeat. He didn't want to puzzle it out. "Let's move on," he said to Adam.

They had lunch in the company cafeteria. Adam said he preferred the down-home food over the more adventurous bill of fare in the executive dining room. "Anyway," he said, "the executives who come in on the weekend aren't much fun. And there are no supersonic pinball games in the dining room."

In the afternoon, they visited two malls, going from collector store to collector store. At the Beverly Center, Virgil grabbed an opportunity to buy a couple pairs of shorts and a new T-shirt. When he returned to the shop where he'd left Adam, the boy was no longer there. Panicked, Virgil finally found him in the store's back room, wheeling and dealing his way through four anime card purchases, none for less than $100. "The storeowner and I both knew what we were doing," he told Virgil on the drive back to his home. "I got no bargains. But I completed my *Sailor Moon* series."

Virgil was tempted to take a spin past his place, to see if it was clear. He decided against it. Better to just stay away for the weekend. There was nothing for him at his apartment and he remembered the terrific sleep he'd had at Adam's. One more night like that and he'd be a totally new man.

After a roast beef dinner that evening, Virgil suggested a card game.

He, the late-shift policeman, Leslie Becker, an officer in his twenties with a gold tooth, Sidney, and Adam played poker, using chips in lieu of money. Five-card stud, anaconda, baseball, all games were new to the boy. But after one or two hands, the chips started piling up in front of him.

Once Adam was in bed, eyes shut, and breathing regularly, Virgil returned to the game, which had progressed to penny ante. Donia was sitting in, too. Howard arrived at ten and took a seat. They played until after midnight. Sidney was the big winner with his three-dollar-and-twenty-cent profit, most of that lost by Howard.

Virgil slept for another twelve hours. When he awoke, he began to wonder if he could become a permanent boarder. He was drinking coffee in the kitchen at a little after one, when Adam raced in. "Don't have a big breakfast," he said to Virgil. "We're going to barbecue for lunch in less than an hour."

Virgil took his second cup of coffee to a chair by the pool. There, he talked sports with Howard, Derkin, and Sidney, who heated the charcoal under the grill. It was nearly two when Adam joined them with a dejected look on his face.

"What's the matter?" Virgil asked.

"I was just on the phone," the boy said. The men tensed. Howard was actually out of his chair before Adam added, "With Nikki." Howard, Derkin, and Sidney relaxed. Virgil didn't.

"What'd she have to say?" Virgil asked.

"I invited her to come to the barbecue. She said she couldn't."

"You mention I was here?" Virgil asked.

"Sure."

Virgil nodded. No wonder she said no.

"Can we play poker again tonight?" Adam asked.

"I think I'm going to head home," Virgil said.

"Won't those people still be waiting for you?"

"Maybe. I'll have to deal with 'em sometime." He flexed the muscles in his sling-supported arm. Not much more than a little tenderness and a lot of stiffness in his shoulder. "It's time I started getting back on track."

≡ 58 ≡

Nikki had only the vaguest idea of how she'd spent the early part of Monday morning. She hazily recalled feeding the dog, feeding herself, showering, dressing, the dozen or more little chores that were part of her daily ritual. She knew she practiced her closing on the drive downtown, with a tape recorder on the passenger seat beside her; she still had the cassette.

She thought she'd had at least two cups of coffee in her office and maybe passed an incommunicative Dana Lowery while heading for the elevator to the courtroom.

She had a foggy memory of Judge Proody arriving, buttoned and looking as happy as a man can with an enlarged prostate. She had some sense of Daspit leaving the table and standing in front of the jury explaining to them about murder in the first degree.

Then it was her turn. No vagueness there.

Though her legs felt unusually rubbery, she got up without any noticeable problem, walked confidently to the jury box, and began her summation.

She reminded them that "the accused is a poet—his family, everybody said so—and as everybody knows poets feel more than other people. They feel a stronger love than ordinary mortals. They feel a darker hatred. When Randolph J. Bingham the third discovered from Jenny Mapes that the woman he loved with all his poet's heart had betrayed him, he made up his mind to kill her.

"He didn't consider that he might be caught or tried or convicted. Randolph J. Bingham the third, a child of privilege, only thought of one thing—revenge. Revenge for the humiliation he was suffering at the hands of the woman he trusted, Shelli Dietz. Even the nanny knew he was being cuckolded. Not in truth—for no evidence has been presented in this court that Shelli Dietz was anything but a faithful and loving woman—but in his twisted mind. He felt he had to do something to regain his self-respect.

"He decided to kill her. He created a plan. Not a very good one, as it turns out. Let his father, his brother, Shelli, the world think he was blissfully unaware of her infidelity. A happy man about to marry is a man without motive for murder. He took his unsuspecting victim and her son to dinner, then returned home and watched television with them, all the while thinking about Jenny Mapes's phone call. You re-member her exact words on the witness stand. She told him that his beloved was 'slutting around.'

"When the boy was put to bed, Randolph Bingham and Shelli Dietz began drinking champagne. And his anger began to grow, eventually erupting into shouts and screams so loud they awoke her young son, Adam. It made the boy a witness to Bingham's presence in the house and state of mind. This was the last thing a practical man would want. But Randolph J. Bingham the third isn't a practical man. He's a poet, with a poet's emotional excesses.

"He took the gun—proven without doubt to be his own weapon—and used it to murder the woman he believed to be his faithless lover. He placed the gun in her own hand. Was this a vain and stupid at-tempt to suggest suicide? Or could it have been a poetic way of telling the world she had been responsible for her fate?

"In either case, the deed was done. Most murderers would flee. Not the poetic Mr. Bingham. He spent nearly seven minutes arranging the body, just so. And in so doing, dropped a crucial piece of evidence—his asthma spray bottle. Mr. Wheeler has tried to tell you that Mr.

Bingham dropped that medicine earlier in the evening, well before the murder. It was found on top of a puddle of the victim's blood. If it had been in that spot when Shelli Dietz was killed, her blood would have been on its surface, too. But the surface of the bottle was clean, except for the fingerprints of Mr. Randolph J. Bingham the third. And no one else's.

"The murderer fled the scene. Mr. Wheeler has tried to convince us that his client left the Dietz home well before the crime. But the shots that killed Shelli Dietz were reported at 2:12 A.M. that night. Seven minutes later—seven long minutes—Gustave Prosser, a neighbor with excellent eyesight, familiar with the suspect's looks and the car he drove, saw him racing from the scene of the crime. Identified him without the shadow of a doubt.

"There's nothing more you need to know. A man of wealth and privilege became so obsessed by jealousy that he brutally murdered the woman he once loved. A talented and caring mother died. A young boy was orphaned. Randolph J. Bingham the third created this sad and terrible and unnecessary tragedy. It's up to you to end it on a note of justice."

Wheeler was an old hand at damage control, but this ship was sinking too fast. He wasn't bad at bailing, but he didn't have the best material at his disposal. His only hope of a verdict of not guilty rested in his ability to discredit the two witnesses who placed Bingham at the scene of the crime and to somehow suggest that the physical evidence was tainted. This last might have been achieved if Proody had allowed him to put McNeil on the stand. Mimi Gentry had damaged Prosser, but hadn't sunk him and the boy's testimony remained rock solid.

Wheeler did what he could. "Adam is a moody, odd child whose memory of that night had certainly been colored and confused by the tragedy. If he did hear the angry voice of Randy Bingham, it could only have been in a dream.

"As for the old porno filmmaker, can you honestly believe anything he might have said? After a night of indulging himself with degenerate images on the television screen, he drags himself to a window and stares out just in time to see my client leave the Dietz house. And he notes the precise time.

"Why? Why did he wait so long to tell the police this amazing thing that he witnessed? Because, ladies and gentlemen, he didn't get the idea to do that until he read the morning paper. That's when he conceived of a way to place himself in the public eye and possibly rekindle his dormant career."

His final argument went on for a little over two hours.

The jury began its deliberation at 3:19 P.M. that afternoon.

At a little after five, Daspit and Nikki were called back to court to hear their decision.

The foreperson, a very large woman who was a buyer for a department store in Culver City, read the verdict to a crowded, murmuring courtroom. Randolph J. Bingham the third was guilty of murder in the first degree.

Nikki was not terribly surprised.

Neither were the defense attorneys, who tried to comfort their weeping client. Judge Proody banged his gavel and announced that sentencing would be the following morning.

Daspit shut his briefcase and stood aside to let Nikki lead the way through the court. She paused to look at the teary-eyed Bingham, who wailed his innocence while an officer waited patiently to escort him to his cell. When she started out again, she discovered that someone had pushed through the crowd to invade her personal space. Jeffrey Bingham stared at her with cold hatred. He was close enough for her to smell his subtle spicy cologne, the scent of cloves on his breath. "I know about you and that lying little half-caste," he hissed.

"Say what?"

"You think you've dragged my brother down to your level."

It wasn't the first time she'd been approached by a family member whose fury had been unleashed by a successful prosecution. That came with the territory. Anger was only a skip away from grief. Usually it too passed with time. Jeffrey Bingham didn't look like a particularly flexible man, however. Not standing twelve inches away with his shoulders hunched and white showing all around his pupils. "You'll get yours, lady. You and the little bastard who lied through his teeth."

He spun on his heel and moved away through the crowd.

"What the hell was that?" Daspit asked behind her.

"That," she said, "was one scary son of a bitch."

Wise held a little victory celebration in his office. White wine and pound cake from a nearby deli. The D.A. was very pleased. The guilty verdict would have its positive effect at the polls. Wise perched on the edge of his desk, beaming at the group of lawyers, clerks, and investigators who'd participated in the trial. Nikki assumed Virgil had been invited, but she hadn't expected him to show up. It would have been interesting if he had.

Twenty minutes into the party, its atmosphere was shattered by the arrival of Dana Lowery. Wise, ever the genial host, greeted her with a smile. "Dana, if I'd thought you needed a glass of cheap wine this badly, I would have invited you."

She marched up to him, a lopsided mirthless smile on her face. "I just wanted to give you fair warning, Ray. I've uncovered the conspiracy. I know what you and that one"—she pointed a narrow finger at Nikki—"have been up to and I'm not going to stand for it. The people of this county won't stand for it either."

Wise grinned at her. "Dana, I don't know why I never realized it before," he said, "but you're as crazy as a dancing bedbug."

"Fair warning," she said again and marched from the suddenly quiet room.

Wise broke the silence by humming *Do-dee-do-do*, then said, "We have just entered . . . the Twilight Zone."

Nikki approached Wise. "What the hell was she talking about? What conspiracy?"

"Only the Shadow knows," he said, going back even further for the reference. He chuckled. "It's finally happened. She's cracked like a walnut."

"Cracked or not, she's up to something," Nikki said.

Wise stared at her and picked up some of her concern. He lost his grin. "Maybe," he said. "We probably won't have to wait too long to find out."

PART FOUR

SUMMATION

☰ 59 ☰

This isn't the end of it, lad," the elder Randolph Bingham said to his second son.

Jeffrey Bingham didn't reply. He was seated on the patio of his father's granite-and-glass home in the Hollywood Hills, high above the heat and pollution that blanketed the rest of the city. He appeared to be staring down on the shimmering lights of nighttime Los Angeles but, in fact, he was seeing nothing but a continuous replay of his weeping brother being dragged away to a cell. Forever. Keats had turned to him, eyes wild and frightened as a spooked horse's, his lips sending out the silent plea: "Help me!" Then the huge hand of the police officer—black, of course—grabbed his brother's shoulder and yanked him away.

"No, sir, we're not giving up on Rand," the elder Bingham said. "I'm meeting with Wheeler and Mimi in the morning and—"

"I'm leaving," Jeffrey said, rising to his feet.

"Stay for dinner, son. It's just you, me, and Divina. The family should be together tonight."

Divina? The family? Jeffrey looked past his father, through the wall of glass that separated them from the rest of the house. Divina George, ever elegant, was lighting the candles on the dining room table. This was his father's idea of family? Some stuck-up black secretary with a kid nobody ever saw who was probably a crack dealer?

The old man was even talking about marrying her. The idea started Jeffrey's stomach churning. His whole world seemed to be turning to shit, thanks to so-called *African-Americans*. Divina. The court officer dragging his brother away. Adam Noyes. The arrogant prosecutor Nikki Hill. Send 'em all back to their fucking beloved Africa. Better yet, send 'em to hell.

"Jeffrey's not staying for dinner?" Divina asked as his father followed him to the front of the house. Was her tone mocking? *It damn fucking was.*

He stopped and almost initiated the confrontation he'd been postponing ever since the miserable evening his father had confessed to him that he'd fallen in love with his secretary. He'd kept his tongue then, knowing the old man all too well, knowing how naive and stupidly unreasonable his father could be. The black bitch had him mesmerized. Even the slightest criticism of their "romance" could result in Jeffrey being not only out of his father's will but out of a job as well.

"Don't worry, son," his father said, misreading his scowl. "We're not gonna let Randy rot in any prison cell."

Oh, God. Poor Keats! The pathetic old fart really trusted that incompetent cornpone cretin who called himself a lawyer to help his brother. "Yeah, well, you take care, Dad," he said.

"Divina's the one takes care of me, son. You should start thinking about settling down yourself."

Jeffrey felt the overwhelming urge to scream.

Somehow he managed to suppress it until he had driven out of earshot of the hilltop house. He steered his Lexus to the side of the road and released a yell so filled with anguish that it brought tears to his eyes.

Afterward he leaned back against the leather seat, panting, the Lexus's frigid air chilling the perspiration on his face. He sat there nearly five minutes, then gulped a deep breath and pointed his sedan back into the world reserved for those with self-control.

When he arrived at the apartment on Sweetzer, his roommate, Doug, was in the living room in his boxer shorts, sipping white wine, and watching a DVD of the movie *The Ice Storm* on the ridiculously huge TV set he claimed was necessary for his work. Doug referred to himself as a pre-published novelist, but in the two years since he'd moved in, Jeffery was not aware of him writing so much as a postcard. Not that Doug would ever have to. A wealthy doting grandmother had seen to that. He would be receiving a monthly allowance of twenty thousand dollars, tax-free, for the rest of his life. Even if he lived to be a hundred, which did not seem likely, considering that he was both promiscuous and careless.

It had been that irresponsible double-header that had led Jeffrey to nip their sexual relationship in the bud shortly after Doug moved in. Now they were just two gay men sharing an apartment and the rent. "Hey, Jeff-ster. Bummer about Rand."

Jeffrey looked at the nearly naked, slightly drunk boy whose eyes had not left the icy long shots on the big screen. "He could get life," he said. "Of course, the possibility of execution still exists. 'Bummer' sums that up pretty well."

"Aw, shit," Doug said, jumping to his feet and deserting the flash-frozen ennui of the movie. He placed his hands on Jeffrey's shoulders and stared into his eyes. "I really am sorry. You know I care about your brother."

Jeffrey nodded and pulled away.

"Have a glass of the chardonnay. It's Stag's Leap '95."

"Not right now," Jeffrey said, heading for the hall that led to his study and bedroom.

"I heard your phone ring about an hour ago," Doug called after him. "Probably left a message."

Jeffrey turned on the overhead in his study, then crossed the room to the phone and its blinking white light. Two hits, according to the LED display. He pressed the "new message" button and heard the screechy rewind as he slipped from his suit coat and started removing his tie.

The first call had been from someone wondering if he knew about the Special Buyers Club his bank was endorsing. It was such a help to today's shoppers that the bank was willing to let him sample its enormous benefits on a three-month trial basis.

With a sigh, Jeffrey tapped the "skip" button. The second call immediately grabbed his full attention.

"Your brother is, innocent," a choppy, metallic voice began. It had an otherwordly hollow sound, like the voice that announces floors in elevators. "I know how . . . you can prove it. Meet me tonight, nine-thirty. Foster's Drugs, Melrose and Beverly. Park in space, along Melrose. Stay in car. Turn on your cellular. It has been off all night. A weapon, may be useful, if you have one. If you do not come, I will assume . . . I have mistaken your feelings . . . for your brother. I will not contact you again."

The message ended.

Jeffrey looked at his watch. It was just about nine. He knew Foster's. It was less than ten minutes away. He was curious about the request for a weapon, but he knew how he could use one. To scare the shit out of somebody, that little Noyes bastard maybe. Then he could get to the truth.

A weapon. He didn't have any handguns or knives, anything like that. However, locked in his closet were three rifles that he'd used on safaris with his father. One of those would do very nicely.

His thoughts shifted to the caller. Who was he? Or she? Someone in the courtroom? Someone who was close to his brother? That wrinkled fat bimbo fraud who ran the Church of the Mumbo Jumbo or one of her thugs? The Goth baby-sitter with the new hairdo? Hell, it could be any of a number of Keats's "people."

He unlocked the closet and grabbed the rifle case closest to the door. A Kleinguenther K-15. Why should he give a damn who it was offering to help? What did he or his brother have to lose?

≡ 60 ≡

Nikki parked the Mazda in Adam's crowded driveway, next to Fallon's Mercedes and Howard's colorful company van. Static from a police car radio screeched through the still night. She was feeling the lousy aftereffects of booze before bedtime, the slight headache and sour stomach, and none of that pleasant glow. That had disappeared a half hour before, at a little after 10:00 P.M., when Fallon had phoned to tell her about the shooting.

Lights brightened the front door and every window of the house and there was a glow coming from behind the building. Shit, she was still wearing her slippers. She'd pulled on jeans and a T-shirt and somehow managed to throw some clothes into an overnight bag. But she'd forgotten shoes. Too late to worry about that.

She gave her name to the uniformed officer at the front door and he moved his bulk aside for her to enter. Howard was standing with two other white men in the dining room, near the kitchen door. Howard was in his usual slacks and Hawaiian print shirt, scowling, the scar a livid streak down his face. The other two men were wearing sport jackets. Detectives.

Fallon entered from the back with a coffee cup in his hand. He was in khakis and what looked like a pajama top—white with blue piping.

Tiny white whiskers powdered the lower part of his face. The anxiety that had been in his voice on the phone seemed to have subsided slightly. He used his free hand to wave her toward the group.

"Nikki, you remember Howard. These are Detectives Rubell and Moss."

"Dave Rubell," the one nearest her said. He was in his forties, medium height, stomach starting to fight his buttoned jacket. Moss was taller, trimmer, and surlier. He didn't bother to give her his first name. She already knew it. Neither man offered a hand for her to shake.

"Where's Adam?" she asked Fallon.

"Upstairs in his bedroom," Howard said. "He's fine."

"Donia's with him," Fallon added. "She's trying to make it clear to him why they're going away."

Fallon had already made it clear to Nikki. Sidney had been in the darkened kitchen, having hot cocoa, when two gunshots—Howard said they were rifle shots—blew out a window facing the pool. Most of the broken glass was concentrated within a few feet of the window, but a few shards found their way to where Sidney was sitting, cutting his face and neck.

He had immediately dropped to the floor, where unfortunately he slid into more glass, slicing the fingers of his right hand. None of the lacerations seemed to be critical. The real damage had been psychological. Sidney, the Vietnam veteran, was suffering a recurrence of post-traumatic stress. He was under sedation. Donia had informed Fallon that she'd been through this with her husband years ago when they'd been younger. She had no choice. They'd be leaving the premises immediately for a hotel. They'd be seeking employment in "a safer environment."

That's when Fallon had called Nikki. Not just to notify her of the shooting but to seek her help in staying with the boy until he could hire someone new to care for him. She didn't know why he felt Howard couldn't do the job by himself.

"So this guy Bingham, Jeffrey Bingham, has been threatening the kid?" Rubell asked.

"Yes," Nikki replied. "This gentleman"—she indicated Howard—

"can tell you about the initial threat, after the boy testified in court against Bingham's brother."

The two detectives looked at Howard. "Yeah. He said something about . . . getting the kid and making him pay for lying on the stand."

"He said he was going to cut Adam's tongue out," Nikki said. "Nice thing to tell a ten-year-old. And he made more threats in court yesterday after his brother's conviction."

"There was a phone threat, too?" Rubell asked.

"Yes," Nikki said. "Only . . ." She decided not to finish the sentence.

"Only what?" Moss insisted.

"It's not one hundred percent certain that Bingham made the phone threat," she said.

"There anybody else got it in for the kid?" he asked.

"No, of course not," Fallon replied. "He's ten years old."

"I've gone over this with Officer Garnett," Howard said. "We saw the guy running out to the road. By the time we got there, he was long gone."

"Car?" Moss asked.

"Black sedan, I think," Howard said. "Maybe blue. Too far for make or model, plates. I should've been quicker out of bed."

"Officer Garnett was downstairs, with his finger up his . . ." Moss let the image go without completing it. "He should've been stepping on the perp's heels."

"There's a lot of property," Howard said. "He was way back by the rear fence when the shots sounded."

"Well, this Bingham fella looks pretty good for it," Rubell said. "Let's go see what his story is."

"We get a warrant first," Moss said. "Otherwise we don't go."

"Kinda late to be getting a warrant."

"Ask the deputy there what she thinks," Moss said.

"You'll need one," Nikki said.

"We'll give it a try," Rubell said. "Mr. Fallon tells us you and Mr. Rule will be staying the night here? We'll have two men join you for the time being, just to play safe."

"Good," Nikki said.

"Whatever," Howard said.

When the detectives had gone, Fallon asked Nikki, "You and Detective Moss have some history?"

"Brief."

"Something about a warrant?"

"He screwed up and cost me a conviction so I made him look like a donkey on the stand. This was about five years ago, but I guess he's not about to forgive and forget."

"Ours is no profession for anyone desiring to be universally beloved," he said.

She flashed on Jeffrey Bingham standing in front of her, threatening her. "No kidding," she said.

≡ 61 ≡

Earlier that night, Virgil had applied his knuckles to a red lacquer apartment door. Almost immediately, feet padded across a carpet, heading toward him.

"Who is there?" a female voice asked.

"Coffin Ed Johnson," he said.

For a few seconds, there was no response. Then the door opened as far as a chain lock would allow. Two-thirds of Annette Bovan's face peered out at him. "You have your nerve, coming here," she said. She didn't seem angry. To the contrary. He thought he'd picked up a little signal that day he invaded Pickett's office. She'd helped Pickett put him in Dutch with the Hollywood cops, but he figured that was nothing personal.

She stepped from behind the door to give him a better view of her body. She was wearing a slip. She looked nice and cool.

"I come in?" he asked.

"How do I know why you are here? How do I know you are not here to hurt me?" She was giving him the playful French sex kitten number. She wasn't bad at it.

"Hurt you? For setting me up with those cops? I knew that was your boss's show, not yours. Do I look angry?"

Her eyes traveled up and down his body. "How did you find me?"

"I'm a detective." He'd conned the information out of Duke Wasson.

"Tell me what you want, or I'll have to close the door."

"To talk."

"Pah. Is that all?"

He grinned at her. It came to him naturally. "We could start with talk."

"How much more could you do, your arm all bandaged?"

"I have my moves," he said.

She shut the door and he heard the chain sliding free. When it opened again, all the way, he stepped into the room. She looked down at the thin silk slip covering her body. "My, my, I should go put something on."

"Not on my account."

"*Asseyez-vous, s'il vous plaît*," she said, indicating a striped sofa. She left the room and was immediately replaced by two Siamese cats, one white, one black. The timing was such that if it had been only one cat, Virgil would have suspected some sort of witch deal. The white cat brushed up against his pants leg. The other stayed back, eyeing him warily.

Annette returned wearing a white kimono with a red Asian symbol over the right breast. It covered her, more or less, from neck to knee. "I see my babies have come to meet you. That is Blanche seeking sexual gratification against your leg. And Noire, bad girl, being so aloof."

"They sisters?" Virgil asked.

"We're sisters," she said. "Would you care for some absinthe?"

"Stuff's illegal."

"It destroys your brain cells," she said, smiling.

"Then bring it on." He moved his leg, trying to shake Blanche loose.

He assumed Annette had put the kimono on over the slip, but when she placed the milky drink in front of him, her gown flared open offering ample evidence to the contrary.

She sat next to him, the black Siamese giving him a wide berth to join her. She asked, "You did not kill him, did you?"

"Pickett? Nope." He sipped the drink. It tasted like licorice. Not brain cell–destroying licorice. Just down-by-the-candy-store licorice with a little added kick. He liked it. "They say a woman did it. I was thinking maybe you."

She laughed. "I liked him," she said. "We were close. It was fun, being a *salope*, a bitch, in the office and being . . . a woman after hours. *Blanche et Noire*, the two parts of me."

The absinthe was warm in his mouth, warm all the way down. The white cat at his feet made a little growl and rolled away from him. She began to purr.

"What happened to your arm and head?" Annette asked.

"A girl shot me."

"And what were you doing to her?"

He smiled. "We all got our secrets."

"Now I am intrigued."

He was suddenly a little unnerved by the situation. The drink. The cats. The woman. He felt like they were all toying with him. It was time to get to the reason he'd come. "You recall seeing any tape cassettes in Pickett's office?" he asked.

"Many. He liked music."

"This was one I don't think you'd buy at Tower Records."

"He received many, what do you call them, demos. Singers and musicians who wanted to perform at the new club. I suppose the club will never open now."

"This tape was bright red," he said. "Like your door."

"Oh, yes, *les cassettes rouges*," she said.

"More than one?"

She nodded. With her free hand, she stroked the black cat's back. "They were not Pickett's. An old man brought them to Mr. Geruso."

"Any idea what was on them?"

"I don't know, exactly. Mr. Geruso would play them in his office. From what I could tell, it was a little girl talking."

"And there were more than one?"

"A bagful."

"Any idea where the bag is?"

"It has been a while since I saw them. Mr. Geruso kept them in his desk."

"You make out anything the girl was saying?"

"No."

"Any idea why the tapes might have been important to Pickett?"

"No idea at all," she said. "I am beginning to feel you did come here just to talk."

Even with the cats and the mind-rotting drink and her weird ways, she was a very sexy woman, laying it out there for him. He and Nikki seemed to be moving further apart; he sure as hell wasn't going to pine for her the rest of his life. Annette was offering him a mighty fine fall-back position. He just wasn't absolutely sure he needed one.

"Talk's it for tonight," he said, standing. "Rain check on the rest?"

"I heard it never rains in southern California," she said.

"I did get your cat off."

She began to laugh. A deep, throaty, French, nasty-girl laugh.

"You're a very funny man, Detective," she said. "Are you a homo?"

"A *homo*?" He chuckled. "Girl, I haven't heard anybody use that word since I was down on the farm."

"Gay, then. Are you gay?" She opened the door for him.

"Nope. Can't say as I am of that particular persuasion."

She nodded. "Then come back some time when you don't feel like talking."

He usually liked hanging out in his apartment, but that night it seemed depressing and confining. He still had licorice on his tongue. He wanted another taste.

He also wanted Nikki. He tried her number.

Her machine answered. He hung up. Where was she at 10:30? He'd heard on the news that she'd won her case. Was she out celebrating? Who with?

He poured himself a shot of tequila. Got that licorice out of his mouth.

Two hours, a lousy TV movie, and five shots of tequila later, he phoned her again. Still the machine. Maybe she was there, phone turned off so she could sleep. He left his name and slightly slurred message, "Ca' me, honey. We gotta talk."

At 3:00 A.M., laughter on the TV awoke him from a drunken slumber. Partially feeling the woozy effect of the alcohol, he phoned once more. Frustrated at getting the machine again, he slammed the receiver back on its cradle, cursing himself for turning down Annette. He wondered what *her* number was.

He finished off the bottle of tequila at four. Nikki was still not picking up. "Me, 'gain," he barely articulated into the receiver. "F'get th' otha mess'ges. Doan wan' you to call me. You lead yo' life, I lead mine, 'kay? Doan call me 'n' I woan call you."

Feeling that strange little tingle you get when you know you've done something really dumb, he passed out with the phone still in his hand.

≡ 62 ≡

It had been after ten when Jeffrey Bingham returned to his apartment. The evening had not gone precisely as planned. The whole thing had been a frustrating failure. A near disaster. He'd heard a scream in the brat's house. The room was supposed to be empty. He might have killed somebody. Worse, he might have been caught.

Doug was entertaining. His guest was a young stud in purple cut-offs and a yellow muscle shirt. The standard hacked green-tinged blond hair, black roots purposely showing. Ersatz diamonds embedded along the rim of his right ear.

"Say hello to Gordo, roomie," Doug said. "Gordo works at the Virgin store. Isn't that a hoot?"

Gordo stuck out a surprisingly well-manicured hand that the AIDS-phobic Jeffrey shied from as if it had been filled with spiders. "Mr. Friendly," Gordo said, withdrawing his digits.

Jeffrey ignored him and rushed to his room. That's where he remembered the damned rifle, still downstairs in the trunk of his Lexus. He should retrieve it, clean it, put it back in the locker. But that would entail another trip past the living room, more conversation with the young lovers. Then, he'd have to bother them again when he returned, explaining what he was doing with a rifle at that time of night.

No.

He'd get the weapon from the car tomorrow when Doug was on his daily two-hour gym trip and the himbo was back cruising, or whatever he did in the morning.

Christ, what a dismal, pathetic, depressing day it had been.

≡ 63 ≡

Nikki sat at her desk on Tuesday, poking at a luncheon salad and wondering what to do, if anything, about the messages that Virgil had left on her machine.

She knew him well enough to realize that, drunk though he may have been, he meant what he'd said about not calling her back. That male pride thing.

She also knew she was not about to simply mark the end of their relationship. Still, those later messages pissed her off mightily. What did he think? That she was getting it on with somebody last night? Didn't the fool know her better than that?

Her mood had swung back almost to the point of "he's not worth all this mental aggravation," when Jesse Fallon called.

"I'm the bearer of unpleasant news, I'm afraid," he told her. "First, the police still have not contacted Jeffrey Bingham. They failed to get the warrant last night. And today, they were told to come up with a little more evidence than a few idle threats to link Bingham to the shooting."

"You said that was first. What's second?"

"Ms. Potter." Fallon had found a seemingly perfect middle-aged woman, a former teacher, to care for Adam. "She's gone. Howard's at

Homeboy, handling some crisis there. I'm at the house now. I hate to ask, but could you spend another night with Adam?"

"What happened?"

"The boy pitched another of his wingdings. Ms. Potter phoned me and took off like a flash when I arrived. He really gave the poor woman a time."

"What set him off?" Nikki asked.

"He claims she went into his workroom and destroyed one of his test models. She says he's crazy. But the damn model is smashed."

"I'll stay with him tonight," Nikki said. She'd been planning on having dinner with Loreen. Her friend would understand. She'd also take care of Bird for her as she had in the past.

"Wonderful." Fallon hesitated. "Can I press my luck? Is it possible for you to be here by four? I hate to ask you, but there's a meeting I simply must make. It could play a part in both our futures."

"That's a pretty intriguing lead-in," she said. "Care to get a little more specific?"

"I want to see how the meeting goes."

"I'll be at the house by four," she said.

≡ 64 ≡

Virgil phoned Nikki at her office and was told by Jeb that she'd left for the day.

"At three-thirty?"

"Mine's not to reason why," Jeb said. "All I know is, she's *went*."

"She go home?"

There was some hesitation on Jeb's part before he replied, "Jar Jar not know."

"Thanks," the detective said. He hung up the phone convinced that the kid was holding out on him. It meant Nikki had been spreading their personal problems all over her office.

He tried her home number. When her machine clicked on, he slammed down the receiver.

His door buzzer rang.

He brightened immediately and ran to the door. "Baby, I—"

Rafe Collins gave him an odd look. "Expecting somebody, brother?" the IAG investigator asked.

"Not really," Virgil said, moving back to his couch.

Collins shut the door and followed him into the apartment. He looked around. "Nice place. Must be a big ticket each month."

"The manager of the complex gives me a break. The other tenants feel safer having a lawman on the premises."

"Smooth work," Collins said. He surveyed the art and African masks on the walls. "You got good taste, Sykes. You been away?"

"No," Virgil said.

"But you haven't been here."

"I been with friends."

"What friends?"

"Just friends. You got something on your mind, Collins? Or you just looking for a place to hang out?"

Collins sat on a leather footrest. "You seem like a good man, Sykes. I just thought you might want to be put wise about something."

"What would that be?"

"Wasson and Puchinski, they're the cops investigating both the Pickett and Geruso murders, they're your buddies, right?"

"Buddies might be pushing it a little. I work with 'em."

"They been building a case against you for a couple days now, brother. And it's coming together."

Virgil knew the son of a bitch was playing him. He'd bought Wasson a drink just the evening before, getting Annette Bovan's address. With Duke, what you saw was what you got. He hadn't seen a hint of any suspicion coming off him. He and Pooch were still working on the woman-killer theory.

"They're investigating me?" he asked Collins. "What's my motive?"

"You wanted to help your partner."

"You say the deaths are helping him?" Virgil asked.

"They sure as hell aren't hurting him. Lemme take that back. They might just hurt him at that, if he asked you to do those murders."

"I'm gonna kill two people, woundin' all those folks on Sunset, just so my partner won't get put down for killin' some ho'? Man, you must be suckin' crack house bedsheets."

"You got any Drano around here, Sykes?"

"Get the fuck out of my apartment, Collins."

"Just trying to be friendly."

"Be friendly somewhere else."

Collins stood up. "I know how it is, brother. You see what's goin' on in the streets, you get a hard-on for the asshole crooks who're living like kings. Pimps, got all those beautiful women. Treat 'em like crap. Hard not to hate 'em," he said. "Hell, I can see wanting to blow 'em away. I hate 'em myself."

"Out," Virgil said. "Go hate your pimps somewhere else."

The man from Internal Affairs started through the door, then turned. "Better enjoy this moment of peace, brother," he said, "'cause your life is about to get very interestin'."

≡ 65 ≡

Nikki, in nightgown and robe at 6:45 A.M., watched from the door-way of Adam's home as a yawning, uniformed policeman bent down near the gate to retrieve the morning paper. He took his time walking back along the brick path and handing it to her.

It was bagged in clear plastic. She wondered why, since there wasn't a cloud in the sky. Maybe they just liked to put a little special touch on things for the good people of Bel Air. *Why settle for just a bag?* she wondered. *Why not deliver the paper between hard covers? Or stick it on one of those wooden spines like they have in libraries?*

She strolled into the kitchen, idly checking the front page through the plastic.

She stopped, chin dropping in surprise at a subheadline: "Deputy D.A. Claims Boss Interference." Under that, in bold type: "Outspoken D.A. Dana Lowery says Raymond Wise is undermining her prosecution of LAPD Detective Daniel McNeil."

Tugging anxiously but ineffectually at the plastic wrap, she entered the kitchen, where Adam was sitting at a table refilling his bowl with a cereal that looked like chopped crayons. His attention shifted from the crudely animated cartoon show on the TV to her struggle. "I use my teeth," he said.

"That's a dumb thing to do," she said, "risk cracking a tooth . . . oh, heck." She lifted the paper, nipped a corner of the bag between her canines and yanked. She was able to probe the resulting tear with her thumb and rip the cover from the paper.

"Something the matter?" Adam asked.

"That's what I'm checking."

It was a story of considerable length. Dana had evidently called another of her infamous news conferences the evening before. Nikki had missed it and its aftermath because she and Adam had been watching a Will Smith movie on video.

This time it looked like Cruella had really gone over the top.

"The acting district attorney is putting roadblocks in the way of a successful prosecution of Homicide Detective Daniel McNeil," the deputy D.A. boldly stated. "He is conspiring, either actively or by benign consent, with those seeking to give McNeil a free ride on the charge of murder."

Nikki knew the magnitude of Dana's ambition and her hatred of Ray, but this was beyond the—

A familiar name caught her eye.

The deputy accused Homicide Detective Virgil Sykes, McNeil's partner, not only of stonewalling her investigators but of purposely interfering in their progress. "I don't know if Mr. Wise is actively helping this rogue cop cover up for his partner," Lowery stated. "But I do know he's aware of Sykes's activities and has taken no action to rein in the pit bull."

Virgil a pit bull? More like a greyhound, lady. Better yet, a wolfhound.
Then her own name popped from the page.

Lowery claims that the connection between the acting D.A. and Sykes is Deputy Nicolette Hill, who, just two days ago, successfully prosecuted Randolph Bingham III for murder. "Hill is Sykes's long-time mistress," Lowery said. "She has used his insider's knowledge of criminal cases to advance her career and ingratiate herself with the acting district attorney."

Day-yum.

She looked up from the paper to see the boy staring at her. She gestured to the TV. "That something you really want to watch?" she asked.

"*Pokémon?* Like I've only seen this episode twenty or thirty times."

"Then do some channel-surfing," Nikki said. "See if you can spot that sour-faced b—the woman who looks like Cruella De Vil. She'll be talking with a bunch of reporters."

While the boy went to work with the remote, she continued scanning the article.

As to why Raymond Wise would interfere with a murder investigation, Lowery replied, "Mr. Wise is a political animal. He wants to be elected. It is not in his best interests for his strongest challenger to successfully prosecute a corrupt member of the Los Angeles Police Department."

"There she is," Adam said.

An apparently unedited tape of last evening's interview was being played on a news network. Nikki watched in amazement as Lowery stated that Virgil "had been questioned by Hollywood Homicide inspectors who thought he may have been involved in the explosion that took the life of local businessman Richard Geruso. Geruso had been a prime witness against Detective McNeil." The *Times* had neglected to mention that part of the interview, probably on the advice of their lawyers.

"Why's she saying all that stuff?" Adam asked. "Virgil didn't blow that guy up."

She smiled at the boy's faith in Virgil.

"You like him, don't you?" he asked.

"Sure. Don't you?"

"Yes. He's a good man. Somebody should stop her from saying all those lies."

"Too late for that," Nikki said. "This is a tape from yesterday."

"This is wrong," Adam said, shaking his head.

Nikki moved across the kitchen to the phone and pressed Virgil's number. Her good intentions were repaid by an irritating busy signal.

≡ 66 ≡

Virgil had had to unplug his phone. The media.

Before the shitstorm had descended on him, he'd planned on going down to Parker Center to see what he could sniff out about the red cassette in Pickett's fist. He was going to do it anyway. It was after nine; Wasson would be on the job. If he was in the field, there'd be somebody at Special Crimes who knew about the damn cassette. He'd go to Corben if he had to.

He stepped through his front door and saw a group of people camped out on the sidewalk in front of the building complex. Had to be reporters.

He backtracked into the apartment. Plugged in the phone. It started ringing immediately. Cursing, he unplugged it again and headed for his back door.

He phoned Duke Wasson from a neighbor's.

"Man, you are persona no way grata around here," the homicide detective told him. "Anybody find out who I'm talking to, I'm gonna lose some of my high esteem."

"You guys confiscate the contents of the Wonderbar offices?"

"Why would we wanna do that? The dead guys may have been business partners, but we all know it wasn't nothing to do with the business got 'em murdered."

"Oh?"

"C'mon, Virg. You know how it works. Murder ain't, isn't, complicated. You got your obvious reason why somebody wound up dead, that's usually the reason."

"And what's the obvious reason here?"

"They were on McNeil's ass."

Virgil's throat was dry. "Just a couple days ago you were saying the murders were probably unconnected."

"I've gotta tell you, Virg, I feel *discomfort* talking to you about this. I don't believe the shit they been saying on TV about you being personally involved, but you and Mac are tight. We shouldn't be having this conversation."

"You really think Mac's guilty of murder?"

"They know he killed the ho'," Wasson said. "They got evidence up the yang. Her blood in his place. On his shoes."

"In his car?" Virgil asked.

"No, but he coulda had it steam-cleaned a dozen times, all I know."

"Could have got his shoes cleaned, too," Virgil said. "But he didn't."

"The ho' didn't bleed much for it to be in the car. You know how Mac is: Women aren't nothing but cum sacks, far as he's concerned. An' he's got zip for an alibi."

"Hell, Duke, with that kind of evidence, you could convict half the guys in the squad room."

"Half the guys weren't fuckin' the vic. And now we made the connect between the hooker's murder and Pickett's."

"How?"

Wasson didn't answer at first. "Shit, Virg. This is a serious breach—"

"What's the connection, Duke? You owe me big time, the way I took care of your cousin."

"Aw, hell. Before Pickett *expired*, he had enough time to leave us a clue."

"Yeah?"

"He grabbed this cassette."

Virgil was sitting up straight now.

"It was the dead girl on it, the one Mac . . . the one he's accused of killing. She's going on and on about her life, things that happened to her that day. Like that."

"How do you know it's her?"

"Stuff she says. She mentions her own name."

"And she mentions Mac?" Virgil asked.

"No. According to the date on the label, she made the tape before they met."

"Then how does it tie to Mac?"

"It's obvious, Virg. Pickett knows Mac is the guy responsible for his death, so he grabs the cassette with the girl Mac killed on it."

"What happens to your logic if Mac didn't kill the girl?" Virgil asked.

"But he did, man."

"There could be a dozen other reasons Pickett grabbed the tape," Virgil said. "Maybe it had to do with the color. Maybe he thought he was grabbing the latest 'N Sync album. The guy was on his way out. His nervous system had been whacked. Hell, maybe he was just grabbing air and the cassette got in the way."

"Look, I know he's your partner, Virg, but he did the crime and he's going down. Listen, while I got you on the phone, you know where Mac's wife is these days?"

Virgil shook his head in dismay. Mac's wife hadn't taken enough shit from him. Now they had the poor woman pegged as the "broad" who murdered Pickett to help out her husband. "No," Virgil said. "Got no idea."

He hung up the phone, experiencing a depression he hadn't felt since those grim days when he saw his brother dying by degrees from AIDS and bad judgment. He'd been helpless then and he was helpless now.

≡ 67 ≡

Nikki tried to phone Ray Wise to tell him she was taking the day off. The line was busy. That meant that all of his six lines were busy. Not even in the midst of the Maddie Gray case had all of his lines been tied up.

She began dialing deputies until she got through to one. A veteran do-nothing named Floyd Florian, only weeks from retirement, who was spending them trying to stay out of everybody's way. "All hell's breakin' loose around here," he complained. "Forget the front entrance. Some guy from Channel 10 nearly knocked me on my ass—"

She interrupted him to ask if he'd tell the D.A. she wasn't coming in.

"Tell him yourself."

"I can't get through, Floyd. All his lines are busy."

"Oh, yeah. It's like an aviary, all the goddamn phones chirping. I hate that electronic chirp. In my place, the goddamn phone sounds like a phone."

"Floyd—?"

"Right. I got an interoffice memo just a while ago with the extension that he is using. It's on my desk some—here we go."

She dialed the new extension and the phone was picked up immediately by Meg Fisher, the woman who handled public relations for the office. "Nikki, is that you?"

"Uh-huh. I heard this was Ray's extension."

"It is. His girls are working the other lines. We're all going a little goofy this morning. Hold on, he's been trying to reach you."

"Your goddamn home phone's been busy," were the D.A.'s first words to her.

"My phone? I'm not even home."

"It's the damned media vultures. My home lines are tied up, too. Even my cellular. The bitch must have given them our numbers."

Virgil's too, she thought. She said, "I'm not coming in today."

"That's why I was trying to reach you. To tell you to stay away. Where are you, anyway? Not with the cop, I hope?"

"No," she said. "I'm staying with the Noyes boy."

"Yeah?" He sounded surprised, but not terribly interested. "Smart thinking. Stay away from any address Dana might know about. That'll keep you at least one jump ahead of the bastards. Whatever you do, don't come down here. It's like a vermin infestation. Take some sick leave."

"I've got cases . . ."

"They'll wait."

"For how long?"

"I'm meeting with my advisers later today, to find out their recommendations. Right now, all I know is that they want me and you to keep a low profile until we can get some of our spin to start."

"Ray, I'm not running for office. I've got work to do."

"Cut me some slack on this, huh?" he asked. "The bitch has me so far on the defense, I'm liable to start biting my own ass."

Actually, she didn't mind staying holed up at Adam's until Wise could get a chair and a whip to drive Dana back into a corner. "Okay," she said. "Can you switch me to my office?"

"That won't work. We've had to put a block on your line. Give me your number and I'll have your clerk phone you."

Jeb called her back in five minutes.

He'd already canceled her appointments for the day. "Figured you'd want to stay off the boulevards," he said.

She told him to clean her schedule for the rest of the week.

"The pit bull called."

"Virgil? When?"

"Twenty minutes ago. When he couldn't get through on your line, he called Johnston"—one of the D.A.'s investigators—"Johnston came and got me. Your man said he's been trying to reach you for a while."

"His phone's been tied up, too. Did he leave a new number?"

"Nope. He said for you to turn on your cellular."

"I would if I had the damn thing. It's at my house."

"I could swing by there and get it."

"And run the reporter gauntlet? No. Here's what I want you to do. Collect the files for my pending cases and bring them to me." She gave him Adam's address.

"That would be whose place, exactly?" he asked.

"We can discuss that when you get here," she said. "Make sure you're not followed."

"Thanks for the ego boost, but the press don't know me from Chris Tucker."

"I'm not talking about them. Just make sure Cruella isn't on your butt."

Jesse Fallon stopped by the house late in the afternoon.

Nikki was going through one of the case files Jeb had dropped off. Adam was in his workroom, the loud rap music *thump-thump*ing in the distance. Fallon seemed in good spirits. He told her he was meeting with several prospective housekeeper-guardians the following day.

"Take your time," she said, pouring hot water into cups for their tea. "The way things are, I'm not going anywhere."

"Your Ms. Lowery is quite a piece of work," he said. "Ray Wise should have tied an anchor to her neck a long time ago."

They carried their cups to the kitchen table. The window had been replaced, but there was still the path along the tile floor that one of the bullets had taken. Nikki tried to ignore it. "Dana isn't a bad prosecutor," she said. "It's politics. Brings out the worst in everybody."

"Perhaps it's time you heeded Mr. Truman's advice and left the kitchen."

"Come again?"

He sipped his tea. It seemed to be to his liking. "It's not quite as political on my side of the courtroom," he told her.

"What you lose in politics you gain in guilt. Setting crooks free to do more crooking isn't my idea of an ideal occupation."

"The thing you have to remember, Nikki," he said, "is that they're not all guilty."

"You offering me a job at Jastrum, Park?"

"Lord, no. I wouldn't do that, even if I could."

"Then what?" she asked.

"I'm quitting the firm," he said. "The reason I joined Jastrum, Park twenty years ago—and the reason I've stayed—can be summed up in two words: Walter Park. Do you know Walter?"

"Not personally. I know of him. He's supposed to be a class act."

"Walter let me know at the onset that I'd probably never become a partner. To compensate, he offered me a certain latitude in selecting my cases."

"You're not going to tell me you only represented clients you thought were innocent?"

"Heavens, no. I'm telling you Walter Park allowed me to take clients who would otherwise have had to rely on apathetic public defenders. Pro bono clients. African-Americans, mainly. Walter has kept the other partners at bay when it comes to me and my 'freeloaders,' as young Nicholas Jastrum is so fond of calling them. But all good things come to an end. Walter is retiring next month. After that, there will be no place for me at the firm. But I'm not quite ready for retirement."

"You going off on your own?" she asked.

"I've been having meetings with some of my satisfied clients who have done pretty well for themselves. I have the backing to start a new firm. But I'll be needing someone younger and more ambitious to handle the bulk of the work. That way I can keep representing my 'freeloaders.' Interested?"

She was extremely flattered. Jesse Fallon was a certified legend. He would have no problem at all attracting the best and the brightest. There was just one drawback. "It's a wonderful offer," she said. "But I'm like a hunting dog who catches the foxes. Helping the fox to escape just wouldn't seem natural."

"To use your analogy, imagine coming upon a fox trap and finding a little puppy, whimpering, with its leg in an iron clamp."

"My experience has been," she replied, "that it's the foxes, not the puppies, who have the coin to keep law firms in business."

"Don't close down your options," he said. "This is nothing to have to decide in twenty-four hours. Take forty-eight. Now, I'd better go see my client."

That evening, at a simple pasta dinner she'd cooked for Adam and herself, the boy asked, "You think Howard has a girlfriend?"

"Probably."

"Guess that's why he can only stay here for a day or two at a time."

"Could be other reasons for that," she said. "Family obligations, maybe. Job-related things."

"I thought I was a job-related thing."

She smiled and said nothing.

"Mr. F. says I'll probably have a new guardian by the weekend."

"Guess he's got a few good candidates."

"Why can't you be my guardian? We get along great."

"You need somebody to take care of you, to take care of this house. It's a full-time deal. I'm in an office every day and sometimes till late at night."

"You can quit. I've got as much money as we'll ever need. I can make you happy."

He was staring at her intently.

She felt vaguely uneasy. It was as if he were proposing marriage. A ten-year-old.

"What makes *you* happy, Adam?" she asked.

"Being with you."

It was not the answer she'd been expecting. "That's very sweet, but other than that?"

He frowned. "I guess it would be when I'm in the workroom."

"Ah," she said. "Then you should be able to understand that's when I'm happy, too. When I'm working."

"What about when you're with me?"

"Yes, I'm happy then, too. And when I'm with Virgil." The last was stretching it a bit, but she wanted to make a point.

"Well, sure with Virgil. That's all part of the way it would work. I didn't think it would be just you and me without Virgil."

"Say what?"

"The three of us. I guess if you want to keep working, that'd be okay. Virgil would go off in the morning to catch crooks. You'd go to your office. I'd go to school and then come home and do my work here. Then we'd have dinner together and watch movies. Maybe Virgil and I and some friends would play poker some nights. It'd be great."

He was so dear. And so serious. She wished to heaven life really was that simple. Her eyes began to mist.

"Don't you think it'd be great?" he asked.

"I think it's time we cleared the table," she said, getting up to break the mood before she started crying.

He followed her into the kitchen. "It can happen," he said.

"Not like you want it," she said, putting the dishes into the sink. "Maybe Virgil and I will get together; maybe we won't. After that, I don't know."

"You don't love me, do you?" he asked, his lower lip trembling.

She reached out a hand. "Honey, I wouldn't be here now, if I didn't care for you."

He let her draw him closer. "But you won't stay with me."

"I'll always be your friend."

He gave her a brave smile. "Guess that'll have to be enough," he said and moved out of her arms.

She watched him walk away. First it had been Fallon with his offer. Now Adam had weighed in with his dreams for her future. Her friend Loreen had been babbling lately about astrological signs. Maybe she should have paid more attention, because something was definitely up with her zodiac.

≡ 68 ≡

Nikki was awakened by a loud, piercing alarm. It took her a while to realize it wasn't part of a dream.

The room was cloudy. Her nose and throat felt raw.

Smoke. Not a lot. But enough.

She was still too sleepy to feel total panic.

The aggravating alarm stopped, followed by an eerie quiet.

Dressed in her makeshift nightgown—a superlarge "Liar For Hire" T-shirt, worn over cotton panties—she staggered to a chair and retrieved the pair of Calvin's she'd tossed there a few hours before. She struggled into them while hopping down the hall to Adam's room.

His rumpled bed was empty.

That's when she panicked.

She yelled his name.

Almost immediately, she heard his response, coming from outside the house.

She ran down the stairs, three at a time.

It was smokier down there, but she saw no sign of flames.

The doors off the dining room leading to the patio were open. She could hear Adam calling her.

He was behind the house in his pajamas, holding a fire extinguisher.

Beside him was a youthful-looking uniformed officer named Swain, who was supposed to have been guarding the house. Swain was talking into a cordless phone. "No need. It's under control," he was saying. "Everybody's okay. It wasn't much of a fire. I stopped the alarm and called off the truck. House is airing out now."

"What's happened?" Nikki asked.

"It was Randy's brother!" Adam yelled. He seemed a little frantic.

"Yes, sir, maybe you'd better," Officer Swain said and clicked off the phone.

"Jeffrey Bingham was here?" Nikki asked, searching the boy for some sign of physical damage, then looking further for mental trauma.

"I was in front, with a clear view of the entrance to the property," Swain said. There was moisture on his upper lip. His face was so smooth, Nikki didn't think he was shaving yet. "Nobody passed me." He said it defensively, as if he expected her to challenge him. She'd save that for others.

"I saw him," Adam said, gulping air as if he'd been running. "I was . . . I couldn't sleep, so I decided to run a few tests on a shark this guy in Palo Alto programmed to shortcut Desdemona."

"Whoa. Slow it down." She thought he was babbling.

"A 'shark' is like a rip-off disc that gameheads come up with to make it easy to move through games. Strictly outlaw. But this one cuts through our number one seller, Desdemona."

It was still gibberish to Nikki, but she recognized the fact that it was nerdspeak, not dementia. "And you saw Jeffrey Bingham here?"

"Uh-huh. I heard this sound, like scraping against the side of the house. I went out on the balcony upstairs and Randy's brother was standing down here in the garden. He was splashing liquid against the house. Right there."

The side of the house was charred. One windowpane had cracked in the heat, but the others were merely blackened. A thin trickle of smoke drifted up through the white foam that had evidently squelched the fire. A few feet away, a message was gouged into the wooden surface of the house. RANDY INNOCENT.

"Man's not getting any saner," Nikki said.

Swain said, "The noise he was making back here sure didn't carry to the front of the house."

"He lit a match," Adam said, ignoring the cop, "and threw it on the liquid and the house caught fire! I shouted and he looked up. That's when I saw who it was. He said something I couldn't hear, then he backed away and started running in that direction. To the back fence.

"I didn't know what . . . I wanted to wake you up, but the fire was going and I thought if I was fast enough—I ran down the stairs to the kitchen and got this"—the fire extinguisher—"from the pantry where Sidney kept it and came out here. The fire was going up the side of the house. I put it all out."

"We'd better get some experts out here to make sure," Nikki said to Swain.

"People are on the way," he said, "but I think the fire's out, too."

"Can I use the phone in your workshop?" she asked Adam.

"Sure." The key was on a piece of elastic that he had tied around his wrist. "I kept forgetting it," he said. "You know, absentminded, like the guy in *Flubber*."

He switched on the light. The room seemed just as purposely disordered as it had been the last time Nikki had seen it. There was a phone next to his fax machine and she headed for it.

"This one's better," he said, pointing to a wall extension. "That one's on my fax line."

He sat on the couch watching her as she punched in Fallon's home number.

Judging by the thickness of his voice, he'd been in deep slumber. He said, "I assume something serious has transpired."

"Good assumption," she said.

Forty minutes later, a weary Detective Rubell put away his notepad. "This time we definitely pay Bingham a visit," he said. "See what he has to say for himself. That scrawled message on the house, he might as well have signed his name." Everybody was still in Adam's workroom. Fallon had arrived within twenty minutes of her call. He'd phoned Howard, who'd joined the party shortly thereafter.

Officer Swain informed them that, though the central air system was doing a yeoman's job of removing most of the smoke, the main house wasn't quite ready for occupancy. Nikki was tired enough to sleep in soot.

"Whoever it was came in through a link fence at the property line in the back," Detective Moss said.

"It was Bingham," Adam almost shouted, as if he felt he had to convince the detectives.

"Looks that way," Moss said begrudgingly.

Nikki and Fallon followed the detectives out of the boy's workroom. Howard wandered off to check the grounds.

"You'll let us know when you have Jeffrey Bingham in custody?" Nikki asked.

"Sure," Rubell said.

"If it comes to that," Moss added.

"Comes to that?" Nikki asked.

"We got a kid who was probably sound asleep a minute before he sees the guy. Looking down from an odd angle. Not the greatest ID in the world. But it's something."

"And there's the message he left," Nikki reminded him. " 'Randy innocent.' Not too many people would share that sentiment."

Moss nodded. "Rube and I'll head over to Bingham's and shake his tree. See what falls to the ground."

Fallon watched the two men make their exit. "Detective Moss could be the poster boy for police arrogance," he said.

"For police ignorance, too," Nikki said.

"Jeffrey Bingham seems to be seriously disturbed," Fallon whispered. "Must run in the family."

Nikki shivered in the night air. She said, "Maybe we convicted the wrong Bingham."

Fallon smiled. "Watch yourself, Nikki, you're starting to think like a defense attorney."

≡ 69 ≡

Jeffrey Bingham was in the extra room that he used as an office-den when he heard his cell phone beep. Sleep had been impossible. Too much roiling about in his head. He'd been watching some absurd worse-than-B movie about butch women in a Malaysian prison that Show-time was using to fill its predawn hours.

He lowered the sound on the television and clicked on the phone.

"They're . . . coming for you," a familiar electronically altered voice informed him.

"Who's coming for me?"

"The police. They know . . . you tried to torch . . . the Noyes boy's home."

"What? I've been here all night."

"The little black boy . . . identified you."

"He's lying."

"Save that for . . . when you get caught. . . . And you will . . . if you don't get moving. . . . I've warned you. . . . It's up to you . . . what you do next."

"Wait. Wait. I appreciate your help. I just don't know what to do."

"One . . . get out of there. Two . . . keep your cellular . . . turned on. When I learn more . . . I'll phone."

"Wait. Who are you?" Bingham asked.

The connection was broken.

Bingham leapt from his chair and slapped off the TV. In a state of semi-panic, he ran to his bedroom. He jammed several items of clean clothing into an overnight bag and tossed a razor and toothbrush into a dopp kit that already contained most of whatever other toiletries he'd need.

Then he headed out.

"What's up, roomie?" Doug asked dreamily from the living room. He was floating on some pharmaceutical cloud with his punch of the evening. Didn't he ever sleep?

"I'd flush your drugs and get rid of your little friend," Bingham said, continuing on to the front door. "Cops will be here any minute."

"Cops? What the hell's going on?"

"That is the question," Bingham said.

His car had just left the underground garage and was moving down Sweetzer toward Melrose Avenue when a dark sedan rolled around the corner. No siren. Just a blinking red light on its roof. He kept facing forward, watching the street. When the prowl car drifted past, his eyes automatically shifted to the rearview mirror.

He saw the dark sedan stop, blocking his garage exit, the blinking bubble throwing a red light against the front of the building, giving it that cheap, neon glow.

Two men got out of the car.

He fed his Lexus just a little more gas and drove away.

His first stop would be the family beach house at Point Dume. He'd have a few days before the police found out about it. He'd wait there until his mysterious savior called again.

≡ 70 ≡

Looks like Bingham is in the wind," Detective Moss informed Nikki and Adam the following morning. He sniffed the air. "Still a little smoky, huh?"

"You get used to it," Nikki said. "You can get used to almost anything, except not knowing when some crazy man's gonna come calling."

Detective Rubell nodded sympathetically. "Bingham's, ah, roommate said he packed a bag and vamoosed, just minutes before we got there. There's a bulletin out on him. We'll hear something soon."

"I say we should've pressed the fag a little harder," Moss said. "He knows where his blow-buddy is."

"I beg your pardon," Nikki said, indicating the boy.

"Randy's brother could be anywhere," Adam said. "Maybe . . . maybe next time he *will* set this house on fire."

"We're doubling the watch here," Rubell said.

Nikki stared at him. "Will that be good enough?" she asked.

Rubell hesitated before replying. "It should be," he said.

"The problem with this place," Moss said, "is there's too much property. That whole wooded area you got behind the pool, where he came in last night, it'd take an army to patrol it effectively."

"That's encouraging," Nikki said.

"If it's not safe here," Adam said, "let's go someplace else."

"I'm not sure that's necessary," Rubell said. "Bingham's on the run. He's going to be more concerned with saving his butt than with risking it by coming back here."

"Of course, some of these guys don't care if they get caught," Moss said. "They're kinda dedicated to what they feel they have to do."

Rubell scowled at him. He turned to Nikki. "Is there someplace else you and the boy can stay for a few days?"

Her home wouldn't work. Reporters knew her unlisted phone number, so they sure as hell knew her address. One or two of them would be camped out there. Wouldn't they be overjoyed to see her drive up with a young boy and two cops? Wouldn't that inspire all kinds of new questions and drag Adam into a whole other sort of mess?

Bingham probably knew her address, too. If he'd found out Adam's, hers would be a snap. "A hotel?" she asked, not quite sure that would work, either.

"I know," Adam said. "The cabin. My mom and I went there last year, when she had her book to finish. We had a great time, just the two of us."

"Where is it?" Moss asked.

"Up near Sequoia Park," Adam said. "Just outside a town called Twin Rivers. No way Randy's brother could find us there."

"Too far out of our jurisdiction," Rubell said. "Let's keep it closer to home, huh?"

"Isn't farther better?" Adam asked.

"Kid's got a point," Moss said.

"You sure about this cabin, son?" Rubell asked. "It's yours and it's empty?"

"I'm sure," Adam said. "There's this old guy named Mr. Hannah. He has a store in town, but he takes care of the place. Gets rid of the spiders and bugs." The boy momentarily lost some of his enthusiasm. Only momentarily. "It's perfect. You'll love it, Nikki. I can bring my junk and work on it. You can do your work, too. It's really quiet.

The trees are amazing. Gigantic. The air's real clean. Not like here. Mom really liked the air. And the smell of pine. And—"

"What do you think, Phil," Moss said to his partner. "They go out of town, we can do a number on this place, set it up so Bingham can't resist. Do the whole staked goat bit. Draw him in."

Rubell thought about it, finally nodded. "Okay. Meanwhile, we'll put pressure on old man Bingham. He's gotta have some idea where his son's holed up."

"Then we go?" Nikki asked.

"Seems like a plan," Rubell said.

It took them just under two and a half hours to get on the road. Very little of that was spent loading the Grand Cherokee. Nikki had just the few items she'd taken from her home two days before. Plus her case files. Adam tossed his things—his clothes and his laptop and a variety of electronic games and gizmos, some finished pieces, other works in progress—into two large pieces of luggage.

Before leaving, Nikki made four phone calls.

The first was to Jesse Fallon. He told her he'd notify Clay Hannah, who cared for the cabin, that they were coming. "I think it's the right move," he said. "I'll arrange for Howard to go with you."

"Already done. Adam wanted it to be just the two of us. And I agree with him that the odds on Bingham tracking us all the way up in the Sequoias are pretty slim. But you don't catch this city girl going up a mountain to some secluded cabin without a brute like Howard along to do the heavy lifting."

"Well, have a good, safe trip," Fallon said. "And while enjoying all that solitude among the giant redwoods, please give a thought or two to my offer."

Nikki promised she would.

Her second call was to Jeb on the special extension. She told him she and Adam were leaving the city.

"Honeymoon?"

"Stop that and listen," she said, not at all amused. "I don't know when we'll be back. Just to play safe, keep my calendar clear until Wednesday. Any changes, I'll give you a buzz."

"Got a number I can buzz you? In case our lord and master Mr. Wise asks?"

"I don't know if there's a phone where we're going," she said. "Probably isn't connected, in any case. Call Jesse Fallon if you run into an emergency."

"I'm your huckleberry," he said.

"Huh?"

"Something I heard in a movie. Don't know why it popped into my head."

"I get any calls?" she asked.

"You mean besides the ones from your hundred or so good friends in the media?"

"Besides them."

"Got a fax from Loreen Battles. Says she tried reaching you by phone, but couldn't. Wants to know if she can sell your dog before he eats up any more of her antique furniture."

Nikki winced. She knew Bird too well to believe he'd eat anybody's furniture, antique or otherwise. But she should have brought Loreen up to date on her situation.

"Anybody else?" she asked, trying to sound casual.

"Sorry. No."

"When Virgil called yesterday, you gave him your new extension number?"

"Uh-huh. He calls again, what do I tell him?"

"Tell him I'm going out of town and I'll call him when I get back."

"You're the boss," Jeb said.

She caught Loreen at her beauty shop. "Don't worry about Bird," her friend said. "Baron gave him a perm." Baron was the stylist who did Nikki's hair. "A whole mess of curls. I'm training the animal to walk on his hind legs so the neighbors'll think I'm dating Rick James."

"I'll call you when I get back," Nikki said.

"You take good care of yourself, girlfriend."

"That's why we're leaving town," Nikki said. "Taking care."

• • •

"It's your . . . last chance. They're leaving . . . the city."

"The police are looking for me," Jeffrey Bingham said. He was sitting on the deck of his father's small beach cottage. "I'm safe here."

"For how . . . long?" the caller asked.

"As long as it takes."

"They'll find you . . . soon."

"What choice do I have?" Bingham asked.

"The choice . . . of forcing the blacks . . . to change their story."

"Some choice."

"Why . . . give up?"

"Even if I knew where they were going—"

"Didn't I . . . mention that?" the caller asked.

Virgil heard the two Internal Affairs detectives pounding on his half-open apartment door. They were not alone, he discovered when he peered out of a window. With them were Duke Wasson and his partner and a uniformed officer. Quite a group.

There was nothing to stop them from pushing the door open a little farther and marching in. No question but that Collins had a warrant in his pocket. Still, they hesitated. Why? Did they think he might be armed and dangerous? Maybe they were right.

"Come on out, brother. We've got a warrant for your arrest. We know you're in there."

The thing was, Virgil wasn't in there. He was across the patio at a neighbor's, getting ready to borrow her phone. He'd tried to plug his back in, but every time he did, it started ringing again before he could dial out.

He watched as the police contingent marched inside his apartment. Wasson was dragging his feet, a sour look on his face, like he'd rather be at home with his wife, practicing his vocabulary.

Virgil's neighbor, a middle-aged woman named Mel, seemed to be amused by his callers. "What've you done now, bad boy?"

"Judging by the crowd, it must've been something top of the line. I better book."

"You didn't make your call."

"No. But it won't take 'em long to figure out why the door was open and nobody home. Do yourself a favor, Mel. Don't tell 'em I was here. you'll get tied up for hours."

"Might be amusing."

"Not the way they'd do it. After they leave, would you make sure my apartment door's shut and locked? It's a big, bad city, after all."

"Guess so. You be careful."

He moved quickly from her apartment, skirting the patio to the covered parking area behind the complex. There, he found his T-bird. But he didn't get in. If they were serious about arresting him, he wouldn't get far in his own set of wheels. He looked at the other parked vehicles. Specifically, he focused on two cars that belonged to an acting couple who'd left the week before to make a movie in Canada. Both cars were convertibles. He didn't have the heart to take the guy's new cream-colored Porsche Boxter. The man's whole sexual identity was probably tied up in that car. The lady's black Saab was older and had a crumpled rear right fender. Not exactly a hooptie, but it was unassuming enough to give him a little camouflage.

Thanks to a misspent youth and a few months undercover in a chop shop, he and the Saab were out of there before Rafe Collins and his crew thought about checking the parking stalls for his vehicle. He'd made his getaway, but he knew it was a temporary one. They were on his ass for something heavy. Since Wasson was part of the welcoming committee, it probably had to do with either Geruso's or Pickett's murder. Or both.

The actress had a phone in her Saab. He'd never much cared for the woman, but he was changing his mind on that, thinking that it was lucky for him she'd been dumb enough to keep her cellular in a convertible. He needed to talk to Nikki. Not just because he loved her, but because she'd know what shit he'd stepped in. He pulled into a minimall and parked. He gave the operator at the D.A.'s office the extension Nikki's clerk had given him earlier.

The clerk, Jeb, picked up fast.

He seemed a little disappointed to hear Virgil's voice. "She's . . . not here."

"I've got to talk with her."

"She's out of town, Virgil. Says she'll ca—"

"Out of town? What the hell do you mean out of town?"

There was silence on the other end. Time to back up and come at him again. "I'm sorry, brother," Virgil said. "It's starting to be a kinda difficult afternoon."

"Difficult all around," Jeb said, showing a little sympathy.

"What's up there?"

"Some dude from IAG comes rolling in about an hour ago and takes Nikki's appointment pad. I try to stop him and he says, and I quote, 'Stay out of this, unless you want to spend three to five getting dicked in your skinny ass.'"

"Big black man?"

"Uh-huh."

"That's be our *brother* Collins. He say anything about me?"

"He didn't say anything about anything. Just took Nikki's appointments. I'm trying to reconstruct from my notes. There are people I have to call to cancel meetings."

"Where is she, Jeb?"

"I don't know. She and Adam Noyes went somewhere."

"When?" Virgil asked.

Some hesitation on Jeb's part. Then: "I talked with her just before I got my visit. She could still be at Adam's. If not, try Jesse Fallon."

Ten minutes later, Virgil was parking the Saab at Adam's home. He let himself in through the gate.

There were faint sounds of rap music coming from the rear. From Adam's workroom, Virgil assumed. He was a little surprised not to see Sidney or Donia. Or a patrolman. Evidently the threat had been lifted.

At least he'd made it in time. Adam was still there. Which meant Nikki was still there, too. He circled the house. The pool and the deck were deserted. The rap music was pounding in Adam's workroom. He had one hand on the doorknob when he felt the gun at his back.

"No sudden moves," a male voice ordered.

"Not moving," Virgil replied.

"It's okay," another male shouted. "I know him. He's a friend of the family. Virgil something. He's a homicide detective."

Virgil recognized the second voice as Officer Lewis Durkin's. He relaxed. He was about to offer his last name, but he censored himself. On the drive to Adam's, he hadn't heard anything on the all-news station about a police officer being wanted, but there was probably an all-points on him. Better to remain simply "Virgil."

The gun stayed against his back.

"Turn around real slow," the gunman ordered.

As Virgil obeyed, the man stepped back a few paces. He was a tall, thin white man wearing a short-sleeved shirt, rumpled slacks, an empty holster on his belt, and a Police Special in his fist. "What're you doing here?" he asked, keeping the gun trained on Virgil's midsection.

"Like Officer Durkin says, I'm a friend of the boy's. I was just lookin' in on him."

The man with the gun cocked his head. "Lucky you're not white or I mighta shot you." He smiled. "Bet you don't hear that too often." Maybe the guy was only doing his job, but Virgil decided they would never be close pals.

"Let's see your ID," the plainclothes said. Durkin, standing nearby, frowned and looked away.

Virgil opened his coat carefully, lifted his wallet out with two fingers. The plainclothes took it, gave it a glance, and tossed it back. He lowered his gun. "Adam Noyes isn't here," he said.

"And you'd be who?" Virgil asked.

The man steadied his waist holster with his left hand while replacing his handgun. "I'd be Detective Erroll Moss," he said almost mockingly. "And I'd appreciate it if you'd leave the premises ASAP. You're fucking up our surveillance."

"Something happen here?"

Moss's eyes shifted to the left. Virgil looked in that direction and saw the scorched section of the house and the gouged words RANDY INNOCENT. "Jesus," he exclaimed.

"Jeffrey Bingham," Moss said. "He'll be back."

"Where's the boy?" Virgil asked.

"Don't worry about him," Moss said. "He's okay."

"What about everybody else?"

"What everybody? The deputy D.A.? She's okay, too."

Good. That was what he wanted to hear. Why hadn't Jeb told him about all this? Maybe Jeb didn't know. Nikki could be a sphinx when she wanted. "And the elderly couple, the Davises?" he asked.

Moss seemed confused. "Oh? Them. They quit a few days ago. Officer Durkin, you want to escort this man off the property?"

Virgil and Durkin watched Moss cross the patio and enter the house. "My nephew works security out at Warners," Durkin said. "He tells me they got something called 'asshole pay,' where you get a bonus for having to put up with certain actors and directors who are real assholes. We have that on the force, I'd be rich as Spielberg."

"What happened to the Davises?" Virgil asked as they skirted the house, heading for his borrowed Saab.

"There was an incident one night. The Davis guy got shot at. So they left."

"Who wouldn't? So Bingham was spotted here, huh?"

"The Noyes boy got a good look at him last night when he tried to torch the place. Moss and his partner went for him, but they were a little late."

"Lost themselves a serious crazyman," Virgil said. Through the front window of the house, he could see the detective talking animatedly on the phone. "No wonder Moss is .38 hot."

"He don't need much excuse," Durkin said.

"Who's he talking to, you figure?"

Durkin looked at Moss on the phone. "Hell, the guy's on the horn half the time."

Virgil wondered if the detective might not be calling Robbery-Homicide to check up on him. He decided to say good-bye to Durkin before the officer got too good a look at what he was driving. He put out his hand and Durkin shook it.

"Where'd Adam take off to?" Virgil asked.

"Some cabin he's got up in the Sequoias," Durkin said. "Him and the lady D.A. That guy Rule is bodyguarding 'em. Not that they'll need it."

"Howard, huh?"

"That's the guy. Scarface."

"Any idea where in the Sequoias?"

"Naw. They don't tell me that stuff."

"Well, you keep on keepin on, Durkin."

He walked off in the direction of the Saab, then turned to make sure the officer wasn't following. Durkin was heading back around the house on his stubby legs. Virgil ran to the car.

≡ 72 ≡

Howard Rule drove the Grand Cherokee with Nikki sitting beside him in the passenger bucket. He was wearing another loud Hawaiian print shirt, uglier than sin, Nikki thought. But it was loose enough to hide a handgun and an ominous-looking weapon that had fascinated Adam when he'd noticed it earlier. It was a black leather sack, hooked to the security chief's belt.

"What's that?" Adam had asked.

"A blackjack," Howard had told him. He'd unhooked it and slapped it into his palm. "Filled with buckshot."

"Why do you need it?" Adam wanted to know. "You have a gun."

"Sometimes, you'd rather not shoot the bad guy," Howard had replied. "Sometimes, if you're close enough, this little baby does the job. No muss, no fuss."

This had satisfied the boy's nimble imagination.

Adam's interests had moved on. At the moment, he was sharing the rear seat with his favorite pillow, earphones, and a cassette machine. He told Nikki he was listening to a dramatic enactment of *The Lord of the Rings*, a "favorite story from my childhood."

Rule was the strong silent type. Or maybe the strong stupid type. In any case, he looked strong, which was the key thing, Nikki thought.

The Grand Cherokee had a phone, which she used to try to reach Virgil. Without success. She wished he was sitting beside her instead of Rule, the three of them heading into the mountains for a nice vacation trip. *Not smart,* she told herself. *Waste of time to go dreaming. Safer to stay a realist.*

Their route wasn't terribly complicated. The first leg was along the Golden State Freeway north in the direction of Bakersfield. The countryside wasn't particularly interesting. Flat open spaces interrupted by fields of garlic and artichokes and oranges, or little residential areas jam-packed with homes all looking as if they were newly cloned from the same Spanish two-story pastel stucco model, with a red tile roof and two-car garage.

Now and then they'd whiz past clumps of fast-food diners, links in a chain, or car dealers with plastic pennants flapping in the breeze. Infrequently, a remnant of a more independent and certainly more eccentric age would appear on the horizon. A huge forty-foot gorilla, for example, to suggest that "You'll go ape over our used-car prices." Or a giant helium hot dog floating over Teeny's Weenies near the end of Highway 5.

The big hot dog got through to Adam, who claimed that he was starving. Nikki was happy to discover that the place had a relatively clean rest room.

When she returned to their table, Adam was alone, still absorbed by his cassettes.

"Where's Howard?"

She had to ask again before breaking through Adam's concentration. "Using the phone," he said, leaving his earphones in place.

Nikki looked around the room and saw the big man hanging up the pay phone. He gave her a grin.

When he'd taken a seat beside Adam, she asked, "Calling your wife, Howard?"

"Not married."

"Girlfriend?"

"Friend," he said.

Rule gulped down his Wicked Weenie, a double hot dog with sauerkraut and jalapeño peppers, without wasting another word. Adam devoured the Cheesy Weenie with melted Swiss cheese and onions. Nikki's choice was a Teeny's Weenie covered with the speciality of the house, a honey mustard too heavy on the honey, that she was barely able to get down.

Then, they were back on the road, stopping again only to let Nikki purchase a few necessary items of clothing at a manufacturer's outlet mall just off the highway at Tulare.

As they headed north along Highway 65, bringing them closer to the mountains, Nikki said, "Howard, you worried about something?"

"Huh?"

"I noticed you've been checking the rearview a lot since we left Tulare."

He shrugged. "Just being careful, Nikki," he said. "We don't want any surprises."

"No, we don't," she agreed.

≡ 73 ≡

The problem, Virgil thought, was that he had no plan.

No, he corrected himself. The problem was that he was a wanted man and he had no plan.

At least Nikki was playing it safe. Hiding out from a loony had its advantages. You could just hole up, relax, let the world go by until you felt like jumping back on again.

That wouldn't work for him. He had to figure out how to get out of the jackpot he was in. Either that, or give himself up and let Collins and the rest take their best shot. He wasn't guilty of anything, other than sticking his nose in the wrong place.

There still wasn't any mention of him on the car radio, which was definitely something in his favor. He stopped off at a supermarket and purchased a Styrofoam tub, ice, milk, and other staples. Maybe two days' worth, he figured. Just to stretch it out, he dropped in on the first fast-food place he could find.

He ate a couple of Arby-que sandwiches under a tree in Griffith Park, relishing his temporary anonymity while pondering his options. A group of young black men were playing ball at a nearby court, hooping full out. He enjoyed watching them almost as much as if it had been the Lakers versus the Blazers. But he wasn't fooling himself. He was just putting off the inevitable. He had more important things to do than get caught up in a game of shirts and skins. Time to roll.

He tossed his lunch refuse into a trash can using his left hand. He wondered, not for the first time, if he still needed the sling. He removed it. His shoulder felt stiff, but not painful. He tried out a few motions and a sting shot down his arm. With a sigh, he slipped the sling back in place and moved on to a pay phone near the park's rest room area.

He cleared his throat to give it a rough edge and dialed a familiar number. Pressing his tongue to the roof of his mouth, he asked, in a garbled voice, to speak with Detective Wasson.

Duke answered with some wariness in his voice.

"Hey, Duke, you been lookin' for me?" Virgil said, speaking normally.

"Gee-zus, what the hell you doin', man?" Wasson asked in an anxious whisper. "We got an APB out on you."

"That's why I called," Virgil said calmly, hoping his mellowness would be catching. "What is it you think I did?"

"Me? Don't lay it on me. It's the shoofly, Collins, calling the tune on this."

"Okay, what's *he* think I did?"

"That you took down Pickett and probably Geruso, too," Wasson said "Not that he doesn't have a reason."

"Which would be . . . ?"

"Goddammit, Vir—goddammit. It's evidence. We been warned to keep it under wraps. You the last person I should be talking to about that."

"We go back too far, Duke. You know I don't go around killin' folks."

"Goddammit," Wasson said again. Then told him about the evidence against him.

Before Virgil could even process the information, the ground beneath his feet started to shift. The brick building housing the rest rooms gave a little shake.

Trembler.

Virgil hung up on Wasson and staggered away from the phone, away from the building and the trees. Away from everything that might tumble down upon him.

Satisfied he was in the open, he stopped and dropped to the ground.

He sat there, finally safe enough in his own mind to look around. Others were reacting to the quake. A crying baby was being held by a young nanny who looked like she might burst into tears herself. Several homeless men who had been lying under an oak tree were now dragging their shopping carts filled with debris out from under its long limbs.

The hoopsters stood frozen on the court as the metal poles supporting the baskets and backstops *ping*ed and swayed.

It had been more than just a little shake. Even though he was expecting aftershocks almost as severe as the original trembler, Virgil got to his feet. Wasson's information was disturbing enough to act as a cure for his earthquake fever.

Nearly fifty miles closer to the quake's epicenter, another fugitive was unaware of its existence. Holding his speed at a nearly respectable sixty-five miles per hour, Jeffrey Bingham had just passed Malibu, heading north. His car had taken a little sideways lurch, but he'd assumed that was the result of a sudden gust of wind.

Even if he'd known about the earthquake, it wouldn't have slowed him down. He was on a mission to get his life back in order. His life and his brother's. As his mysterious helper had said, Adam Noyes was the key.

As much as he wanted a chance to get his hands on the boy, Jeffrey had played hard to get. "I'm not driving anywhere unless I know who you are and why you're doing this."

"Why is this so important?" the caller had asked.

"So far, all of your advice has got me nowhere."

"It has kept you . . . out of jail."

"Yeah. I owe you that. But I have to know whom I'm dealing with."

"I am . . . someone who . . . you met once."

"Where?"

"Where do you think?"

"At work?"

"No."

"I don't like this game. At a bar?"

"Why does . . . this matter? Why not simply accept my help?"

"Why are you helping me?"

"I am helping . . . myself," the caller said. "Helping you . . . helps me."

"Explain."

"No more questions. We both . . . wear the scars . . . of our defeat. We both have reason . . . to hate the Noyes boy . . . and others like him. That is all I have to say." *Click.*

≡ 74 ≡

Though Nikki and the others didn't know it at the time, the epicenter of the 5.2 earthquake had occurred in the Fresno area, only fifty-five miles away from where the Grand Cherokee was now stopped.

They'd been traveling up the side of a mountain when the narrow road beneath them had started to shake. It had lasted for only a few seconds, but to Nikki it had seemed a lot longer. As the vehicle had begun to slide to the edge of the mountain, Howard Rule had jammed his foot on the brake and yelled "Ho-lee shiiiiit!"

Saved from the prospect of sailing out into space, then a hundred feet or so down the side of the mountain, they waited while rocks and dirt and some flora rained on the Cherokee.

Adam had torn off the earphones even before Rule's yell. He sat pressed against the seat, staring out of the window at the dusty air. "Earthquake?" he asked.

"Oh yeah," Rule said. He was ghostly pale. Nikki wondered if she might not be, too. When the dust started to settle, he put the vehicle back in gear and gunned it on up the mountain, hugging the safe side of the road.

Occasionally they met a vehicle heading down, its occupants looking as dazed and as grateful as they. They passed several fallen trees, small redwoods, rotted at their core, and drove around a number of large pieces of mountain that had been dislodged by the quake.

It was nearing six o'clock when they arrived at General Sherman Road, the main stem of Twin Rivers. Hannah's Market was, as Fallon had described, two blocks past the town's only traffic light. It was an ancient squat building situated between Planchard's Early Bird Dinners, a white clapboard building with a big display window, and the Mariposa Inn, an old two-story hotel with a wooden stairwell going up one flight to a porch. One empty rocker was on the porch. Three others lay on the sidewalk in front of the hotel.

A jagged lightning bolt of a crack cut through Planchard's plate-glass window, and what looked like three generations of the Planchard family—grandfather, son, and grandson—were examining it with some caution.

The exterior of Hannah's Market appeared to have withstood the quake rather well. The sun-bleached smoky gray wood frame of the old store seemed undamaged and the small display window was intact, though some objects behind it, notably food cans and boxes of detergent, had fallen over.

Inside, Nikki and the others were greeted by toppled shelves and tumbled goods. She asked a plump elderly woman with worried eyes for Clay Hannah, and was surprised when she called to a man in his late forties standing in the middle of the chaos. His hair was dark, graying at the temples. He was short and muscular, with the tanned, rugged good looks of an outdoorsman. He was dressed in a dark green T-shirt, khaki shorts, and workmen's boots.

"You want my dad," he said, when she'd explained why they were there. "I live in San Diego. Just paying a visit in time to help with the cleanup."

His dad was more the Clay Hannah she'd been expecting—the same height as his son, but softer and plumper and maybe thirty years older. "Some shaker, huh?" he said, grinning as if it had been a merry adventure. Then he sobered. "Heard it sent some travelers off the mountain. Glad to see it wasn't you."

Young Clay asked Howard if he'd mind giving him a hand with the shelves. Adam said he'd help, too.

Old Clay handed Nikki a ring of keys. "They're all labeled," he said. "Front door, back door, shed. That little one might just come in handy. It unlocks the generator. Quake mighta knocked down the power wire heading out there. You should find a full tin of gasoline, case you need it for the engine."

"Looks like you're okay here," she said, indicating the lights.

"Got the electricity, but no phones."

"I guess we should buy some food," she said.

"All taken care of." He frowned. "Least it was. If the power's off, some of the frozen food might get a little thawed 'fore you can get to it."

"How far away are we?"

"Close to an hour," he said. "The boy's daddy went looking for solitude when he bought the cabin from Jason Ducat. Was his downfall, too."

"How's that?" Nikki asked.

"Been closer, maybe Doc Olibert coulda made it out there in time." He looked at Adam, who was happily "assisting" Howard and the younger Hannah hoisting up a food shelf. "Good seeing the boy smiling and enjoying himself. Musta been real tough on him losing his dad that way."

"It was a while ago," Nikki said.

Clay Hannah nodded. "I always hoped the little fella don't come down too hard on himself."

"Himself? Why would you think that?" Nikki asked.

"He was the one bought the turpentine his daddy drank down."

"Adam? He couldn't have been more than four."

"About that. Marched in here and said his mom was down the street at Miss Jelico's dresses. Sent him with a ten-dollar bill to buy some turpentine."

"Any idea why his mom needed the turp?"

Hannah shrugged. "It's one of them things people need sooner or later. And speaking of later, you might want to get going. Case the power's off, it'll be easier and safer getting the generator started in day-light."

"Safer?" Nikki asked.

"Sure. You gotta be careful up here in the mountains. This is brown bear country."

Welcome to Bear Country Safari, Nikki thought. She wondered if the geezer was just one of those rurals who got their kicks by throwing a scare into the big city tourists. Or, maybe he was just giving her the lay of the land. "These bears, it's sort of a live and let live situation, right?" she asked hopefully. "They don't bother you if you don't bother them?"

"Not exactly," Hannah said. "They used to keep to themselves. But they're protected animals. You get into twenty kinds of trouble, you shoot a bear up here. And the bears aren't stupid. They've picked up on that. So they go where they want and do what they want. You gotta keep your food locked up tight. Garbage, too. They're hungry critters. Not so long ago, a five-hundred-pound mama bear ripped the trunk off a car to get at a stick of chewing gum."

Damn!

"Nikki," Howard Rule called to her from across the room. "Sun's going down and we ought to get going. You about ready?"

Ready? Was she ready? *Does a bear—no, don't even think about it,* she told herself.

≡ 75 ≡

A highway patrolman was stopping vehicles as they approached Route 117.

"What's the problem, Officer?" Virgil asked. He wasn't terribly worried that the man might recognize him from the material Duke Wasson said they'd sent out. He might have been a little more cautious if the man had been black. He could tell the first time the guy spotted him that he wasn't looking for a black murder suspect. White lawmen seemed to carry a vague image in their heads. If they're looking for a black man over six feet tall with his arm in a sling, any African-American male who fits that general description will do. Even Virgil, who'd removed the sling and was being very careful with his arm. But if they're not looking for you, they're looking through you.

For this one, Virgil was like Patrick Swayze in *Ghost*.

"Quake caused a few problems up the mountain," the CHP said, looking at the cars piling up behind the "borrowed" Saab. "Got some fallen trees and rocks. Two cars went over the side in the quake. No telling what kind of kick the aftershocks will have."

"Thanks for the warning, but I've got to get up there."

The highway patrolman nodded, still not facing him. "Good luck," he said, waving him on.

He started up the road in the Saab. So far, it'd provided such a fine, comfortable drive he wondered if the actress would consider selling it. Stuck to the dash was the Post-it map Jesse Fallon had drawn.

For him, the jury was still out on Fallon. The lawyer seemed too damned stuck on himself. When Virgil had called his office, he'd been away. His secretary had refused to give up his whereabouts. She suggested that Virgil leave a message, though she wasn't sure when or if she might be speaking with Fallon that day.

Screw that.

He got McNeil's lawyer Porky Porcello to call Fallon and say it was an emergency.

When Fallon returned the call, Porky put Virgil on the phone. "They say you can read minds, Mr. Fallon," Virgil said. "Mine should be screaming that bad things are gonna happen unless you tell me where Nikki and Adam are."

The elderly lawyer agreed to meet with him at Porcello's office in fifteen minutes.

Virgil used the time to inform Porky that he might be needing his services. "How much trouble are you in?" the defense attorney inquired.

"On a scale of one to ten, I'd say about fifty."

"Give me a dollar and tell me all about it."

He didn't tell him all. He left out his presence at Pickett's office the night of the murder. What he emphasized was the connection between Rafe Collins and Deputy D.A. Dana Lowery.

"So, you're saying it's a bullshit charge, based on your refusal to cooperate with them in their effort to send Mac down the tubes?"

"More or less."

"And you don't know anything about either Pickett's murder or Geruso's?"

"No," Virgil lied. He knew a few things, but there was no way he could explain that to Porky.

"To your knowledge, all they have on you is an object with your prints, found in Pickett's office near the body?"

Virgil nodded.

"And you were in that office two days prior to the murder, when you might have dropped the object?"

"Uh-huh."

"I hope those pricks do arrest you. We'll sue the slime off 'em."

Virgil didn't feel that optimistic, but he liked the idea of having Porky to back him up. Of course Porky didn't know all the facts and he hadn't done so well keeping Mac out of prison.

The receptionist rang to say that Fallon had arrived.

Porcello let them use his office while he stepped out for a smoke. It took no longer than a king-size cigarette for Virgil to fill Fallon in on why he needed to know where Nikki and Adam were.

"There's a warrant for my arrest in connection with the murders of two pimps named Pickett and Geruso," Virgil said. "The reason for the warrant is that something of mine was found in Pickett's office near his corpse. A tiny badge given to me by the Bay City Sheriff's Department."

"And?" Fallon was waiting for a punch line.

Virgil obliged. "I gave that badge to Adam four days before Pickett's murder."

Fallon frowned, then smiled. "You're suggesting what? That a ten-year-old boy committed two murders?"

"It's one of the possibilities."

"Assuming that the little boy could, why in the world would he?"

"You tell me. He's seeing a shrink."

Fallon stared at him and didn't blink. "Not because he has displayed any homicidal tendencies, I can assure you."

"Geruso was blown up in his car. Somebody dropped some Drano into his gas tank. Sound like any little genius we know?"

"Quite a stretch," Fallon said. "And all of it based on a badge left in Pickett's office? Didn't I read he and Geruso had been partnered in a new nightclub and restaurant named Wonderbar?"

"Right."

"Well, then, that could explain the badge. Adam and several other members of Team Homeboy had a meeting with them concerning the integration of electronic gaming boards in their new establishment. He could have dropped it then."

"He never told me he'd met those guys," Virgil said. "Why would he have kept it a secret?"

"You really do leap to conclusions, Detective. Just because Adam didn't bring it up in conversation doesn't mean he was trying to keep it a secret from you."

"Look, I'm as skeptical as you are about a kid, even a very bright kid, doing hits on two street-tough adults. Maybe Adam dropped the badge during his sales pitch, like you said. Maybe he lost it somewhere else and a third party we know nothing about found it and left it behind when he, she, or they killed Pickett. I don't know. What I do know is, one: I don't want Nikki to be in a cabin in the wilderness with a little boy who may have knocked off two hard guys. And two: Adam is the only one who can get me off the police hook about the badge, because he knows damn well I couldn't have left it there. So, for either reason, I'm driving to see 'em."

"I want to talk with him first," Fallon said, reaching for the phone on Porky's desk.

"I've tried calling the town," Virgil said. "Thought somebody at city hall might tell me where the Noyes property is. The lines are down because of the quake."

"There's a phone in the Cherokee," Fallon said.

As they discovered, that didn't work either. The car was in the dead zone of the mountains.

"Tell me where they are," Virgil said.

Fallon hesitated.

"If anything happens to Nikki—" Virgil began.

"No melodrama, please. I'm as concerned about Nikki's safety as you are. For different reasons, I hasten to add. At the same time, I don't want you running up there and abusing the boy, either mentally or physically. You may ask him what happened to the badge you gave him, but you are to accuse him of nothing. Understand?"

Virgil nodded.

"Don't shine me on, Detective. If your actions cause Adam Noyes even a moment of discomfort, I shall make your life a living legal hell. Are we clear on this?"

Virgil looked up to see Porky approaching the office. "We're clear," he told Fallon.

"All right. Then let me draw you a map to the cabin."

Two and a half miles up the mountain road, cars were stalled, motors off. In front of him, a middle-aged man in bib overalls and a white undershirt sat sideways in his pickup, facing the open driver's door and dangling his work boots over the narrow running board. "A sequoia fell across the road up ahead," he told Virgil. "Been here forty minutes. Folks up front been here twice that long."

"The quake hit over three hours ago."

"Well, Mr. Tree didn't fall just then. Took his sweet time poppin' his roots out the earth, then takin' his slide."

"Okay, so it's been a problem for two hours. How long does it take to move a tree?" Virgil asked.

The man in the overalls chuckled. "No time at all, if you're talking about trees like you got down on the flats. Welcome to sequoia land, my friend. Welcome and wait."

≡ 76 ≡

The Grand Cherokee traveled seven miles along macadam before coming to a weathered wooden sign on a post that stated simply, NOYES. Beside it was an unpaved, untended road that wormed through the giant sequoias. The Cherokee jounced along its twisted, rock-strewn path. Adam said, "My dad kept it rough and rocky to discourage anybody from coming to see us. He wanted to get away from it all up here."

"Mission accomplished," Nikki said, searching the dusky woods for signs of life. She noticed that Howard's interest still lay behind them. "Something back there?" she asked.

"Nope," he said, eyes shifting direction. "But there's something up ahead."

The cabin sat surrounded on three sides by a forest of towering trees, a two-story matchbox lost in a giant's woodpile. Fifty yards or so from its front door was a medium-size lake, in the center of which was a flat floating raft. "Used to be able to catch fish in there," Adam told them. "I haven't tried for a long time."

"The raft for swimming?" Nikki asked.

"Uh-huh. Mom used to like to swim out there and sunbathe. It's anchored to the bottom of the lake."

"Maybe we can do some fishing and swimming while we're here," Nikki said.

"Maybe," Adam said, but it sounded as if that wouldn't be a priority.

Howard drove the Cherokee near the rear door of the building before parking.

The sun was starting to sink below the treetops but there was still enough light for Nikki to see that the quake had taken a slight toll on the outside of the cabin. Several windows were cracked but none seemed broken. The rear door had twisted from its jamb and was swinging free, a sight that filled Adam with alarm. He began shouting about insects, while Nikki searched the surrounding woodland for brown bears. Fear feeding on fear.

Howard hopped from the Cherokee, told them to "Sit tight," and strode to the cabin. He pushed the back door completely open, waited a few beats, and entered, gun drawn. Light suddenly glowed at the rear windows. They had power.

A few minutes later, Howard appeared at the back door and waved them in.

The cabin had been designed for comfort and convenience. A large kitchen was filled with almost as much gadgetry as Nikki's own. Some of the utensils were scattered on the floor, but most were in their holders or niches. Heading forward, she paused at a pantry. More floor clutter, but the boxes and plastic containers looked undamaged.

In front of the pantry was a wooden stairwell that Adam ran up two stairs at a time, carrying one of his pieces of luggage. The rest of the downstairs was taken up by one large room that served as a combination living and dining area and den. The latter featured soft leaf green leather chairs facing a large TV monitor and a tower of music decks that someone, the late Jerome Noyes probably, had taken the trouble to secure to a steel frame. Nikki wondered if he'd been worried about earthquakes.

More of the green leather chairs and a sofa formed the living room grouping around a stone fireplace. Soot and some pieces of stone had been shaken down by the quake. Wood carvings and Indian sculptures that had hung on the walls were now decorating the throw carpets and hardwood floors. Paintings—by Shelli Dietz?—had also shaken down, their glass and moldings cracked and shattered.

There was another stairwell beside the front door. Nikki used it to climb to the first floor, where she was greeted by piles of books that had been tossed from shelves lining the light brown walls of a small sitting room. A floor lamp with a heavy brass base was in place beside a chocolate velvet chaise longue. A maple-wood table was leaning on two legs against the head of the chaise longue. Nikki used the tip of one index finger to move the table upright. She stepped over the books and moved into an unlighted hall.

Doors led off the hall to a series of four small bedrooms. Adam had already claimed one of them. He was sitting at a desk, the drawers of which were lying on the floor. He'd emptied his suitcase onto the bed and had withdrawn an assortment of objects that he'd laid out on the desk.

"Need any help in here?" Nikki asked.

"No," he replied with uncharacteristic rudeness. Then he added, "I'm kinda busy now. Something I have to do."

Nikki could tell he was fighting to stay calm. She nodded and backed out of the room, closing the door behind her.

At the end of the floor was a double bedroom, with mullioned doors opening onto a rough wood balcony. The shelves and other flat surfaces were clean, but in the dresser drawers she discovered an assortment of powders and creams and perfumes. In the closet were stacks of art paper and boxes of chalk and pastels, some of which were broken, probably during the quake.

She tested the bed and decided she might as well make the room hers, since Adam had chosen one of the smaller rooms. She unlocked the doors and walked out onto the balcony. Below, Howard was removing luggage from the Cherokee.

She scanned the woods.

Something moved in the distance. A car.

She blinked and it was gone. A trick of the light? A shift of shadows?

She went downstairs.

Howard had piled the luggage near the staircase. He had a hammer and screwdriver and had removed the back door, which was resting against a wall. "Gonna try and hang this straight again so that it fits tight. Keep out the bugs for the kid."

"Keep out the bears, too, while you're at it," she said. "I think I saw a car on our road."

She had his attention. "Really?" he asked, stepping through the doorway. He looked off through the trees. "I don't see a thing. You sure?"

"No. Actually, it didn't seem to be moving. Just parked out there."

He looked again, then shrugged. "Getting too dark. We'd better put the door back on."

He picked up three butt hinge frame leafs, repositioned them one at a time, and screwed them to their original places along the door frame, tightening the screws deeper into the holes that had been gouged out when the quake had ripped the door free. "They gonna hold?" she asked.

"Not forever. With luck, until I can find a lumberyard to repair the damaged sections. Give me a hand with the door."

He did most of the work. She simply held the door in one position while he tightened the center leaf hinges along its edge. Together, they lifted the door and worked the knuckles of its hinge leafs into those of the frame. Howard wiggled the pivot pins into place and, with a satisfied smile, swung the door open. When he closed it, it fit snugly against the frame. "Gonna take more skills than I have to fix the lock, though. It'll have to be replaced."

"An unlocked door isn't going to make for carefree sleeping tonight," she said.

"I could nail it shut," he said, "if it'd make you feel better."

"Absolutely," she said, thinking about that car in the woods, or whatever it was. "Don't spare the nails."

The freezer was packed with food. Steaks. Chicken. Duck. Vegetables. Fruit. Desserts. All clearly marked. Several cases of expensive California wine were stacked at the back of the pantry, the bottles protected by bubble wrap. She freed a bottle of merlot and pulled a cut-up chicken from the freezer. The wine was too good to be used for cooking, but when your back's to the wall . . .

Anyway, she'd drink it while she cooked, so some of it would be disposed of properly. To be polite, she asked Howard if he'd like a glass of wine. She was pleased that he declined. If he was going to be their white knight, she wanted him to be able to stay up on the horse.

When Adam joined them, she thought for a second that he'd been drawn to the fragrance of garlic and wine and olives and mushrooms and minced ham and green onions simmering in butter on the stove. But he headed straight for Howard and the hammering.

"You got the door back on," he said. "Great. But what's with all the nails?"

"Lock's busted. The nails will secure the door till we can get it fixed."

Adam seemed to study the nails for almost a minute. Then he turned away and asked, "What's for dinner?"

"Chicken," she said.

"Fried?" he asked hopefully.

"Not exactly," she said.

Chicken with Marchand de Vin sauce, whipped potatoes, a tomato and lettuce salad with vinaigrette dressing, and chocolate cream pie. A damn good meal, if she said so herself. Which she had to, since neither of the males did. They ate everything on their plates. Howard had seconds and Adam put away two slices of pie. But there were no spoken compliments. And very little conversation.

Then they were gone.

Adam raced back upstairs for some "special project." Howard went outside, via the front door, to return the hammer to the tool shed and see what else was out there.

Nikki cleared the table and loaded the dishwasher. Then she picked up her overnight bag and the packages from her speed-buy session at the Tulare Outlet Center and carried them up to the bedroom she'd selected.

A chest of drawers was against one wall.

She filled two of them with her things. Then she opened the closet again and looked in at Shelli Dietz's art supplies. Beside a box of art brushes was an unopened bottle of turpentine in a cardboard box and a half-empty bottle that had fallen over on its side.

Shelli must've used the stuff for cleaning her brushes.

That explained why she got the baby Adam to buy her a bottle. But how did the bottle get into her husband's liquor cabinet? Had Shelli put it there? Had she deliberately led her abusive husband into gargling with a toxic fluid?

Only one person might have the answer to that question, and Nikki was not going to raise it with him.

She looked at her watch. Nearly eight.

She returned to the den section of the big room downstairs and turned on the television. Her intent was to get some news of the quake, but none of the nearly ninety stations was wasting time on local news. Not when there were guns to shoot and sutures to sew and presidential misconduct to explore and reexplore down to its last minutiae of detail and beyond. She turned off the TV.

Eight-thirty.

Had Howard come back from the shed? What could he still be doing out there?

She crossed the room and looked out of the window. At total darkness. The shed was not that far from the main house, but she couldn't see it. Surely if he was out there, he'd have a light on.

He must have come back and gone up to one of the bedrooms.

She walked to the rear stairs. Howard's one piece of canvas luggage was still where he'd left it when he unpacked the Cherokee.

She ran up the stairs and began checking bedrooms. Three were still empty.

Adam's door was shut. She could hear his gizmos chirping and whirring.

She knocked.

Was that a window being closed in his room? Of course not. The cabin had no screens. The boy would not do anything to invite bugs into his room. She knocked again. "Adam?"

"Nikki? Come on in."

He was playing a handheld game while a foot-tall toy robot clinked and clunked its way across his desk. "Retro," he said, indicating the robot. "Retro and cheeso, but I like it."

"Have you seen Howard?" she asked.

"Nope. Isn't he here?"

"I'm beginning to wonder," she said, trying not to let too much of her apprehension show. No sense spooking the boy until he had to be spooked.

"Maybe he drove into town. Or is the Jeep still here?"

"Good question."

She went back downstairs. Through the rear window, she could see the Cherokee right where they'd left it, shining in the moonlight. From there, she could just make out the tool shed, too. It looked like the door was still open.

She lowered the window and shouted, "Howard? You back there?"

No answer.

"Howard?" she shouted a little louder.

Nothing.

She shut the window and locked it. Then she ran to the front door and attached the double lock. Feeling a little more secure, she took stock of the situation. Assuming Howard hadn't gone for a late-night hike in unfamiliar, bear-stocked woods, something had happened to him. Make that someone. Someone had happened to him. Hurt him? Killed him?

She and Adam were next.

She grabbed the phone on the coffee table. Dead. She let it slide from her fingers back onto its cradle.

Howard had a gun. Lost to them now.

But there was another gun. The Police Special she carried in her purse.

Her purse.

She ran back to the bags by the rear stairs. Just luggage. No purse. The damned purse was in the car. The car that was parked just feet from the back door that was now nailed shut. To get the gun, she'd have to go out the front door and circle the house, hope that the car was unlocked, root around for the purse, hope that whoever was out there hadn't already found it, and then—

Why belabor the point? She was not leaving the cabin. Only dumb women in novels and movies pulled stupid stunts like that. She was going to stay right where she was. Safe in a locked house.

A chill ran through her body.

Howard had gone to the tool shed. He'd taken the keys to the shed, which were on a ring with the keys ... to the house.

Too late, she heard the scape of metal on metal and saw the handle of the front door begin to turn.

She wanted to run but her feet wouldn't cooperate.

The front door opened. Jeffrey Bingham entered the cabin. His hair was dank and uncombed, his clothes rumpled, his eyes wild and unblinking. He raised the rifle he was carrying until it was pointed at her chest, grinned, and said, "Hi, honey, I'm home."

≡ 77 ≡

Bingham had arrived in Twin Rivers just at dusk.

A kid who was applying putty to the display window at Planchard's Early Bird Dinners told him how to reach the Noyes cabin. There had been other townsfolk he could have asked, but the boy was so caught up in his work that Bingham doubted he'd remember one thing about him.

In case the situation turned unpleasant at the cabin.

He was so anxious, he almost missed the turnoff.

It was growing dark. He wanted to drive right in. When you track your prey to their lair, you don't give them time to work up their courage. His father had taught him that. Unfortunately, he had no beaters to risk death by going ahead of him to flush out his quarry.

But wasn't that function being filled by his mysterious helper?

He smiled at that realization.

During their last communiqué, the mystery man had said, "They will be . . . at your mercy."

"It's just the two of them, then?" he'd asked.

There had been brief silence on the other end. Then: "When you arrive . . . there will be . . . just the two."

He parked the car in the woods. He could see the lights of the cabin through the trees. He didn't think they could see him.

He heard hammering. Then silence. Then more hammering.

Taking a chance, rifle in hand, he moved cautiously through the trees on foot until he had a clear view of the rear of the cabin and their vehicle. The back door was shut and someone—he couldn't see who—was pounding nails into it from inside the house.

Probably the arrogant black woman. Thinking nails could keep him out. He'd drive his car through the back of the fucking cabin, if it came to that.

He would wait silently, motionless, observing their lair until he was certain he could control the situation.

The hammering ceased.

Then the food smells began. Wonderful odors that caused his empty stomach to twinge and growl. Fifteen or twenty minutes of that and he could stand it no longer. He had to make his move.

He stood, holding his rifle at port arms, and headed for the cabin.

He was nearing the front door when it opened.

He ducked back and watched as a huge man made his exit.

Who the fuck was he? Why hadn't Mr. Mystery mentioned him?

Had he made the wrong turn and wound up at the wrong cabin?

No. There was the Grand Cherokee Mr. Mystery had described.

The big guy circled the house.

Bingham stalked him, making a wide circle around the front of the cabin, the better to see the big man heading for a small shed. Bingham's night vision had kicked in. He brought up his rifle. He placed his sights on the man's broad back.

Can I pull the trigger? he wondered.

Probably not, but you never really knew until the last second.

Bingham was distracted by a scraping noise from the cabin. A door or window opening. He could see no movement, but the light from the cabin's interior momentarily robbed him of his night vision.

Slowly, enough of it returned for him to get a fix again on the big man. He was leaning forward into the open shed.

And then—! Bingham blinked. A black bird, possibly a crow, soared through the trees and dived at the big man. It just missed him, zooming past. It did a loop and headed back.

Though Bingham heard nothing, the bird must have made a noise, because the big man straightened fast. He turned to face the bird just as it dived straight at him.

The big man dropped to the ground, rolling as he did, and yanking a pistol from his belt. Bingham stood transfixed as the man tried to get a bead on the flying object that had missed him again. This time, it flew off into the woods.

Shakily, the big man got to his feet. He stuck the gun back into his waistband and, cautiously scanning the woods for the bird's return, reached out to close the shed.

That's when the amazing bird reappeared.

Bingham had hunted in jungles throughout the world and he'd never seen any feathered creature quite like it.

The bird hovered thirty or more feet over the big man's head, then speed-dived until it was directly behind him. It hovered there, nearly motionless, then seemed to leap forward, sinking its beak in the small of its victim's back.

The big man looked like he'd been struck by lightning. His heavily muscled arms flew out straight and his legs bucked and folded under him.

He fell forward on his chest, shaking and twitching, while the bird continued feasting on his back.

Bingham's hunter's genes kicked in. He wanted to down that remarkable bird. He caught it in his sights.

And it was gone.

Bingham searched the now-dark sky. Gone.

He waited a few minutes to make sure the creature had really departed. Then he scuttled forward to check the bird's prey.

The big man was still alive, breathing raggedly. Bingham couldn't tell his condition. Maybe the blood loss . . . he looked closer, squinting. The man was wearing some horrible-looking Hawaiian shirt, but he could see no blood on it. Not even a tear where the bird's beak should have struck.

Was he hallucinating?

Was this really a man lying in front of him, or some fantasy?

He poked at it with the toe of his tennis shoe. Solid flesh.

Had he shot the man and blocked it from his mind?

He shivered and looked up at the sky.

Maybe this was all a sign. He should get back in his car and drive away. Leave this place.

Then he saw the ring of keys hanging from the shed door.

Well, maybe he could take care of a few things before running off.

The first person he saw when he entered the cabin was the arrogant bitch who'd taken away Keats's freedom. She was gawking at him, obviously shocked to see him there. He could feel her animal fear and he reveled in it.

"Hi, honey, I'm home," he said, pointing the rifle at her.

She straightened, apparently drawing courage from his attempt at humor. "Call me grouchy," she said, "but this doesn't strike me as the ideal moment for an *I Love Lucy* reference."

"No no no," he shouted. "It's mockery. You don't get it."

"Explain it to me." She was growing more confident, he could see. But he was still in control.

"I'm mocking my father," he said. "Every night he comes home to his brave little black woman. Tonight I'm coming home to mine."

She stared at him. At the gun and him. "What did you do to Howard?" she asked.

"He the big stud with the bad taste in shirts?"

"Uh-huh."

"I didn't do a thing to him. But he's not feeling so good. A birdie told me."

"Where is he?"

"That's not important," he said. "The question is: Where's the little bastard?"

"You mean Adam?"

"What other little bastard would I be asking about?"

"He's in town, at the hotel," she said.

"Don't lie to me," he said, tightening his finger on the trigger. Then he froze.

The bird was in the house. It had just zoomed behind the woman. He stepped to the side, trying to see it.

The woman seemed puzzled by his movement.

"It's here, damn it," he shouted, hating the hysteria in his voice.

"What's—"

She went rigid. The bird flew away from her as she sank to the throw rug, twitching spasmodically, moaning from deep in her throat.

With a startled cry, Bingham took a backward step and banged against the front door, shutting it.

He dropped the rifle, turned, and began clawing at the door.

He heard a little purr as the bird bit the back of his neck. Immediately, his limbs became useless. He plummeted headfirst against the wooden door. Then he was lying on his side on the floor. Everything hurt. He seemed to be experiencing a total body spasm. No control of arms or legs. Or eyelids. Couldn't even blink. Why was he awake? Why wasn't he experiencing the peace of the unconscious?

He saw the bird fly to the rear of the cabin.

Would it come back? Would it attack again? His eyes filled with tears. His tear ducts seemed to be the only part of his body that still worked.

PART IV

Verdict

≡ 78 ≡

It was nearing ten o'clock when Virgil turned off the macadam onto the rocky road to the cabin. He'd spent hours waiting for the sequoia tree to be removed. Finally on the road, he'd wound up creeping behind a long line of traffic that seemed to think the speed limit was 5 mph.

He'd rolled into Twin Rivers a little after the town had closed down for the night. No real problem. He had Fallon's map.

The roadside sign was exactly where he'd expected it.

What he hadn't expected was the dark Lexus sedan parked on the road to the cabin. According to gas receipts in the glove compartment, the sedan belonged to Jeffrey D. Bingham.

Bingham? Virgil had thought he'd had the situation figured, but if Bingham had trailed them to the cabin, his calculations had been 180 degrees off. It was like they said: Forget the fancy bullshit, and put your money on the most obvious explanation.

It was just as well he hadn't bothered to use the sling, once he started up the mountain. He'd only have to take it off again. He needed both hands free.

He touched the Lexus's hood. Stone cold. Not good. Bingham had been there long enough to do a mess of damage. Virgil drew his pistol. He didn't know why Bingham had decided to stick around, but if the man had harmed Nikki in any way, it would be a costly delay; he would be dead.

The detective approached the rear of the cabin, gun in hand. Maybe if the back door was open . . .

It wasn't. It didn't budge.

Cautiously, he circled the cabin, pausing to peek into windows. Nothing. The downstairs area seemed to be unoccupied. He moved closer to the front window, and from that angle could see most of the room, including Nikki lying on the floor motionless.

Forgetting caution, he ran to the front of the house. The door was locked. He stepped back, raised his right leg, and smashed his heel into the door handle. The lock gave and the door swung inward.

He ran to Nikki. She was unconscious. The skin was broken behind her right ear where she must have been struck. Her hands and feet had been securely tied. "Oh, baby," he moaned as he knelt beside her. He placed his gun on the floor and then put his arms around her. His plan was to carry her to the sofa, but he'd forgotten his wound. He'd barely begun to lift her when an unbearable pain shot down his arm. "Sorry, honey," he said, lowering her back to the carpet.

That's when he saw the man lying near the wall, just under the window. Like Nikki, he was unconscious and bound.

Virgil fought his confusion to focus on the immediate need. He ran to the rear of the cabin, to the kitchen, and found a bread knife.

He carried it back to the living room and knelt beside Nikki again. He was positioning the knife to sever her wrist ties when he felt a ripple of air against his neck.

Almost immediately, there was the sensation of two bees stinging his neck and back. All strength and coordination left his limbs.

He was already tumbling forward as the bread knife slipped from his useless, twitching fingers, bounced against Nikki's leg, and rolled to the floor. By then he was down on his side, gurgling and growling, arms and legs doing a Saint Vitus' dance.

His mind was working.

And his eyes.

He saw something that resembled a black bird fly across the room and then hover near the front stairwell.

Adam walked down the stairs, holding what looked like two TV remote wands, one in each hand. He was controlling the bird, which Virgil realized wasn't a bird at all but some kind of toy aircraft.

Adam directed it to make a perfect three-point landing on the floor, just inches from Virgil's face. So close he could read the manufacturer's name on the Taser secured to the model hovercraft by a plastic sheath.

Adam put down the two remotes and walked toward him. The boy's handsome face looked sad. "I'm sorry you came up here, Virgil. You're my friend."

Virgil didn't even try to talk. He knew the effects of the Taser. It would be another five minutes or more before his nervous system would start to react normally.

From his pocket, the boy withdrew a blackjack. Virgil wondered idly how he'd come by it. "I'm sorry," Adam repeated, raising the sap. He had only a boy's strength but the way the weapon worked, it was strength enough.

When Nikki awoke later that night, her nostrils were filled with the smell of gasoline. Her head throbbed and the bindings were chafing her wrists.

She felt liquid splash against her legs and saw Adam, dressed in pajamas decorated with dinosaurs. He was pouring gas over the room and over Jeffrey Bingham, who was lying on his side, facing away, hands tied behind him. Bingham didn't react. Which meant he was unconscious. Or dead.

Nikki moaned and turned her head, discovering another bound body beside her. "Virgil," she cried. His eyes remained shut, but he was breathing. There was a knot the size of a walnut on the left side of his forehead, matching the healing gunshot wound on the right. In spite of the situation, she was struck by the thought of stereo head wounds.

Adam's green eyes were studying her, completely without expression. "Too bad, so sad," he said and continued to soak the room.

"Burning down the place?" she asked, trying to match his nonchalance.

"Uh-huh," the boy said. "Ropes'll burn, too, see? Though I'm not sure that'll matter."

"How you going to explain your miraculous escape?"

"You saved me, Nikki. With your last breath, you pushed me through the front door."

"You really are a little monster," she said.

"It's what my mom called me just before I shot her." He wasn't bragging or gloating. It was a flat statement of fact.

Nikki fought off the chill that swept through her. She thought of the questions she'd had about the case against Randy Bingham. "You found Randy's gun?"

"Uh-huh."

"And his champagne glass?"

"There's this drug called clomethiazole," he said. "Mom used it when she had trouble sleeping. You're not supposed to drink when you take it, because it can really knock you out. I put some in Randy's champagne. After he passed out and I killed Mom, I washed his glass to get rid of the dregs. There was no more champagne in the bottle and a clean glass wouldn't have looked right. So I just put it back on the shelf."

"Why'd you kill her, Adam?"

"She was a bad person. The world's better off without bad people."

"How was your mother bad?"

"She rejected me. She and Randy were going to get married. And they were going to get rid of me by sending me to some prep school far away. I think it was his idea, but Mom went along with it.

"Rejection. The worst thing somebody can do to you. Mom explained it to me in this very cabin years ago. She was talking about my dad. He was planning on going away and not taking us. She said he was rejecting us, which was why we didn't help him, even though he was screaming and running around and must have been hurting really bad after he drank that turpentine."

Nikki stared at the little boy, the little monster his mother had created. She feared him, but she also felt a pang of sorrow for him. She was too much of a survivor, however, to let that stand in her way. She'd run right over him to save Virgil and herself.

A moan from Jeffrey Bingham briefly distracted the boy.

"Why are you doing this now?" Nikki asked.

"Come on. You're smarter than that. I just told you. You rejected me, too, and you know it. It would have been perfect. You and me and Virgil. We'd have been a great family. Much better than mom and *Randy*. But you wouldn't let that happen."

"Damn," Bingham said, coughing and attempting to sit up.

Nikki tried to ignore him, concentrating on the boy. "So you're going to kill all of us for something I did?"

"I'm really sorry about Howard, and I surely didn't think Virgil would follow us up here. There's nothing I can do about that. The world will definitely be better off without *him*." He indicated Bingham.

"What's going on?" Bingham demanded. "What's happening?"

Adam put down the gasoline tin and approached him. He removed a blackjack from his pocket. Nikki recognized it as Howard's. The boy hit Bingham with it just above the temple. He held back on his swing.

Bingham grunted, but was still conscious, eyelids fluttering. Adam used the sap again, harder this time. That did the job.

"I have to hit him just right," Adam told her. "No concussion or anything that'd look weird when they examine whatever's left. Poor Howard, I think I caved in his head. He's outside, dead. Too big to drag in here, but I got him close enough to the cabin that I think it'll look okay."

"How will you explain Howard's head wound?" Nikki asked.

Adam pointed to Bingham. "He's the one did it all. He brought it on himself, threatening us. Maybe he really would have tried to act on his threats without my urging. I've been calling him on my cell phone using my techno voice, working him up, getting him to do things, telling him how to find us."

"Why?"

"I've been using him. I used him to scare off Donia and Sidney, 'cause I thought that'd make it easier for us to get together. Then you rejected me and I decided to use him again." He frowned. "The thing is, I just don't know enough about how they investigate fires up here. I think it must be pretty basic. But they still will probably figure out that the fire was set. So they'll believe crazyman Bingham set it. Just like they believe he tried to burn the other house."

Virgil started to stir.

With a moan, he sat upright and saw Nikki. "What—" He winced and frowned. "Man, that feels bad."

"I didn't want to hurt you," Adam said.

Virgil turned to him. "You're some little fella."

"He says he's going to kill us," Nikki said. "Barbecue our bones."

"Good thinking," Virgil said. "But you screwed up."

"Screwed up how?" Adam asked.

"I imagine you plan on blaming everything on Bingham over there."

"So?"

"So you screwed up. They're gonna realize it wasn't him tried to burn your house in Bel Air," Virgil said. "And when they start with that . . ."

"What are you talking about?" the boy said, showing signs of anger.

"The message you scrawled. 'Randy innocent.' Jeffrey Bingham doesn't call his brother 'Randy.' He calls him 'Keats,' like the poet. Old man Bingham'll know that, probably some close friends, too. You screwed up."

"Yeah? Well, I'll take my chances," Adam said petulantly. He put the gas can on the floor and began to pace up and down. "You know, you screwed up, too, Mr. Perfect. Yes. I'll prove it."

He ran up the stairs.

Nikki said, "That 'Keats' stuff is jive, Virgil. Nobody's going to pay any attention to that. Won't do *us* any good, even if they do."

"Sure it's jive," Virgil told her. "I'm just trying to keep him busy. Feel around under your legs."

She did. Something sharp poked the tip of her finger. "Ow."

"It's a bread knife. I was starting to cut you free when he hit me with that flying Taser of his. Start sawin', baby."

She'd barely begun when she heard the boy bounding down the stairs. She hid the knife under her leg.

Adam was carrying his tape recorder. He placed it on the floor near Virgil. He reached into a pocket and withdrew a red cassette. "I played through a bunch of these on the trip here. Pretty boring stuff, most of it. But this one's good."

"You got this when you broke into the office?" Virgil asked.

Adam's head was turned to Virgil, so Nikki tried to position the knife blade against the ropes binding her wrists.

"When I broke in, yes. I had to kill Mr. Pickett. That wasn't part of the plan. Mr. Geruso was the only one I set out to kill. After we followed him around and you told me what a bad man he was, I arranged for Homeboy to go to a meeting at the Wonderbar offices, so I could scope the place out. See what I could see.

"Mr. Geruso didn't stick around the meeting very long. I heard Mr. Pickett tell the secretary that he was making his afternoon trip to the Victoria. So that's when I figured on the Drano bomb. Took a cab there the next day, found his neat-looking red car, and the rest is the rest.

"Then, that night I thought I'd take a look around Mr. Geruso's office, see if I could find anything to help your friend, Detective McNeil. I knew the layout and I'd checked the lock the day before. I used a credit card and a screwdriver, just like they said to do on the Internet. And it worked."

Nikki had the blade against the ropes, but the boy had stopped talking and she paused.

"What exactly were you hoping to find, Adam?" Virgil asked.

"I dunno. Something that your friend might use to prove Mr. Geruso was a liar. I'd read somewhere that when you search a room, you look for the locked stuff first. So, I pried open the one locked drawer in Mr. Geruso's desk and that's where I found a bunch of red cassettes in a bag. There was a gun there, too, but I didn't touch that. I figured the tapes must be important. I was carrying them out when Mr. Pickett grabbed me. I guess he'd come into the outer office and was waiting for me."

Nikki began to move her wrists up and down, rubbing the rope against the knife blade. It was an awkward process.

"He was yelling at me and squeezing the breath out of me," Adam continued, "and I guess I freaked because I started kicking him. I gave him a good bite on the arm and twisted free. He was blocking the way. And he knew who I was. So I got out my pepper spray and blasted him. Then I Tasered him. And while he was rolling on the floor, I looked around for something that I could use to kill him. The paper-weight was made to order."

"When you were tussling, you dropped that badge I gave you," Virgil said.

The boy shook his head. "So that's where I lost it."

Nikki felt the knife bite in finally.

"Because of that badge, they're blaming me for Pickett's murder," Virgil said.

"Too bad," the boy said. "I guess I screwed up twice, huh? Well, Mr. Perfect who knows everything, you listen to the tape, while I finish up."

The female voice on the cassette was singsongy and slightly nasal, echoing in a room. The speaker was talking at some distance from the recorder.

It's so me. I try to make my life better and it gets worse. I leave my beautiful Ricky G for this old fart who I think will at least be nice to me. And he starts whaling on me worse than Ricky ever did.

Nikki was only half listening to the tape. She was focusing on Adam, willing him to leave the room.

Then he did.

This is it. No more playing punching bag for little Patience. But it's gonna be so hard. Got to stay low for a while, at least until he cools off. He's the baddest drunk I've ever seen. And he's a cop, which makes it even worse. He says he'll kill me if I leave . . . Ooop, cab's honking. Outta here.

A few seconds of white noise and the voice returned. She sounded depressed.

Me again. Guess who just phoned? Crazy cop. I don't know how he found me so fast. He was playing nice man. Apologizing. Saying he's thought it over and he agrees it's for the best we don't see each other anymore.

Nikki continued to saw her bindings, but she was paying attention to the tape now. Her eyes met Virgil's. They both knew exactly what the girl was saying, even before she spelled it out.

"He said he has some stuff of mine that I left in his dryer. Panties and tanks. He wants to see me tonight, for old times' sake, and return my stuff. I don't trust him. But he knows my phone number, which means he knows my address. And I hate to just blow off the Vickie Secret panties. So I guess I'll see him. But that's it. He's too scary. So, off I go to say good-bye forever to the big man with the little dick, Detective Big Deal Mac-Neil."

The rest of the tape seemed to be blank. It hissed on while Nikki sawed at her ropes and stared at Virgil. He looked like he'd just taken another hit on the head.

Behind her, Jeffrey Bingham groaned and coughed.

"Virgil," Nikki called, more harshly than she had intended, "focus in on what's happening here and now. I've almost got—"

"Where's the little bastard?" Bingham asked. "I'm gonna kill him."

"Shut up, fool," Nikki hissed. "You'll draw him back here."

Her hands were free and she bent to cut the ropes binding her ankles.

"Give me the knife," Bingham ordered.

"Don't tempt me," Nikki said, crawling across the gasoline-slick floor to Virgil.

His ropes were severed quickly, but he didn't seem to care that he was free. "C'mon, honey," Nikki urged, "let's make it out of here. Then we can worry about Mac and his problems."

"Hey," Bingham said. "Do me."

"Wouldn't I just love to," Nikki said, moving across the floor to him. She could feel the tension in his body as she sawed his wrist bindings.

He seemed to be vibrating. As soon as the rope separated, he grabbed the knife from her hands and began freeing his ankles. He was muttering a homicidal mantra. "Kill the little bastard. Got to kill the little bastard."

Nikki stood unsteadily and began helping Virgil to his feet. Bingham rushed past, nearly knocking her down. He was headed for the rear door. She started to tell him that the door was nailed shut, but decided to let the jackass find that out for himself.

She was concerned that Virgil was so out of it. "Come with me, honey," she said, pulling him toward the front door.

The gasoline fumes were almost overpowering. Virgil allowed her to lead him, but when they were only a few feet from the safety of the outdoors, he pulled his arm away.

"Gotta get that tape," he said.

"No time."

He ignored her warning, running back to the Walkman in the other room. She ran behind him. She was conscious of movement along her peripheral-vision line. Adam was on the stairwell, carrying a book bag. He froze when he saw she was no longer bound.

"Youuu!" Bingham screamed from the rear of the cabin.

Adam flew down the stairs and out the front door into the night.

Bingham strode across the room, in no particular hurry. Nikki watched him pick up his rifle, check its load. He walked to the front doorway and stood there, staring out into the night.

Suddenly, he made a quick ducking motion.

The toy hovercraft with its deadly sparking Taser shot over him and into the gasoline-filled front room.

≡ 80 ≡

The hovercraft's arrival was Virgil's wake-up call.

The spark of that damned Taser would send the whole place up in flames, with them in it. Bingham evidently realized this, too. He rushed out of the house onto open ground.

The hovercraft buzzed the living room, just missing the gasoline-slick walls.

"Come on, Virgil!" he heard Nikki call. "Now!"

Virgil's fingers were like uncooked wieners as he tried to pry the red cassette from the machine. Finally it popped loose, and he jammed it into a pocket and ran to the front door. He saw that Nikki was just ahead of him. He could feel the fresh air on his face when—

He was on his back on the floor, staring up at exploding lights and the hovercraft heading for the far wall. He tried to stand. He was facing the half-open front door. He'd run into the damned door as it was swinging shut. He turned and saw the Taser connect with the gasoline-soaked wall.

A tsunami of flame rushed toward him, just as small but strong hands grabbed his bad arm and yanked. The pain was so intense he allowed himself to be pulled forward through the door.

He was conscious enough to kick the door closed after him. That kept the backdraft from following them from the house and claiming them. Nikki continued pulling him. Into the lake.

At first, it was just a weird sensation of shoes sloshing through water. A distant memory of boyhood disobedience involving Sunday shoes and an inviting bayou. Then the silty ground beneath his feet gave way entirely and he was in the water up to his chin.

Nikki's hand left his arm as she fell forward with an *Owwww* of surprise before disappearing underwater. She surfaced again almost immediately, spitting out a mouthful of lake and sputtering.

Virgil reached out to steady her and was reminded of his wounded shoulder. His waterlogged sport coat was too heavy for him to lift his arm through the water. "Can you swim, honey?" he shouted.

"Hell of a time to ask," she said, treading water. "Sure. You?"

He was shrugging off his soggy coat, kicking off his shoes. "Uh-huh," he said.

Suddenly the night brightened. Virgil turned to see the cabin completely engulfed in flames. Tongues of fire leapt out to lick the nearest sequoias. A blast of heat reached his face.

"Getting hot here," Nikki said.

She turned and swam away from the heat through the dark water. Using just one arm and his legs, Virgil managed to follow her to the raft in the center of the lake.

They were both hanging on to the side of the raft when Nikki asked, "You figure there's anything dangerous in this lake?"

"You mean like 'gators and snakes?" he asked.

"I'm not talking about Bigfoot. Definitely 'gators and snakes."

"No on the 'gators," he said. "Snakes, who knows?"

Nikki swung sideways and awkwardly levered one leg onto the raft and pulled herself from the water. Virgil, working with only one arm, had a harder job of it. But he got himself onto the raft, too. He lay on his side, panting.

"I don't see either of them," Nikki said. She was staring at the woods surrounding the burning house.

Virgil saw that the trees were beginning to catch now. Hundred-year-old wood was turning into kindling. There was no sign of human life, not that he was sure the boy and Bingham belonged in that category. "They could be halfway to town by now," he said.

A red carpet of flame rolled out along bush and foliage. As it neared the Grand Cherokee, the door on the driver's side flew open and Adam tumbled onto the ground. The boy was momentarily frozen by the blaze that was bubbling the paint on the vehicle's hood.

Virgil felt Nikki's fingers suddenly grip his ankle.

He twisted his neck to look at her. She seemed to be in torment. "He can't," she said.

"Who can't?"

She pointed to a spot at the far end of the lake where Jeffrey Bingham, the not-so-great white hunter, was lining up his shot on an unmoving target.

"Adam, run!" Nikki shouted.

Virgil saw the boy shake off the fire's mesmerizing effect. He took one step and a shot rang out above the crackle of the fire. Adam screamed. There was a second shot, but no scream followed that.

In the glow of the flames, Virgil saw Nikki's eyes fill with tears. He slid across the surface of the raft until he was beside her. She was staring at the boy lying motionless beside the burning vehicle.

"The fire'll be on him any second," Virgil said. "Better for him if he is dead."

She turned and moved close to him. He wrapped his good arm around her, holding her.

Over her shoulder, he saw Bingham standing between them and the burning cabin, pointing his rifle in their direction. "Aw, shit," Virgil said as a bullet ripped into the top of the raft, inches from his head.

He pushed Nikki into the inky water and rolled in after her just as another shot echoed across the lake. Nikki's head popped above the water's surface a few seconds after his. Quietly, they circled the raft, putting it between them and the man with the gun.

His good hand clutching the edge of the raft, Virgil chanced a glance at shore. He was dismayed to find Bingham standing in front of the burning cabin, holding his rifle low as he searched the lake for them.

Virgil felt Nikki's body brush against his. "He's still there," she said. "Fool thinks he's gotta bag his limit."

"He has to leave soon," he said. "Folks'll be coming to fight the fire."

"He'll probably try to kill them, too," she said. "He's totally twisted."

They'd been whispering but not softly enough. Bingham tensed and stared directly at them. He was bringing his rifle up to a shooting position when the Cherokee blew up. Bingham wheeled in that direction, saw the flaming vehicle, and began to laugh.

As he was turning back to them, the cabin gave up to the flames. The front wall fell forward with a *whoosh*, sending sparks through the air. Some of them must have reached Bingham's gasoline-soaked clothes, because suddenly he, too, was aflame.

With a horrible yell, he jerked the rifle's trigger, sending bullets into ground and sky, while he twisted and turned trying to escape the fire that was now a part of him. Too late, he tried to run into the lake.

He missed by only a few feet.

Virgil turned away from the sight. Nikki continued to watch, without expression.

After a while she said, "Do you think Adam . . . ?"

"No chance," he said.

It was nearly an hour before the truck from the Twin Rivers Fire Department arrived. Nikki and Virgil spent another several hours on the raft, watching the firemen battle the flames. When it seemed that the blaze had been reduced to embers, they swam ashore.

The firefighters, surprised by the couple's emergence from the lake, were quick to carry them over the ashes to the truck, where they were provided warm blankets and black coffee. The chief told them that the fire had razed a large section of woodland before burning itself out.

"We're not equipped to put out a full-blown forest fire," he explained. "Usually we just let 'em burn. Figure it's nature's way of thinning out the forest, getting it ready for new trees."

Virgil explained that nature hadn't had much to do with this fire, and twenty minutes later he and Nikki were talking to state troopers.

The story that they told was an abbreviated version of the truth. Naturally, nothing was mentioned about Virgil's "wanted" status, or the murders that had taken place in L.A. But they did cover Adam Noyes's arson and Jeffrey Bingham's rampage. And they told the lawmen where they might find the charred remains of Adam, Bingham, and the unfortunate Howard Rule.

The sun was starting to come up when they were set free.

For some reason not even the fire experts could explain, neither the Saab convertible nor Bingham's sedan had been touched. The troopers held on to the latter. Virgil reclaimed the "borrowed" Saab. Nikki drove them down the mountain.

Five hours later, they arrived at her home in Ladera Heights. Their plan was to move on to Loreen's house if they spotted any reporters. But the media vigil seemed to have ended. There were phone calls to make. Jesse Fallon had to be notified about Adam. Ray Wise would have to start proceedings for Randy Bingham's release. Virgil needed to have a long talk with Duke Wasson about the murders of Luther Pickett and Richard Geruso. But first, there was sleep.

As it turned out, the phone calls didn't even rate second priority.

≡ 81 ≡

The charges against Virgil were dropped.

In addition to Nikki's testimony that the late Adam Noyes had admitted murdering both Richard Geruso and Luther Pickett in her presence, the boy's workroom yielded corroborating evidence—printed Internet pages on how to construct a Drano bomb, a mechanic's textbook on servicing the Lamborghini Diablo, and several of Patience Dahl's tapes.

The day he was officially pronounced an innocent man, Virgil visited McNeil in prison. His ex-partner was initially happy to see him. "Heard you and Nikki had a rough time up in big-tree country."

Virgil nodded but didn't return McNeil's smile. He wasn't in a smiling mood. "You killed that girl, Mac."

"The fuck you talking about?"

"Patience Dahl," Virgil said. "She tried to get away from you and you found her and beat her to death."

"You're fulla crap, *partner*."

"She fingered you in her diary."

"This is bullshit. That bimbo could barely write her name, much less keep a diary."

"A verbal diary," Virgil said. "On tape. It got a little damp and the quality's not so hot, but it's pretty convincing."

"This is a con, right? You wearing a wire, *partner*?"

"No wire."

"I been in your corner from the start," McNeil said. "I saved your life."

"Not something I'd forget."

"You gonna testify against me?"

"Not unless they force me."

"You really think I did it, huh?" McNeil asked, a crooked smile on his face.

Virgil nodded.

McNeil stood. "Well, hell, then, you're in the wrong place."

"But you aren't," Virgil said.

The prisoner nodded. "I suppose I should be thankful you won't be on my jury," he said, and walked toward the guard at the door.

Virgil watched him leave. "You could do worse," he said to no one in particular.

Daniel McNeil was found guilty of the murder of Patience Dahl in the second week in October. Perfect timing for Prosecutor Dana Lowery's campaign to make maximum use of the victory. Raymond Wise, meanwhile, had been left with the unfortunate task of freeing Randolph Bingham, an innocent man who had been wrongfully convicted.

Which essentially is why Dana Lowery became the first woman to be elected district attorney for the county of Los Angeles.

The day after the election, Nikki submitted her letter of resignation. Then she phoned Jesse Fallon to see if his offer of a partnership was still on the table. It was. Together they decided that the firm of Fallon, Hill and Associates would hang out its shingle shortly after the new year.

That left Nikki with her first period of downtime since graduation from law school. Virgil helped fill the void. One morning late in November, a van stopped in front of her home. It contained his furniture and other possessions from the Hollywood apartment. And him. "It's time," Virgil said.

"Damn right," Nikki replied.